T0365137

THE ORDER

DAN MORRIS

iUniverse, Inc.
New York   Bloomington

The Order

iUniverse books may be ordered through booksellers or by contacting:

iUniverse
1663 Liberty Drive
Bloomington, IN 47403
www.iuniverse.com
1-800-Authors (1-800-288-4677)

ISBN: 978-1-4502-2736-0 (sc)
ISBN: 978-1-4502-2737-7 (ebk)

Printed in the United States of America

iUniverse rev. date: 5/5/2010

CHAPTER 1

Throughout civilized history there have always been conspiracy theories. Some were so laughable that they never had a chance of being proven or disproved. One thing they will always have in common is that they are extremely difficult to prove. Most begin as mere speculation while others are simply so far fetched that they can only be the product of some whacked-out nut case, thus, they don't have a snowball's chance in hell of being true. How many of them are true is rarely known since their premise and substance are almost certainly encapsulated in secrecy. The reason we consider them at all is that once in awhile one will turn out to be legitimate. So we tend to give all of them a fare shake. Considering everything, we have to admit that whenever powerful and influential men and women lack transparency, preferring to make contentious deals in back rooms, they open themselves up to speculation. Is it no wonder that they end up in the crosshairs of conspiracy theorists?

Man's uniqueness is rooted in his innate capacity to reason and his ability to act with a free will. Although, there is a strange dichotomy attached to this phenomenon. His resulting, and sometimes unpredictable behavior has become one of his many curses; a reality-based double edged sword. His highly evolved intellect and diverse emotions are the very things that get him into trouble with others. Man's very attributes are the ingredients for a trap of his own making; one that he inevitably will fall into when he is sneaking about. Yes, there are those among us that are prone to do the unthinkable. We have conspiracy theories because we think, feel, and rationalize over the behavior of others. Conspiracy theories are ideas and concepts that people plant in the minds of others and once they take root there's no telling what they will grow into.

Certainly, a person's character and emotional flaws are easily coupled with his urges. Together, they form a recipe for perfecting an ambitious quest for public achievement with global domination being their crowning glory. This type of person has no problem reasoning and justifying his aspirations. He is convinced that he is serving the common good of all and that other paths are destined for a lesser good or even evil. In the shadow of these circumstances, is it no wonder that disaster and chaos await those few who are out to capitalize on the herd mentality of the many?

Conspiracies are bold attempts to create change with unorthodox methods. In this day and age conspiracies are more global than ever before. We all have to be vigilant and challenge choices and paths that are cloaked in secrecy. Not only should checks and balances permeate our hearts and minds; they should be articulated and well grounded in the U.S. Constitution.

Considering the current political climate and our country's state of affairs, the story that will unfold within these pages has the potential for becoming true. There is a gray line between what is real and what has the potential for becoming real. Who among us has the scrutinizing logic and ability to distinguish between fact and reality? Sadly, we may not discern the truth until we face the future. That's right, not all answers are apparent. However, they're out there somewhere waiting to be discovered. We are living in a fertile environment for growing a credible conspiracy. We need to be watching and taking notes. Our awareness is the key to our future.

The issue for man is not all that complex because everything seems to boil down to motive and need. When a person feels compelled to hide his motives he is actually creating a safe haven in which to work toward his goals and objectives. No matter how ruthless or devious his work, the ends will justify the means; so he rationalizes.

One of man's biggest challenges for advancing any struggle is to seek like minds in order to build a consensus. He will always need a power base if he is to succeed. No single man can accomplish everything. That is left to God or some other form of deity with elevated, supernatural power. A conspirator who operates in secrecy to achieve universal goals, at a minimum, sees himself as a demigod, destined to rule. Conspirators, like birds of a feather, tend to flock together. If there are two people of like minds in a city or a country for that matter, it is only a matter of time until they find each other and join forces.

Not surprising is that many people seem to be ordained by their own nature to keep certain matters cloaked in secrecy. One could say that such individuals come by this secrecy trait naturally like a child is drawn to his or her mother. For others, secrecy is a learned characteristic.

Things that are learned means that there is some sort of educational setting or mentoring scheme. In other words, there are teachers and there are students.

Secret societies will always use some sort of vetting process where students are spotted for their attributes, assessed for their loyalty, and recruited for their potential to serve the cause. The vetting, testing, and recruiting process must be stringent, and thorough. The process must also be cyclical and never-ending for the protection of members and for ensuring that the mission remains secure.

Not surprising, is the fact that only the most loyal and adept of initiates are permitted to advance to the inner circles of any secret society. A secret society's success is often guaranteed only by having the right people working in an environment governed by a strict enforcement of its rules. When this occurs, it creates a great deal of difficulty for any conspiracy theorist to expose even the existence of the organization. Investigators usually wind up lacking the proof they need for exposing the often sinister goals of secret societies. Actually, if goals were ones widely accepted by society, then there would be no need for secrecy. Herein is where the above stated proverbial trap is found. Can a group of self-appointed and anointed masters dictate what is right for all others? Is this concept even logically sound, let alone ethical? If a true conspiracy is to be destroyed before it achieves its goal, then the catalyst for its destruction must come from within its membership.

Any member's actions and reactions to external stimuli will; either pave the way for advancement within any given society, especially a secret society, or will inhibit his or her access to sensitive information. The adept are the ones that are imbedded the deepest inside any given secret society. They can go no deeper than the center or nucleolus of the organization. Often they are so far inside that they are unreachable by many of the outer cells. The inner circle, by virtue of their positions, has the ultimate, definitive authority and influence. They rule and dictate from the position of secrecy. The outer circles only know them as "the top," "they" or "them." The innermost circle rules and dictates with autonomy and anonymity.

One important segment of the retention and advancement process becomes exceedingly clear in the way the society conducts its secret rites. Rites are always designed to test and reinforce unshaken loyalty with words and oaths, and this aids an initiate in connecting the dots in a clear fashion. Initiates must always work within a framework and never step out of bounds.

However, oaths alone are merely empty words and shallow promises. Words, one could say, are nothing but dust blown about in the windstorm we know as civilization. So a secret society must cement words by adding substance and action; consequences, not just direction. There is one last thought here for giving credibility to secret conspiracies. Behind every coup that toppled a government, there was a secret conspiracy.

There is much to learn about the structure of secret societies in order to gain a clear understanding of how they work. However, right now, other matters deserve attention.

On this night, action coupled with the notion of consequence will overshadow a crucial and essential meeting of one outer cell within a secret society. All consequences have to be dire or they risk being ineffective.

Tonight, a rural Texas meeting is taking place in a country club setting. The regular members, all dues paying men and women, have left following a long day of golfing and socializing. All the domestic help, to include kitchen staff, are gone for the night. A group of six figures sit in a private room around a large mahogany table. The lights are dim and the shadowy silhouettes fidget in their cushy leather chairs.

Normally, there would be seven to ten attendees at such a meeting, but, that is not the case tonight. A decision must be made concerning an absent member. In the dim light the member's faces are not discernable, and their voices are deep and low, nearly indistinguishable from one another.

The group rarely meets in the same location or on any standard day, week or month. Meetings are usually determined by need and circumstance. A voice cracks the hushed silence only after a member returns from making a sweep of the premises. His voice guarantees the group's privacy.

A briefcase is placed on the table in front of one of the figures. If an observer had been standing behind the man he would only have seen the latches flick open and the lid rise. A large envelope is removed from the case and the case is shoved aside with a backhanded wave. A stack of photographs are removed and tossed onto the center of the table.

One by one, the photographs are picked up and passed around to the others as one man spoke.

"On the back of each photograph, you will see a date and a location stamped. You will notice that each meeting is between our Walter and a man named Jonathon Pickerington, a noted journalist who specializes in investigative reporting for a syndicated magazine."

"Have the nature of these meetings been discussed with Walter?" A questioning voice came from the far end of the table.

Another voice asked, "Who took the photos and why were they taken?"

"As you are all aware, we operate in cells within a layering of inner and outer circles. A member of another cell gave these photos to me, yesterday. The photographs were taken over a period of two months and they were all taken in Houston. Now, let me answer your question as to why they were taken. A close colleague of Pickerington is a member of The Order. Pickerington confided in him that he was working on uncovering a secret political society. Pickerington even asked our man for some help in unraveling the nature and structure of our organization. One of our Houston associates initiated some surveillance and was able to take these photographs. Last night, our associate was able to surreptitiously enter Pickerington's apartment and make off with his notes on this matter. Two names of people sitting at this table were mentioned in those notes. I'm sure more would soon follow."

There was a long drawn out moment of silence around the table before someone finally spoke. "Acquiring the notes from Pickerington's apartment does not remove them from his head, let alone his computer."

"The Order's cell in Houston has already remedied that situation. His computer's hard drive has been replaced and there was a fire in his apartment. Unfortunately for Pickerington, he was killed during the break-in at his apartment. At a police news conference, today, a spokesperson announced that the robbers who killed Pickerington also set the apartment on fire to destroy evidence."

Another voice chimed in with a question: "Now, what about Walter?"

"Walter is our problem. One of us will have to carry out the task, don't you think?" The task, a deadly sanction, was an implied or understood necessity.

The voice at the far end of the table sounded off again. "I know we have to act quickly, but, we also have to act smartly. Once Walter learns about Pickerington, he might spook and go to the authorities and that means we will all be under investigation. None of us want that kind of attention. We also have to find out if Walter has compiled any additional records on us or The Order's activities."

Dan Morris

"Those are all good points and we need to come to some kind of a consensus and do so quickly."

A nervous hand places a pair of spectacles on the table and then the man rubs his eyes with his palms. "I don't know about all this. I've been part of The Order for a decade and we have never had to resort to violence. Maybe we should turn this matter over to others who have more experience at this sort of thing. I don't know if I have the stomach for murder."

The man's concerns did not go unanswered. The situation was growing graver by the minute and out of necessity each of them would have to state his position. A new, steadier voice joined the debate.

"Our allegiance is to The Order and not to any notion of self interest. We will always carry out The Order's mandates, regardless of the risk involved. Just remember, The Order has been around for a long time; long before any of us were members. We all have taken the same sacred oath of allegiance. If we are to advance the right political ideals that The Order was founded on, then we all must do our part. The Order has brought about the deaths of many others who have run afoul of our commitment to effect change in an otherwise weak society. All the cells in all of our member states have to be willing to act and do so at a risk. Should we become exposed, we will all have a monumental price to pay. A few dead bodies strewn about our path is a small price to pay for the greater good. We all agreed on this before when we pledged our oaths."

A response from one of the attendees stirred the debate into a moral issue. "That's easy for you to say. After all, you have been a prosecutor and now you're a judge. You are content to look men in the eye and send them to death row. I'm a minister and I am concerned with saving souls not dispatching them."

The debate that was materializing was only the latest resurrection of an old and frequent rift between the two men. They had argued on many occasions, before. Their depth of commitment for membership in The Order was beginning to show signs of strain. The minister had moral limits on his dedication to The Order and the judge didn't.

"Yes, I am a judge. Who gets the blame when a hardened criminal is set free? You surely know the answer to that question- that's right, the judge is condemned. Am I biased when it comes to justice; you bet I am. Chief Justice Oliver Wendell Holmes of the U.S. Supreme Court once said that he does law, not justice. Well, I am the opposite; I do justice every chance I get and that means I sometimes have to twist and bend the law to achieve that justice. Isn't this one of the things The Order is all about? Let me ask you a philosophical question. What is the difference between justice, vengeance, and self-defense?"

The challenge carried the sting of a scorpion, and it was beginning to fester into an old wound for the minister. Yes, beneath the minister's pious exterior a dilemma was beginning to take root, one that hinged on self-judgment. Inside all men, at one time or another, there was some type of moral conflict that needed to be resolved. The minister had been a member of The Order for ten years and during the full scope of that time he had always wondered if he was doing the right thing. Perhaps, poor Walter had had the right idea.

The minister knew he was a man of God. The judge; well that's a different story. How could a judge be a just person if he lacked the moral insight of a man that served God? There were times when the minister thought the judge was born with the devil in him and that translated into him being a man that surely lacked morals and ethics. After all, he openly set aside the dictates of his elected office to pursue a personal agenda.

The minister knew that he was out numbered in this forum so he began looking for a way out of the disagreement. He would find one, he always did. Besides, he was well aware that dissension would not be tolerated by The Order. Dissension with conviction would be construed as disloyalty and with that there would be sanctions, harsh sanctions. This was a solemn time when their cell had to debate not the need of a death sanction for betrayal, but rather how and who would carry out the deed. Sure, he was beginning to regret voicing his concerns, but, they should expect it because, after all, he was a man of God. He had pledged himself to God long before he had even heard about The Order.

Obviously, he had pushed his point far enough and he certainly did not want to be the focus of another meeting, a meeting he would not be invited to. He did not want to attain the same status of poor Walter. A feeling of paranoia was beginning to invade his psyche and he knew it was real and justified.

Another voice from the dark confines of the table intervened. "Will you two stop this petty philosophical bickering so we can get back to Walter? Lawyers and ministers always have to have their say and now you two have had yours. No one is going to ask either one of you to take out Walter. I move to have this done by someone outside of our cell, by someone who is more attuned to this sort of thing. We need to turn this matter over to a professional. The Order has such people at its disposal. I will take this for action and I will move on it quickly. I'll keep you all informed. I want to leave each and every one of you with one thought, though. We are all part of this conspiracy and that means we all will have a hand in Walter's demise. Just because his assassination will take place out of our sight does not mean we are not part of it. I hope that point is clear should any of you have any ideas contrary to what we have agreed to."

The judge made some unintelligible grunting sound and the minister gave a sigh of relief. Understandingly, the judge was running low on patience, but, the minister was displaying extraordinary guilt for being part of sentencing a friend and a good person to death.

At times like this there would always be some members in the room who would have serious misgivings about having a minister in their cell. Rumor had it that there were ministers in other cells that would have no problem taking a life to preserve The Order. The crusades, and many other wars, were proof that killing for the sake of religion was an acceptable practice, indeed, a noble thing. However, the minister was not a Templar or some church sanctioned crusader that was willing to kill. He was simply a minister who had gotten into a secret society that was allegedly designed to right the wrongs of society while pushing for a manipulated or grass-roots political correction. His original motive for joining The Order was a righteous one. Anyway, that was what he had thought at the time he had joined.

At this point in his life, the minister was no longer driven by scripture. He was reduced to being a pawn in a deadly, immoral game. His own fear and guilt were beginning to consume him.

Once the meeting was over, the minister sat alone in his car watching the others drive away down the lane into the dark. So many times he had told troubled parishioners that fear was the absence of love and love was the absence of fear. Now, he found himself doubting his commitment to a spiritual way of life. He knew that God expected him to follow the Ten Commandments. He was adrift in a sea of doubt and the current was carrying him farther away from his faith.

Yes, it was only a matter of time until he would have to answer to God, to his human values, and to the law. Worse yet, he would, sooner or later, have to answer to The Order. He sat there in the dark praying for courage to do the right thing. Unfortunately, no matter how things turned out, his loving wife would also have to suffer.

He thought about The Order, its importance, and perceived value to the world. Now, and ironically, The Order might even be a threat to the entire country. Hell, even the entire world. He had to ask himself, in the end would The Order turn out to be a big joke that no one would dare laugh at? They think they are so high and mighty, even cultured in the highest intellectual sense. They probably see themselves as God's Chosen Ones. That is if they even believed in God. What a hypocrisy The Order was turning out to be. Most members probably didn't believe in God.

No matter how long he sat there and prayed, he still felt like a hypocrite. A man, a minister, who had turned a blind eye to God, now sat alone in the dark, praying in the name of Jesus. As he prayed, he wondered if God would see him as a spiritually diseased man and dismiss his words as those of an empty and faithless nonbeliever. Hopefully, God would see him as a sincere man reaching for heaven in search of his misplaced faith.

At length, he got out of his car and knelt down on his knees. The asphalt was hard and coarse. Worry over his trousers becoming stained or torn was the farthest thing from his mind. His eyes filled with tears as he prayed with sweaty palms that were squeezed tightly together. He had never prayed with this intensity before. He had to do this because he was on the verge of being spiritually bankrupt. His words flowed uncontrollably with passion.

"Oh God, I know what you see in my heart is dark and evil and that I have been acting with a misguided faith. Please God, shine your loving grace on me and give me strength along with the wisdom to use it wisely. Show me the way, God, to do your bidding. Allow me, Lord, to rise up in this lonely parking lot as a better man. Give me some sign that you have heard my prayer. Father, I know that I have sinned and now I ask for forgiveness. In your loving name I pray. Amen."

The hour was late, past midnight, and it was cooler out here in the country. In fact, dew was already beginning to settle on his car and the surrounding shrubs. The minister stood up on trembling legs and reached out to open his car door. In the dark confines of the parking lot he heard a car door slam shut. Someone from The Order, it has to be! Had they heard his every word as he prayed to God? If so, they would all soon know how he truly felt. This was not the sign he had asked God for. He would now be confronted with greater challenges and his path would become a deadly one.

He did not recognize the car that sped away into the darkness. The car's headlights did not come on until it had left the parking lot. Who had seen him and heard his prayer?

CHAPTER 2

Following a long day of tedious report writing that verged on becoming languid, Frank McLaughlin, Private Investigator, had had his fill of tapping away on his computer's keyboard. He was more than ready for a break as he stood, stretched, and yawned. As if nudged by an invisible hand, he stepped outside in an attempt to shake the office staleness from his head. The change in air brought on as much freshness as it could in a large city like Dallas. At least the outside air leaned toward invigoration.

It was mid-October and the ninety degree days had waned to the low-to-mid eighties. A light fall breeze ruffled the hair on his bare forearms and he rubbed them as if the temperature was much cooler than it actually was.

He eyed his old Nissan pickup that was nestled in the shade of a huge old oak at the corner of the parking lot. The office was nestled among other businesses on a small hill. In front of the office were two flower beds that were tiered like small terraces. They were propped up by old weathered railroad ties that had turned ash-grey in color over the years. The flowers had already begun to wilt from the seasonal change, except for a few pansies. Fallen leaves were beginning to carpet the parking lot. The scene was a far cry from the definitive seasonal changes he remembered from his childhood in Southeastern Ohio. Oh how those memories were spectacular. The older he became, the more homesick he was for the solace that could be found in those foothills to the Appalachians. He remembered an old saying: "You can never go home." He knew the hills would be the same; but, what about the people and cultural atmosphere? At last he concluded that the world would have appeared differently to him when he was a young man. Over the years, his perception of the world had changed due to experience, time, and circumstance. At least he could cherish his youthful memories.

Frank observed that some of the vehicular traffic that was whizzing by already had their headlights turned on. Soon it would be dark. Everything he was seeing seemed to be telling him that this work day had come to an end.

He locked his office door and headed to his pickup, hastening his pace to escape before some forgotten, work-related task had a chance to call him back inside. After all, he had kept his shoulder to the grindstone all day long without any break other than a few trips to the restroom. In fact, he hadn't even taken a lunch break, choosing to munch on snacks instead. Thankfully, at the moment there were no luring hunger pangs that needed satisfying.

Trail Riders; that's where he needed to go so he could unwind. He hadn't been there all week and that meant there was tavern news that needed to be caught up on. Hopefully, Phil would be there and they could play a game or two of pool. Beth, the bartender, would discretely fill him in on any missed gossip. Who knows, maybe Jill would be there hovering over the juke box, blowing smoke rings toward the ceiling. Everyone in these small bars tended to ignore the new smoking band. With any luck, some old country-western tune would entice her into a couple of slow dances with him. Holding Jill close as they swayed to classic tunes had a way of soothing his nerves. There was not a day so hectic that she couldn't make him relax and unwind.

Frank was pleased over his choice to make Trail Riders his hangout. He enjoyed chatting with the regulars who were never shy about telling their one-sided stories about lost loves, bad jobs, and misdirected adventures. He liked to think the tavern's ambiance truly reflected the main stream, blue-collar culture that helped build and maintain the country. Such places, in many instances, reflected the true roots of Americana.

The traffic was accident free and moving along at a good clip so he arrived in only a few minutes. Trail Riders had no windows so the security cameras that covered the parking lot gave a great deal of comfort and reassurance to the patrons. Despite being Friday, there were not many cars in the parking lot. That would drastically change over the next couple of hours.

Once inside, Frank asked Beth if Phil or Jill had been in yet and she said, "You bet. They'll both be back later about the time the band gets here. Jill is going to help me tend bar if we get busy. They both have been asking about you."

"I've been swamped with paperwork this week. How's it been for you?"

"Give me a couple of minutes, will you? There's something I want to talk to you about."

"You bet, just shove a Bud Light my way while I wait." He was anxious over the prospect of someone wanting to talk to him about something other than work.

Once Beth had taken care of the more mundane tasks of preparing the bar for a busy night and attending to the few patrons that were already there, she returned with Frank's Bud Light. She demonstrated her resolve to talk by pulling up a stool on her side of the bar.

Obviously, what she wanted to discuss was not for the ears of others because the volume of her voice was reduced to nearly a whisper.

"I hope we don't get interrupted so I can get this all out in one shot." Beth started to light a cigarette then changed her mind for some reason that was only known to her. Like everyone else, she didn't care about the new ordinance.

Frank got the impression that Beth had rehearsed what she had to say and she feared a cigarette dangling from her mouth would somehow pull her off track. He matched her posturing by leaning closer until they were almost nose to nose, heads bent for focus.

"I'm not from Dallas. I've been here about fifteen years, now. Actually, I grew up on a ranch just outside of a little town in Texas called Childress. It's near the Oklahoma border at the edge of the Texas panhandle. It's one of those sleepy little places where there's no crime and the air is clean. In fact, there's not much going on there at all." She gave a sigh just short of being apologetic.

"I'll never forget those early years back on the ranch when I was growing up. Those days will always be a big part of my life. My best friend was Charlene O'Keefe. Charlie was what we all called her and besides being my best friend, she was also a first cousin."

Beth cleared her throat and scanned the bar for anyone needing a drink. She also gave in to the temptation of lighting up the cigarette she had previously stuffed back into the pack. Her eyes told Frank that she was searching for the best words to continue with as she blew smoke up at the ceiling. She had placed her free hand on the bar and Frank reached over and squeezed it gently to reassure her. He sensed that she was surely about to build up to something important and awkward to talk about.

"Charlie was popular in high school; as much as I was, anyway. In our junior and senior years we double dated more times than I can count. I guess we were typical, though, because, like others our age, we always acted coy with the boys and a little giddy with our girlfriends. I think we were just normal teenagers from a rural area."

Frank and Beth both nodded there heads in agreement over her summation. Besides, the comment was rhetorical so no response was needed.

"Anyway, I guess you get the point about Charlie being my best friend. There was one thing that really stood out about her, though; it was her talent. Boy could she sing. She had a voice that could capture your soul; if you know what I mean. She even sang at our high school prom and the crowd went wild. She sure grabbed the spotlight that night." Beth broke out with a sincere smile of admiration as she recalled the event.

"After we graduated, it was no surprise to anyone that Charlie started singing with a country-western band. The next few years went pretty fast, especially for her mom."

Beth's voice became resonate, more confident as she continued to speak. "By the time Charlie was twenty-one, she was on the road with a popular band until she settled out in Phoenix, Arizona. As far as we were concerned, you know, the rest of the family, living in Arizona was like living in another country. It sure wasn't Texas and it sure wasn't Childress County."

Beth flinched and glanced away from Frank as she reacted to the front door creaking open and letting in some of the parking lot light. She looked relieved when she saw that it was only one of the regulars popping in for an after work beer. "I'll be right back as soon as I take care of this guy."

Frank was curious about where all this talk was headed and what it had to do with him. Finally, he concluded that if nothing else, it was good background information on Beth's life. Besides, there was a certain amount of warmth associated with being a confidant.

Once the customer was taken care of with the same flirtatious charm and stroking words that guaranteed a good tip from the clientele, Beth was again seated across from Frank.

"Now where was I? Oh yes, Charlie had settled in Phoenix and that was somewhat unpopular with most of the family. I wanted to blame some one or some thing for Charlie taking off like that, but, I couldn't come up with who or what to nail it on. Oh, at least Charlie called home to her folks once a week and I got a call from her once in awhile. Her mom, who was also my Aunt Jane, seemed to take it all in stride. At least the calls let us know that she was alive."

"Well Beth, we all have to strike out on our own sooner or later. Look at me. I grew up in Ohio and here I am sitting in a Texas tavern.

Look at where you are. Dallas, Texas may not be Phoenix, Arizona, but, it isn't exactly Childress County, either." Frank didn't press the issue any farther.

"Yeah, I suppose you're right. If Charlie hadn't taken off, I would probably be sitting in the living room back home in Childress telling Charlie that we should have taken a chance at doing something else with our lives than being homebodies. However, that isn't the important part of what I'm trying to get at."

"I figured there had to be something more to all this." Without being rude, Frank hoped his comment would move Beth's story along.

When Beth began to speak again, her voice had acquired a mournful and troubled tone and that alerted Frank that a shift in Beth's story was about to occur.

"When Aunt Jane passed away, Charlie was right there to comfort her dad. She did everything that was expected of her, and more. Don't worry Frank; I'll spare you all the touchy-feely details on everything that was said during and following the funeral. Things like that are always intense. The real change came about two months later."

In spite of a pause, Frank didn't have to coax Beth to reveal the sparse details surrounding a mysterious time in Charlie's life. The lull in conversation was brief and only sufficient enough for Beth to take a couple of deep breaths and for Frank to gulp a swig of beer.

"If I hadn't already moved to Dallas at that time, I might know more about what happened. All I could get out of my uncle was that Charlie ended up in the hospital in Yuma, Arizona and then was transferred to another one in Phoenix. No one could pry any more information out of him. Hell, no one even knew anything had happened until it was all over. Whatever it was, it must have been serious, though.

"The first hint that something was up was when one morning, my mom gets a call from my uncle who said he was going to Arizona to help out Charlie. A couple of weeks passed before he came back and then he just said he went to visit and ended up hanging out there. Everyone knew that there was more to it than that. When my uncle got there he called home and sounded concerned. Two weeks later he called and sounded upset about something. The next thing we knew he just came back home and brought Charlie with him. For the longest time, they just kept to themselves. This is all some kind of a big secret between Charlie and her dad. You and I both know that a father has more at stake than an uncle. At any rate, no one, especially me, knew what to make of it. Maybe it will always be a mystery for the whole family."

"How long ago did this happen?" Frank queried.

"This was all about fifteen years ago. This all happened right before I landed here in Dallas."

Frank shot a puzzled look at Beth and then asked: "So why are you telling me all this?"

"Well, there are several things I want to run by you, Frank. First, it has to do with Charlie's career. You know, she never sang again. That's right, whatever happened in Arizona, it ended her career. Second, she quit calling me. That's right; she had quit calling me, her best friend. We were always so close. It's like she dropped off the end of the world.

"Third, after all these years, Charlie is still living at home with her father on the ranch. They have been doing a really great job at keeping to themselves. You don't know how all this makes me feel. I mean we weren't just best friends- we were and are family.

"Now, are you ready for the kicker? Two weeks ago, I get a letter from Charlie and now she has been calling me every day. She's acting like she never left in the first place. After all these years without my best friend, she's right back in the middle of my life. So here I am, sharing my life with someone who is almost a stranger. She's acting like she never left. I'm so confused. I don't know what to make of all this."

For a moment, Frank's mind wandered back to a time in his own life. Somehow, this all reminded him of something odd that had occurred during his youth. There had been this elderly couple that lived down the road from his home. His mother had been friends with the couple, although not close enough to know a great deal about them. The only thing he remembered about them was that he sometimes saw the old woman driving an old Packard. Her name was Ethel and she cleaned homes for a living. She had been friendly enough and always waved when she drove by. Frank rarely saw Ethel's husband who almost never left their home. Frank's mother told him that the old man had been bitten by a copperhead snake when he had been pruning some flowers in his yard. That had been over thirty years before. The old man was rarely seen by anyone after he had been bitten and that often led to a lot of gossip and concern about his well being.

Sometimes, people would speculate and start rumors. On occasion, the rumors were alarming and that fed everyone's imagination. People would say that the old man had died and his wife had buried him in their back yard. Usually, when people were on the verge of reporting their suspicions to the sheriff, someone would see the old man walking around his yard. They said he seemed to walk around like one of those zombies in an old horror movie.

One afternoon the old woman came running out of her house to the edge of the road yelling that her husband had been bitten again by a copperhead. Frank's mother fetched her car and they all helped the old man into it and took him to the hospital in Athens. A week later, the old man was out and about knocking on doors and asking about people he had known and neighbored with, thirty years before. Some of them had passed away. At any rate, the new snakebite had reversed the effects of the first one, and as a result the old man had renewed his original lease on life. He simply picked up where he had left off. The question now was: Had a similar phenomenon occurred with Beth's cousin, Charlie?

"Beth, sweetheart, you have just got to take this one day at a time. You don't know enough to analyze it. Whether you want to admit it or not, Charlie has been an integral part of your life for as long as you can remember. Even in her absence, she had a place in your heart and mind. The fact that you are sitting here telling me about this is evidence that you still care about her and she is still part of your life. Sometimes, the best part of caring for someone is to not ask the sensitive and personal questions. So what if there is some terrible, dark secret lurking in the shadows. Open up and let some light in and the shadows of doubt will grow smaller. Right now, I think Charlie needs you and you have to be there for her. You have to do that unconditionally.

"I hope I've been of some help to you, Beth. Should you need to lean on me for support just say the word. You have my phone number. We're friends and that means I will be there for you whenever you need to talk."

Frank started to lean back on his bar stool when Beth reached across the bar and put her hand behind his neck. She pulled him close and kissed him lightly on the cheek.

"Frank, you are a true friend and I'm glad you feel the way you do about helping me get through this. In fact, I do need you to do something for me. In a few minutes, Charlie will be walking through that door. After all these years, I hope I will recognize her. She will be staying with me for a couple of weeks and I am really antsy about this."

Instantly, Frank realized he had opened widely the door of commitment and that meant he had fallen into a trap of his own making. All those years in the military and he was still vulnerable to volunteering. Perhaps he could find some wiggle room for how much he would have to get involved.

"So, what is it that you want me to do? I mean she doesn't even know me."

"Hey, you're the private investigator with all these stories of how you find out things about people. What's that word you always throw around? Oh yes, elicitation. Just elicit all you can and give me some advice. I want you to hang out with us and keep me from putting my foot in my mouth. You have all that behavioral training and you're always talking about how important it is to be objective. I'm too close to the situation to try any of that. Come on, you said you would help."

"Alright, you got me. I'll do what I can to help you out. Besides, I like a good challenge and live for the opportunity to defy the odds while testing my abilities. Just remember, sweetheart, there is a risk involved whenever you step into the unknown areas of someone's mind. Matters of the heart can be a quagmire at times. Remember, it's only human to get off track when you take chances. The important thing is that we don't let this get out of hand and allow it blow up in our faces. The last thing I want is to contribute to breaking up a life long friendship. I'll do what I can, but the thing you have to do right now is be there for your friend."

"Terrific. I'm glad I don't have to take this on totally alone." The tension in Beth's face relaxed a little. "That beer's on me, Frank."

"Wow. My services have been bought and sold for the price of a Bud Light."

"Funny, Frank. That's not what Jill tells me. She says you're a pushover for a slow dance. Don't worry, buddy, I'm not the jealous type. Besides, just wait until I get my arms around you for one of those slow dances."

Anticipation of Charlie's arrival began to snowball for both Beth and Frank and there was nothing either one of them could do to stave off their anxiety.

Beth busied herself by engaging a couple of regular patrons with idle bar talk. There was an awkward uneasiness in her demeanor that culminated with her dropping a glass behind the bar. The sound of the shattering glass prompted a few acknowledging and playful hoots from the customer ranks. The distraction was in line with her sometimes playful nature and that had a calming effect for Beth.

Frank's thoughts raced off in a different direction. The anticipation over a mystery was already bouncing around in his mind like a ping pong ball. Anything that had the potential of turning into intrigue always excited him. Right now, his intuition was pulling him toward Beth's cry for help and his determination for answering that call was beginning to grow by leaps and bounds. Besides, investigating suspected insurance fraud and routine auto accidents rarely aroused this level of excitement; this was a totally different challenge.

Frank's eyes caught sight of some movement on the overhead security monitor that covered the parking lot at the front door. He raised an eyebrow when he saw a Ford pickup pull up out front. A woman got out on the drivers side. Setting up a little straighter, he shot a look at Beth, who then also turned her attention to the monitor. Most female patrons don't arrive driving an old pickup. Oh well, this is Texas, the pickup capital of the world.

The look on Beth's face confirmed that this was the anticipated moment. Surely her stomach was in a knot and her heart was beginning to race.

Frank took a deep breath and felt sorry for Beth as she braced for the meeting. Even though Trail Riders was Beth's turf, the neon beer signs that decked the walls were now casting shadows instead of projecting an inviting sense of warmth and merriment. A tenuous reunion in a bar filled with drinkers on a Friday night left the two old girlfriends unsure of themselves. So much could go wrong or everything could work out just fine.

Beth quickly sprang into action when she saw a customer sitting next to Frank. She ran around the bar and pulled him away to the juke box, handed him two one dollar bills and told him to make a few more selections. With an empty stool now by Frank's side, Beth locked eyes with Charlie. Her plan was obvious, she would immediately usher Charlie over to Frank and introduce them. This would give her some extra time to see if there was any noticeable uneasiness between her and Charlie.

Fortunately, there appeared to be a mutual self-surrender of devotion between the two women. Frank saw the tears streaking down their cheeks and this was a good sign; an expected and natural occurrence. The two women rushed toward one another and that caught everyone's attention. A brief silence settled over the bar as everyone watched with approval, even though few of them, if any, knew who the stranger was or why she was there. At least the new arrival was friendly and posed no threat to the regulars. The over-riding feeling among the patrons was a recollection of the time a Southern Baptist woman had sashayed into the bar and immediately began to preach the horrors of drinking and carousing. That incident sent some patrons scrambling for their vehicles.

Frank wondered what the two out-of-touch friends truly felt they owed to one another. He also wondered about Charlie's motive for reviving her old ties to Beth. There had to be a good story in there somewhere and Frank wanted to learn the details. After all, curiosity was one of his curses and he always gave his best effort to learn the root causes behind every story.

At least for him, the night was turning out to be great even though things were playing out in a smoke-filled barroom. The most important outcome, for whatever the future held, had to be preserving the title of 'friend' when it came to Beth. Finding a good friend had little to do with where that special person was found. Barroom to church, farm to foxhole, people are no better or worse than what they say and do.

Soon the captive silence began to fade and the bar was again abuzz with idle bar talk. Beth had turned Charlie's attention to Frank and for the first time he had a good look at Charlie. Her hair was red, flaming red, hung straight nearly to her waist, and it was aglow like a candle's flame. Walking toward him disclosed that she was extremely slender and her tight jeans made him do a double take. She did not have large breasts, but they appeared firm with nice cleavage. Maybe she was athletic or simply no stranger to strenuous ranch work. Of course, good genetics could not be ruled out. At any rate, she was packaged nicely.

The closer she came the more he noticed her face and skin. She was graceful in form and fair in feature. Her cheeks and forehead were sprinkled with freckles and her lips had just enough gloss to make them look full. She extended a hand as Beth introduced her.

The glow from the dim lighting could not hide the fact that her eyes were green, on the verge of turning hazel. The eye color had to be a family genetic trait because Beth's were the same. All and all, everything fit nicely with the Irish name of Charlene O'Keefe.

Frank knew that if he ever had a minor weakness or failing it came during that awkward moment when he was meeting an attractive woman for the first time. In this case, he sensed that Charlie must have been harboring a similar anxiety because, for an instant, they both only looked at each other and smiled as if at their own nervousness. He then hoped that Beth hadn't given him too much of a buildup. He was one of those men that struggled over meeting attractive women for the first time. Hopefully the ice of awkwardness would melt quickly.

The scent of Charlie's perfume was luring, but not overwhelming. Her voice was very distinguishable. "I'm pleased to make your acquaintance, Frank. Beth speaks highly of you. I must admit, you do not look the way I thought you would."

Charlie's voice was magnificently charming and that made an incredible impression on Frank. For a woman who had been out of circulation for so long, she had a lot going for her. He instantly understood why she could have been a terrific singer. She projected a quiet charm that could easily be misinterpreted as seductive. However, he doubted that she was anything but a friendly gal from the country who displayed a sense of natural charm; the home grown variety. However, there was always that chance that she had acquired her charm from being an entertainer. The truth was probably a combination of all these things. She would no doubt fit in no matter where she went.

"I am likewise pleased to make your acquaintance. In a pleasant way, you are every bit as pretty as I have been told, and more so. Tell me, Charlie, what do you think of the big city of Dallas?"

"It is a big place, a very big place. I haven't seen enough of it to form an opinion yet. I suppose it's like most big cities. They all seem to have their good and bad points. I guess any place is no better or worse than the people who live there." Her wide smile and friendly tone made her a good candidate for being a public relations person.

Returning Charlie's smile, Frank responded in a way that made it easy for her to say more. "I don't know if Beth told you, but, I grew up on a small farm in Southeastern Ohio. When I got to the big city, I had to learn a new set of skills to survive while maintaining a degree of sanity."

"No, we haven't had time to talk that much about you. However, I can see that we have one thing in common. We both come from a rural setting and we know life is different in the big city."

She placed her purse on the bar next to Frank and scooted up on the stool next to him. Since she didn't know anyone else in the bar besides Beth, she seized the opportunity the empty stool next to him provided. Her move spared both Beth and Frank from having to voice an invitation.

"What can I get you to drink, Charlie?" Beth kept her distance to allow Frank to take over for her.

In spite of her boldness, Frank realized that Charlie was no common barfly or a rough and tumble cowgirl. At some point in her life, she had acquired an education that amounted to more than just high school parlance. Maybe she hadn't spent all of her time away from home singing in nightclubs. Then there was the possibility that her demeanor came from having a good upbringing.

Frank knew that it was his job to do more listening than speaking, otherwise, he would not learn as much as he wanted about Charlie. Often during his life, Frank had learned too many hard lessons when it came to conversing. Yes, the greatest art in conversation is silence. So he made a mental note to only ask open ended questions and make comments designed to allow a free flow of cordial conversation. Besides,

Charlie appeared to be a very charming and interesting person. Briefly, he wondered if maybe Beth had read too much into Charlie's absence from there friendship. Beth could be jumping to too many conclusions.

Looking at Frank's empty Bud Light Charlie answered. "Let me have a Bud Light, too. I haven't had a beer in ages."

Frank gave a nod to Beth that he would like another one himself.

Apparently, Charlie didn't need much prodding to talk. Surely, she wanted to make a favorable impression on Frank for Beth's sake. Naturally, there was one other possibility; if she controlled the conversation then she had a better chance of steering their conversation to more comfortable topics. At any rate, she took the initiative to keep things rolling.

"So, what is it you do here in the big city, Frank?"

"Well, I thought you would never ask. No, I'm only kidding." He was noticeably hesitant. "I do private investigations, mostly for insurance companies. It pays the bills and I get to set my own schedule. You could say that I like my independence." Frank placed extra emphasis on insurance company work to down play his other work. He preferred not to come off as the stereotypic TV image of a private eye.

"What about all that neat, sneaky stuff, do you get to do any of that? I bet you have to have all the same gadgets that cops do, don't you?" Her tone had turned a little harsh and she wasn't looking Frank in the eye when she spoke.

He sensed an element of investigative knowledge coupled with a lack of confidence in law enforcement. Especially noteworthy was the slanted emphasis she used when she said the word "cops." Frank decided to file her sarcasm away in the back of his head. More than once, he had noticed how people give something away about themselves in the way they use words; this was one of those times. Tidbits of information have a way of adding up over time.

"Yeah, I do have a few things that help me get the job done. The difference between me and the cops is that I will use my stuff a lot quicker because I worry more about my reputation for giving the most service for my fees than the police do for their salaries. They are always prioritizing because of budgets. I don't earn my living as a public servant looking out for the tax payers. I charge more money when I use my gadgets so if someone wants me to pull out all the stops and use everything, and they have the money, I'll give them what they want in the way of a stellar performance. I'm a business man that sells his skills. You could say that I'm a bit of a mercenary. A client gets what he pays for."

Charlie sighed and said something that was nearly inaudible. Frank thought she said, "It figures."

"Have you ever done criminal cases?" Now, she was looking Frank in the eye.

"Sure, I have done some."

"Can't that get a little dangerous?"

"Sometimes any case can get a little rough. One problem with criminal cases is that they don't usually pay a lot. Although, once in a while, especially with capital cases, a court appointed attorney is allowed to hire a private investigator. I've heard of a few guys making a pretty penny on those high profile cases. Of course, the rich always get the best."

Charlie wrinkled her nose indicating she was harboring a little disgust over the criminal justice system. Frank wondered if maybe she had hit a brick wall following some run-in with the law. The law is not always equal and rarely is it just. It's simply a flawed system, but, better than what anyone could find in other countries.

Beth placed their drinks on the bar in front of them. "Hey, you two, lighten up. You aren't having a spat already are you? This is a bar so you should be laughing and whooping it up."

"No, not at all; she just wants to know a little bit about what I do for a living."

"Don't worry, Beth; I'm not going to beat him up and throw him under the bus. He seems to be too nice of a guy for that. I just get a little moody sometimes. Don't worry, I don't intend on putting a damper on the night. You have my word on that; both of you." Charlie realized that her mood was edging toward being grumpy. There were some touchy things in her past and she had to find a way to not let them control her.

She nodded at an empty pool table and launched the challenge that few men could refuse. "When was the last time a woman kicked your ass in a game of eight ball?

"Well, if you really want to know, that did happen once. Let me tell you that little story before we start playing.

"Years ago, I was sitting in a small bar in Houston. I had gone there a few times and it was sort of a rough place, at times. There was this video slot machine in the back and this woman asked me if I wanted to split the cost of playing it. I went for it and we both popped ten dollars in it. I don't know how it happened, but, the next thing I knew the damn thing was spitting out all these tickets and she was screaming like a banshee. I thought she was going to have an organism right there on the spot.

"I knew it was only a video machine and couldn't pay off. Yeah, right! The next thing I knew she was stuffing the tickets into an envelope. She sealed it put her initials over the seal and asked me to do the same. She then gave it to the bartender and asked me to meet her there the next night at 7:00 p.m., sharp. I know, this wasn't exactly legal, but, I did it anyway.

"We met the next night, a Friday night. The bartender handed the envelope back to us and when she opened it there was $400 in it. Now what do you think of that?"

Frank was doing a good job of baiting Charlie because she gave him this puzzled look and then asked: "What in the hell does this have to do with a woman beating you in a game of eight ball?"

"I thought you would never ask. I'm just setting the scene for you. Anyway, we went out for a nice dinner and then returned to the bar. We got there just in time for all these guys to arrive. They worked out in the gulf on oil rigs and were in town to have a good time. They had more money than sense.

"The woman I was with wore this tight leather miniskirt and she was a knockout. The place started to fill up with these oil well guys so she suggested that if we wanted to play pool, we should grab a table while we had the chance. There was no way these guys could not notice her. I beat her three games in a row and then I got a little sloppy and she beat me. She didn't beat me too bad, but bad enough. Everyone was having a good laugh at our expense.

"The next thing I knew, these guys wanted to play, too. We played doubles and then things began to change. First, the guys wanted to play for a dollar a game along with the price of the next game. Then it went to five dollars; then ten and then twenty dollars. Before I knew it, we almost lost all the money we had made on the video slot."

"Sounds like those guys were reeling you and your lady friend in." Charlie showed signs of feeling sorry for Frank.

"That's when things got really crazy. The biggest thing I remember was seeing fifteen one hundred dollar bills on the table. My wallet was empty and so was my friend's purse." Frank shook his head in disgust and then frowned.

"Come on Frank, she didn't exactly beat you in a game of pool. Now did she?"

"Well, I guess not. What she did do, though, was tell me to sit down and relax. Then she broke the racked balls and started running the table. Those poor guys never got a shot. The whole game was her putting balls in pockets; left, right and center. When the game was over, she scooped up the money and suggested that we get the hell out of here.

"They were still throwing rocks at us and cursing us when we spun out of the parking lot." Frank was smiling, ear to ear.

"I would say you two were lucky to make it out alive. She was a ringer and a hustler and that doesn't always turn out the way you want it to. She just used you, Frank. I would say she risked your life in the process." Charlie's analysis was mostly on the mark.

"Yeah, you could say that. She did split the money with me, though. We stayed friends for a long time. Oh yes, there was one more thing. I asked her how she came to be such a good pool player. You know what she told me?"

"I'm all ears."

"She said that three years in a row she played in the finals at the Las Vegas championships. A couple of nights later she demonstrated a bunch of trick shots and they were all really amazing. Anyway, I've never seen anyone shoot like that again. Don't worry, Charlie, I'm not a hustler. But, I am a competitor and that means I will do my best to beat you. In other words, I won't give you a break just because you're a girl."

"Thanks for the warning, Frank. I'll keep that in mind." She was heading to an empty table.

They had three games under their belts when they were shaken from their concentration by the band's arrival. They were testing their equipment. Frank was hanging his head a little lower than when he and Charlie had started. He had only won one game.

Beth had her hands full taking care of the bar and somewhere along the way a young lady had arrived to take care of customers who were filling up the tables near the dance floor.

A cute gal in tight fitting jeans was adjusting the microphone and Frank was already thinking about the prospect of dancing with Charlie. However, Charlie's demeanor began to drift off in another direction.

Charlie dashed all hopes for Frank having a night of dancing with her when she snuggled up next to him and said, "You know, I had a long drive here and the time has gotten away from me." She rubbed her stomach. "I haven't eaten all day and I'm famished. Also, I don't think beer on an empty tummy is all that good for girl. What do you think?"

The only logical response to what Charlie was saying was to agree. "You know, you are so right. I just realized that I haven't eaten dinner either. I know a great little restaurant not far from here. What do you say we go get something to eat? Come on, it's on me."

"You don't have to buy me dinner, Frank. I'll split the tab with you. There's nothing wrong with going Dutch with a girl. Besides, I do think that it's a good idea for you to take me. The truth is, I don't know my way around Dallas and I could get into trouble out there in the dark."

"That settles it then. Let's tell Beth what we're up to. She might get nervous if we just up and leave." Frank was handing Charlie's purse to her as he spoke.

On another level, he was trying not to read too much into what was taking place. However, in the back of his mind there was this tiny thought about Charlie feeling a bit uneasy over watching the cute gal with the band singing to the crowd. If there hadn't been such a dramatic shift in Charlie's singing career, way back when she was in Arizona, she would probably want to compare notes with the girl that was about to perform.

Beth was firm when they announced their plan to go out for dinner. "I want you two back here at closing time. Charlie and I have a lot of catching up to do. In fact, you should be back here by midnight unless you're going to hang out in some all night diner."

Beth's concern registered well with both of them. Frank nodded okay and Charlie bounced back with, "Yes mommy."

Half an hour later, Frank and Charlie were sitting across from one another in a quaint little Italian restaurant. They were relaxed under the spell of some soft Italian song, and had they been fluent in the Italian language, they would have recognized it as a love song. Frank forced his best façade of casualness and prodded slightly.

"Beth mentioned that you used to sing professionally. She said you had a beautiful voice and everyone was really excited for you."

"Well, that was a long time ago. Things have a way of changing. At the time, I was old enough to leave home; just not mature enough. I guess you could say I was extremely naïve and made some mistakes that turned out to be costly. Anyway, this is not something I feel comfortable talking about." Her response closed the door for any additional conversation on the topic.

Frank let her off the hook by a surprised glance at his wristwatch. "Wow. It's after eleven. We better wrap this up or Beth is going to be ticked off at both of us."

Precisely at midnight Frank pulled to a stop in Trail Rider's parking lot. Music from the band was blaring through the front door that had been propped open for a bit of fresh air.

"Well, I guess I had better deliver you to Beth." He was watching Charlie's face for a reaction.

She fidgeted a bit and then lit a cigarette. "Can't we just wait out here? I'm really not in the mood to sit around and listen to a bunch of drunks."

"Well, we could sit out here until the place closes up and everyone empties out. I might fall asleep on you, though." Frank was trying to send a message about the reality of what Charlie was suggesting.

"Frank, let's go in and see if Beth will just give us the keys to her place. That way you can go on to your place and I can take a nap. I know Beth will want to stay up late talking, but, I'm just worn out. I was up before daylight so it has been a long day for me. Do you get my drift?"

"You're right, Charlie. I'm pretty tuckered out myself." He got out of his truck and wandered inside to confront Beth.

Beth displayed a bewildered look when she saw Frank walking in alone. She wasted no time getting to him to find out what was going on.

"Where's Charlie? Did something happen? She's alright, isn't she?"

"She's sitting in my truck. She's beat. It's been a long day for her. She wants to know if you will give me the key to your place along with some directions."

"I wondered about that myself. Let me get the keys and write down some directions for you." She was reaching under the bar for her purse.

Several men spread out along the bar were asking for another drink and Jill was fidgeting impatiently while she waited for Beth to fill an order for the tables near the dance floor. "Hold on everyone. I'll be right with you." Beth yelled out with an annoyed tone.

At such a late hour patrons had a way of displaying their impatience, and to a point, their arrogance. They already had a few brews under their belts and their fun meters were peaking. This was the part of the bar scene that Frank could do without. He was not the type of person that was prone to being a night owl.

Beth shoved a key and a crudely drawn map at Frank. "Here, it's not far from here so you should have no trouble getting her there. My cell phone number is written down with the directions. Make sure Charlie keeps her cell phone on in case she falls asleep. Oh yeah, make sure she locks her truck up and make sure you see her to the door with her luggage. Do you have any questions?"

"No, Beth; I think you covered everything." Since patrons were beginning to get antsy over not having her undivided attention, Frank turned and headed toward the door.

Frank had Charlie follow him in her truck because it wouldn't have been safe leaving it at Trail Riders. The trip to Beth's apartment only took a few minutes. Charlie only had one large suitcase and a knapsack. He did the manly thing and grabbed the suitcase. "How in the world did you get this thing into your truck?" Frank grunted as he hoisted it to the ground.

"My dad put it in there for me. He's a tough guy for his age."

"Well, there's something to be said for the rigors of ranch work." Frank was glad the bulky suitcase had wheels on it.

"My dad only ranched part time. Ranch work helped him fit in better with the community."

Charlie's comment opened the door for Frank to pry a little. "So how did your dad earn a living the rest of the time?"

"He was a deputy sheriff for as long as I can remember."

Charlie's answer caused something to bounce around in the back of his mind. Earlier in the evening Charlie was asking about the justice system and law enforcement. He filed these bits of information away for possible future use.

Once Charlie and her luggage were safely inside Beth's apartment, he allowed her to see him to the door.

"Frank, I apologize if I somehow messed up your night. I didn't mean to. You really seem like a nice guy and I would like to see more of you. That is if it's alright with you?"

"Well, if you want to dance with me you will have to pay the fiddler." He was all smiles.

"Exactly, what is it I will have to pay this fiddler?"

"How about helping out around my office a little once you and Beth are caught up? You can even tag along with me on a couple cases. Does that sound fair? I might even take you out to dinner again and it won't be Dutch. That is if you're interested."

"You have a deal, buster. I think this is going to end up being a fun trip." She winked, smiled, and to his surprise she grabbed him by the collar and pulled until their faces were close. She kissed him softly on the cheek then eased the door shut. The last thing Frank heard was the deadbolt being locked. Now, he had more than a casual interest in her. Hopefully, he was not only drawn by the mystery surrounding her, but also drawn to her as a person. All indications pointed to a possibility for some romance and that was indeed a bonus.

He couldn't help wonder why there was no evidence of a man in her life other than her father. After all, Beth had told him that the two of them had quite a record of double-dating. Everything aside, Charlie appeared normal in spite of the inside information from Beth.

CHAPTER 3

Frank was more tired than he had realized and the sleep that followed was extremely restful. The next morning he awoke energized. The day promised to be an easy one, and for that he was thankful. He liked Saturdays and tried to keep them as open as possible. Once he slipped into his robe, he headed to the kitchen cupboard and grabbed a glass. After tossing in a couple of ice cubes, he filled the glass to the brim with cold orange juice from the fridge. This ritual kept him in step with his Saturday morning routine.

He slid the patio door open, and with drink in hand, he strolled over to the chase lounge. After a long drink from the glass, he sat it down on one of the two patio tables. By this time any hint of the night's chill had dissipated. The setting appeared serene as he stretched out on the lounge. Lacing his fingers behind his head he stared up at the sky. It was pale blue, streaked with long, high feathery clouds. A great day was in the making.

Absorbing the warmth of a new day, Frank couldn't help reflecting on last night's events. Everything pointed to an interesting new challenge. All challenges involving human behavior tugged at his natural instincts and lured him into another realm, one where he desired to roam. He would always be a student of life. People and their varied fates, coupled with their circumstances, became a live stage upon which he could ad lib at will. Each and every person in his life had all been teachers in his reality-based classroom. Yes, the whole world was his university, theater, and universe.

Something, years ago, had knocked Charlie's life out of balance with her career, and her childhood friendship with Beth. Beth had always been her confidant. Adding fuel to the smoldering mystery was some obscure connection to the criminal justice system. The whole affair seemed to be rooted in some event or circumstance that had played out in Arizona. The end result seemed to be isolation, following a return home. It had also been a show-stopper to her career as a country-western nightclub singer.

Now, all these years were missing from her life. On the other side of the coin, Charlie was now ready to reach out to Beth in an attempt to restore some degree of normalcy to her life. Perhaps, she had come to terms with the fact that her father would not always be around to care for her and protect her. Support, stability, and order were things that had to be high on her list of priorities. Frank realized that coming to Dallas to see Beth, after all these years, was a monumental leap of faith for Charlie. She was betting heavily on this trip; she had to be.

Fearing that he would doze back off to sleep if he spent any more time in the warming sun, Frank decided to get up and take a shower.

Noontime rolled around quicker than he had expected and boredom began to settle in. Pacing about the house proved useless. Finally, he switched on the television, but, was only mildly entertained by the president giving yet another scholarly and eloquent speech on the sad financial state the country had fallen into. As expected, the president couldn't resist stating how he had inherited the country's financial woes from the previous administration's blunders and inaction. No doubt there was some truth to the president's assertions since the previous administration had over spent while pretending to be conservative. There was little to support anything to the contrary. People were loosing their homes and jobs at a record pace while the country was waging two wars half way around the world. Businesses were failing and the stock market was declining. In spite of the dire economic situation, the president and a liberal congress were pushing for bigger government and increased debt. Frank couldn't understand how it was possible to spend your way out of debt.

Frank was intrigued by the way successful politicians always managed to keep the general public in a state of fear and alarm. He wondered if the whole political system wasn't designed as a mechanism to maintain job security for elected officials. The most desired politicians were always the ones that were gifted when it came to manipulation in the name of leadership. Ethical and insightful citizens had to be asking themselves if they were being led in the right direction or being led like lambs to slaughter. In Frank's opinion, there was always an aspect of political life that leaned toward being metaphysical with one smoking mirror after another.

However politicians plied their art, it was only that, an art and not a science. Frank wondered why universities taught courses as political science and not political art. No wonder courses in terrorism are taught in political science classes because violence has a way of driving politics. The only thing that was surely flourishing was controversy.

Concerning the president, Frank thought the man never had a clear, detailed plan for any of the challenges that were facing the country. What he had was the ability and intellect to tap the skills of others who had expertise in the various fields where challenges were running rampant. No single man, even the president, can be an expert in everything. However, whenever the experts come up short, the blame would fall on the leader's shoulders and that meant the president. There was also something to be said about the company the president was keeping.

One disconcerting note was that the president tended to select his czars from people with questionable backgrounds. Some conspiracy theorists and political analysts were already waving red flags and questioning the president's motives over his selections. The question now becomes; where is the president really trying to take the country? Could a single person at the top of our governmental pyramid be duping the masses for some hidden purpose? We were indeed living in scary times.

In general, Frank had another theory when it came to politics. Throughout our country's history, the pendulum always swung between right wing conservative over to the left wing liberal positions. After eight years of Republican rule, it was time for the pendulum to swing back to the Democrats and liberalism. The danger is in the pendulum swinging too far in either direction. The country already had its fill of Republican domination that kept coming up short. Sadly, the Republicans were spending like liberals and that made people wonder which ones were representing what.

Had the pendulum not swung back and continued on course to the right then we would no longer have a thriving two-party system. The point of no return has never been clearly set. Lacking a two-party system, there would be no reason to vote; that is unless we were voting for the individual and not a party line. When would we ever decide on whether we wanted a democracy or a republic? Frank always thought the founding fathers had made our country a republic.

Frank figured that no matter where the pendulum is positioned, at any given time, there would always be critics and maybe that is the way it should be. Think of the irony if a category of "None of the above" was ever placed on a national ballot and the majority of voters checked that block at election time. There would be no vote of confidence, only a realization that our government was broken. There was one upside notion to eliminating our two-party system, though. That would be doing away with all parties and allowing us to vote for the candidate and not down a party line. Maybe that was what President George Washington meant in his farewell address when he warned about the perils of having a two-party system.

Somehow, all of the treacherous waters and storms facing this country, now or in the future, would be weathered. They always were. However, regardless of what politicians do in the name of making us safe and prosperous, there will always be something going wrong.

The ringing of his telephone jerked Frank back from his cerebral essay of contemporary politics. Thankful for the interruption, he made his way to the phone and answered with a simple "Hello."

Charlie asked; "Hey. What are you doing today?"

"I'm not doing anything, in particular. I bet you guys were up all night going through a talking marathon."

"We had a good time talking with each other. There was no competition, no vanity, only a leisurely talk about sentimental things. We laughed ourselves to tears talking about all those crazy things we did as teenagers. Beth and I both had to call it quits around five this morning. It was like we were having a two person pajama party."

Frank couldn't resist saying, "I bet Beth's butt will be dragging at work today."

"Oh, you know it. I just woke up and see that she already left for work. She left a note on the dresser. I caught my second wind about an hour ago and just got out of the shower."

"You sure do sound chipper, Charlie. As for me, I'm bored to tears. I'm glad you called. Do you have any plans for the day?"

She was quick to respond, "I'm wide open. Do you want to hang out?"

"I can pick you up in say twenty minutes. Is that okay?"

"Terrific! I'll be ready. See you when you get here."

"I'll be out of here in five minutes, sweetheart." He almost regretted adding the term "sweetheart." He hoped it wasn't too forward and familiar for greeting a new friend. After further consideration, he had to admit that they were making inroads when it came to forming a closer friendship.

After knocking on Beth's apartment door, he waited nervously like a teen on his first date until the door opened. The sunlight lit up her green eyes and they sparkled with energy. His eyes were locked on hers and he had to force himself to break contact. The sheen in her red hair was every bit as breathtaking as her eyes. The only distraction in all her natural beauty was the age wrinkles that had crept in around her forehead and eyes. But, she was aging gracefully and that lent her a special splendor and charm. Attractive women like Charlie had a way of complementing their age in a sophisticated and eloquent way. At any rate, he felt that she was prettier than he was handsome.

"Well, Mister Private Eye, are you going to stand here all day gawking at me or are you going to take me somewhere?"

"Sorry, my mind was somewhere else for a moment. As for taking you somewhere, I don't really have a plan other than showing you my office. After that, we can just make it up as we go. How's that sound?"

"Some of the best times I ever had happened without a plan."

He was mildly surprised when Charlie took hold of his hand as they walked to his pickup. He had no sure fire way of knowing if they were going out on a date or just paling around. He guessed time would tell.

The drive to the office at this time of day on a Saturday was easygoing because traffic was light. Naturally, in a large city like Dallas there was never a time when there was no traffic. During the ride, Charlie constantly leaned over toward him in an apparent display of affection. He liked the attention she was giving him.

Frank concluded that Charlie had a gift when it came to socializing and being with someone. He figured she would show the same consideration to any man she was spending the day with. In the back of his mind he wondered if she would demonstrate any public display of affection. After all, she had not done so the night before. Maybe her casual manner and affectionate tone was only her way of thanking him for taking the time to show her around and giving her a tour of his office. He hoped she wouldn't be disappointed with the office because there really wasn't much to it.

As soon as they pulled up in the parking lot at his office, Charlie made it clear that she was not just killing time. She was sincerely interested in what it was like to be a private investigator; especially in a city as large as Dallas. She was firing questions, left and right, about the variety of work that went along with the job. The energy in her questioning was like an enchanting spell and the effect was warming. He wasn't only impressed with her enthusiasm, he also felt very comfortable in her presence. Even if there was no romance in the making, she would become a very good friend. Childress County, Texas must have a lot going for it when it came to producing women with a degree of charm.

After an hour, she was skilled at doing basic research on his computer. She was self-confident in a relaxed way. There was no slow drifting from one program or action to another; she was focused and quick with the keyboard. Unlike her singing career, she was no stranger to a computer.

Frank was the patient type who was happy to teach the finer, routine aspects of working in a private investigator's office. The personal computer was an indispensable tool for his vocation. He was always amazed, and grateful, when he found such a quick study for his work. However, work in the office required a different skill set than plying his trade in the field.

Charlie looked across the table at Frank after printing out two practice investigative reports. "What do you think?"

"I not only see that you are pretty, you also have a great deal of talent. If you are around long enough, I would like you to work with me. Don't worry; you'll earn your way in this office. How's ten dollars an hour sound?"

"I never expected to make any money. I thought we were just hanging out. Do I have to talk to you like a boss?" She wasn't smiling when she popped this question.

"No. We can be pretty lax in this kind of an environment unless there is a client in the area. In that case, we will have to maintain a more formal composure. How do you feel about this kind of an arrangement?"

"Hey, Frank, I think we both will know where to draw the line when someone is around watching us. Just don't expect me to hold back too much when we are alone, though. I mean, we are kissing buddies, aren't we?" She had that coy feminine posture that was not only fresh; it was also girlishly cute. Frank was also wondering when that first big kiss would come his way. Hopefully, he wasn't reading too much into the situation.

He nodded and smiled, acknowledging that they had formed a clear understanding that there was a personal relationship forming between them. She was indeed a beautiful woman with intelligence and that was all the chemistry he needed to form an opinion about a relationship.

Frank walked over to the little fridge in his office and pulled out a can of Pepsi; his proclaimed elixir of life. He split the contents in two paper cups and handed one to Charlie.

"This is one of my little weaknesses. I am almost addicted to Pepsi and that is something you will have to get use to." He held his cup up toward her to make a toast and she did likewise. "Here's to the future and the good times it holds for us."

"Here, here, I'm for that." She touched her cup to his and they both drank like they were sipping a fine French wine.

He smiled and headed to the restroom to relieve himself. "Excuse me. I'll be back in a minute; nature calls."

Charlie glanced out the front window at something that caught her eye. A black Lexus pulled up in front of the office and a woman got out and headed toward the office door. Without as much as a knock, the door swung open. Charlie knew that Frank's office was a business place and that meant it was opened to the public. Inside her mind, she hoped the woman was not Frank's girlfriend. That would certainly spoil her day.

At least this was a Saturday and there was no "open" or 'closed' sign in the window. What bothered her was that she knew that Frank did not intend to work today; he was going to spend the day with her. The woman must have seen her so Charlie couldn't ignore the woman's presence. Besides, maybe the woman's arrival would turn into a new case and she could work it all the way through with Frank. She was beginning to feel like she was already on the clock.

At first the woman didn't speak, she only stood there as if hesitating. Charlie quickly sized up her appearance. She was at least two inches taller then Charlie and dressed conservatively with navy blue slacks and a white blouse. Her hair was short and feathered back. Her hair was also black as coal. However, it was not her clothing or hair that distinguished her, it was her jewelry.

Charlie thought it took a lot of nerve or a degree of arrogance to wear what appeared to be a diamond wristwatch and a pearl necklace. Going about town dressed like she was and without a male escort was an open invitation to any potential mugger who might spot her.

Charlie put her best foot forward and greeted the woman. "Good afternoon, I'm Charlie. How can I help you?" She extended her hand in her best country tradition, like a true Texan.

Charlie fully expected the woman to be snobbish, and for a split second, she wondered if the woman might not take her extended hand. Surprisingly, there was no reluctance at all on the part of the stranger. Not only did she take Charlie's hand, she shook it as if they were old friends.

"I'm pleased to meet you Charlie. Is Charlie informal for Charlene?"

"Why yes it is."

"I guessed as much. Excuse me. My name is Felicity, Felicity Whitman. I was hoping to catch Mister McLaughlin in. I'm sorry, I don't have an appointment." Felicity's voice was businesslike, but not in any way threatening. In spite of her affluent façade, Felicity seemed pleasant.

"You're in luck, Felicity. Frank is in the other room and should be out in a few minutes." Charlie immediately regretted her boldness and familiarity by referring to Frank by his first name. Oh well, it was a small office and things like that should be expected.

Charlie assumed the role of hostess. "I don't have any coffee or tea to offer you, but, I do have a Pepsi."

"Actually, that would be nice, if it isn't any bother. I'm a little dry and some sugar and caffeine would be a nice boost."

Now that the ice was broken and the tone was cordial, Charlie wasted no time getting them both a can of cold Pepsi. She also concluded that everyone that appeared wealthy was not necessarily stuck up.

Both women took a seat on opposite ends of a couch that was in the front office. Charlie couldn't help wondering why such a person as Felicity needed a private investigator. Then again, maybe she wasn't here for any special need- only time would tell.

Nervously and suddenly aware that this was a private investigator's office, Charlie craned her neck so she could scope out the parking lot. She wasn't sure what she was looking for, but if it appeared, she knew she would recognize it. Felicity's Lexus and Frank's Nissan were the only vehicles in sight. What she did notice, though, was a darkening sky.

"Oh great, it looks like we could be in for a real storm." Charlie's announcement caused Felicity to twist about for her own look. She sighed with disgust when she saw the dark ominous clouds beginning to gather.

"This is Texas, just when you think you know the weather, it can change in the matter of minutes. We can't even trust the weatherman, anymore." Felicity looked at her flashy wristwatch as if she had a schedule to follow.

The wind blew the door open with a bang followed by a flash of blinding lightening, a clear indication that the storm was closer than either woman had expected. Thunder shook the heavens and everything around them. Charlie sprang into action, shutting the door, and securing it with the deadbolt.

As if on cue, Frank emerged from the other room. "Man oh man alive, where did that storm come from?" No sooner than he spoke, he noticed they had company.

Frank was standing right in front of the two women before he realized it, and his face took on a questioning look. He reacted without any prompting by extending his hand to the new arrival.

"Frank, this is Felicity Whitman and she popped in just ahead of the storm. She's here to see you, on business. Felicity, this is Frank McLaughlin, Private Investigator." Charlie was able to salvage the moment of surprise for Frank by performing her first official duty as his assistant. She knew her introduction was flawless.

"I'm pleased to make your acquaintance, Felicity. How may I be of service to you?" From the change that was quickly taking place on Felicity's face, he was keenly aware that something was distressing her.

"Please, have a seat here." He offered her one of the stuffed leather chairs that was directly in front of his desk. Before she could sit, there was another loud crash of thunder and with it came the drenching sound of a torrential downpour outside. The combination made the hair stand up on all their necks and arms. There was a noticeable shiver from all of them.

Charlie wanted to be privy to the discussion, but, she agonized over whether it would be proper to remain in the room. Since she had already, to some degree, established a rapport with Felicity, she elected to stay and took a seat on the couch. She felt she was now involved, unless Felicity or Frank took exception to her presence. There was no reaction to the contrary from either of them.

"Well, Mister McLaughlin, I guess that's the proper way to address a private investigator. Is that alright?"

"I believe we will both be more comfortable if we go by first names. The important thing is that you get everything out without any more discomfort than is necessary."

"Thank you, Frank. I appreciate you putting me at ease. This may take awhile. I'm not interrupting your day, am I?"

"No, I think the rain put a damper on that. Go ahead and let me know what's going on so I can see how I might be able to help."

"My husband is Reverend Matthew Whitman. He's a protestant minister in Plano. We have been happily married for eighteen years and we still love each other with the same passion and dedication we started out with. I couldn't have asked for a better man to go through life with. He has always been there for me, through thick and thin, and all I want out of life is to be there for him."

"From what you're telling me, I would say you really have a good thing going for yourselves. I hope things keep working out for you."

Frank knew he was hearing the sweet part of the story so he began bracing for the bitter. After all, Felicity didn't walk into his office without a problem and it was apparent that her problem had something to do with her husband.

Frank remained quiet, giving Felicity time to come up with the right words to justify her reason for needing a private investigator. He sensed that her stomach was knotting up a bit and her heart was beginning to beat a little faster.

"My husband's congregation is a fairly large one. I'd say somewhere in the neighborhood of two thousand. There are a lot of heavy-hitters that attend services on a regular basis. The front pews are filled with judges, bankers, politicians, and by all outward appearances, they are pillars of the community."

"I would say your husband has a pretty good power base of devoted worshipers. He must have quite a bit of clout in the community as a result. It's nice to know that the rich and powerful attend church." Frank was still waiting for the bomb to drop.

Deep inside his heart and mind, Frank had some doubts and reservations when it came to the rich and powerful. There were always the possibilities of corruption and misplaced values. Things that are held as divine; like morals, virtue and honor, have a way of gaining second class status when money is involved. Even men who strut about on moral high ground know that fewer people would notice them if it wasn't for their money and power. The most vile and heartless criminal will surely know the Lord's Prayer by heart. Behind the most righteous façade there is a man or woman with something dark to hide. Everyone does his or her best to only put their best foot forward. People in the public eye have a vested interest in maintaining a flawless and virtuous appearance.

The time Frank took to have these thoughts was long enough for Felicity to ready herself for what to say next. "Now that I have run my mouth about how great my marriage is and how well my husband is established in the clergy and in the community, I know you are wondering why I'm here."

"Truthfully, Felicity, that thought is crossing my mind."

"Well, here goes." She glanced over at Charlie for quick eye contact to demonstrate that she too was included. Just as quickly, her eyes reconnected with Frank's. Somehow, she was comforted that her story was also falling on another woman's ears.

"First, I want to make something perfectly clear. My husband is not having an extramarital affair and neither am I. We love each other dearly and we have never had any problems with our marriage. When you hear what I have to say, there is no cause to speculate on or question our devotion and loyalty to one another." She paused long enough to search the faces of Frank and Charlie for any questioning or challenging reaction to the contrary.

During this moment, the only sound that could be heard was that of the storm that was making a nuisance of itself outside of the office. A sudden flash of lightening followed by an earth shattering clap of thunder nearly caused everyone to jump out of their skin. Briefly, the lights dimmed and everyone wondered if the electricity was about to go out. Luckily, it didn't.

Satisfied that she was making her point, Felicity continued. "When two people like Matthew and I, have lived and worked with each other for as long as we have, you learn to read each other quite well. Often, we are able to read each other's thoughts and anticipate each other's next move and words. We are friends, lovers, and soul mates. It is nearly impossible for us to keep secrets from one another. Note, I said nearly impossible."

"Felicity, if it is any consolation, I fully understand what you're saying. I also know that success in marriage is much more than finding the right person; it's also a matter of being the right person. Your sincerity speaks volumes of the love you have put into your marriage. I can only take your word that your husband has placed the same amount of effort into your marriage. I'm no marriage counselor so my opinion is limited and only based on my observation of you."

Frank was now poised for the critical point that was on the cusp of being delivered. Secretly, he hoped this was not going to turn out to be some weird domestic squabble because Texas was a No Fault Divorce state and there wasn't a lot that private investigators could do unless there were children involved and even that had strict limits.

"Felicity, do you two have children?"

"No, we don't have any children. It's only the two of us. In fact, we were high school sweethearts back in Kansas. Our parents were farmers. My parents still are, but, Matthew's parents didn't do so well when there was a two year drought. His father gave up farming and opened up a hardware store. We never had much experience with a big city until we came to Plano. Why do you ask?"

"No particular reason." Frank told a small white lie. "I'm sorry. I didn't mean to interrupt you."

She shook off the interruption and continued. "Lately, Matthew has been acting very strangely. I tried to approach him to find out what was bothering him and he dismissed my inquiry as frivolous. He told me that it was church business and that I shouldn't be concerned. He said things would work out. The problem is; he is a nervous wreck. Whatever he is dealing with is not some miniscule bit of church business. He's not sleeping well or eating right. Whatever weight he's carrying is weighing him down and destroying his health.

"The other night I woke up and he was not in bed with me. I went about the house looking for him and found him out on the patio praying. I couldn't hear what he was praying about, but, he was sobbing uncontrollably. I mean he is a man of God and a man of great integrity. I'm scared half out of my wits for him. He won't open up and let me in to share this burden, whatever it is. I somehow get the distinct impression that he is trying to protect me from something; something horrible."

Frank watched the tears streaming down Felicity's face as she fought for control- a control that was slow in coming. He still did not have enough information to assess the problem. At this point, he did not want to speculate for fear of being totally off the mark. Past experience told him that strong emotional states, like the one Felicity was exhibiting, had a way of clouding the real issues.

There was a host of possibilities that were running rampant through Frank's mind and somehow they would have to be sorted out in order to make sense of why Matthew was acting as he was. The man's abnormal behavior was an obvious result of some thoughts and feelings associated with a deed or situation. Maybe it was criminal in nature or an ethical slipup that would go badly for a minister should it become known. If Felicity's concern was on point, then there was probably a good reason for her husband's fear. Of course, there was always the possibility that she was over reacting to or misinterpreting a situation and there was no legitimate cause for concern.

Yes, he would have to be extremely skeptical about the information Felicity was feeding him. Was she expressing some misinformed intuition? After all, she was awfully close to her husband and a long distance from the facts, or was she? Before he would run with the case, he would need more background. Also, a full blown investigation could become awfully expensive for a client.

"Felicity, tell me about your husband's friends and the parishioners that he closely associates with. Also, I need to know about any extracurricular activities that he is involved in." The more prying and prodding he did the better he could assess the case.

"Of course, as the minister of a flourishing church, there are the ordinary groups that any church has such as; bible study, choir, youth groups and working with church elders and deacons. Naturally, he has to deal with such things as deaths, births, baptism, weddings and some personal crisis someone might have. He has a very typical ministry." She stared up at the ceiling as if trying to think of something out of the norm.

"Does he belong to any social groups or clubs that require special attention?"

"Well, it is not a formal club, but, it does consist mostly of church members. They always go off somewhere and meet. For a period of time, I tagged along as did the other wives. The guys always talked about current events and politics. The wives were routinely excluded from the nuts & bolts parts of their meetings so we decided to just sit off to ourselves and talk about things that interested us. After a few months, the wives, including myself, just quit going."

"Where do these meetings take place and how often do they take place?" The idea of men meeting off to themselves was something Frank thought was worth dwelling on.

"There has been no set time or place for the meetings. They happened whenever one of them came up with some topic that was controversial. I usually didn't find out about them until Matt told me he had received a phone call from one of the guys. Most of these men belong to the church and are well thought of in the community. This is all just harmless man stuff and nothing I would be concerned about."

Frank couldn't help thinking that Felicity had no clue about how naïve her words sounded. Considering her concerns about her husband, she was placing way too much trust in the credentials of these church-going men than some people put in their own family members. Yes, she was either naïve or afraid to rock the boat of this group of men who were holding themselves out as pillars of the community. There was no way Frank could let this ride.

"Look, Felicity, you came to me worried to death about your husband and now you're steering me away from a situation that may be the clue to this whole affair. Trust me, I have been doing this for a long time and I have a good reputation for ferreting out the truth. I have to be thorough. I can't leave this stone unturned. I want a list of these men and notes on everything you know about them. I want to know where they work, what they do, their descriptions, and if you can, a description of the vehicles they drive. Don't worry; I know how to be discreet. You're just going to have to work with me on this."

Felicity rolled her eyes and fidgeted in her seat until she agreed to Frank's terms. She realized that she couldn't be half committed and expect results. Besides, how could it hurt if Frank found a little dirt on these guys? Bad information on people could prove valuable under the right circumstances.

"Felicity, once I take this case and start running with it, I'm going to need all I can get from you. Don't worry, I will come up with my own information and when we put it all together, we will know what has to be done next. I'm going to make it as easy as I can for you. I have some worksheets for you to use as you collect information. This will keep you focused and, in the long run, will save you money and save me time. Speaking of money, we need to discuss the terms and agreement of the contract that we will both have to sign. Yes, we have to put this all in writing."

Frank walked over to a filing cabinet and began pulling papers out and placing them on top while Felicity sat patiently waiting for the next step. She also took the time to assess her situation, especially when it came to long-term members of her husband's church. She tried to calculate the relativity and reality of the opposing views that she and Frank had exchanged. On a deeper level, she knew that Frank had chosen the appropriate approach and response for focusing a hard look at the men who often met with her husband. After all, they did meet without witnesses and never gave any details about their long discussions.

She also hoped that Frank and Charlie didn't think she was ignorant about human nature. Additionally, she knew that there were differences in people's values and that they were not always as they seemed. For good or not, to her, church members were like family, and that considered, it was painfully difficult to accept that those who are closest may also harbor secrets; dark ones. Without a doubt, she would have to work openly and honestly with Frank if she was to get accurate results. She was now blatantly aware of how wrong she was to filter Matt's meetings and associates to fit her own opinions and experiences. Could she be loosing her objectivity to personal feelings?

This afternoon's meeting with Frank and Charlie gave notice that personal bias was yet another strained force of life that she would have to reckon with. At least, she was now able to recognize her sometimes naïve nature and with that insight she would be vigilant for it, should it raise its ugly head again. Next time, if there was a next time, she would come prepared and avoid looking gullible.

"Felicity, this is the part of the process that is always a bit awkward for both me and a client. Getting through the financial details of a case is, unfortunately, a hurdle that must be cleared. I am filling in the portions of a standard investigative contract that are best suited for this type of a case."

Felicity's eyes were focused on the end of Frank's pen as he began to fill in the blanks. She listened to him as he explained.

"This contract states that you have retained my services to represent you as your attorney-in-fact in a matter of deep importance to you. In other words, you are empowering me to act in and for you, in your best interest, to look into your husband's activities that have resulted in strong concerns over his emotional state, safety and security. Being your attorney-in-fact does not mean that I am an attorney; it only means I am acting on your behalf. I am a private investigator and not an attorney. You are also giving me authority to expand the case to resolve personal and family issues that may arise, unless you give me new direction. To this end, you are tendering $5,000 to serve as an expense retainer in this matter."

"I knew this was going to be expensive." She added her understanding about the retainer.

Frank continued to move along. "Allow me to further break this down for you. My hourly fee for local work is $100 plus expenses and fifty cents per mile when I drive. Any work that becomes a full day's effort or requires overnight stays such as out of town work will be $600 per day plus expenses and mileage. This is the biggest break you will get from the $100 an hour rate.

"You will be provided a detailed invoice that accounts for all time and expenses. In case you are wondering about the work that Charlie does on your case, you will be charged $20 per hour plus any expenses she incurs. Charlie is the only go-between we will have during this case. You will also receive a comprehensive investigative report that will articulate our findings. If you don't want the report mailed to you, you can pick it up here at the office. Do you have any questions at this time?"

"That's a lot of money, Frank. I guess I'll just have to trust that you will only do what's needed. I knew it would be expensive. I just didn't know what all it would entail. Maybe I have watched too many private eye shows on TV." While speaking, she was digging through her purse looking for her checkbook.

Frank couldn't leave Felicity with the idea that he would take advantage of her and milk the case like some private investigators do.

"Look, I have plenty of work on my plate right now, so I'm not hurting for more business or money. In fact, I'm going to have you do as much as you can to help me so I can keep the cost as bearable as possible for you. That's why I'm not going to move on this until you complete these worksheets. Whenever you come up with something that has merit, I'll work on it. I'll also have Charlie do as much as possible to keep your expenses down. The last thing I want to do is to go off half-cocked on wild goose chases. I have better things to do with my time and I have a reputation in the community to think about."

Felicity wrote out the check and attached a business card and then slid it over to Frank. Frank, in turn, slid the contract over to Felicity to review and sign. Frank did a double take when he looked at Felicity's check. The check was not written on a personal account, it was in the name of a business. He read it twice before commenting.

"I'm a bit confused about the check and your business card. What is the Plano Temple of Devine Messages? And what is After Death Communication, and who is Madam Abigail, Psychic Medium?"

Frank's puzzled look and questions did not phase Felicity.

Outside, the storm was still attacking the elements. There were still flashes of lightning and claps of thunder with an almost deafening roar of torrential rain. In spite of all the distraction and gloominess, Charlie clearly heard what Frank had asked. She leaned forward to make sure she would not miss a word of explanation from Felicity.

Frank sat poised, waiting anxiously for an answer to the questions that were buzzing around in his head. A few seconds ago, he thought he had a complete understanding of Felicity's case and her naïve anomaly. Now, the situation was far from perfect. Perhaps, she had more to do with her husband's odd and recent behavior than what Frank had previously detected. The case was beginning to look more distorted and puzzling. Frank and Charlie equally wanted to make sense of everything and find clarity.

Finally, as if an aching tooth was finally coming out, Felicity began to explain. "If the questioning look on your faces indicates that you are questioning my sanity and emotional state, I will have to do my best to put you both at ease. However, I don't want to take up too much of your time explaining, especially, if I am on the clock and being charged."

"No, Felicity. We can take our time and this time it won't be charged to your account. As far as today is concerned, we had nothing planned. Even if we did, the rain would have changed those plans." After speaking, Frank glanced over at Charlie looking for her reaction. She nodded her approval.

"All right, you asked for it. Abigail was my mother's first name and it is my middle name. My mother had some rare talents when it came to spirituality. Back where I came from, in Kansas, she was a local medium who ran a small church of devout followers. I'm not going to go into any detail about her church, other than it had a central theme of After Death Communication. This was the belief system that I was reared under. Yes, to make things clear, I am talking about communicating with the dead.

43

"When Matt and I were married, he was fully aware of my beliefs and upbringing. He was also aware that I had inherited my mother's gift of being a medium. One of my beliefs is that Western culture is ignorant about what happens when a person dies. I have validated my belief in Spiritualism many times during my life. Most Christian churches, aided by contemporary materialism, have obscured the existence of life after death. Evidence of the reality of an afterlife has routinely been suppressed by Church doctrine. All thoughts and behavior are subject to evolve like everything else in the universe. Life tends to run in cycles and currently the cycle of belief in the afterlife is beginning anew. The world is about to engage in a new renaissance of spiritual realization and I am part of that phenomenon. Contemporary belief in Spiritualism is a resurrection of old beliefs.

"As a medium, part of my mission is to enhance spiritual growth by monitoring and recording life events given by people who now reside in the afterlife. The dead speak through me. Let me make that point clear, that is what I do as a medium.

"Ethically, I do not filter out or distort the messages I receive. Those who seek my services are entitled to everything I am able to receive from the other side. I operate under the same ethical rules that you do as a private investigator. You give me the facts as you find them and I deliver messages from the afterlife as I hear them.

"As you can imagine, there are those in the public sphere, and in many churches, that ardently oppose any attempt to approach and facilitate afterlife communication. These people have narrow minds instead of open ones. They suffer from the herd mentality that comes from some Christian churches. In the pits of their shallow minds many people have to see Spiritualism the Church's way or no way at all. Today, many people believe that anything spiritual that does not follow their belief path must be accomplished by evil practitioners who serve Satan."

Frank agreed with the concept Felicity was speaking to. "I have seen the same thing on two of my biggest cases. I think before people condemn a philosophy they should first walk in the shoes of their opposition to know and experience their ways. What a person doesn't know, he can never understand, so he has no right to condemn it."

"Thank you, Frank. When I'm having a dialog with someone who has passed from this life into the next, I am often not sure if I'm speaking with an evil spirit or a good spirit. All I can say for sure is that the spirit is in the same spiritual condition as it was in the physical world. I believe this life coexists with the next one. Here, in this life, a spirit has a physical element or image, and in the next life it loses its physical essence. When it crosses over, it is entering another purer stage of higher growth. During the process, spiritual beings do not forget the ones they left behind. In fact, they understand more about them than ever before.

"Finally, all this adds up to me not wanting to damage my husband's work which focuses on the here and now- this life of materiality. In the Temple of the Devine Message, I have provided a forum for acquiring a great deal of solace for the living and an avenue for giving guidance to them by way of their deceased loved ones. I have helped them deal with their grief and secure a degree of closure. I don't think that makes me evil. In doing this, I use my middle name in honor of my mother and that puts a safe distance between what I do and what Matt does. Actually, Matt has been my best supporter in this initiative."

The core of what Frank was seeing in Felicity's and Matt's relationship was one of trust, cooperation, and understanding. "I can see that over the years the two of you have nurtured a strong bond. I have to congratulate you on this achievement." He stopped short of dismissing any conflict between them that might exist.

"The reason I am writing my check to you on this account is to conceal what I am trying to accomplish with your services. Do you have any doubts or reservations with what I have told you?"

"No, there is nothing significant that I need to drill into. However, I was not really prepared for such a long-winded explanation. However, that said, I found this to be very interesting and it is background that I needed to know about. Since I am going to represent your interests, I need to know the full scope of them, the big picture, if you will, regardless of how sensitive or common these things seem."

Felicity looked relieved when she understood that Frank was still taking her case. "Some people react with more emotion than you have when I let the cat out of the bag regarding Spiritualism. I was worried about you thinking I was some kind of a flake. I was especially troubled and somewhat embarrassed over, how naïve I sounded earlier."

Both Frank and Felicity looked over at Charlie for any sign of a reaction from her. "What? I have no problem about any of this. I think this is all very interesting and I'm looking forward to learning more. This after death communication business is not something that people talk about where I come from. The only things folks talk about back in Childress County, Texas is the weather, cattle, and horses. Frank, was there any of this paranormal stuff back where you came from?"

"Yes, I have to admit that I'm no stranger to the paranormal and Spiritualism. I was born and reared in Athens County, Ohio. The town was founded in 1797 and Ohio University started up in 1803. There was even a state run asylum there. Athens has the reputation of being the most haunted place in Ohio. There are many accounts of spiritual presence there. I don't suppose either of you have been there, have you?"

Charlie shook her head no and Felicity said, "No I can't say that I have."

"Athens is tucked away in the foothills to the Appalachian Mountains and the place is rich in history. Since everything that had to do with Spiritualism began prior to the Civil war, you should know that Athens County borders what is now West Virginia, along the Ohio River. My point is that the place was extremely rural with a unique aura about it. Even the Shawnee Indians wouldn't hunt or camp in the area because they considered it sacred ground."

"Sounds like a really cool place, if you ask me." Charlie was quick to comment and by the look on Felicity's face, she was just as impressed.

Satisfied that he was getting his point across, Frank continued. "In the mid-1800's the Koons' family lived there on the highest point in the county. It was a ridge point called Mount Nebo. Jonathon Koons was married to his wife, Abigail, and they had nine children. Large families were common in the area. In spite of being self-educated farmers, they were well-versed in the politics and the philosophies of their time.

"Early in 1852, the family began to read newspaper accounts about the famed Fox Sisters of New York and the growing phenomenon of Spiritualism and séances. Jonathon began to travel all over Ohio to attend séances and eventually learned that he also had a great ability for being a medium. Once he returned home, he quickly learned that his wife, Abigail, and his oldest son, Nahum, also possessed the same psychic abilities.

"Through a series of séances, the family soon developed quite a rapport with some spirits. These spirits began to give instructions to the Koons' family mediums. Following these instructions, the family built a one room log cabin dedicated to spiritual work. The room was not all that large and elaborate; it was roughly 12 x 14 feet with shuttered windows and a single door. Following more orders, a variety of musical instruments were put inside for use by the spirits. Furnished with benches, the Spirit Room could accommodate about 20 people. There was a wide variety of spirits that would attend and they eventually numbered 165. One of the spirits was said to be that of the buccaneer, Henry Morgan, who had died in 1688. Yes, with all those instruments being played by spirits, the room often became very noisy. Sometimes, spirit hands would appear and write messages on blank sheets of paper. The room's notoriety gave it national and even international fame.

"The Spirit Room and the Koons' family were investigated by many believers, skeptics, journalists, and people of established character that all pointed to this not being a hoax of any kind. There was little, if any financial gain for the family. Another family, the Tippie family, that lived about three miles across the valley from the Koons' family, started up their own spiritual venture, but, it never became as famous as Koons' place.

"In 1858, the Koons' family closed their Spirit Room and moved to Illinois. After they left, their old home and the Spirit Room log cabin were burned to the ground by unknown persons who objected to Spiritualism. Most of the Tippie family relocated to Colorado. I have to admit that I did once take a Tippie girl to our high school prom. That's another story, though.

"The bottom line is; I come from an area that is famous for its rich heritage in Spiritualism. I could go on and talk for hours about the area I grew up in. I only want to make a few final points here. First, I fully understand the concerns you harbor for your husband's ministry should your work in Spiritualism become public. Second, I find it interesting that you, your mother, and Mrs. Koons all share the name of Abigail.

"Finally, as far as my own experience with Spiritualism, well that is for another discussion. On a deeper level, I think everyone has some unexplainable thing in their past that hedges on the paranormal. I'm thankful that humans are blessed with the power to reason and the ability to feel emotions that are more advanced than any other species on the planet."

Felicity rubbed her eyes, not from boredom, but, from an empowering feeling she felt from listening to Frank. "Without a doubt, I found my way to the right private investigator. No other one could be more suited for my case, Frank."

Following a mad dash through the rain, Felicity was gone. Alone with Frank, Charlie walked over to him and put her arms around him. "Like Felicity Whitman, I too have come to the right place. Sometime, I hope we can have a long talk about my past, also. I've never met a man as honest and open as you, not ever. I have a lot to learn from you."

"Charlie, every one of us has a lot to learn from life and from those we encounter. I believe we owe it to ourselves to be students of life.

CHAPTER 4

Walter Welch's hand trembled uncontrollably as he lifted a glass of bourbon whiskey to his lips while glancing out the study window at his home in Argyle, Texas. Torrents of rain slammed the window panes as gusts of wind whipped through the stately trees that surrounded his mansion. The weather was not what was driving him insane with fear, though. The image that daunted him from his computer monitor was the source of his torment. There it was, big as life; an article from the Houston Chronicle. The headline was a chilling one: "Local journalist slain in his apartment."

Jonathon Pickerington had been his friend for nearly thirty years. They had been more than mere roommates while attending Stanford University. Their friendship was genuine, not one built on ceremony or politeness. Unlike many college peers, Jonathon's friendship remained steadfast and never waned under any challenge. Once, they had unknowingly tried to date the same girl. When they found out, the dispute was settled by both of them withdrawing from the contest.

Not once had they lost contact with one another. Their friendship had not been one of those that tabloids kept track of. Walter's banking exploits had made him a millionaire many times over and he was able to keep his public signature confined to the business world. He had been involved in several law suits that had not amounted to a hill of beans. Everyone knew how law suits have a way of following wealth. As for Jonathon, the man made his living by being in the public eye. As an investigative journalist, he was always making enemies in wealthy circles and making an equal number of friends among the disadvantaged and uninformed. His name had been shouted on the airways and his face

48

plastered all over newspapers, magazines, and television. Whenever Jonathon went to court, the media went with him.

By design and honesty, Walter had no scandals nipping at his heals or lurking in the shadows. However, he did have one ugly skeleton in his closet and lately it was not setting well with his ethical standards. Like an ugly wart on his rump, it was out of sight from public view, but not out of his conscience. Unfortunately, he knew right where The Order was in his life. It was out of public sight, but not far enough away to avoid being a source of moral agitation. The Order was his curse in life; joining it had been the biggest mistake of his life.

More than a year had passed since his wife died from cancer. Every day, week after week, month after month, while that agonizing disease tortured his wife, Jonathon was always right there for both of them. They had shared that same painful path out of devoted friendship and a strong sense of loyalty. The path began with diagnosis and ended with her being lowered into a cold grave. Even on his wife's death bed, she was glad Jonathon was there to comfort them. Somehow, she knew that Walter would need Jonathon's emotional support and reassurance.

Now Jonathon was gone; the victim of a savage attack during a break-in. But, was his death the result of a botched burglary or was it a by-product of a powerful political conspiracy?

Nearly three months had passed since he began feeding information to Jonathon about The Order. There was no doubt that The Order was capable of murder. Members of The Order had resources at their disposal and there was no option off the table when it came to the organization's secrecy. The Order's tentacles reached deeply into all facets of contemporary society to include politics, and if its presence was discovered, there would be hell to pay.

Throughout his decade of membership, Walter was slowly able to piece together The Order's true mission and ultimate goal- world domination. Slowly and methodically, The Order was setting the world on a collision course with chaos and pandemonium. Because The Order was imbedded in secrecy and orchestrated by egotistical madmen who were over-paranoid, there could never be a way to expose the organization's depth and reach without risk. The Order had access to destructive powers of the highest magnitude.

Somewhere in its innermost circle there had to be some sort of governing board that ensured the steady growth and power of the organization. The gains were too important to allow any member to take his eye off the ball. Any powerful organization, like The Order, had to have men willing to pull in the reins or unleash the whip. Few men knew who or how many executives were at the helm and no one could second guess their ruthlessness. Madmen can be extremely methodical and deliberate. Also, they were exceptionally cunning, so to identify one of them, a person would have to look in the most unlikely places. This was why Walter's inside information was so crucial.

Cleverly and clandestinely, Walter had been able to bit and parcel together a loose mission statement for The Order. The mission statement was a tiered and extremely abstract one that went the full spectrum from the country's destruction to its resurrection. Once he had enough information to establish a credible theory concerning national and state agendas for The Order, he confided in Jonathon.

In general terms, The Order wanted the U.S. President, whoever that might be at the most opportune time, to fail with regards to the nation's economic and national security policies. The Order had to create a monumental rift between Republicans and Democrats. Once this was done, the country's credibility and effectiveness to govern would deteriorate to a point where the citizens would become so disillusioned that they would cry out for new leadership; The Order's leadership. No member of The Order had an ounce of loyalty to the country. Any member of The Order that believed in its premise had to be guilty of sedition of the highest degree.

Unwavering dedication to the right President and a friendly Congress was what the country needed to remold its beliefs and recover from the hardest of times. What it did not need was the destructive voices from the bowels of The Order. Walter often wondered how he had allowed himself to be duped into joining such a disgusting organization.

With a political revolt underway, The Order would unveil its own political party. This was where all of the outer circles, at the state and local levels, would come out of the closet as the country's saviors. They would use a grass roots approach and finesse their new clout to take control of a new emerging government to restore order. On the surface, they would display the highest of ethical standards and work for the rights of all citizens. Of course, in the interim, there would have to be marshal law. After all, a heavy hand would be needed in the beginning to restore order. What a cruel farce for the country to endure. In reality, martial law would last forever.

Naturally, all of the old politicians that did not conform to the new party's dictates would be barred from the political process. Similar restructuring would occur in other countries that were global heavy-hitters. In the new world, under a single governing body, there would be no war because all former countries would be reduced to a single entity.

In theory, all would prosper, to some extent, under a new financial and health care system. Oh, there would always be regional conflicts, but they would be put down quickly with decisive military might.

The Order's aim would appear noble on the surface. The only things missing would be justice, freedom, and a sense of fair play. Judges would no longer consider writs of habeas corpus. In other words, citizens accused of crimes would not be able to petition the courts or appeal their decisions because detained people would have few, if any, rights. Our Constitution would become nothing but a mere relic in some government-run museum; that is if it was ever seen again. Elements of The Order's manifesto would be incorporated into a new Constitution, one that was in line with the times.

In retrospect, Walter figured he had joined The Order because, after amassing his wealth, life suddenly became droll; a boring arrangement of routine tasks that only required mundane logic. Within weeks of joining The Order, he began to doubt the wisdom of his decision. Many of the members of his circle displayed an enormous amount of ruthless, merciless temperament. Some even bragged about how they abused their public power and authority. Judge Jeremiah Fullerton was the worse one of them all.

Many times, Judge Fullerton spoke of how he was destined for greatness. In his mind and once underway, his exploits would be chronicled in the annals of history as the right man at the right time. He would one day be appointed to the U.S. Supreme Court so he could play a major role in dismantling the status quo of an outdated government; one that had been so steeped in tradition that it had failed to progress with the times. He often laughed when he commented that the hanging judge of the Old West would pale in comparison to him.

Another one of his cries for change included public executions. In the proverbial sense, it was not the severity of punishment that deterred crime; it was the certainty of it. He was convinced that his philosophy would make the country stronger than ever before. Of course crimes against the state could never be tolerated. The judge was quick to acknowledge that the highest and most inner circle of The Order already had tagged him for the U.S. Supreme Court. In the mean time, he had his eye on a higher elected office such as state governor, congressman, or even the presidency.

There would be no checks and balances for the government once he was in power because The U.S. Constitution of today would become a relic of the past. What a horrible little dictator the judge was. Actually, after careful consideration, Walter did feel that there was a place in

American history for Judge Fullerton. However, he most surely would end up being chronicled as shameful.

Now that Jonathon and his wife were gone, all Walter could expect from life was some self knowledge that came too late and appeared as a crop of un-extinguishable regrets. In fact, if the truth was known, there wasn't much left of his life. Most certainly, Jonathon's murder was the work of The Order and it occurred because of the information Walter had given to him. The Order seemed to have eyes and ears everywhere.

Looking outside, he wondered if assassins were already on his property with orders to silence him. They would probably torture him first to find out where his copies of the evidence were hidden. They would offer no mercy for his weary soul. Out here in the country, they could work uninterrupted because they would know that he lived alone, isolated from the public.

He needed to act quickly to go into hiding. He had about $50,000 in cash tucked away in his home safe. However, one thing that he did not have in his home was the evidence. He was fully aware that The Order would soon learn of his traitorous attempts to expose and end their secret organization.

Normally, the unexplained disappearance of an adult, especially a wealthy one, would be a frightening experience for one's family and friends. However, he had no family to speak of and his best friend had been murdered. He did have business associates who would be concerned about his whereabouts, though. Irene, his secretary, would have to be given some sort of ruse to cover his absence. He would tell her that he was going camping, a test of sorts for his survival skills. Such adventures were used by him for team building by some of his executives. He would simply tell Irene that he did not want to be disturbed and that she was to only call him on his cell phone in case of an extreme emergency. She could simply leave a message in case he was in a dead zone with respect to cell phone coverage

Carefully, he packed two suitcases and a rucksack. Within thirty minutes, he was ready to head out the door. He called Hank, his caretaker, and gave him the same ruse he had given to Irene.

He was glad that he had taken the time to obtain a concealed handgun permit. He removed a .45 caliber Llama, semiautomatic from his gun cabinet. He filled four magazines, putting one in the pistol, and the others into his rucksack. The clock was ticking and he knew better than to waste any time. He tossed everything into his Ford Expedition. He was glad that he had parked it inside the garage because the storm was still wreaking havoc outside.

Within minutes, he was driving down his private driveway toward the main road. Headlights were darting back and forth at the other end of his driveway. Immediately, he went into survival mode and flicked off his own headlights. He drove off into the grass behind a clump of trees and took his foot off the brake so not to let the other driver see his brake lights.

His heart began to pound with deep throbs against his chest cavity and even though he knew better, he feared the sound would be heard over the engine and storm. Even though it was impossible for anyone to hear his throbbing heart, he instinctively took long deep breaths to bring it under control. He regretted not keeping himself in better shape.

His worse fears were confirmed when the car stopped short of the house and the headlights were switched off. The assassins were already here for him. Two of the car's doors opened and he could see two men get out. He knew they were experienced because they had disconnected the inside dome light so their presence would not be exposed. They walked in half crouched positions toward the house. Although he could not see clearly because the storm blocked any moonlight, he assumed they were carrying handguns.

Copying their actions, he removed the dome light from his Expedition. With shaky hands, he rummaged through the rucksack until he found a hunting knife. At this point, speed was as important as stealth. Using the trees and shrubs for concealment, he quickly made his way to their car. In less than twenty seconds the air was hissing out of both rear tires and he was trotting back to the Expedition. He was scared, and for good reason.

Thankfully, the storm was covering his movements and he went undetected. He still had one more surprise for his would-be assailants. The wooded acreage that surrounded his estate was enclosed by a high stone fence. Normally, he left the gate open. Now was a good time to lock his intruders inside in order to buy more time for his escape. He knew the road well so he opted not to turn on his headlights until he was clear of his property.

Since it was the weekend, he had no difficulty thinking of the perfect place to hide out until he could think more clearly. Without a plan of action and some immediate and achievable goal in mind, he was only adding a little time before his life ended. Ideally, he wanted to put an end to The Order and return to his life as a successful businessman. Presently, there was no clear way to make things work out the way he wanted them to.

The drive to the Oklahoma border via I-35 took less than an hour. He had no recollection of the trip other than the relief he felt when he crossed the Red River into Oklahoma. Many times, he and his wife had made this trip during their marriage. The destination's name never changed, but, the place's appearance had undergone many improvements. Now there was a motel on the premises and that meant fewer people left when they became tired.

Winstar Casino had turned into a class act with thousands of slots and some gaming tables. Naturally, blackjack was the casino's featured card game. The food ranged from fast food to fine dinning. The thought of food generated hunger pangs and suddenly he couldn't remember the last time he had eaten.

Right now, ensuring that he had a room was the most important thing. He would not chance using a credit card for payment, though. Surely, The Order had the means to track the use of any of his credit cards. The last thing he wanted was to have those assassins slipping into his room in the middle of the night and abducting him. Currently, they had no idea where he was and that was comforting. After paying cash for his room, he removed his belongings from the Expedition and secured them in his room. He had asked for and received a room on the second floor. Ground level rooms had windows that could be easily breached.

He took the added precaution of not parking his Expedition in the motel's parking lot. Instead, he drove over to the casino where more than two thousand vehicles were parked. His vehicle would blend in just as easily as he would. The asphalt parking lot was dry, but, that would not last long. The storm he had left behind in Texas was not far behind. Flashes of lightening were already crisscrossing the southern sky.

Inside the casino, patrons were threading their way through the crowd. The sight reminded him of October Fest in Munich, Germany where drunks bumped into each other in search of friends and more beer.

Following a good meal, he couldn't resist a quick game with the quarter slots. Sure, he had the money to play the higher dollar slots, but, winning some money was not important. He only needed to relax and regain his bearings. All the laughter and cheer, coupled with all the ringing bells and rousing announcements of big winners had a subtle way of taking his mind off his predicament.

Suddenly, without any warning, the loudest roar he had ever heard blasted down from the ceiling. His first thought was that a tornado was striking the casino. All voices either fell silent or joined a monumental gasp. The most distinguishable sounds that could be heard were those of the slots. An announcement came across the public address system, informing everyone that the noise was only rain striking the casinos metal roof. There was no cause for alarm. The announcement was all that was needed for people to continue what they were doing before the rain.

The stormy diversion only lasted about an hour before he was able to walk back to the motel without getting soaked. The trip only took him about ten minutes by foot. Once he was in his room, he undressed and showered. He turned down the bedding and scooted over onto scented clean sheets. He didn't bother turning on the television. Instead, he turned on a radio, selecting a station with soft, easy listening music. There was so much to think about that he didn't know where to begin.

Each time he thought about The Order and his particular circle, one name kept popping up. Matt Whitman, the pastor, was the only voice of reason that came to mind. Matt had always been very vocal with his criticism of issues that Judge Fullerton favored. All outward appearance indicated that Matt was an ethical man with strong morals. If there was any chance that he had an ally within the circle, then that man was certainly Reverend Matthew Whitman. Matt usually objected with a great deal of passion whenever the judge veered off course on moral or ethical issues. If it wasn't for a little backing from others who were more prone to being mild-mannered, Matt would probably have been eliminated from the group, years before.

The decision to contact Matt was a heavy one. Confiding in anyone at this point would be a risk-taking venture. The first time he had met Matt was during his third meeting in The Order. If words had been swords, Judge Fullerton would have used his to cut off Matt's head. They were in a bitter argument over capital punishment. The judge dug his heals in to support the death penalty for habitual criminals, regardless of the crimes committed. As an example, he wanted any criminal found guilty of four thefts to be executed. According to his rationale, any person found guilty that many times for thievery, could not be rehabilitated.

Matt's opposing position was that some people committed theft only to support their families because the economy was in such a slump that there were no jobs. Criminal enterprise was the only way they had of surviving. The death penalty for non-lethal crimes was cruel and unusual and a violation of the Eighth Amendment to the U.S. Constitution and was out of sync with the "eye for an eye" punishment that was set in scripture.

The argument took on a new face when Matt suggested that when theft became equal to murder, then a criminal was inclined to kill when stealing because the punishment would be the same. The end result would be more murders. The punishment should fit the crime for justice to be done. In the case of the judge, the law was an instrument of force and nothing else. Others at the meeting had to intervene and put a stop to the debate when the judge's comments were reduced to name calling and profanity. According to him, a man of the cloth had no say when it came to criminal justice because a minister should only be concerned with a man's soul and not with the way he answered to society. On more than one occasion, the judge urged Matt to withdraw from The Order because he was too soft. Matt usually responded to the judge's objections by telling him that he would pray for the judge's soul. He also urged the judge to worship more often and pay more attention to God's word when he did attend services.

There was not an ounce of compassion in the judge and there was an abundance of it in Matt. The judge had a reputation for having a heavy hand and Matt had a reputation for extending a helping hand. In the case of these two men, opposites did not attract.

After all this thought, the question for Walter was still there; call Matt or don't call him? There was also another question that needed to be answered. What on earth should he do with the evidence he had hidden. So much of the evidence was circumstantial, except for a few pages. Most likely, some authority like the Federal Bureau of Investigation (FBI) would easily laugh him out of their office for lack of substance. Conspiracy theories abounded in all corners of life. When did something quit being a theory and start being something credible?

He concluded one thing, though. The Order wanted to see what he had so they could do some damage control. Knowledge was certainly power in any game. What if the FBI had other evidence that supported the existence of The Order and its evil intent? Maybe there was some missing piece of the puzzle lurking in his evidence stash and someone inside the Justice Department needed it. He wasn't sure he had the key to exposing The Order or not.

In the mean time, there were assassins out to serve his head up on a platter to The Order once they put their grubby little hands on his evidence.

Not knowing who to trust had become a very discouraging dilemma for him. Sooner or later, he would have to make some kind of a play or die for nothing. Somehow, dying would only dishonor Jonathon's friendship. There was no way he could allow that to happen.

His cell phone was on the nightstand next to the bed. Matt's personal cell phone number was programmed into it. All he had to do was pick his phone up, flip it open, and punch a couple of keys and Matt would answer. Once that was done, several things could occur. First, Matt would not know anything about him and his life long journalist friend, Jonathon. Second, Matt could turn out to be deeper entrenched in The Order than he had supposed and would remain loyal to it. Third, Matt could bait him and lure him into a trap. Finally, Matt could turn out to be more than ready and just as eager to take on The Order. Any of these positions could be set in motion if he would only pick up the phone and call.

Following a deep breath, Walter picked up the phone and turned it over in his hand. Quietly, he sat there trying desperately to determine his next course of action. The phone was the tool, but, should he call, what should he say? At least the phone gave him distance and that translated into security. His mind was swirling about without direction in spite of having a full understanding that he was a hunted man.

An old saying drifted into his confused thoughts. "If you are going to battle, ride toward the sound of the guns." That's right, hiding out was only a temporary state and not an answer. One thing he had, without question, was the measure of whatever was left of his life. He had to make it count for something. His soul was not pure, but, it was the only passport he had to the next life. His next move had to be decisive and as wise as he could make it. Surely, a man of God would understand that.

The Order had been reduced to a sinister and dark shadow in his life; one that had once been presented to him draped nobly in the folds of eloquence. If only he had initially seen it for what it really was; a dishonoring evil.

Walter nearly dropped the phone when it suddenly rang. At first, fear clouded his vision as he looked to see who was calling him at this late hour; or was it the early hour of morning? Instead of a number appearing in the small screen, there was a name. There it was as if by some divine design: "Matt."

The clock on the nightstand read 3:02 a.m. A simple flip of the wrist was a defining moment in his life and he had everything resting on it. The gambling that was being done at the casino failed to compare with the risk he was about to take.

"Hello, this is Walt; what can I do for you, Matt?"

"That was fast, Walt. You must sleep with your phone at your ear."

"I have a lot on my mind these days. You must have a lot on your plate, too, for you to be calling at this time of the night, or should I say morning?" Walt's tone was noticeably hesitant and marked with despair.

"I'm not going to apologize for calling at this late hour, Walt. What I have to say to you can't wait for normal hours. I've been up for hours praying for the courage to make this call and now God has given me what I asked for. After you hear what I have to say, you will have to gather your own courage."

Instantly, both men were aware of the other's tension and apprehension. At this point, Walter was obligated to wait for Matt to clarify the purpose of the call. Obviously, Matt had some moral duty to perform and Walter was not about to break Matt's train of thought or curtail his objective.

"Walter, this week God has awoke something in me that I should not have allowed to fall asleep. For several days, now, I have not had a single restful moment. Explaining all this to you is only the beginning for me. It's only a matter of time until I share your fate. At this point, I have an honest voice, so listen closely to what I have to say." Matt paused for a reaction.

"Please continue, now that you have my full attention."

"As mortal men, we sometimes walk blindly and in agony toward our final peace. If we have faith in God and a sense of right and wrong, justice if you will, we will find our peace. Once found, our peace will cleanse our souls. This is what I am thinking as I tell you what you need to know."

"Matt, I appreciate your honor and your moral values. Personally, you never had a proper place in The Order. Men of true character, such as you, would only hinder The Order's efforts to corrupt a country of good will; our country. We cannot allow the United States of America to collide with the destructive forces of such evil, as The Order's."

Walter knew what Matt was going to warn him about. All the signs were there: the man had a relationship with his God and he had an unwavering aptitude for decency. Concerning Matt, he had no ill thoughts or reservations about him; he felt nothing but kindness. Over the years, Walter had many occasions to observe Matt and all that he had seen led him to believe that this minister would never offer a gift horse full of angry Greeks to any man. The time for accolades and politeness was over. Now, it was time for laying their cards on the table.

"Walter, the other night our local circle of The Order had a secret meeting. You were not invited for good reason. You were the subject of a great concern, especially for the judge. They had irrefutable evidence that you're a traitor to their cause."

"What sort of evidence did they have? I mean, it must have been overwhelming to jump to such a conclusion." As the words slipped from Walter's lips, he knew what the evidence was.

"Do you know an investigative journalist by the name of Jonathon Pickerington?"

"Yes I know him. He has been my best friend for the biggest part of my life." Walter was waiting for Matt to confirm what he already knew.

One of Jonathon's pals, also a journalist, just happened to be a member of The Order's circle in Houston. Your friend, Jonathon, confided in him and asked him to do research on suspected members of The Order. This was background research on the members of our circle. The Houston circle took it upon themselves to murder your friend. They even took the hard drive to his computer and faked a break-in. The police think that Jonathon returned home unexpectedly and found the intruders ransacking his apartment. Because Jonathon saw their faces, they killed him. I know differently, and now you do, also."

"How did our circle conclude that I gave Jonathon his leads? That's quite a jump from circumstantial to fact."

"The answer to that question is simple. I saw the evidence myself. Members of the Houston circle started out by placing Jonathon under constant surveillance. They had photographs of you giving Jonathon an envelope, the same envelope that they recovered from his apartment."

"What do they intend to do about all this?" Walter knew that his question was rhetorical.

"They have already started the process. Men from out of state are on their way here to kill you and recover any evidence about The Order that you might have. Do you understand what I am saying, Walter? These men are going to torture and kill you. They think that they are soldiers for a righteous cause; they are here for The Order."

Walter paused long enough on the phone for Matt to relax. "Why did they not do like the Houston circle and take me out on their own?"

"That's an easy question. No one really had the stomach for it, except the judge. Do you know what else, Walter?" Matt didn't wait for an answer. "I bet that I'm now on the same short list as you. I caused a little fuss and stayed behind when the others left the meeting. Anyway, I thought I was alone. I prayed to God right there by my car, in the parking lot. I don't know who it was, but, someone saw me and overheard me praying. They sped off with their lights off. I'm now like you- a cooked goose. I'm their weakest link outside of you. I think its time we join forces; don't you think?"

"Please Matt. You don't have to convince me. All you have done is connect a few dots for me. The Order's out of town assassins have already been to my home. I was lucky enough to get away by out foxing them. It was all a matter of timing. Had they arrived a few minutes earlier or had

I been a few minutes later in getting away, they would have had me and we would not be having this conversation. I already knew about Jonathon and put two and two together. Right now, I'm on the run and hiding out. Don't bother to ask me where I am because I won't tell. I'm sorry you are in the middle of this, I really am."

"Oh Walter, I'm just as sorry as you. You're a descent man and don't deserve what is happening." As expected, Matt's first concern was for Walter.

"Look here, Matt. I have my copy of the information I put together. Most of it is about the judge." He told Matt a white lie. "I have it hidden in a good place where no one should find it. I propose that we meet somewhere and discuss what I have. If it was good enough to kill Jonathon for, it must be valuable and damaging to The Order. After we discuss it, we can decide if you want a copy for yourself. It might turn out to be good insurance for you. What do you think?"

"How about meeting some place public and busy, say in Plano? If these guys are following either one of us, I don't think they will try anything in front of a lot of witnesses. Walter, you give me a call at about 2:00 p.m. on Wednesday afternoon and tell me where to meet. I don't want to know ahead of time in case I'm being followed."

"That sounds like a good plan to me. I'll give you a call about ten minutes ahead of time. Please be careful."

"You be careful, too." They both shut their phones off at the same time.

CHAPTER 5

When Frank pulled into the parking lot at his office, the first thing that caught his eye was that Charlie was already there. She was sitting in her pickup listening to music on her radio. He didn't get a chance to hear what song was playing because Charlie jumped out and started prancing off to the office door before he had a chance to hear. He had to admire her exuberance and enthusiasm. Not only was she setting a good example for herself, but she was also setting a good one for him to emulate.

"Good morning, princess." Frank spoke too fast, he thought. Hopefully, he wasn't talking down to her as if she was a child.

"No royalty here, I'm afraid. I'm just a country gal with a good work ethic."

Frank tossed a complementary smile her way so she would know that he was pleased. Should she continue to work out, he wondered if she would stay permanently. Naturally, he would have to ante up more money to make it worth her while. Also, he had no idea what was happening with her father or what other forces might pull her back home to Childress.

Once he had unlocked the door and they were inside, another idea crossed his mind. "You know, Charlie, I think you need your own key to the office." He walked over and opened one of his desk drawers and slid a key over to her.

"I guess this means that I'm not a screw up. A vote of confidence is a good thing, isn't it?" She was grinning as she worked the key onto her key chain.

"Yes, it is a good thing. In fact, I have never given anyone else a key to my office, not ever. I guess this is a sign that your ranking is notching up higher on my hit parade list."

"I'll do my best not to let you down. If we ever have a big fuss, just remember one thing, I won't stay mad. I might try to get even in some small way, but, I won't let it fester. Every time I did that, I had a hard time trying to get over it." Her tone dropped as she dealt with some old emotional wound.

"The first thing you need to do each morning is check the answering machine and write out the messages for me. Don't delete them in case I want to hear one of them myself. The second thing you should do is check the fax machine. We get most of our insurance cases by fax. You can go ahead and set them up in the computer. If I know I'm going to be late, I'll give you a call. If you get stuck on anything, feel free to call me. The only bad question is the one that's not asked."

"Does that mean I'm only going to be working in the office?"

"Oh no, you don't get off that easy. Some weeks I do most of the office work in one day. I'm not about to have you sitting around filing your nails while I'm out doing all the work. Actually, I'm going to have you with me most of the time. Should you still be hanging around here after a couple years, we can see about getting you a private investigator's license."

He just tossed her a bigger carrot than giving her a key to the office. He knew that he was taking a lot for granted. But, he did like her and he did see a great deal of potential in her.

An hour later she had entered two new insurance cases into the computer, swept, mopped and straightened the office up. She was a flurry of activity and didn't volunteer much in the way of conversation. Once she focused on something, she didn't let up until it was finished. Frank figured that she trained horses the same way. She was patient, focused, and thorough.

After he reviewed the entries she had made in the computer, he relaxed. "Do you have any questions?"

"As a matter of fact, I do have something I want to ask you about. After dealing with our new client, Felicity Whitman, you said that you were saving your own experiences with the paranormal for another discussion. When do we get to have that discussion?"

Obviously, her anticipation for hearing more from Frank on the paranormal had been hounding her.

"Are you really that interested in my old stories?"

"You bet I am, boss. This is really a new and fascinating topic for me. Until the other day, I never gave such a thing a second thought. Come on, we have time right now, don't we?" She was pleading.

"When it comes to the paranormal there is one thing you have to understand. Describing things that sometimes defy logic can strain the

English language. Scientists demand irrefutable proof before they etch their findings in stone and publish them in a journal. Acts of faith or matters that abound in the ethereal regions of our minds are a little trickier. I think that our spiritual self is not only a mirror image of our physical self; it is also an actual place that coexists with everything in the universe. It's a parallel land."

"That's pretty deep, Frank. I'm not sure what to make of it."

"Don't get me wrong, I believe in the power of faith. However, I'm not a religious person, at all. My deeds and actions reflect what I am inside. I never have been and probably never will be a Bible-thumping Christian. I'm more at home in the wilds of nature than I am in some church. When I speak to nature, she talks back to me. That's the way I grew up. In my world, nature does not play politics or have denominations. Nature is the deity."

"I know where you're coming from, Frank. Going to church to find faith is like going to the police station or a courtroom to find justice. Maybe we can have that discussion someday when I can be more open-minded. Any way, you can move on because I understand what you're trying to say."

"Okay. Like you, I look forward to that discussion. In the mean time, I have to admit that I dreamed a lot as a child. I had daydreams, night dreams, nice dreams, and nightmares. We can escape in our dreams or we can become trapped by them. Sometimes that was good and sometimes that was scary. I'll skip the small stuff and head to my first significant dream. I was only twelve years old at the time. At least a half dozen times over a period of a month, I had the same horrible dream. The details were not only vivid, they were terrifying. I dreamed that my mother was driving our car and in the passenger seat there was another lady. Her name was Ethel. I was sitting in the back seat behind Ethel. There was a horrendous crash and the car went tumbling into a ditch next to a railroad track. Then everything went fuzzy for awhile. When my vision cleared, I was crawling along the railroad track. I rolled over and looked back at the car. My mother was underneath it and Ethel was squirming in the grass, moaning with pain. The car that stuck us from behind was on its top and the passengers, both of them, were climbing out the windows. They were drunk."

"That's an awful dream, especially for a kid. What happened next?" Charlie was caught up in the dream's drama.

"Another car pulled over and three huge men got out and two of them lifted our car up from the back bumper and the other man pulled my mother out. My next vision was of me, dazed, sitting on the front steps of Sheltering Arms Hospital in Athens."

"Frank, that wasn't a dream- that was a nightmare."

"No, I wasn't only having a nightmare. I was dreaming the future. My dream was a precognition of what was coming. After having this dream for two weeks, it did come true just as I have described it to you. My mother ended up with a punctured lung and Ethel ended up with a broken leg. As for the three men that saved my mother by pulling her out from under the wreckage. Well, that had an odd twist to it. Those men were brothers and they were on the run for armed robbery out of Columbus. A month later, they were killed in a shootout with police in the mountains of West Virginia. The point here is that even bad men can do the right thing in an emergency."

"That's quite a story. So you can dream the future?"

"Let's just say that I have, on several occasions. I have also arrived at a conclusion that most precognitive dreams are not changeable. A few are, but very few. These dreams, for the most part, are only a reflection of what is in the universal plan for us. I have found that the older I get, the less I have these types of dreams. However, I still do have them, from time to time."

He looked into her eyes and saw that she was giving his story a great deal of thought. Maybe she was even comparing them to some of her own. He wondered what her dreams were like.

"So dreams are the largest extent of a person's paranormal experience?" Her question was pointed.

"No, dreams are just the beginning of it. Allow me to focus on another aspect of my paranormal experience. As before, I will skip the small stuff and go for the mother load. This is a longer story. That is if you are up to it."

"Boss, if you want, you can take me off the clock. Since there is something to this, I don't want to miss hearing about it."

"What's all this boss crap? You can't kiss me like you did the other night and only think of me as your boss."

"Old habits are hard to stop, Frank. As far as that kiss, well I meant it."

"That's good to know before I begin exposing my soul to you. If any of this got out, people might think I was a bit weird."

"Oh, believe me, Frank. You don't know what weird is until you hear about some of my emotional baggage."

It was only a matter time until she would confess what happened to her in Arizona and how it caused her to give up a promising singing career.

"Alright, Charlie; ready or not, here we go. I had a break in my military service after Vietnam. I returned home to Ohio during that time. I landed a job as a deputy sheriff in Franklin County. That's where the state capital, Columbus, is. I hung around with another deputy, Jim.

"One night in December, I was on patrol duty. It was snowing like crazy and the roads were a mess. It was just after midnight when the dispatcher sent me to Green Lawn Cemetery. The caretaker had been there earlier and heard some kind of a disturbance. He said the noise came from the mausoleum and that he was not about to check it out on his own."

"This is going to get really creepy, isn't it, Frank?"

"Oh yes. This is only the beginning of a series of events that leads to a surprising end. Maybe I should say that these things never really end. Hold on to your britches, Charlie. Here we go."

Displaying a little animated humor, she stood up and pulled on her belt. "I got them."

"After I plowed my cruiser through the snow and finally arrived at the mausoleum, I was in for a shock. There were no tracks anywhere, only fresh snow. Once I stepped into the archway of the entrance, I saw a pile of broken glass from the front door. The glass was on the outside and there was none on the inside."

"Wait a minute, Frank. That means it was broken from the inside. Whenever you break glass from one side, the broken pieces end up on the other side."

"See, you do have an investigator's mind. That's not all of it, though. There was some blood on the inside floor where the glass had been struck."

"So, Frank, what else did you find on the inside?"

"I couldn't get inside. The door was still locked."

"What did you do then?"

I was saved by the patrol car's radio. The dispatcher called and told me that the cemetery was in the Columbus city limits and that the Columbus police were on the way. I did stick around long enough to talk them, though. That's when things really began to get bizarre."

"Go on, don't stop now, Frank. This is getting good."

"One of the officers had been on the force for nearly twenty years and he told me that this wasn't the first time they received a call like this.

Some officers thought it had always been some kind of a hoax and others thought it was something supernatural. You'll like the next part.

"Back in the late 1800's and into the early 1900's there was a famous magician by the name of Howard Thurston. He was born in Columbus, and along with Harry Houdini, he was one of the world's greatest magicians. He perfected levitation, hundreds of card tricks, and sawing women in half and then restoring them whole. It took eight railway cars to carry his show as he traveled around the country. In 1936, Howard was doing a show in Miami, Florida when he had a heart attack. After a few days in the hospital, he died of pneumonia. Right before he died, he vowed that he would come back from the dead. People that had seen his acts believed that he could pull off that trick, too. They thought it would become his greatest trick of all."

"Now that's an incredible story, Frank." Charlie was impressed by the whole tale.

"Oh, the story isn't over yet. I'm only about half way through. You see, I couldn't let the supernatural aspect of this thing go without looking into it. A couple of nights later, I was having a beer at a local bar with my pal, Jim. I told him the whole story and he was just as taken with it as you are.

"We got the bartender to give us the yellow pages of the phone directory so we could find advertisements for Spiritualism. Surprisingly, we came up with a long list. One of them really caught our eye, though. It was a listing for the First Spiritualist Church of Linden. I told Jim that I would call the next day to find out the days and times when the church was open. As soon as I got the information, I told him I would call and we would go from there. He agreed."

"You have more surprises for me, don't you, Frank?"

"Oh, you have no idea, sweetheart."

"I would never have thought that there were so many people following Spiritualism. I mean, I find it surprising that they are listed in the phone directory. I bet they get a lot of crank calls and some badgering from other churches." Her eyes were growing a little wider with excitement.

"Well, we live in a strange world that is full of goofy people and surprises. Fortunately, we are even lucky enough to live in a country that is open enough to allow almost any religious or philosophical path.

"Now, let me to get back to my story. The next meeting at the First Spiritual Church of Linden was on Wednesday night at 6:30 p.m. Jim and I were equally and overly excited about the prospect of delving into such an esoteric adventure. Books and movies are one thing, but, something that is hands-on is another. There are people that look and there are people that do, I'm a doer."

"You have that old fashion frontier grit in your crawl, Frank."

"Thank you, I think. Anyway, we decided to take separate cars in case one of us wanted to leave early. Separate vehicles proved to be a wise choice.

"The streets were icy and covered lightly with a fresh snow so we left early to make sure we were there in time for the service to begin. I got there first and hovered out front in my parka until Jim arrived. The temperature had fallen to a point that could only be described as being bitterly cold. I have never been comfortable with cold weather. I guess that's why I live in Texas. For the most part, Texas has moderate winters compared to Ohio.

"Once we were inside, things began to get stranger by the minute. First, let me describe the interior for you. The layout reminded me of a slice of pie. I think you know what I mean. It was shaped like a wedge; rounded in the back and narrow down in front where the stage or pulpit began. To get on the stage, there were three steps on each side. In the center of the stage, or pulpit, there was a lectern. Behind the lectern there was a row of chairs. There were two isles dividing oak pews and enough room to seat about one hundred people."

Charlie interrupted with a comment. "You're describing a standard looking church. Although the ones I remember back home were rectangle in shape and not wedge shaped."

"That's the same impression that I had when I walked in. However, now we're going to depart from the norm. In most churches there are stained glass windows, a crucifix replica of some sort, and if there are any paintings or statues, they are Christian oriented. That was not the case in this church."

"You mean there was nothing on the walls?"

"No, I didn't say that. There were paintings. There were three or four on the walls on each side of the pews."

"All right, Frank, I'll bite. What were the paintings of?"

"The paintings were of Indians. To be more precise, they were of Native-Americans. Although, at the time, I wasn't sure what Indian tribes were represented by the paintings. The feathers were what threw me. They were sort of thick and finely fluffy. Most of the feathers were white. The faces were very noble looking with soft eyes. The clothing they were wearing was very traditionally ceremonial looking. I will explain the paintings and feathers later on before I wrap up the story. I promise."

"Okay. But, I'm going to make a mental note in case you forget."

"Jim and I blended in with the others as they arrived. We sat toward the back in the center of the congregation. The pews were full by the time the service began. To this day, I can't remember what the sermon was about or who gave it. I think it was a standard Christian service and somewhat boring. I do remember that we sang songs from hymnals that were in wooden slots in the back of the pews to our front. Like in any other church, a collection was taken up. No one was pressured to give any particular sum of money. Jim and I both gave a dollar."

"Okay, Frank. What makes this Spiritualist church service any different from any other church service? Other than the paintings, your description of the church and service sounds pretty standard to me."

"Oh no, the service was far from being over at this point. Sitting in the row of chairs behind the lectern were two men and two women. They were mediums. One at a time, they went to the lectern and did their best for those in the congregation and for those spirits that had crossed over to the other side."

"What do you mean by crossed over?"

"When a person crosses over, they leave the physical world and enter the spirit world. In other words, they had died. The mediums were funneling communications between the two worlds. They were facilitating after death communication."

"Exactly how does that work?"

"I'm gong to give you two examples from that night. The way I understood what was going on is that the messages were originating from the spirit world. The messages were more of a recollection of something from the past; something that the spirit thought was significant enough to bring up to validate the spirit's presence.

"In the first example, the medium was standing with his eyes closed and speaking to some unidentified person that was sitting in the congregation and speaking on behalf of someone that had passed over. The message went like this: The sky was dark and a heavy snow had fallen. There were four white horses pulling a sleigh. The sleigh was not the common variety that people saw during winter months. The sleigh was a black hearse. There were windows on both sides of the hearse and people that were lined up along the street could see inside. The coffin was small, it was only about four feet long and it was pure white in color. The day was a cold and somber one and that matched the sad emotions of the people that were attending the funeral.

"Suddenly, an elderly lady stood up from a pew to the right of us and farther up front. Her response sent shivers down my spine. She explained that during the winter of 1930, her little sister had died from some kind of a fever. The funeral had taken place right there in Columbus. A heavy snow had fallen and there was no way to postpone the funeral so a sleigh hearse was used. Her sister's coffin was white. The hearse had been pulled by four white horses. The lady asked the medium what her sister was trying to say. The answer was simple, yet to me, it was spectacular. The medium said her sister only wanted to let her know that she had been aware of how difficult her death had been for the family. She also wanted to let everyone know that she was in a good place among friends and family. Even though she had passed at a young age, her spirit was still maturing. She also wanted the lady to know that when it was her turn, she would be there to welcome her."

Tears were streaking down Charlie's cheeks. They were a mixture of sadness and of happiness. "I don't know how to explain how this has hit me, Frank. How did it strike you?"

"I felt the same way you do. It was a moving moment. Significant events, whether good or bad, have a way of leaving life-long impressions on us. What we become in life is based on what we experience."

"I can't argue with that, Frank. The worse things in my life came as a surprise. I tried to fix one and it nearly crippled my outlook on life. Don't ask me what that was. Someday, if the timing is right, I will talk to you about it. Let's get back to your story. What is the other example that came out of the church service?"

"The next medium that came to the lectern came up with something totally different than the first one. She was a lot younger than the other mediums. She couldn't have been more than thirty-five. I didn't pick up on any outstanding features; she was plain, ordinary. She did not wear any makeup.

"She began much the same way as the previous medium had. She did a superb job of tuning out the congregation. Her trancelike state was just as intense as the last medium. Her communication went like this: She described the scene as if she was looking through the lens of a movie camera. She was acquiring images of traveling through hills with thick forests of elm, oak, and walnut trees. There was one large weeping willow and a small apple orchard by the edge of a meadow. The grass in the meadow was turning brown and apples were falling from the trees. Below the orchard was a small pond with some cattails shooting up on one end. Beyond the pond there was a barn that was badly in need of repair. There was a chicken coop next to a barnyard. The farmhouse was an old two-story home that needed paint. It had both a front and a back porch. There was a metal tub filled with rainwater sitting on a stand near the back porch. The aroma of freshly baked apple pie rode a gentle breeze as it drifted across the barnyard. A heavyset and elderly, white haired woman in a blue and white print dress was placing the second of two apple pies in the window to cool. A skinny, gruff looking little boy who was wearing coveralls without a shirt started walking toward the pies. His face and hands were dirty and he needed a haircut. He tried to touch one of the pie pans, but, it was too hot to handle. The other one was only warm because it had been sitting there for awhile, cooling. He took this pie and ran around the house to sit on a large gray bolder. He was stuffing handfuls of pie into his mouth until the shrill sound of the old lady's voice struck terror into his heart. She took what was left of the pie from him and told him to go to the willow tree and break off a switch. He was going to receive a whipping for his misdeed because there were other mouths to feed and he had acted selfishly."

Charlie gasped out loud. "I could see the same thing happening to me when I was little. I can't remember ever doing it, but, I certainly was capable of it."

"The message meant much more to Jim because he jumped up out of his seat and nearly ran out of the church into the cold. I chased after him. When I caught up to Jim, he was leaning up against the wall of the church hyperventilating. In spite of the cold, he was sweating profusely. 'What's the matter, are you sick?' I asked him. Before he could answer, he wiped tears from his eyes. He told me that he took that pie and he did get a licking from his grandmother for taking it. He was made to get his own switch from the weeping willow tree. Jim was scared to death because he didn't understand the meaning behind the message. He told me that he was sorry, but, he couldn't handle any more of this Spiritualism stuff. After that night, Jim refused to ever discuss what had happened. He made me promise to never bring it up again.

"I think it had been a defining moment in Jim's life that he would always regret and never forget. I think that licking he took made him vow to never steal anything again, as long as he lived. And, I believe it was the reason he went into law enforcement. Until the day he dies, he will pay for that apple pie he took."

"How do these mediums find out about all these things in people's lives?"

"They talk to everyone involved, especially the ones that have crossed over. That's right; they talk to the dead in their spiritual form. Their spirits are very much alive and willing to talk. I think that it's that simple. Just because someone dies, it doesn't mean they don't have messages for the living."

"All right, good buddy. You witnessed these things, but they didn't happen to you. You made me think that you had experiences, too." Charlie knew that she had a commitment lever with Frank and she wasn't going to be shy about pulling on it.

"Wait a minute, missy. I didn't say that I was finished, did I?"

"No, you didn't. I'm sorry I jumped the gun." She was embarrassed that she had spoken too soon.

"Remember, I haven't explained the feathers on the Indians in the paintings. That will fit in with the rest of my story. I would thank you for a little patience here." He was all smiles at this point.

"After two months had passed since that memorable visit to the First Spiritualist Church of Linden, I still had some skepticism running through my veins. I needed a clear and decisive validation. Every day I racked my brain for a way to either validate or invalidate after death communication. Then one day, out of the blue, it came to me.

"It was a Wednesday and I had the day off. I arrived early at the church, at about 4:30 p.m., with the hopes of finding the pastor there preparing for the evening service. The church had a residence attached to it and I suspected that was where the pastor lived. The day was warm and pleasant for a change so I was only wearing a knit sweater. Alone, I lacked the same boldness I would have had with Jim tagging along.

"I knocked on the door with heavy knuckles. Men do that sometimes to cover up any signs of fear. I call it the bravado approach."

"So that's what men do when they are low on testosterone?" Charlie couldn't resist a little antagonizing.

"Yeah, that's one of the things we do. This time it turned out to be overkill. When the door opened, I saw the sweetest looking lady. She could have been my grandmother. She had long hair that had a mixture of texture that went from wavy to curly. I noticed that her hair was turning from grey to white. She greeted me with a smile and when I told her that I was interested in Spiritualism, she shook my hand, firmly.

"She told me that she was about to bake some eggplant and if I would like some, she would bake two. Since I hadn't eaten lunch my stomach let me know that any offer of food would be greatly appreciated. Besides, the invitation opened the door for spending some one-on-one time with the lady. I gladly accepted the invite. She seated me at a dinning room table and went about preparing the eggplant.

"She was a slender lady and moved gracefully. It is funny how, after all these years, I am able to remember such details about someone I only knew briefly. The wrinkles in her face lent her character and a sense of nobility. However, it was her eyes that captivated me more than anything else. She had the kindest and most sincere eyes. She was wearing black slacks and a white ruffled blouse. Her engagement ring and wedding band were simple with a modest diamond. The tone of her voice had an element of professional authority. It all came together when she told me that she was actually a psychiatrist by trade. She had her practice in downtown Columbus. Her husband, she told me, was an engineer with the telephone company. Their credentials identified them as well-educated professionals. Becoming a psychiatrist is no small scholastic achievement.

"There was no doubt about her background throwing me for a loop because I was expecting to encounter a little old lady from the country that worked with roots and herbs. At any rate, she was no gypsy. She was a fine cultured lady with professional credentials."

"I see your point, Frank. I would have expected someone like my Grandma Emily. She always came up with all these old remedies whenever one of us got sick. I think she came from a long line of medicine women. She was one fourth Indian and it showed."

"Getting back to my story, I knew I was dealing with someone that could see through anyone trying to con her. So I took the high road and approached her with more caution than was probably needed. Partly out of curiosity and partly as a means to establish rapport with her, I asked her about the Indian paintings. See, I told you I would remember."

"Well it's about time. All this waiting was driving me nuts." Charlie was once again on the edge of her seat.

"The lady gave me two important pieces of information about those paintings. First, the reason for the strange looking feathers was that they were all Indian spirit guides. They were a great source of inspiration when it came to working with spirits in the afterlife. Second, and this nearly floored me, all those paintings had been painted by people living in Columbus. They were painted many years before. The paintings were part of the church's local heritage."

"That's really cool, Frank. I would say the church was lucky to be able to get their hands on the paintings. I can see how they could inspire people."

"Oh, my dear, that's not the half of it. You see, all of the paintings had been painted by blind people." Frank paused to allow enough time for the concept to sink in.

For the first time, Charlie was speechless. She just sat there staring in uncontrolled thought. After a few minutes, she finally stated her conclusion.

"The painter's hands were guided by Indian spirits. I think the paintings are actually a form of after death communication. I can't see any other way for this to happen."

Smiling at Charlie, Frank expressed a feeling that they were sharing with each other. "I guess great minds do think alike."

"I'm not going to flood you with questions, Frank; because I know you have more to tell me and you'll most likely cover everything I could think of to ask you about."

"Thank you. I see you're catching on. For a few minutes, I'm going to leave the First Spiritualist Church of Linden and flip back in time to those tender years of my youth. I must have been about eight years old when this happened. Death always leaves an everlasting impression on us.

"It was a Saturday and my mother was at work. As usual, my grandfather was looking after me. It was after lunch and I had been outside in the back yard playing. I came in for something; I can't remember what, exactly.

"When I walked into the living room, my grandfather was stretched out on the floor. Even at my age, I knew there was something seriously wrong. I tried to talk to him. I even tried to shake him, but, he was out cold. I ran to the neighbor's house, a Mrs. Timmons. She ran as fast as she could behind me and followed me through the back door. After seeing my grandfather's condition, she immediately called an ambulance. After the ambulance took my grandfather away, I stayed with Mrs. Timmons until my mother could get there.

"I went with her to the hospital. I sat in the waiting room impatiently waiting on any news from my mother who was with a doctor at my grandfather's bedside. I knew my grandfather had died when I saw my mother crying. It was one of those sad moments that always seem to haunt a person for the rest of his life. The hardest part for me was those two days at the funeral home when everyone came to pay their respects. I was close to my grandfather and whenever I'm in Ohio, I still like to visit his grave. Now that I think about it, I need to do that more often."

Charlie became teary-eyed, again, after listening to Frank. "I remember my grandmother's funeral. She was my grandmother on my mother's side of the family. I didn't want to be there, but, somehow I knew I had to. I understand what you must have been going through."

"Thank you. I appreciate your sentiment. I really do."

"You're welcome." Charlie plucked a tissue from a box on the desk.

"In order to put all this into perspective, I have to tell you some things about my grandfather. You see, he was a Mason. No, he wasn't a bricklayer. He had belonged to the Fraternal Order of the Masons. He had not only been a member of both the York rite, but, also the Scottish rite of Freemasonry.

"When dressed up for ceremonies, he always looked so distinguished. Whenever he attended some function in the Scottish Rite, he would always wear his kilt. When he attended something for the York Rite, he would always wear his white helmet with a plume on top and his sword strapped on his side. He reminded me of an English officer in some army regiment.

"As you could imagine, being a male, I was extremely fond of that sword and was absolutely mesmerized when he allowed me to hold it. After he died, I hunted high and low for that sword and never could find it. Now, let's fast-forward back to my visit with the pastor at the First Spiritual Church of Linden"

"I think I can see where this is going." Charlie muttered.

"You're right on target. I explained it all to the pastor, just as I have to you. I asked her if there was anyway to get one of the mediums to contact my grandfather to find out what happened to his sword. Do you know what she told me?"

"I have no idea."

"She caught me off guard; that's what she did. She said why waste time waiting for one of the church mediums to ask my grandfather when we could do it right now. I was sitting opposite from her at the table. She reached across and took both of my hands and asked me to visualize my grandfather as I remembered him.

"He was a tall bald man with a lanky frame. He wore glasses and smoked a pipe. I still think of him whenever I smell the aroma of apple or cherry blend tobacco. He had a black friend who lived down the street, and together, they would take me to the country to pick berries. Not long after my grandfather died, my mother sold the house and we moved to the country. I never cared that much for city life and my fondest memories of my childhood come from when I lived in a renovated eighteenth century log cabin along the Hocking River. It was a harsh life, but a very rewarding one.

"I'm sorry, I didn't mean to digress. My childhood is another matter for another time.

"For the next few minutes, I concentrated on my grandfather with all my heart. The pastor's face began to change. I swear she slipped into a trance, right before my eyes. Her voice shifted back and forth between a manly tone and her own sweet and gentle tone. She appeared to be having a conversation with herself. Once she seemed to be fully connected with my grandfather, her trance became more relaxed and casual. Finally, she sort of faded off to somewhere else; she was no longer there with me."

"The scene you're describing seems frightening to me, Frank."

Ignoring Charlie's concern, he continued. "I must have sat there a full five minutes, watching her blank face. I had this strange feeling like we were sitting in a room within a room and that room was not in this world."

"Come on Frank, how did it end?"

"It ended when she slumped in her chair and started to breathe heavily like she had been running across the yard. The whole ordeal had exhausted her. She wasn't faking this because I know worn-out when I see it.

"Once she caught her breath, she told me that she had a nice talk with my grandfather and that I shouldn't worry about his sword. The unfortunate reality was that we had fallen on hard times and the money he received from his retirement and what my mother was bringing in as a waitress was not enough to make ends meet. We always seemed to come up short toward the end of the month. Each time we needed money he would take his most prized possession, his sword, down the street to the Texaco gas station and hock it with the owner. Each time he got ten dollars for it. Unfortunately, he passed away before he could get it out of hock."

"You mean she actually knew it was a Texaco gas station and it was down the street from you grandfather's house? I mean that is spooky. Did all this make sense to you, Frank?"

"Mostly, everything she said made sense to me. However, I didn't know what kind of gas station was down the street from my grandfather's house. I was sure that we needed money because that was pretty common to us. I was absolutely positive of one thing, though, and that was what I had to do. After thanking the pastor for the eggplant and her efforts in contacting my grandfather, I went home to think and rest. Early the next morning, I drove to Athens. The gas station was closed and out of business. But, that old Texaco sign was still there. Now, I had the validation that I had been looking for; after death communication does exist and it finally put me at ease about a mystery that had nagged at me all my life."

"I guess that makes you a believer then, doesn't it?" Charlie's eyes were just as piercing as her question.

"Let me tell you what I think. I think there are some charlatans out there along with the real McCoy's. That's why it is so important to validate. You aren't only validating your messages; you are also validating the medium. In their line of work, they need validation. Every unknown thing we face in life must be looked at with both a sense of optimism and a sense of skepticism. This is true, even when we have to face ourselves."

"Man, I sure have a lot to learn, Frank. I don't know if I will be able to sleep tonight with all this running through my head."

"I think you will do just fine."

CHAPTER 6

Bernardo Pisano was known most commonly by his acquaintances as simply Bennie. He grew up in Queens, New York and because he combined a heightened sense of caution with being extremely streetwise, he had never been arrested. In fact, he had no record of any adverse contact with the police.

Bennie had a large barrel of a chest, a thick neck, huge arms and a disproportionately small lower body. However, the most noteworthy features about him had to do with his face. Like most Italians, he had thick black hair, bushy eyebrows, but it was his face that distinguished him. His face was heavily pockmarked. The pockmarks could have come from some disease such as smallpox or it could have come from some genetic defect. The bottom line was that no one was about to ask him about his face because he had a history of explosive behavior. This fear factor kept others at bay.

Additionally, any family gene that would have given Bennie any degree of height was sorely absent. He was only five foot six inches tall and that caused him to be a bit self conscious. In an effort to compensate for his shortness, he often wore shoes with oversized heels and that occasionally made him prone to stumbling.

Perhaps, his family genes contributed heavily when it came to making him lethally dangerous. If there was such a thing as genes that produced a sociopath, then they were abundantly present in Bennie. Overall, he was extremely sensitive about his physical deformities and that contributed to his desire to become a hit man; killing helped him compensate for his physical shortcomings. Not surprising, to Bennie's credit as a hit man, during his forty-four years of life, he had racked up an impressive twenty-three kills.

He had never been arrested because he had an unrestrained passion for being cautious. With rare exception, every detail of each of his assignments was the result of him being excessively methodical and calculating. He preferred to work alone and was known for not wanting anyone to know about his involvement in a hit, except for his handler. He especially did not want the client to know his name or anything about him other than he was gifted and dependable when it came to killing. An explanation is in order to clarify this point.

Bennie was an asset in a pool of assassins. He received his instructions from an untraceable organization known as HITS which stood for Hostile Interactive Threat Service. Depending on one's perception, HITS could only be characterized as being a highly skilled and anonymous security organization that delivered results. Only a limited number of agents carried out assigned tasks. Agent selection was a long, thorough, and drawn out process. Additionally, HITS only serviced a select number of reputable long-term clients. The existence of HITS was not known to the law enforcement community. Although, there were rumors about a new group of elite contract killers. HITS was certainly an elite organization serving affluent clients in an extremely professional manner.

On his present assignment, Bennie was disillusioned over having to work with a partner; even though his partner was also a member of HITS. Working with a partner, in Bennie's mind, was a liability. In this line of work, one mistake was career-ending. All of his begging and pleading fell on the deaf ears of his handler. If the truth was known, the biggest drawback for Bennie was that of having to split the fee with another HITS member. He and his partner were destined to butt heads.

Bennie's one vice was gambling and it preyed largely on his financial status and ego; it was a weakness in his nature. He owed a great deal of money to a casino in Las Vegas and he had to pay up or risk being barred from all casinos. His inner voice kept telling him that some day he would surely wind up being a big winner and when that happened he would walk away from both his vice and his chosen profession. Then, and only then, there would be no more killing for him. He was convinced that his destiny included only sunny beaches and an affluent lifestyle. He could see himself as a socialite wearing fine clothes, driving luxurious cars and dinning in the finest restaurants. In the mean time, he would have to tolerate working with a partner named Ivan Vanic.

Ivan was an immigrant from Russia. He was thirty-five years old and had been in the U.S. for ten years. His father had been a hit man for the Russian Mafia back in Saint Petersburg, so it was not surprising that his father's influence had brought Ivan to this line of work. Family traditions die hard.

Ivan's uncle had also emigrated to the U.S. from Russia. Often when his father and uncle met in front of Ivan, they would brag about their exploits as hit men. They had learned their skills as agents in the Russian KGB and successfully demonstrated them during the Afghan and Chechen wars. Once the wars had ended and following the break-up of the Soviet Republic, they turned to the Russian Mafia, the old Vory. During those days, they focused their skills on killing witnesses and settling vendettas on behalf of organized crime figures.

Ivan's uncle was the first to immigrate to the U.S., entering as a skilled carpenter when housing starts were booming. Of course, that was only a front. At the time of his uncle's entry into the U.S. the old hit man organizations; Murder, Inc. and the National Crime Syndicate, were already phasing out. HITS had been a secret spin off of those organizations and it had a keen eye for talent that was not readily known by any of the old killing organizations. Fresh new faces from overseas meant less liability for business as usual. Since no one knew of its existence, HITS could not be infiltrated or compromised.

Ivan was tall and lanky with sharp, cold eyes. Unlike Bennie, he had a juvenile record for assault. His admiration for his father and uncle drove him to emulate their conduct, as best he could. That was especially true when it came to their past careers as hit men.

During his senior year of high school in Tampa, Florida, he had assaulted a football star from a rival team for a mere forty dollars. The money had been collected and paid by players from his home team for the express purpose of tipping the odds in their favor during a championship football game. When confronted by the police, those that had hired Ivan then ratted on him for a guarantee of leniency. Later, they had their arrests expunged. Since Ivan had no bargaining chip, his arrest remained on the books as a juvenile offense. Instead of learning a lesson in right and wrong, he learned to be cautious about the people he worked for. The secrecy surrounding HITS had a special appeal to Ivan.

Ivan preferred organized crime hits and never, under any circumstances, would he undertake a hit on a spouse over a domestic disagreement. The risk of passionate hatred turning into soft guilt was too high. Unlike Bennie, he had no problem working with a partner. After all, regardless of who pulls the trigger, both are charged for the crime. Still, there was that lingering memory of betrayal when he had been a juvenile.

Ivan's weakness was that he had an eye for women and a craving for sexual intimacy. Next to family pride, sex was his true weakness and vice. The intensity of his sexual fantasies testified to his wickedness. Several of his fourteen kills had been women. He made two of his targets undress so he could enjoy a quick sexual fantasy before shooting them. The others, he undressed after he had shot and killed them. Each time, he had lingered behind long enough to hover over their bodies and fantasize about what he could not have. He was a sick and depraved man. His addiction to porn movies came as no surprise.

Ivan was completely deprived of having any social skills when it came to the opposite sex, and because of that curse he had never had a girlfriend longer than a one night stand, and some of those involved an exchange of money. More often than he cared to think about, he had been turned down when he had asked a woman out.

Bennie and Ivan had a strained working relationship when it came to this assignment. They had no idea why someone wanted Walter Welch taken out. The standard hit was fairly straight forward. Once you got in town, you took a day or two to check out the target's habits, haunts, and routines. During that time, if there was a good opportunity, you went ahead and took out the target. Otherwise, you assessed what you had learned and planned a place and time that afforded the most secrecy and best opportunity for success. This time, however, their handler had tossed in an additional twist.

The quicker they accomplished their additional task, the quicker they could get on with the hit and leave town. The handler wanted Walter watched to see who he was meeting with. Walter also had in his possession some information that could be damaging to the client. Getting their hands on that information was Bennie and Ivan's first order of business. If Walter didn't freely relinquish the information then they were cleared to abduct and torture him in order to get their hands on it. The only thing the handler could confirm about the targeted information was that it included a list of names of people that had high profile affiliations. The complexity of the assignment created too many opportunities for things to go wrong and that bothered Bennie.

This necessity for having two hit men was because one would have to remain with Walter until the other retrieved the information. With a degree of certainty, Bennie did not have much faith in Ivan satisfactorily accomplishing either task. Bennie decided to play everything by ear until they were finished.

In the mean time, both men sat in their hotel room killing time until morning. Since they had already lost Walter once at his home, they had to wait on their handler to call with new instructions. Bennie ordered food and drinks brought to the room while Ivan watched the adult channel on the television.

Bennie had rented the room with a fake driver license from Illinois. Each of them had three sets of identification and credit cards. The car they were driving was a rental.

Without any outward expression of thought, each of them wanted to blame the other for the botched run at Walter's home. However, neither one of them could come up with any single thing they could blame on the other. Although, after some thought, two theories did come to mind. One was that Walter was already on the run for some unknown reason. The other theory, and the worse case scenario, was that Walter was expecting a hit on his life from the client, whoever that was. All Bennie was sure of was that Walter had made fools of them by leaving them stranded at Walter's estate. The other issue bothering Bennie was that without success, there was no payoff.

Ivan was a chain smoker and when he watched porn, he smoked non-stop. Agitated over having to miss a steamy part of the movie, he left the room to buy another pack of cigarettes. The food arrived as soon as he left.

No sooner than the food arrived, the phone rang. Bennie instinctively knew it would be their handler since no one else knew the phone number. Partially to reduce the noise so he could hear better and partially to irritate Ivan when he returned, Bennie turned the television off.

"Hello." Bennie gave the universal greeting.

"Hello, Sam, this is James. Are you alone so we can talk freely?" During this trip Bennie was using Sam as his first name and the handler was using James as his name. Even though Bennie had a solid working relationship with his handler, he had no idea what his true name was. This was good operational security for both of them.

"Yes, my buddy went out for cigarettes."

"Good. I can be open and frank with you." The handler's voice was low and breathy. Bennie had the impression that the handler's real voice was being mechanically disguised by some device. In this line of work there was always a fear that the phone lines could be tapped. Also, a voice imprint could identify a person.

"Go ahead, let me have it." Bennie knew something was up.

"In the morning, I want you to go to the home of a Matt Whitman, a local minister. I checked and his home address is listed in the phone directory. I want you two to keep an eye on him for a day or two because he is a known associate and friend of your target."

"I think we can handle that alright."

"Should these two men not meet within three days, then I want you guys to go back to the target's home. By some off chance, he might go back there. He may even be hiding something there that we are interested in." Bennie suspected that there was something else on the handler's mind.

"How are you two getting along, Sam?" Something in the handler's tone alerted Bennie that something was truly up.

"It's touch-n-go, but, we're doing alright. I have to admit, though, he wouldn't have been my first choice for a partner."

"I understand. I want to change the terms of your contract. Once the information is collected and the job is finished, I want you to use your own discretion when it comes to your partner. He is no longer stable enough to be trusted. I have good information that because of his sexual proclivities during two of his previous assignments that law enforcement now has an interest in him. I can't afford to have the police keeping an eye on him when he is working for me. Once you take care of this little problem, you will collect two fees; yours and his. Do you understand what I am saying to you?" The handler was being as pointed as he could over the phone.

"I read you loud and clear, boss." Bennie exhaled noticeably to indicate that he was not surprised. On another level, he gave a sigh of relief.

"Boss, I think I will be coming back by car. I hear tell that those Louisiana swamps and bayous are pretty this time of year. The diversion will give me enough time to get the smell and trash out of the car."

"Take your time, Sam. Like always, I only want a clean job with no hiccups. Should anything else pop up, I'll give you a call. The same goes for you." The handler did not wait for an answer, he just hung up. He never was one to chit-chat.

Now that the call was over, Bennie relaxed in one of the cushioned chairs in the room. Not only would he now be able to pay off his gambling debts, he would have a few thousand dollars left over.

Suddenly, another thought crossed Bennie's mind. He had to take out a fellow hit man because of his sexual obsessions. Bennie wondered what his handler would do if he learned about his gambling obsession? He had to quit gambling, that was all there was to it. Otherwise, he could end up suffering the same consequences as Ivan. No one wants to go through life looking over his shoulder.

Ivan barged into the room with a fresh pack of cigarettes in hand like he was late for an important meeting. "Hey, why is the television off? You knew I was watching it."

"Oh, I don't think you lost your place. The plot in a porn movie isn't hard to follow." Bennie felt justified in being sarcastic. He was also confident in knowing he would have the last say when it came to Ivan.

"If you have to know, I turned off the television because our handler called with some new instructions." Bennie paused so Ivan could ask about the new instructions.

Ivan must have figured that new instructions could wait and the most important matter at hand was to get the television back on. He didn't have to fumble with the remote very long before getting back to the adult channel. In the matter of seconds, his eyes were wide with excitement. It also didn't take long for the room to be clouded with cigarette smoke.

Bennie only smoked occasionally because he had sinus problems. He liked mildly flavored and very expensive cigars. He walked out of the room and headed to the lounge where he could enjoy a good shot of bourbon and a nice break from Ivan.

Ivan had two annoying idiosyncrasies, sexual deviance and chain smoking, and the combination had drawn him a death warrant. It was bad enough being a hit man, but it was even worse to be such a jerk. People in this line of work should go out of their way to appear normal and be nice to others.

CHAPTER 7

Frank felt guilty about dousing Charlie's head with so much information on Spiritualism. Hopefully, he hadn't overwhelmed her to the point that she was mystified beyond redemption. Esoteric matters that tended to defy science also had a way of dividing people that were deeply entrenched in their own traditional belief system. Contemporary mysticism was a long way from day-to-day acceptance and people sometimes could not find any similarities between what they already took for granted and the Spiritualism approach. Depending on a person's state of mind, Spiritualism was either a bright path to enlightenment or a dark road to hell.

Charlie had every right in the world to doubt the authenticity of Spiritualism. In the mean time, she sat quietly there in the office consumed by her thoughts. Frank was aware that he had thrown a great deal of persuasive commentary at her. The feedback she had returned, so far, was that she was convinced that Spiritualism was real. Maybe, she was only trying to figure out what to do about her new revelation. How does one go from acceptance to practicing? Frank recalled an old adage: "When the student is ready, the teacher will appear." However, Spiritualism was not a subject that he was qualified to teach.

"Hey, earth to Charlie, are you hungry?" He decided to nudge her back from her thoughts.

She bounced back with a jerk and wide, bright, alert eyes. "I'm sorry. I sort of zoned out on you. This has been one interesting day for me. If you like, I'll buy you dinner. What do you think? I mean, it's the least I can do since you kept me on the clock when we really weren't working."

"Oh, that's alright. You were what they call a captive audience. Dinner is on me for you putting up with an afternoon of my crazy stories." He over dramatized his apology.

"I'll let you buy dinner on two conditions. One, I get to buy you lunch tomorrow. Two, if you get take-out so we can eat it at your place. I'm not looking forward to going back to Beth's apartment and fixing a sandwich and then sitting around staring at the walls or watching television. Also, I'm not in the mood to go hang out with her at the bar. I promise I won't keep you up late." She produced an irresistible pleading look on her face. Women had a knack for doing that.

He faked an indulging look. "Oh, all right. Now you know I'm a sucker for a face marked with pity." He also didn't care if she did keep him up late because he enjoyed having her around.

"Now, I'm not forcing you, buddy. If you want, you can watch me drive off so you can go sit at home alone and do whatever it is that bachelors do when they're alone."

"No, I don't sit at home alone. Leo will be there to make sure I have company."

"I'm sorry, Frank. I didn't know you had a roommate. I just assumed that you lived alone."

"Charlie, you will like Leo. He's a great guy. Actually, he's a blonde with long hair and he's my best friend."

"Is he anything like you?"

"No, he's nothing like me. He's a lot quieter with a different style of charm."

"Well, boss, maybe I shouldn't intrude. It was kind of rude of me to push myself off on you and wiggle my way into your home."

"Oh, you're pissed, now. You are calling me boss again. I thought we were past that." He had her going, but, wouldn't let it get too far out of hand.

"No, I'm not pissed. I guess I was just taking things for granted."

He decided to let her off the hook. "Leo, all fifteen pounds of him, is a cuddly ball of fur and he will love you."

"You asshole, you were playing with me. Okay, I can take a joke. Just remember, someday, I will pay you back." They both broke out in laughter. Their banter was playful and had a bonding effect.

"What do you want, Chinese or pizza?" He took the liberty of narrowing the choices to things he liked.

"Chinese sounds like a good idea. I'll take whatever you take, as long as it's not spicy."

"Great, cashew chicken it is. I'll call in the order now and we can swing by and pick it up on the way to my place. You can leave your truck here and I'll bring you back later to pick it up. With the price of gas skyrocketing, there's no sense in wasting it."

Frank placed the order and they were out the door within minutes. Along the way to pick up the order, he stopped by a convenience store for a re-supply of Pepsi. He couldn't remember how much Pepsi he had at home, but, a person can never have too much of it.

Once they were at his front door, he let Charlie juggle the boxes of food and Pepsi while he unlocked the door. He liked how well they worked together. They made a good team.

By the time everything was spread out on the kitchen table, Leo came strolling down the hallway. He was a little reluctant at first and decided to sashay over to Frank and rub against his leg.

"Oh what an adorable little guy you are. You must be Leo." Charlie bent over to run her hand down his back. Leo arched his back is response. "Can I hold him?"

"Sure, go ahead and pick him up. He likes being held. Anyway, he will until I put his food down. Just be careful, though. He gets carried away sometimes when you touch his tummy. I think he's overly ticklish there. He'll get his back feet kicking and even bite. He just loses control."

Once she picked him up, she sat down on the couch with him on her lap. Like a revved up a little motor, he began to purr loudly. That is, until he heard the clank of his food dish hitting the floor. In a flash, he left Charlie sitting alone on the couch.

Frank walked over to the cupboard to get two glasses for the Pepsi. When he opened the door, he saw a set of wine glasses and suddenly he couldn't remember the last time he had used them. In a wine rack that sat on the counter there were several bottles of wine. Would serving wine be a better touch than serving Pepsi?

In a split second, he made the decision, and went for broke. Why not, after all, why shouldn't he pamper Charlie a little? She was about to get an extra treat and it was a far cry from Pepsi. As an added touch, he pulled out two candle holders and candles. Besides, after drinking all that caffeine-laden Pepsi all day, they deserved a more extravagant upgrade. He rushed around as fast as he could to set things up so it would all be a surprise.

At last everything was ready. He lit the candles and switched off the lights while Charlie was thumbing through a travel magazine that she had picked up from the coffee table. The look on her face told Frank that his idea was a hit.

She walked over and put her arms around him, held him close and kissed him gently on the lips. "That's a nice touch. I appreciate it, I really do. Thank you."

She released her embrace and turned around to sit down. He followed and pulled out her chair to seat her. The ambiance around the kitchen table was warm, inviting, and the perfect setting for unwinding and conversing.

She brushed her red hair back out of her face, but a few wavy strands settled back over her cheeks. Frank saw her green eyes sparkle kindly at him and that made him feel good. He was drawn to her in a way that signaled something more than a budding friendship. The candle flames danced about when the air conditioner came on. Reflections of the flames could be seen in her eyes.

She looked down at her plate as she took the last bite of her food. Then she glanced up, her eyes meeting his. She smiled as she sipped wine from her glass. "Frank, can I ask you a question?" She asked while setting her glass back down on the table.

He drained the last bit of wine from his glass and set it down while locking eyes with her. "Sure, fire away." He was expecting some romantic inquiry. However, that did not come.

"What would you have done with your life had you not become a private investigator?"

He wondered if Charlie was intentionally drifting away from what could become a more romantic moment. "I guess I can tell you. It's no big mystery." Although he was momentarily disappointed, he gave his best answer.

"Years ago, I had a friend in Florida. I met him through his brother, who was an attorney in Ohio. The guy was a professor at a university. He taught marine biology. The man had quite a history. He was an older gentleman who had served in the Navy in Japan during the Korean conflict. While he was there, he took up SCUBA diving and underwater photography and filming. When he got out of the Navy, he went to college on the G.I. Bill. He earned extra money showing his underwater pictures and films while giving lectures to any group that would pay. Eventually, he earned his PHD, married a journalism major, and they had a son, late in their lives. However, his big love was sailboats."

"That's all interesting, Frank. But, what does that have to do with what you might have become?" She was pressing him for a direct answer to her question. She thought he was being evasive.

"Be patient, I'm getting to that. You should know by now that my explanations are rarely brief. Anyway, the man's wife did not like sailing the way he did. So she would stay home with their son during the summer months while he island-hopped around the Caribbean on his forty-foot sailboat. As a side note, the small sail at the front of a sailboat is called a jib. Jib was the first name they gave to their son."

"Hey, that's pretty cool. I like that." She sounded genuinely impressed.

"It gets better than that. All the furniture in their home came from the ocean. Their dinning room table was the door off of a sunken shrimp boat. The bench seat around their dinning room table came off of an old sunken Spanish galleon. Galleons were unique ships. They were popular during the fifteenth and sixteenth centuries. They were used as both traders and warships. You see their likeness in all those old pirate movies.

"Ned, that was his name, would take me out on his sailboat for short afternoon trips in the keys. He would drop anchor among the mangroves and we would go swimming.

"He kept his boat at the Deep Six Marina at Key Largo. One day, he introduced me to a couple that lived on their fifty-foot sailboat. Like Ned and his wife, they also had a little boy that was in elementary school. The school bus came to their slip in the marina to pick up their son. Now how many boys get to grow up living on a sailboat? The man's wife was an artist and she painted seascapes. He, on the other hand, made custom underwater reefs for movie sets. Here's the best part. Whenever life got unbearable for them, they just pulled up anchor and sailed to parts south. They island-hopped, strolled hand in hand along deserted beaches, poked around small tropical islands, and lived their dreams. They had the guts to live the life most of us can only find in our dreams.

"So, you ask me what I would have done if I hadn't become a private investigator. Well, you know I have my military retirement coming in each month. When I'm finally ready, I would like to become an affluent beach bum. All I need is a sailboat and the right woman to share my seagoing adventures and exploits with."

"Wow! I would never have imagined you doing that. I don't know what to say. That's about the most romantic notion I have ever heard. That's such a beautiful life goal to have."

The sight of Charlie's delightful response was a feast for Frank's heart and eyes. Her persona was so fresh and innocent at this moment. Her eyes were clear with sincerity and he could see a sense of purpose beginning to surface. She truly wanted to learn all she could about him. He was convinced that her interest in him was more than casual.

"Tell me, Frank, when was the last time you went sailing?"

"Last year I went sailing with a new buddy. We sailed out of a marina at Morgan City, Louisiana. He had a nice sail boat, a forty foot Hunter, and even though he allowed me to take the helm, I'm not sure my heart was in it." He was dredging up a sad memory that he wasn't quite over yet.

"I don't understand. What was wrong?"

"It all had to do with the purpose of the trip. I sailed out cradling an urn. I scattered the ashes of my last love over the sea in the Gulf of Mexico. It was the only way I had of honoring her death and finding some degree of closure."

He turned his head and stared out the patio glass door. Clearly, he did not want to discuss it any further. After a minute, he looked back at Charlie.

"Okay, Charlie. I have exposed part of my soul to you. Now, it's your turn. Tell me some guarded secret that you're holding."

Already, she was beginning to regret starting this little game. She should have known that it would become a tit for tat.

"Well let's see. When I was two, I flushed my neighbor's goldfish down his toilet. That was a shameful act and it bothered me for a long time."

"That's a nice try, Charlie, but, you're not getting off that easy. You just can't expect to weasel out of this with such a lame story. I bet you just made that story up, didn't you?"

"You saw through it, huh?"

"I'm afraid so. Let's go sit in the living room." He quickly cleared the kitchen table and followed her into the living room where he joined her on the couch.

Frank took a bold chance. "I'll make a deal with you, Charlie. I'll let you ask me anything you want, if you will tell me why you quit singing."

"Huh! Don't you know? I haven't talked about this before, except with my father. I'm sorry, but, I'm going to have to hold back a lot. I won't give you the whole story, only the general reason behind it. I just can't tell everything. First, however, I want your word that you won't repeat any of what I tell you. That goes for Beth, too. Do I have your word on that?"

This was an unexpected twist for him. He had already told Beth that he would try to find out why Charlie quit singing and what happened to her in Arizona. Now, in exchange for some of that information, he would have to promise not to tell anyone, including Beth. How on earth did he end up operating in the murky gray area between honor and betrayal? The world of ethics can be very limiting and unforgiving.

Finally, he arrived at a compromise, even though it was not a clear cut one. "Alright, I promise. But, you know Beth is your friend and she wants you to trust her. Just promise me that one day you will talk about this with her. At least tell her enough to demonstrate your friendship."

"I can live with that. I'll tell her a little, but, not as much as I'm going to tell you. And remember, I'm not going to tell you everything either." The zone they had established was as neutral as it could get considering the circumstances.

"Let me begin by explaining my feelings about this. I'm not anyone's trophy and I never will be. No man should look at me like I'm some prize to be won at the county fair. That's what a singer or entertainer is to some men. She's nothing but a damn prize.

"When most men see you strutting around on stage singing and see how other men gawk at you like you are some kind of an idol, well, they want you. They think they have to have you. However, it's all fake and temporary. When the novelty is gone, so are the trophy hunters.

"They also think that because you work in a nightclub, that you're a piece of meat. They never see the real person that you are. They're always trying to use you; some for money; some for status; some to feed their egos; and others only want you to satisfy their lusty urges. Men can be real animals that only see women as nothing but their prey.

"When you finally come to your senses and see through their deceit and resist them, they want to get rough with you. All most women want is to be loved and that's no different for an entertainer. It's that simple, I only wanted to be loved for who I am and not what I am. I'm not a sports car to be driven hard, shown off, and then dropped off at the junkyard. I'm a human being and I'm a woman."

Frank recalled an old song sung by Helen Redding titled "I am woman, hear me roar." He remained poised for the rest of Charlie's story.

"Things got out of hand one night and something bad happened. Everything ended badly, so I pulled the plug on my career. If I wasn't seen, then I couldn't be a target.

"Don't ask me what happened or what didn't happen as a result. It was handled and that's the end of it. Maybe someday I will tell you and maybe I won't.

"You have been taking your time with me without pressuring me. Right now, I think you are just as curious about me as I am about you. At least you are treating me like a real person and I like that."

She reached over and took his hand, squeezing it gently. The last thing she wanted to do was drive a wedge between them. He had ignited a spark in her heart and she wanted it to grow into something more, something bright and warm. Currently and realistically, the only thing that could douse that spark was him pressing the issue of what occurred in Arizona.

Frank's mind was headed off in another direction. He would uphold his reputation for loyalty, but would not leave this conversation without making a few points.

"The world can be a cruel place, Charlie. Many truths are self-evident- just look at the nightly news. Governments everywhere send their young men and women off to war to settle global disputes or to exact revenge, always under the auspices of protecting their country. The country's soldiers kill for their country out of a sense of duty. Every killing scars their souls, wrecks their bodies, and when they return home, they encounter an ungrateful nation. Then they are told to make ready for the next war. There is no end to what they go through. Many make the ultimate sacrifice, giving their life. No soldier escapes giving. That's right, they all give something. Not all wounds are physical."

Charlie was getting the gist of what Frank was saying. "I understand that all wars are not justified. I think many countries are like bullies, they like pushing other countries around."

Frank didn't let up. "Sadly, we also see religions trying to destroy other religions over who has the correct path to the afterlife and who has God's ear or who has the true God. Then we come to the environment. Everywhere you turn, you can read about men raping the land and pilfering the oceans out of greed. Our youth are poisoning their bodies with drugs in search of the best high for escaping from an unfulfilling world. Street gangs do drive-by shootings against rival gangs. Politicians use clever words and deceit to gain power and then they take rights away from the very citizens they are sworn to serve and protect. The world is steadily sinking into ruin and decay. So it's not surprising that men use women as toys. It's a sad state of affairs when mankind feels they have to exploit others, especially women.

"Charlie, I have no idea what happened to you. Whatever it was that you went through was wrong because what I see in you is a good-hearted woman with character. As you get to know me, you will find that I am always coming up with proverbs that speak to whatever we are dealing with. Right now, I'm thinking of one. Here it is: "Reputation is what you are in the light; Character is what you are in the dark." You have decent character, Charlie, and I'm drawn to it."

Frank had already concluded that whatever had happened to Charlie in Arizona had something to do with the criminal justice system. That impression came from her words and tone. He had gleaned that much from her on the night he had met her. No matter what she had gone through, he would do his best not to let it happen again. He squeezed her hand in return and she twisted around on the couch until he embraced her from the back. She nestled close and kissed the back of his hand.

From behind her, he leaned close until they were cheek to cheek, so they were facing across the room. Another old proverb came to mind as he kissed her cheek: "We ask four things of a woman; That virtue dwell in her heart; modesty in her face; sweetness in her mouth; and labor in her hands." Charlie had all of these things going for her. Were they falling in love with one another or were they just getting closer?

"Frank, is there any more wine? What about some music?"

"Sure, I'll be right back." He picked up another bottle of red wine from the rack, plucked two clean wine glasses from the cabinet. But, he didn't stop there. He pulled some cheese from the fridge and some crackers from the pantry. He placed everything on a wooden tray. Then, because Charlie was a redhead with Irish blood running through her veins, he put a carefully selected CD in the player.

He quickly grabbed some pillows and a blanket from the bedroom and tossed them on the floor in front of the couch. Charlie scooted off the couch and arranged the blanket & pillows on the floor. By that time, Frank arrived with the tray. As he poured wine in their glasses, the speakers came to life with an old Irish tune; "When Irish eyes are smiling."

There was no talk about Arizona or her singing career. There was, appropriately, conversation about old Irish songs that stirred the heart. Frank told her about his all-time favorite song.

"When Irish eyes are smiling is a beautiful song, but, my favorite is Danny Boy. You know, it was a ballad written in 1910 and first recorded in 1915, in time for World War I. It was subject to interpretation and the one I like best goes like this: It was a message from a father to his son. His son was leaving for the war. Sadly, the father had already lost his other sons to war. The lyric in the song; 'The pipes are calling,' of course, refers to the bagpipes being played at a funeral. I can't count how many times this song has brought me to tears. During my military career, I saw way too many sons die. That's why I detest war so much. Unfortunately, there will always be war and there will always be sons coming home in flag-draped coffins."

They both sat there with tears in their eyes and streaking down their faces. Charlie spoke first.

"I can't imagine what the horror of war is like. I once read that there are a thousand faces of death. I'm sure a soldier sees many of them. As for the song, 'Danny Boy', as well as 'When Irish eyes are smiling,' my mother used to sing them to me when I was a little girl. She said her mother sang them to her. The Irish will never be without passion.

By the time the wine and food were gone and the music had stopped, they were both fast asleep next to each other.

CHAPTER 8

Maybe it was the wine, or it could have been that she had slept nestled up next to a man she now trusted. Whatever the reason was, Charlie woke feeling safe, secure, and fully rested. She murmured some polite word of thanks to Frank, although he probably didn't hear what she was saying because he was only now wiping the sleep from his own eyes.

They looked at each other and smiled. No words were really needed to acknowledge how much they now meant to one another. The last few days had flown by so fast that it seemed as if it was only a smidgen of the actual time. Somehow it all added up to love at first sight. She felt like pinching herself to see if maybe she was only dreaming. Oh well, if what she was feeling was a dream, she hoped this one would last a long time.

Charlie stood, stretched and then extended a hand down to Frank. She pulled him to his feet and led him to the sliding patio door. Holding hands, they walked outside. She rested her head over onto his shoulder and stared east at a newly born copper sky. The sun was also waking up to a new day.

She looked at the great ball of light as it rose skyward. "I hope today is as good as yesterday."

"Yes, I hope so too. We had a good day yesterday and a good night last night. Isn't it funny how almost every living person and creature on the planet looks forward to the sun rising? The sun's rays give us warmth and its brightness allows us to see so many of the things that are hidden from us during the night, yet, we seem to take it for granted. Maybe those who practiced the old religions and worshiped the sun and the moon had it right."

"You have an odd way of looking at life, Frank, but I like it. To you, the smallest thing has some marvelous meaning. Because of you, I'm beginning to realize that nature holds all the greatest treasures and gives us the most wonderful pleasures." She looked over at him and smiled.

Frank's tone turned to one of disappointment. "Unfortunately, dear, we have to go to work so we can pay the bills. You don't want your first paycheck to bounce, do you?"

"Even if the check bounced, I wouldn't be disappointed. I'm a lot richer today than I was a few days ago. There's more to life than money." She followed up by gently squeezing his hand.

"I'm sharing the same sentiment with you, Charlie. However, we also need to be pragmatic because we live in an unforgiving world that demands money for basic services. That, my dear, means we have to go to work."

"First, you big spoil-sport, you have to get me to my truck so I can get back to Beth's to clean up and change clothes."

"Okay, I'll grab a quick shower first and then I'll drop you off at your truck. While you're gone, I can check for messages."

Once Charlie was gone to get ready for work and all the routine office tasks had been taken care of, Frank relaxed behind his desk. Officially, he now had a girlfriend. He knew little about courting and figured he had a long way to go in understanding the mind of a woman.

He had removed a can of Pepsi from the small office fridge and sat it on his desk. He stared at it for a long moment, testing his resolve to quit drinking it. He tapped his fingertips on the desktop and admired the can as if it might be his last. He chuckled to himself before popping the tab and taking a large gulp. The thought of asking Charlie to help him cut back on drinking Pepsi crossed his mind. Like so many other things, too much soda and caffeine would damage his health. These were medically proven facts.

Frank looked at his watch and was suddenly anxious to see Charlie walk through the door. His forehead began to ache because he had taken too big a drink of ice cold Pepsi. He hated a brain freeze. Maybe he wouldn't drink so much of that damn stuff with Charlie being there to keep him occupied.

He leaned forward and shoved the Pepsi can over to the edge of the desk thinking he would not be tempted if it was farther away. Before he could lean back in his chair the door opened quickly and Charlie walked into the office, pausing only slightly while she closed the door. "Hello, sweetheart," he greeted her crisply, but with affection.

He stood up, intending to give her a hug, then didn't. Something caught his eye in the parking lot. Recognizing Felicity Whitman's black Lexus as it pulled into a parking spot, Frank alerted Charlie. "There's Felicity. She must have that list of names and background information for us. Maybe this case will start picking up steam."

Indeed, Felicity was carrying a cloth tote bag that was bulging at the seams. The closer she came to the office the more determined she appeared. There was no doubt about it, there was something bothering her and she was wearing her worry on her face.

"Look at her face, Charlie. Something's up. Just in case, grab a pad and pen."

While speaking, Frank also pulled a pad from the desk drawer. Experience had taught him that recording some perplexing information was better done by two than by one. They would compare notes and then ask questions until they had a good understanding of what was happening. Success was better achieved with teamwork.

When Felicity burst into the office, she also burst into tears of fear and concern. Charlie immediately rushed to her side and seated her on the couch. With a calming tone, she went about comforting Felicity as only one woman could to another. The instinct and art of comforting often escaped men.

Frank brought a box of tissues from his desk and handed them to Charlie. He decided to take the lower road of patience and returned to his desk so Charlie could work her maternal magic.

"I'm sorry. I didn't mean to fall apart like this. It's just that something very bad is about to happen. Poor Matt, I don't know what to do about him." She was choking back sobs in the midst of her slurred speech.

Charlie handed a tissue to Felicity and then took one herself. While Felicity dabbed her eyes dry, Charlie wiped the long streams from Felicity's chin. Both tissues were quickly stained with mascara. After a few minutes, the tear ducts seemed to dry up as calm was restored. Sometimes, all it takes is being among friends and allies, especially when they are rallying to your side.

Frank decided to add his own touch. He retrieved a cup and filled it with ice and Pepsi. At the moment, Felicity could make better use of his elixir than him.

She took the fizzing cup and drank from it. "Thank you. I know I look like a mess right now. You have no idea what I have been going through during last night and this morning."

"Well, my dear, that's what we're here for. Don't forget, we're partners in this."

"Thank you, again. Any kind words right now are surely appreciated."

Frank was eager to get down to business so he picked up his pen. "Now what happened last night?"

"It has been a long and exhausting night. Shortly after midnight I felt the covers move and realized that Matt was getting up. I pretended to be asleep until I heard the French doors open out onto the patio. I put on my nightgown and followed. I hid behind some tall shrubs and watched him walk out into the flower garden. Everything looked so spooky."

"Keep going, Felicity. You're doing fine." He wanted her to keep talking, hoping she wouldn't fall back into another crying spree.

"There he was, kneeling down next to the roses. He was praying and although I was alarmed, I knew that was a good thing. That's what men of God do when something is bothering them. The next thing I knew, a cloud had moved along and the moon was casting its light over the garden. That's when I saw it. You don't know how it scared me."

"What did you see, Felicity? What scared you?" Frank was becoming anxious.

"On a stone next to his knee, there it was. My Matt, my poor husband has a pistol. There it was, glaring in the moonlight. Why does a man of God carry a pistol when he prays to the Lord?"

"Could you hear his prayer?" Frank figured the key to needing a pistol would be found in Matt's words. Hopefully, the prayer had nothing to do with suicide. He had seen that one before.

"At first, I wasn't close enough to hear so I missed the first part of the prayer. All I could get from it was that he was asking for courage to do something and guidance to make sure he did the right thing. Whatever this weight is, it's heavier than any he has ever had before."

"What happened next?"

"Another cloud moved in, blocking out the moonlight. I only wanted to wait long enough to make sure Matt wasn't going to do something awful to himself. When my eyes adjusted to the darkness he was standing again. I stayed there until he put the pistol into his pajama pocket. I was sure that he would be okay so I rushed inside the house and slipped back into bed and pretended to be asleep. He didn't get back in bed with me, though. All he did was pace around the room and stare out the windows. I think he was watching for something or someone. Someone's after him, aren't they? What do you think?"

"I think you have a good point there. To me, this looks like he was standing guard over you as well as himself. Has he said anything to you about any of this?"

"No. He hasn't said a word to me about what's going on. We did have a short talk this morning, though." She paused long enough for Frank to ask the obvious question.

"What did you talk about?"

"He said that there were a lot of things going on in the parish and he thought it would be easier for him to handle things if I went away for a couple of weeks. He thought that going back to Kansas to see some of my relatives and old friends would be good for me."

"What did you tell him?"

"I said I would think about it. What I really wanted to do was borrow some time until I had a chance to talk this over with you." Felicity's eyes darted back and forth between Frank and Charlie.

"That was some fast thinking on your part and you did the right thing. Have you told me everything that has happened?"

"No I haven't. There's more. There's a notepad next to our phone and I saw that he had made a note and then tore the page off. I took a pencil and shaded over it. He is going to meet someone this afternoon in Plano. They are supposed to meet at 2:00 p.m. I asked Matt what he's going to do today and he told me nothing in particular; only a few housekeeping errands for the church. I've lived with him long enough to know that he wasn't telling me the truth. He couldn't look me in the eye when he was talking."

Frank put down his pen, folded his hands together and placed the tips of his index fingers to his lips. "Felicity, I want you to check into a motel some place and call me with the phone number and the room number. Here's my cell phone number." He handed her a business card.

"How long will I have to stay there?"

"Until I tell you it's safe to leave."

Charlie reached over and touched Felicity's arm. "Everything will be just fine. Please, don't worry. Relax by the pool or watch movies."

"Do you know where Matt will be around noon?" Frank had his pen at the ready, again.

"He will be wrapping up a fundraising meeting at the church with the Cancer Society. After that, I don't know what he will be doing, other than that 2:00 p.m. meeting somewhere in Plano."

"Good. That will give me time to set up surveillance. I'll need a photo of Matt and a description of what he will be driving." Frank looked at his wristwatch.

Felicity reached down and picked up the cloth tote bag she had brought in with her." I have all that right here along with everything else you wanted me to bring in about those guys he meets with." She handed the entire bag to him.

"Great. Now don't worry about anything. One of us will be in touch with you as soon as we have something. In fact, you'll hear from us even if we don't have anything. It's 10:15 a.m., and we have a lot to do in the way of preparation. You gave me your cell phone number the other day so I can get in touch with you quickly if there's some emergency. Right now, just do like Charlie said and relax." He stood up to let Felicity know the meeting was over.

Charlie walked Felicity to her Lexus and gave her an assuring hug. She even stood in the parking lot and waved until the Lexus was out of sight. Returning to the office, she found waiting for her the beginning of a new chapter in the private investigation business.

"What the heck is all this stuff?" She was scratching the back of her head in bewilderment.

"Since you will be helping me use these things, I guess I should give you some training." He picked up a set of earphones that were attached to a dish like object by a cord. "This is a Bionic Ear and booster. With this we can listen in on a conversation a hundred yards away. This little gizmo attaches to it so we can record any conversation we're intercepting." He held up a small mini-recorder.

"What if they're whispering?"

"That's no problem for this equipment. We can hear a bird clear its throat. It even has a Bionic Booster to reduce background noises." He was smiling because he knew she was impressed.

"I bet something like that sat you back a pretty penny."

"Not really. This is one of the best ones you can buy and it only cost a couple hundred dollars. If you are real ambitious, you can make one yourself for a fraction of the cost. You can get everything you need at Radio Shack and a hardware store."

After holding and examining the Bionic Ear, she set it back down on the desk and picked up a small plastic box that was about two inches square. She turned it over and saw that it had a magnet attached to it. "What's this thing?"

"That is a mini GPS tracker and not only does it cost more to purchase, it also costs to operate it. If we want to relocate a vehicle that we know will be out of our site for some time, then the GPS tracker is what we use. All we do is slip this under the fender and attach it with the magnet. When we're ready to locate it, all we have to do is log into a computer and activate our account. A satellite image will come up on the monitor and give us the coordinates. Then we can go right to it. In our case, we will use a laptop computer also linked to a satellite. That's pretty cool, huh?"

"This is James Bond stuff."

"A private investigator can never have too many gadgets in his line of work. The best part is that it all gets billed to the client and our chances of success jumps way up there." Frank was beaming with pride.

"Now, over hear we have two sets of binoculars. One is for ordinary daytime use. The other one is more sophisticated. It's what we call night vision goggles. We will use it to see in the dark. We might not need any of these things, but we're taking them along just in case."

"What are these little ear things for?" She picked up one and stared at it.

"Those are Expo Radios. We use them to talk to one another whenever we have to separate. Most people won't even know we have them on. Not only can we talk to one another, we can also hear what people are saying around each other. Here, you'll need this little microphone. All you have to do is fasten it out of sight to the inside of your blouse. Before we leave, we're going to test all this in the parking lot. Remember, we always check our equipment before going out on a case."

During the next forty minutes, they judiciously rehearsed and tested the equipment outside in the parking lot, except for the night vision goggles. They were tested in the back room of the office with the lights off. Frank knew that there was quite a bit for Charlie to grasp in such a short time. Fortunately, she already had a demonstrated aptitude with the computer and that was in her favor. At least these new gadgets were not technologically challenging to operate. Frank recalled how much difficulty he had learning to use a spectrum analyzer to isolate cell phone signals for interception, a procedure that is now against the law.

The inside of Frank's little Nissan pickup quickly took on the look of an overstuffed electronics lab. Each piece of equipment was neatly sorted into shoeboxes with exceptional care not to mix any accessories. Experience had taught him that when time was critical, it was too late to organize.

It was already 11:50 a.m. and the clock was ticking. Once inside the truck, Frank insisted on double checking to ensure they had everything. Because Charlie had enough spinning about in her head, he decided to do all the voice notes himself. He spoke clearly with exaggerated slowness into a voice activated recorder. He named the client, gave the date and time, and identified both himself and Charlie. He then specified that they were in route to the target church to initiate surveillance.

Charlie needed no special explanation for Frank's official posturing. She knew that this could all become extremely important when it came to the business of private investigation. She was also experiencing a slight rush of adrenalin because she was aware that a good surveillance could make or break a case. It could also lead to something more exciting. Additionally, not knowing what they might get into left her feeling like she was in some movie drama. For her, all this had a special appeal to it.

Fortunately, the church had a large parking lot with an abundance of large shrubs and trees. Frank announced to the recorder that they had arrived at the target address. Casually driving through the parking lot, they were able to confirm the target's vehicle; a red Ford Explorer. They also confirmed the license plate number. Felicity had been thorough.

They took up their surveillance position at the far end of the lot, in the shade of a large tree. Frank wrapped his hand over the microphone of the recorder before speaking to Charlie because he didn't want to activate it when he spoke to her.

"Let me explain something, Charlie. If, for any reason, Matt decides to exit the parking lot by driving past us, we will need to display a cover for being here; a cover for action. In other words, we have to have a good reason for being here. We will hide our faces by kissing each other."

"Is this a trick, Frank?" She wasn't sure if he was pulling her leg or not.

The look on his face was all the answer she needed. He wasn't kidding. That term he used; cover for action, was a clear indication that this was how things were done in his world. He was quoting from either his experience or some doctrine linked to his tradecraft. She was convinced that he had an enormous repertoire from which to draw on. Each day she worked with him was a learning experience.

"Come on Charlie, we're going to stroll around the parking lot. We'll hold hands so people will think we're casually passing through. When we go by Matt's vehicle, I'm going to bend over like I'm tying my shoe lace. While I'm kneeling, I'll attach the GPS mini-tracker to his vehicle. If we don't need it, we'll retrieve it later.

There was no reluctance on Charlie's part. She was already feeling cramped in the little pickup with all that equipment jam-packed in with them. Within ten minutes they had accomplished their task, left the parking lot, and sneaked back to the pickup.

Nearly an hour passed when Charlie learned a new lesson about conducting surveillance. "Honey, I have to, you know? I have to pee."

Frank pulled out a paper sack and removed some tissues and a jar. He handed them to Charlie. Here, take this jar and pee in it. I'll look the other way."

"I heard about this somewhere. I can't remember where. I wish it wasn't daylight. Can't you go for a walk? Walk behind that tree for a minute." This wasn't an easy adjustment for her.

Frank scanned the parking lot for people and when he didn't see anyone, he got out of the pickup. "Please, hurry up." He spoke with urgency and an added emphasis.

Frank hid behind a tree for a few minutes. Figuring she would be finished peeing, he peaked. She waved for him to come back to the pickup and he recognized the gesture as confirmation that she had finished relieving herself.

After getting back into the pickup, he spotted a car pulling up and parking out on the street. He wondered why the driver didn't park in the parking lot. After all, it was nearly empty, except for the few cars that probably belonged to the people from the Cancer Society. The meeting must have been breaking up because people were filing out of the church and getting into their cars.

Within minutes, the only vehicle parked directly in front of the Church was Matt's. The car that had parked out on the street did not move. "Give me that Bionic Ear. I want to listen in on what those two in that car are talking about."

Charlie was amazed at how quickly Frank zeroed in on the two men in the car. She started to lean toward the Bionic Ear to hear better, but didn't need to. The men's voices came in extremely audible and loud enough that Frank had to turn the volume down.

At first their conversation seemed mundane. One man was angry at the other because he wanted them to leave so he could purchase cigarettes. The other man seemed to be in charge and nixed the request. The voice of the man that seemed to be going into nicotine withdrawal sounded younger than the other one. The younger voice began to challenge the other one by hurling a few unpleasant remarks his way. Shortly, their conversation began to sound more revealing, and alarming.

One overheard question in particular was startling to both Frank and Charlie. The question was: "Do you really think this preacher will lead us to Walt?" The question had an electrifying effect that seemed to numb Frank and Charlie.

They both gasped, but it was Frank that put things into perspective. "I would say we have some competition in the area. We're going to have to be on our toes from hear on out."

Charlie acknowledged the situation. "It looks to me like Felicity's concerns are real."

"It's evident that something is amiss." Frank put his finger to his lips to request her silence. Hopefully, they would hear more from the two in the car.

By 1:45 p.m. Frank was on his second Pepsi along with a snack; a snickers candy bar. Charlie was still nursing her Pepsi, fearing that if she drank too much she would have to pee in the jar again. Both of them were fighting off leg cramps from sitting so long. The cramped quarters were having a worse impact on Frank because he was taller. He was nearly to the point of chancing getting out of the pickup for a quick stretch. However, that would not happen.

In the wink of an eye they went from being slumped in dull boredom to being wide-eyed alert. Right before their eyes, Matt was getting into his vehicle, the red Ford Explorer.

Frank and Charlie simultaneously glanced at the two men sitting in the car out on the street. They were ducking down in their seats to avoid being seen by Matt. Frank and Charlie did likewise.

"Charlie, we need to think about tactics here. Not only do we not want Matt to know that we're watching him, we also don't want these two jaspers in that car over there to know we're watching Matt. For our safety and the sake of our case, we can't allow those guys to know that we are on to them."

"Okay, but can't we just use that mini-GPS device?

"No, that won't work for this. It takes time to activate the satellite account and we need to keep our eyes on Matt. We can't let him out of our sight, not for a moment. The mini-GPS tracker is for locating Matt's vehicle after half an hour or so has elapsed. At first, I think we should get in behind Matt ahead of our new guests. We can do some jockeying after we get down the road."

Frank was having trouble drawing on his past experience because the ideal vehicular surveillance is done with more than one car. The surveillance system used by the U.S. Army is an adaptation of the one used by the British in MI-6 and it requires a minimum of four vehicles.

"So what are we going to do?"

"Reach behind my seat and get that cloth bag. The things inside should help."

When Matt drove out of the church parking lot he did them a favor without knowing it. He drove in the opposite direction that the two men were headed in. Frank drove out on the street and right past the other car. In his rearview mirror, Frank saw the other car making a u-turn. Frank smiled and mumbled "so far so good."

Charlie began pulling things out of the cloth bag. Among the things she was retrieving were; sunglasses, a black wig, a false beard, and several different kinds of magnetic stickers. She couldn't resist asking, "Are we going to a costume party?"

Frank laughed out loud. "In a manner of speaking, we are. We are combining two tactics here. First, we are conducting what is known as a loose surveillance. A loose surveillance is used when trying to determine contacts and intentions of a subject. The second tactic is known as counter-surveillance and that is directed at those two guys in the car that's now following us. In our loose surveillance mode, we risk losing Matt. In our counter-surveillance mode, we risk being burned. We have to be prepared to do a lot of juggling here.

"When we are on long stretches of road we can let the other car pass us. When we are in more congested areas we will have to change how we appear so we can pass the other car without alerting them or allowing them to recognize us. The stickers are for the windshield and rear window. The disguises are for us."

Charlie started to giggle. "This is not only exciting, it's flat out fun. Do you think they will notice if I put the beard on?"

"Now aren't you the funny one."

During the next ten minutes they only changed their position twice. Now they were right back where they started, directly behind Matt. The other car kept changing lanes behind them, but it didn't attempt to pass. They were keeping a safe distance. Once, Frank caught the passenger using binoculars. The man didn't seem to be paying any attention to Frank's pickup.

The convoy ended up traveling north on Preston until reaching Highway 121. Out of habit, Matt turned on his turn signal to make a turn onto Highway 121 South. Frank did not use his turn signal in case Matt changed his mind at the last minute. Frank had used that trick before to see if someone was following him. When someone commits to a change of direction by using his turn signal, he would draw attention to himself by not following through. Thankfully, Matt didn't have the same background as Frank.

After a few minutes, Matt made another left hand turn onto Legacy. Although in different lanes, all three vehicles made the same turn. The car with the two men in it was three cars behind Frank's pickup when it got caught by a red light. Frank knew that when the light changed to green, the other car would be traveling hell bent for leather. Frank liked that old western term. The driver would be whipping however many horses he had under the hood of the car he was driving.

Frank continued to diligently record every aspect of the trip into his voice activated recorder. In the back of his mind he had visions of Charlie transcribing the recording into an investigative report. An objective and accurate report is what makes a client feel they have gotten their money's worth. It's all in the details.

In the rearview mirror, Frank could see the other car weaving recklessly through traffic to catch up. The occupant's focus was on catching up to Matt and that meant they weren't aware of Frank and Charlie's presence. In Frank's opinion, the two men's heart rates were racing as fast as they were driving.

The traffic suddenly came to nearly a halt as they reached the intersection with the Dallas Parkway. This was a very busy intersection for two reasons. First, there was a traffic light on each side of the parkway for vehicles wanting to use the frontage roads. Second, because the speed limit on Legacy was reduced significantly for a heavily used business area. No matter which way anyone looked they could see businesses; mostly trendy shops, cafes, and restaurants. People everywhere were strolling along window shopping or heading for their favorite eating establishment.

After crossing Dallas Parkway, Matt turned in on the first entrance to the right. He immediately veered right again on the very next street and was lucky enough to find a parking spot. After parking and securing his vehicle, he crossed the street and walked into the Café Express.

"Quick, Charlie, follow him inside to see if he is meeting anyone. Just read the menu or buy a soft drink. I want you to take a good look around, but don't stay any longer than you have to. And get me a cold Pepsi if they have it."

She didn't need any prodding because her legs were about to cramp from sitting. Frank backed his pickup into a parking spot half a block from the café where he had a good field of view.

Things were happening so fast that Frank didn't have time to turn off his engine before the other car with the two men in it passed them by and parked across the street on the same frontage lane, directly in front of Café Express. The driver backed into a parking place just as Frank had. They had a good view of the front door of Café Express and a partial view of the side while Frank had a good view of both the front and the side of the restaurant. The passenger immediately got out and entered the café behind Charlie. The man had short hair, was tall and lean, and wore jeans with a knit polo shirt. Frank was unable to get a good look at the man's face.

Frank realized that neither he nor Charlie had put on their Expo Radios. This made Frank uncomfortable because Charlie was out of his sight and he still didn't know what kind of a mess Matt had gotten into or why someone else was also following him. The Expo Radio situation would be corrected as soon as Charlie returned to the pickup because Frank didn't like sloppy work, even when it occurred under demanding circumstances.

Frank knew only well that there were no predetermined solutions for all problems which can arise during surveillance. Presently, one concern he had was eye contact. Hopefully, Charlie could avoid direct eye contact with Matt and the man that entered the restaurant behind her. Any subconscious notice of Charlie by either man could cause a later recognition of her. Maybe he was making too much of the situation. After all, Matt didn't have any counter-surveillance training; anyway, none that Frank knew of. As for the other man, well the jury was certainly out on him. Unfortunately for Charlie, she did not know that one of the men from the other car had followed her inside.

The next thing Frank noticed was Matt coming out a side door and taking a seat at a table in a fenced area for customers that preferred sitting outside. Should Matt meet someone outside, the circumstances would be perfect for using the Bionic Ear. Finally, the possibility of a good break was at hand.

Charlie walked out of the café's front door carrying a sack. Her jaw was set, indicating that she was miffed about something. She surprised Frank by walking down the sidewalk behind the truck instead of directly to it. After a few minutes, she worked her way through some shrubs and slipped back into the pickup, unnoticed.

"There's a real creep in there, Frank. I caught him looking at my butt. He wasn't just glancing; he was trying to undress me with his eyes. When he was looking, he even spoke to me. He said I had a nice ass. Can you imagine a total stranger talking like that to a woman, especially in a public place like this? I wanted to smack him, but, I looked away from him and moved on up in the line."

"Was he a tall lanky guy with short hair and wearing jeans?"

"How did you know?" By the tone of her question, her anger over the man's offending behavior was not about to dissipate any time soon.

"He was the passenger in that other vehicle that has been following Matt." Frank's tone was one of noted concern.

Deciding not to dwell on the incident, Charlie changed the topic. "That café is really cool. When you order food, they give you a pager to let you know when your order is ready. Matt went out the side door and sat down with his pager. I guess you saw him."

"I certainly did see him and I'm glad he went outside."

Charlie looked down at the Bionic Ear and said; "I guess that means we can still put that thing to good use, huh?"

"You are absolutely correct. Now it's a waiting game to see who shows up."

CHAPTER 9

Reverend Matt Whitman sat nervously at a sidewalk table outside the Café Express. The pager that would signal that his food was ready sat on the table in front of him. The only way he had to control his tension was to stare blankly at that damn pager. He fought the urge to just get up and run away. If he only knew where to run in order to find a safe haven, he would do it. That is, he would run away once he knew his wife was safe.

Poor Walter! The Order's assassins were already chasing after him. Once they kill Walter, they will surely turn their sights on the only other loose end; and Matt knew that would be him. These killers certainly had no compunction over killing a minister; a man of God. After all, they had no sense of guilt when it came to killing anyone. Some men must be born without any sense of morality. The shiniest part of their character had to be their devotion to evil. However, Matt believed that evil, any evil, could only shine as the bright flames of hell. How interesting; there are two different kinds of light in the world of religion; one for evil and one for good. He could certainly turn that into a good theme for a sermon.

Matt drew in a deep breath and felt his stomach tighten. Rubbing his forehead with the tips of his fingers, he wondered how he had allowed himself to get into this predicament. What had the members of The Order seen in him that made them think he would be an asset to their cause? Maybe they somehow thought that having a minister by their sides, they could somehow deflect public scrutiny. That was it. They had wanted to appear innocent by associating themselves with Christianity. They had used him only as a pawn. This would not be the first time that Satan used good men while pursing evil goals.

Now his ears were ringing and his head was pounding because of elevated blood pressure. All this was brought on by his stupidity and naiveté. Yes, he was angry at himself for falling for The Order's propaganda. Suddenly, the pager sounded off loudly and began to vibrate across the table. He was thankful for the distraction.

He had been sitting there adrift in a fog of regret when a simple little pager called him back. Gladly, he welcomed the chance to stand up. The last thing he wanted was to be so preoccupied with his thoughts that he lost his sense of awareness to his surroundings. Three different influences were bearing down on him at the moment. Walt was out there somewhere and he was late for their meeting. Hopefully, nothing had happened to him. Also, the assassins were also out there somewhere and he had no idea what they looked like.

Unfortunately, he was also unaware of what he had going for him; there was a private investigator out there that was interested in saving his troubled hide.

Matt went inside and picked up his order, then returned to the table. After taking a couple of bites from his sandwich, his thoughts settled on something that was more important than his own life. He feared for the safety of his wife, Felicity. His thoughts always returned to her.

During all the years he had known and loved her, he had never kept anything from her. His guilt was eating away at his soul. Should something bad happen to her, he would be devastated beyond redemption. He had to make sure that she left town, on his terms, without suspecting that his life was at risk. There was no doubt in his heart and mind that she would not leave knowing that he was in danger. After his meeting with Walter, he would make sure she went back to Kansas to visit friends and relatives. Some day, when all this was behind him, he would set down and explain it all to her.

Out the corner of one eye, he spotted Walter standing on the sidewalk. He was hesitating. His eyes were wide and he looked edgy, as expected. Walter looked around in every direction as if sizing things up. He walked toward the table as if he half expected a bomb to go off. Tucked under one arm was a newspaper.

"I thought you weren't coming. Is everything alright?" Matt was genuinely concerned about Walter.

"No, everything isn't alright. Those killers are still out there looking for me. Besides feeling like a sitting duck, I'm a nervous wreck over this whole ordeal. How about you, are you doing okay?"

"I guess I'm doing alright. I'm about as nervous as you are, though."

"Matt, remember how Judge Fullerton always said that the best way to take over a government was to take out the number two position, fill the vacancy, and then eliminate the person in the number one position?"

"Yes, I remember. How could I forget all his fiery, long-winded orations? He had the mind of a madman. I always thought he was the proverbial loose cannon. He sounded scary, especially when it came to his aspirations for grabbing a key position for himself. Why do you ask?" Matt hadn't expected to be talking about Judge Fullerton's stability or his ambitious nature.

"Matt, I want you to take a good look at this." Walter slid the day's newspaper across the table to Matt.

After Matt read the headline to himself, he repeated it out loud with pronounced astonishment; "Lieutenant Governor of Texas Slain."

"Do you know what this could mean, Matt?"

"Are you implying that Judge Fullerton is behind the assassination?"

"We both know how unstable the judge is. Too many times, he tried to create new law based on his radical ideas when he ruled on cases. He's psychotic and one of the most egocentric men I have ever known. He thinks the whole world should revolve around him. We have both heard him say, on numerous occasions, that he could take out anyone who stood in his way. The man's a monster of epic proportion." Walter paused to allow his words and assertions to sink in.

"I don't know, Walter. Do you really think The Order would allow him to assassinate a government official and then let him make a bid for the man's position?"

"Let me give you a civic lesson when it comes to the Lieutenant Governor's Office in Texas. The Lieutenant Governor holds the most powerful position in the state. He controls the work of the Texas Senate. He's also elected separately from the Governor. He's actually the President of the Texas Senate. The Texas Constitution allows the Senate to write its own rules. The Lieutenant Governor has a great deal of influence when shaping state policy. Should something happen to the Governor, guess who takes over? What better credentials could a man have for running for the presidency than being a state governor? Hey, it worked for George Bush, didn't it?"

Matt's eyes scanned the front page until he saw another lead for an article. It was about Judge Fullerton so he turned to the next page to see what it was about. "Oh no, look at this, Walter." Matt slid the newspaper back over to him.

After reading the article, Walter felt compelled to comment. "I'm not surprised to see Judge Fullerton addressing the Texas Legislature next week. He's even giving his address on the day after the Lieutenant Governor's funeral. His timing may be tacky, but it will be a time when the assassination is fresh on everyone's mind. All Texans will be paying attention."

Matt shook his head with both disappointment and concern. "It says hear that he is known for taking a strong stance on illegal immigration, crime, and the status quo of a failing, ineffective federal government. He is expected to side with the growing number of Texas citizens who are calling for Texas to succeed from the Union. That's bull. He wouldn't go for that unless he thought he didn't have a chance at the White House. He's just trying to garner more support for his ambitions. Some people are drawn to radicalism."

"Everything that's happening can't be attributed to coincidence. Most of the information I have pigeonholed is on Judge Fullerton. He has too big of an ego and too big of a mouth to get by unnoticed. For years, he has been telling me how he has the inner circle of The Order in his pocket. Lately, however, he has been disgruntled over The Order's inaction. He has no patience when it comes to his ambitions or the fights he picks. He's more of a threat to The Order than I am. He's the one they should have a contract on, not me." Walter was wringing his hands as he sat there trying to come to grips with his situation.

Both men sat quietly for a few minutes. In spite of the sun's warmth, there was a chill in the air and with it came a sense of loneliness. Fear was what they were experiencing. Their fear was a reminder that the cold finger of death was pointing in their direction and there was little they could do about it. The Order had once burned brightly for them as a symbol of hope. Now, that hope had withered into the ashes of despair, The Order was trying to fix things by destroying them. The Order was willing to kill in the name of peace and do so without any regard for what was just.

"Walter, I am sitting here with you because of the grace of my Lord and savior. He will help us find a way out of this mess; that I am sure of."

"You have more faith than I do, Matt. I just can't understand how a truly benevolent God would allow me to get into this fix. I have been a good and honest man and I have prospered from it. I have always worked for the good I could find in this world. My reward shouldn't be this kind of punishment."

"Together, we are going to weather this storm, Walter. We will emerge stronger than before."

"I hope you have enough faith for the both of us, Reverend. At least you're not alone. You have God and a wonderful wife. As for me, I have lost my wife, my best friend, and my faith in God."

"I'm sure your wife and best friend are alive and living well in heaven. Heaven is a paradise filled with perpetual sunlight. Things are really great there. In fact, there aren't even any clocks because life there is eternal. Once you arrive, there are no deadlines or ultimatums; there is only love and contentment. As for your faith, I don't think it is lost, it is only temporarily misplaced. Reclaim it and some day you will join your loved ones in paradise. This is God's promise to you."

"I don't know about all that, I've been told that there is also light in hell."

"The only light in hell is from the fires of damnation. Heaven is lit by the pure white light of love, and that my friend, is wielded only by God. This is the only light God has in store for you as long as you keep your faith in Him. Remember, heaven is His kingdom."

"All that sounds nice, Matt, but, if you haven't noticed, we're in a real pickle here." Walter kept alternating between calling his friend by his first name, Matt, and by his title of Reverend. One minute he is seeing him as a friend and the next minute as a pastor. Sometimes men do such things when they are under pressure. Under stress they tend to reach in different directions at the same time. He was so confused.

"Please, Walter, neither of us should be looking for pity because of the mess we've gotten ourselves into. It's time for us to stop complaining and to start sorting through our options so we can find the best way out." Matt was attempting to reassemble their composure. After all, ministers were also leaders.

"No matter how much I fear for my life, Matt, I'm not about to offer any concessions to The Order if it means compromising any of my ethical standards. Besides, I don't even personally know anyone in The Order's inner circle. I know names only and I can't swear to their legitimacy of membership. Judge Fullerton is the only one I know of who might have a contact there. Plainly, there's no use asking him to intervene on our behalf. I won't even consider dishonoring myself by asking him for help. I prefer death to dishonor. In fact, if I thought it would do any good, I would kill the judge myself."

"Walter, I don't think I will be of any use to you in this matter unless you have a change of heart. I don't think I could be involved in killing anyone. Killing goes against everything I believe in. As a man of God, I can't ignore any of God's Ten Commandments."

"Give me a break, Matt. Under the right circumstances, we are all capable of taking a life. Could you stand idly by and watch someone rape or kill your wife? You see, we all have our limits; a line we will cross. In every battle, the last man standing wins. Who do you think wins when there is no man left standing? I'll tell you who; it's either God or the Devil. When you do nothing at all, then you're not taking either side and that means you have lost your faith. I really do want to get mine back."

"Don't worry, Walter, you haven't lost your faith. You've only set it aside for a little while. Already, you're reaching out to it so you can bring it back."

"Reverend, I only want to do what I think is right; no more and no less. Currently, I only have one viable weapon at my disposal. I have a file on The Order and Judge Fullerton is all over it. I'm not afraid to use that weapon. Even my file might not get me any further than a run-of-the-mill conspiracy headline; but, it's better than nothing. One thing is for certain, though. I have enough to create some serious doubt concerning what is going on in this country. I'm confident that I can put one hell of dent in the judge's armor."

Matt started to say something; then realized the magnitude of Walter's words. He watched the table for a minute, paying particular attention to Walter's clammy hands, which were continuously being folded and unfolded. Walter was in deep thought. Even a condemned prisoner will try to think of a way out of an appointment with his executioner.

Matt leaned back in his chair and glanced over Walter's shoulders at the sidewalk. Pedestrian traffic had died off and that left a clearer view of the parking areas. It was almost 3:15 p.m. A waiter began to clear the table of their trash. In the midst of all this, Matt noticed a parked car with two men inside. The car had been backed into its parking space and that was unusual. The man in the driver's seat was watching his passenger fumble with some piece of equipment. Since Matt hadn't noticed the car before, he had no idea how long it had been there. A voice inside his head was shouting that something was not right about the two men.

Even though Matt's voice was nearly a whisper, it still projected a sense of alarm. "Walter, lean over to me, I think some guys are watching us. Don't look around. They are in a parked car and they have some sort of a device. It looks like a little black umbrella or dish attached to a handle. I've never seen anything like it before. I swear one of them is always keeping an eye on us."

"What you're describing is a parabolic microphone. I've used them on hunting trips and when taking photos in the woods. It's like a stethoscope. With this device, you can hear things at a distance that no one else can. If that is what these guys have and they have been using it on us, then they have heard every word we have said. They might be the two guys who have been after me. Now that we have been seen talking to each other, they will be after you, too. I'm so sorry that I have gotten you into this mess." His voice was so low that it was nearly inaudible to Matt.

"What are we going to do, Walter?"

Walter kept playing the ringer tone on his cell phone to cover up their whispered conversation. He had no idea if the distracting noise was doing any good. "I'm going to do my best to draw them away from you so you can make your getaway. I wish the sidewalk was more crowded because that would make it easier for me to lose them." Walter's eyes were searching the area behind Matt.

Matt asked, "What are you looking for?"

"I'm looking for a plan and my limitations. I'm not as young as I once was, you know? Okay, I think I have it. When I get up, I want you to go back inside. I'm going to walk down the street and hopefully, they will follow me. I'll circle around the block and come up on the other side. I parked over on the other side of Legacy in that tall parking garage; the one past that little cemetery. All you have to do is make sure they're following me. Once you're clear, all you have to do is hightail it to your car and get out of here. Don't worry about me, I'll call you later."

"Please be careful, Walter. Your plan is going to make you a highly visible target and that means things can go wrong, more for you than me. These guys are dangerous; remember, they're working for The Order and it was The Order that had your best friend murdered. You're not only my friend; you're also my only ally so I can't afford to lose you."

Neither Matt nor Walter had the slightest inkling that there was another team, a friendly team that had also been listening to their conversation with a parabolic microphone.

Walter did not acknowledge Matt's concerns with any additional words. His eyes and the look on his face did all of his talking. Walter stood and began his walk down the street and Matt headed back inside the Café Express.

CHAPTER 10

Dumbfounded, Frank and Charlie sat in Frank's pickup. They were both wearing shock and disbelief on their faces. Danger was just over the horizon and they both knew it. Ordinary people, at times like this, would split and run. However, cowardice was not what was expected of a private investigator, especially one that was ex-military. Frank and Charlie were soldiers in the same manner as mercenaries. Honoring their written contract and their word to Felicity Whitman was nothing they could now question or run away from. This case was turning out to be a lot more involved than an ordinary insurance investigation or some domestic infidelity issue. A significant amount of risk was now present and that would test their mettle; probably more than once before they were through.

Surprisingly, it was Charlie who broke the silence and uttered the first words. With an outward display of bravado, she zeroed in on how important it was to accept the risk and continue. "I think we need to be on our toes from here on out. What do you think, Frank?" She gave no hint in her tone that they should back away from the potential threats and challenges that lay before them.

Before she spoke, Frank had given some thought to having Charlie stay in the pickup while he followed this new actor, Walter. Apparently, Walter's life was the one that was in immediate peril. He was also the one who obviously had the key to what was driving Matt's despair, and consequently making Felicity fear for her husband. A successful case meant getting all the answers and they were getting too close to quit now.

There would be plenty of time to scrutinize the recorded conversation that had taken place between Matt and Walter. "Charlie, do you have your Expo turned on? We have to make sure we can communicate."

"Yes, I'm wearing it and I'll switch it on right now. I'm ready, willing and able to get this show on the road."

"Okay, partner. I'm going to stay as close as I can to Matt's friend, Walter. I want you to tag along behind me. Make sure you stay close enough to keep me in sight. You'll be covering my back so it's important that you keep me informed. Do you understand?" Frank hoped that Charlie would be out of harms way while covering his back. Their personal security was just as critical as gaining information.

"I hear you loud and clear, boss." Addressing him with the title of boss was always an indication that she was irritated with him. Of course she understood the importance of staying within sight of him.

They had taken too much time discussing what to do because the two men from the other car were already shadowing Walter. In a way, Frank figured this was a good thing because that meant Matt was safely out of the way and inside the Café Express.

Frank easily kept track of the two men from the car. He labeled them Mutt and Jeff based on their appearance. The younger man was tall and lanky while the older one was short and stocky. As a pair, they stood out with unquestionable distinction among the dwindling number of shoppers and window watchers. Frank was also aware that they had also been using a parabolic microphone so they, most likely, overheard Matt and Walter's conversation. Since Mutt and Jeff were not paying any attention to him and Charlie, they most likely were not aware that they had any competition.

There they all were, sprawled out for half a block. Leading the pack was the target for assassination, Walter, who was keenly aware that two dangerous men were following him and that they most likely would torture him for the file's location before killing him. He truly feared for his life. Next, there was Mutt and Jeff, the paid assassins who were focused on their objective, Walter, with a high degree of tunnel vision. They displayed no actions to indicate that anyone was remotely aware of their presence. Frank, the knowledgeable observer, trailed next in succession. After listening to and recording the revealing conversation between Matt and Walter and having spotted the assassins, Frank was the most informed of the pack. Frank's only backup was his new partner-in-training and girlfriend, Charlie. She was the least experienced, but, she was the most enthusiastic and optimistic of them all. So far, she was performing admirably. Thankfully, Matt was temporarily out of the picture, having made it to his car.

Soon all of them had completed the first block and negotiated the first turn, a left one, and that left them heading toward Bishop Street. By now, they had all fallen into a comfortable routine. Complacency always seemed to occur right before a decisive and exigent event and this instance would prove no different.

With a high degree of purpose and forethought, Walter slowed the pace to nearly a foot-dragging stroll. His intention was to slow his pursuer's pace. He faked appearing listless and nonchalant as he leisurely made another left turn around the corner onto Bishop Street. Once he was out of sight, he broke into an all out run, heading for Legacy as if the devil himself was after him. He was putting as much distance as he could between him and his pursuers. He knew that once they rounded the corner and saw him running, the race would be on.

His goal was to reach his car and escape before they could catch up to him. His life depended on this last ditch effort. However, his body was not in sync with his will to survive. The lurking perils of high cholesterol, lack of exercise, hypertension, and a long history of burning the midnight oil at full speed ahead was about to take its toll. Successful businessmen often pay a high price for wealth. Success often turned men into work addicts.

Legacy was abuzz with vehicular traffic in spite of the hour. Walter's chest was heaving uncontrollably as his lungs gasped for oxygen. He chanced a look behind him and saw his pursuers running frantically to catch up. This frightened him to no end. He pressed his body harder because he was now committed to his survival. Motivated by fear, he pressed his long strides to gain distance, an effort that was lacking.

Cars and small trucks squealed to a stop and swerved to keep from hitting him. Once across the intersection, he saw that familiar and ominous sight that now stood as an omen in his mind. It sat elevated above the sidewalk, supported by a concrete wall. He figured that he would soon live in such a place. It looked so out of place in this affluent and public setting. The streets and walkways were lined with an inordinate number of sidewalk cafes and trendy shops. He was baffled over why developers had built around a tiny cemetery. As a business man and developer himself, he would never have built in such a place. Nonetheless, he was there, running along side an ever enduring home for the dead. Some of the tombstones were leaning as if they would topple over at any moment.

He realized that he would have to push himself beyond any limits he had physically reached before because the assassins were gaining on him. They were nearly a quarter of the way past the cemetery as he reached the end of it. Not only was he out of breath, but terror was paralyzing his limbs. Never was he so determined to do something as he was at this moment. He was begging his iron will and body not to fail him.

Walter did not know that on the other side of that ghastly cemetery there was another man running to intercept him. In short order, Frank realized that he was in better shape than his competing adversaries so he had shifted to the right of the cemetery and accelerated past them. He rounded the end of the cemetery just in time to see Walter enter the tower parking garage. Walter stopped for a few seconds and leaned against the wall, fighting for enough oxygen to continue.

Charlie, being the lesser athlete, chose to continue following the two assassins. Between gasping breathes, she spoke into her Expo to inform Frank about what she was doing and he acknowledged her. Those Expo radios were worth their weight in gold.

Once Walter had entered the parking garage things began to fall apart for him. The upstairs struggle was proving to be too much for his failing body. He had no idea that his oxygen deficiency would soon become irreversible. By the time he reached the second level in the stairwell he was experiencing a cold sweat accompanied by nausea. He fell against a wall and collapsed, sliding down it. Gagging, he nearly vomited as he fell into a heap on the floor. The sensation he was experiencing was frightening to the point that he felt death from over-exertion was a real possibility.

There was a crushing pressure in his chest; it felt like an intolerable blunt weight forcing itself against the walls of his chest and radiating down his left arm and up into his neck and jaw. He could only describe it to himself as constricting and viselike. The suddenness and severity of the pain was a clear message that he was in serious trouble. Just as frightening was the expected certainty that the assassins would soon be there, towering over him.

Frank burst out of the stairwell and ran to Walter's side. Frank was fully aware that Walter was expecting cold blooded killers and not someone who would be sympathetic to him. Frank quickly read and understood Walter's symptoms. A woman and a small child were walking to their parked car on the same level. Frank barked orders to the woman to call 911 and request an ambulance.

The scene was apparent to her so she did not question or hesitate to make the call. Her only concern was that she did not want to expose her child to seeing a man die so she kept her distance instead of offering to help.

Frank began to reassure Walter that help was on the way and that he should relax. The truth be known, Walter had physically and emotionally over extended himself and that had resulted in an extra surge of adrenalin into his circulatory system. Frank recalled a first aid class given by an Army physician and how clinically he had explained what happened at times like this. Even younger men of military age had experienced events like Walter's, especially during combat. Walter was in a fast spiral into oblivion and certain death. The oxygen in Walter's blood was steadily being used up and that meant his brain was beginning to fail. His consciousness and sight was dimming as if by the turn of a dial. Soon they would switch off permanently. Fortunately, this did not occur before the arrival of the emergency squad.

The two medical technicians were quick to begin CPR. Under the new rules for emergency first aid, chest massage was the most critical aspect of a rescue like this. However, the damage was already done. For whatever reason, Walter's heart never decided to resume its responsibilities. A technician turned to Frank and simply said, "I'm sorry. We did all we could. My best guess would be that he died of ventricular fibrillation. We will transport him to the hospital so a doctor can make the official call. By any chance are you a friend or a next of kin? We're also going to need some information from you for our report."

"No, I don't know the gentleman. Maybe you can get some information from his wallet. When I found him I asked that lady over there to call for help because I realized that he was having a difficult time of it. For awhile, I thought he was going to make it. However, by the time you arrived, he was fading fast. If you had been a minute later, I would have been performing CPR on him."

A curiosity driven crowd had gathered around the scene and Frank noticed the short stocky assassin among them. He did not see the other man among the on-lookers. Within seconds, he knew why.

He began to listen intently to his Expo Radio as Charlie was having a conversation with someone. Another crisis was in the making and it demanded Frank's attention.

Charlie was face to face with the tall lanky assassin. She chose her words carefully because she knew Frank would be listening. "So what are you going to do with that knife, asshole? Just because you have me cornered hear in the stairwell doesn't mean you're going to have your way with me. There's a crowd up there and if I start yelling they will all be down here. I'm sure one of them will stick that knife of yours where the sun doesn't shine."

Charlie's message was clear and still echoing in Frank's ear as he dashed frantically toward the stairwell. Now his adrenalin was flowing. Except in his case, his body was in good enough condition to make good use of it without any harm being done.

When he burst into the stairwell and looked down at the next level, he witnessed the lanky pervert as he used his knife to cut one of the straps to Charlie's halter top. With his other hand, the man jerked the strap down violently enough to expose one of Charlie's breasts.

Overcome with rage, Frank took the steps three at a time and upon reaching the landing where Charlie and her attacker were standing, he engaged the assailant. With the full force of his weight and momentum, Frank crashed into him. The force was so fierce and overwhelming that the knife flew from the assailant's hand and tumbled down the stairwell with a tinkling sound. Frank punched the man squarely in the face and then followed up with a foot to the groin. As an added measure, he grabbed the man by the back of the head and pulled down as he thrust his knee upward. The man then began to tumble down the stairs. As he tumbled, a pistol fell out onto a stair step.

The man stared at the pistol, but was unable to rally the wherewithal to attempt retrieval. The now bloody-faced man scrambled to gain enough footing to effect a retreat. Frank wrapped the pistol in a handkerchief and stuffed it into his pocket. Somehow, Frank knew he would have to deal with this knucklehead again.

In an act of pure chivalry, frank pulled off his shirt and handed it to Charlie. She wiggled into it and then threw her arms around Frank's shoulders and held him tight, but she didn't fall into a litany of uncontrolled whimpers; only a couple of short sobs escaped her mouth. "Please, Frank, don't think I'm a sissy. It's just that the guy was so creepy. If you hadn't come, I would have tried to fight him off. If he had knocked me silly, then he would have probably tried to rape me right here. That animal needs to be locked away in a cage somewhere. I went through something like this once before and I'd rather die than go through it again."

"Don't worry, Charlie. You're in good hands now. And, you're no sissy." Frank took her hand and walked down the stairwell with her. Once they were outside, they saw Mutt and Jeff jogging along next to the cemetery. The younger man was in obvious pain. There was no reason to worry about Walter because he was no longer among the living.

CHAPTER 11

After eighteen years of service on the bench, Judge Jeremiah Fullerton had managed to develop his own personalized strategy for dealing with criminality. Looking around his chambers at all the law books, he frowned at how useless they had been for dealing with criminal behavior. In his opinion, the questions of why and how crimes were committed had little relevance when it came to administering justice. He found it most disheartening when he had to follow United States Supreme Court rulings that dealt with the fourth amendment and the laws of arrest, search and seizure. He looked at his name plate and spoke out loud to himself, because he was alone in his chambers, out of earshot of his clerk and bailiff. "Judge Jeremiah Fullerton. What a nice ring my name has, but being a judge just isn't enough. It is only a stepping stone to my true destiny."

Yes, someday his name would be a household name and there wouldn't be a day that went by when his name would not appear in every newspaper in the country. One of his first official acts as President of The United States would be to phase out all forms of rehabilitation in the federal prison system. Confinement facilities were for punishment only, and under his leadership, billons of dollars would be saved through the elimination of rehabilitative treatment for criminal behavior. Chain gangs and hard labor would replace behavior counselors.

Hell, he would be in charge of the entire nation, and under his rule, the entire system would be overhauled. Most importantly, he would oversee the highest, most secretive, inner circle of The Order. His position would place him at the forefront of all governmental institutions on the planet. The heads of every country of the world would have to clear all policies through him. He would never again have to look up to any other human being.

Unfortunately, in the interim, there were other matters that demanded his immediate attention. He had his own personal checks and balances to attend to. He wasn't about to allow any loose ends to cast any doubt on his standing as a candidate for any office whether it was the U.S. Supreme Court, the state governor's office or the oval office in Washington D.C.. He was quickly and truly becoming the master of his own destiny.

Reaching under his desk, he grasped the handle of a briefcase and set it squarely in front of him on the desktop. He flipped the latches and opened it. Stacked on the left were hundred dollar bills totaling $50,000. On the right was a .40 caliber semi-automatic pistol. The pistol was clean and that meant it was untraceable. He had even disassembled it and wiped each component and cartridge shell clean of fingerprints and then reassembled it wearing gloves. The origin of the cash was cleverly concealed; clean, laundered money. Originally, he had thought of the pistol as personal insurance. Now, he realized the pistol was paramount to the money. The money would only be used as a last resort even though it was a significant part in his strategy.

There was a special entrance and exit door in the courthouse for judges and that cleared the way for him to avoid any inspection of his briefcase. He enjoyed the privileges that came with his position. At some point in his future, there would be no limits to his privileges. As long as he held an iron fist over all others, he could be just as arrogant and self serving as he wanted.

After closing the briefcase, he walked out of his chambers with all the confidence of a saintly public servant. Ten minutes later, he was driving out of the secure parking garage. He was quickly approaching another milestone for this chapter of his career.

An hour and twenty minutes later, he crossed the border into Oklahoma. The sun was slipping away to the west and shadows were beginning to creep across the countryside. Traffic had thinned along I-35 and he was just south of Ardmore.

The sun was about to rest after giving a full day of labor to this part of the country. In a few minutes, it would sink from the western sky and this was exactly what he wanted; a cloak of darkness. He turned west toward that sinking orange ball and drove along Highway 70 toward Lone Grove. Traffic was nearly non-existent and that was comforting. He pulled off the highway and stopped at a gate to a farmer's field. This was a good time to collect his thoughts and calm his nerves. He had to ready himself for the task at hand.

He recalled where the seed to his plan had taken root. A year had passed since that afternoon in his chambers. As awkward as the time had been, he had handled it wisely. He was now glad that he had taken such copious notes when he met with that sociopath of a defendant, Jess Farley. The man's arms, neck, hands and face had been covered with hate-centered tattoos. All those body marks were clear evidence of Farley's psychological profile.

He had told the man's attorney that he wanted to speak with his client alone. After sitting there staring at each other, consumed by their own respective anger, a truce was quietly declared. For Farley, victory sprang eternal; for the justice system, there was only failure.

The private meeting was fortuitous for the judge, in spite of having to free the man on a technicality. The police and prosecutor had been overzealous when they filed a kidnapping charge against Farley. The case had taken a turn for the worse when the defense attorney produced a marriage license that bonded the defendant to the victim, in holy matrimony. The license had been issued in a rural county courthouse in Oklahoma. There had been too much smoke and not enough fire when authorities focused on Farley's close ties with the skinhead environment. Farley's new eighteen year old bride, the alleged victim, had invoked her marital privilege not to testify against her husband. Without a victim, there was no crime. Sadly, the young bride had been indoctrinated into the cruelty and violence of an Aryan subculture. The photos of the girl's bruised wrists were still imbedded in the judge's mind. That was the source of the probable cause police used for searching and seizing the restraints Farley had used on her. Unfortunately, there was no law against consensual bondage between a man and his wife.

In the future, once he had his way, such technical defenses would no longer find their roots in the U.S. Constitution. In fact, they would be racked up as horrible mistakes in history. Chief Justice Earl Warren nearly wrecked the entire justice system while restraining law enforcement with his leftist rulings. President Eisenhower should have vetted Warren more thoroughly about his views on the Bill of Rights. Anyway, that was all history now. At least, in retrospect, freeing that degenerate hate-mongrel that day paved the way for something more important. The end had certainly justified the means.

The young man that had set in his chambers that day was destined to do his part, albeit unwittingly, in righting the wrongs of the country. The young man had worn his swastika tattoos like badges of honor. Now, this neo-Nazi hate monger would be served up on a platter of justice; a justice served by one Judge Jeremiah Fullerton.

Next, while wearing gloves, the pistol was removed from the briefcase and the judge made sure there was a round in the chamber and the safety was turned off. When needed, the pistol would be used quickly, and decisively. Darkness finally settled in and it was time to move forward with his mission.

He had been parked there for twenty minutes and not a single vehicle had gone by. Five minutes later, he was driving down a secondary county road. The terrain was hilly and heavily forested. The judge slowed to a stop as a family of raccoons crossed the road in his headlights.

The judge had used a psychological ploy on Farley; one that had reduced the chance of betrayal. Farley had been promised more jobs and more money and that translated into an opportunity for Farley to gain some financial traction for his movement. If the life of a Lieutenant Governor was worth $50,000, then what would the life of a U.S. official be worth? Surely, the life of the United States President was worth a million dollars.

Eventually, his headlights illuminated a small white cross on a dilapidated tree. This was the agreed on entrance. He exited his vehicle and approached the metal chain link gate and lifted the latch. Before dragging the gate open, he looked around to make sure he was alone. Everything appeared to be going according to plan.

After driving through the gate, he closed it and studied the trees and brush. The lane was dirt and filled with ruts and potholes. He drove slowly and cautiously along the lane. The lane wound in serpentine fashion, winding like a snake until it ended at an old barn with faded paint. A dented up pickup was parked in front of the barn. A dim light could be seen through the spaces between weather-worn boards. So far so good was all he could manage to think as he sat behind his steering wheel.

An idea crossed his mind. He opened the briefcase and removed the pistol and placed it inside his belt at the small of his back. When the time was right, he would pull it out and make good use of it. His evil intent was making him nervous so he took a few deep breaths to calm himself. Some day, he would not have to clean up his own loose ends; he would have others do his dirty work for him.

When he approached the barn door, it opened for him. The judge recognized the young woman that had opened it. She was Jesse's wife, the now infamous Mrs. Farley. Her presence posed a small obstacle; nonetheless, it was one that could be easily dealt with. The judge cast a warm smile her way. "Good evening Mrs. Farley. It's a pleasure to see that you are looking so well."

During the past year, her appearance had taken on a new look and the change was dramatic. She no longer looked weak, timid, and tormented. She was now callused and wore a hardened face. Her eyes were cold and defiant. As ruthless as the judge was, he had to admit that her confident demeanor was further proof that she had assimilated quite well into her environment and new lifestyle. No words or greeting came out of her mouth; only a nod toward the center of the barn.

Jesse Farley sat alone, poised proudly in front of a large Nazi banner draped from the ceiling. On a worn and chipped table in front of him he had two stacks of papers and a revolver of some sort. This barn undoubtedly served as his command post; a place where his loyal followers could safely rally. Now, Judge Jeremiah Fullerton was entering Jesse's den as his honored guest. Jesse stood and shook hands.

"Welcome to my headquarters, Judge. I'm glad you made it alright. I'm also glad that we share an honorable goal. Working hand in hand, I think we can bring about some much needed change in this country. I can't wait for the revolution to begin."

As a judge with a high degree of intellect, Judge Fullerton knew he would never share any meaningful relationship with the likes of Jesse Farley, other than as his executioner.

"I appreciate your comments, Jesse. You look to be in good health so life must be treating you well. Not only do we, as individuals, need to be in good health, but, so does our country. I applaud your service and dedication." The judge's words were intended to make Jesse and his wife relax and feel like they were in the presence of a true believer and friend.

Judge Fullerton saw that Jesse's wife was wearing a holster with a revolver nestled in it. "Are we all alone?"

"Absolutely, feel free to speak your mind. I have no secrets from my wife."

The judge's eyes focused on Mrs. Farley. "How much does she know about our arrangement?"

"She knows everything. In fact, she was my lookout when I blasted that lily livered liberal Lieutenant Governor. I can't believe he was in favor of equal rights for all races." Jesse showed no remorse over what he had done. His pride was apparent. He would probably have killed the Lieutenant Governor for the pure gratitude of serving his cause. The money was only icing on the cake.

125

"Does anyone else know about this other than you and your wife?" The judge's question was an effort to identify any potential for compromise. "Only the three of us in this room know anything about our deal."

That was the confirmation the judge was looking for. "Excellent. Now, I have an open-ended question for you. What would your followers think of you taking out a Lieutenant Governor?" The question was only a distraction. "Can we all sit around the table here while you deliver your thoughts and views?" The judge didn't like Jesse's wife standing off in the shadows.

Jesse waved his hand for his wife to join them at the table. As expected, she sat next to her husband. That positioned them at arms length from the judge.

"Let me explain where I'm coming from, Judge. I have formed my own splinter group of the Aryan Nations. We're hard core and we mean business. What Tim McVeigh did when he bombed the federal building at Oklahoma City was in line with our view of the federal government. The tyranny of the federal government cannot go unchecked. The killing of 168 feds would only be a drop in the bucket for my group. I'm willing to do anything to bring the government to its knees. Don't get me wrong, I'm not stupid. I know that once we win our revolution, we will need experienced politicians who are willing and capable of looking out for our own race. We need someone like you to lead and represent our interests. I'm honored that we are on the same side."

The judge evaluated the irony of Jesse's assessment and misunderstanding. In truth, Jesse couldn't be more out of sync with the reality of the situation. The judge's goals had nothing to do with race. Power and control was driving his political ambitions. He had to force himself to restrain from laughing out loud. The likes of Jesse and his group would be the first to go once Judge Fullerton became President Fullerton. There wasn't a strong enough word in Jesse's limited vocabulary to describe how much loathing the judge had for Jesse and his cause.

"In the interim, Jesse, what would you like to have?" At the moment, Judge Fullerton had only an academic interest in Jesse's cause and movement.

"Ensuring that the purity of my race endures forever is driving my life. To this end, I need to put guns in willing hands and that means I need money. Unfortunately, many of those willing hands are rotting away in prison. As a judge, you can help me free them. The money you are paying me will buy the guns I need. We are going to end up being a great team. Together, we are going to give this country the shot in the arm that it needs. Your money will come as a surprise to my brethren. Don't worry, my friend, I know how important secrecy is. My followers will only be told that the money came from an anonymous contributor who shares our ideals."

Judge Fullerton looked at his wristwatch and saw that time was getting away from him. The time had arrived for him to close the meeting and clean up all the loose ends. The time for words had come and gone. He flipped open his briefcase and spun it around so Jesse and his wife could see the stacks of hundred dollar bills. He watched as Jesse and his wife began to remove the stacks and flip through them. This was all the distraction that was needed.

The judge reached behind and retrieved his pistol from the small of his back. With the wave of a hand he knocked Jesse's revolver off the table. Anticipating that Jesse's wife might draw her revolver, he decided to shoot her first. At this range, there was no way he would miss. The barrel jumped and the supersonic report from the muzzle was deafening in that old barn. The bullet struck her squarely in the forehead, knocking her over backwards in her chair. Before the echo of the first shot had a chance to subside a second round split through the barn's stale air. That bullet struck Jesse in the face, spinning him around until he dropped to the floor with a thud. His body wreathed for a few seconds and then became still.

Judge Fullerton stood up and walked around the table to view his handiwork. Both of the Farley's were dead from massive brain damage. Only minor twitching could be seen. As insurance, each of them received two more direct head shots from the judge's pistol. Bleeding was minor. Since neither of the victims had any preconceived notion or warning of what had been in store for them, they did not have to experience any fear or attached terror. Both kills had been quick and clean. Death by violence is, by and large, in the province of the foolish, reckless and heartless. Both of the Farley's had lived violent lives so it was only fitting that they died a violent death. Any nobility that might have been attached to their cause would not be shared by the general public. Like most radical causes, their movement was destined to self-destruct.

There was no need to set fire to the barn. The judge didn't care if the Farley's corpses laid there rotting for days, even weeks. The only thing he needed to do at this time was to put distance between him and the barn. After turning his vehicle around, he stopped long enough to look at the barn in his rearview mirror. An inner voice was telling him that he had committed the perfect murder. Furthermore, he had no bitter regret for his actions and he certainly had no moral anguish over what he had done to the Farley's. With deliberate forethought and refined calculation, he had severed his ties with two repulsive people; criminals. They had unwittingly served a greater purpose; one that had nothing to do with their life goals.

He looked at the briefcase that was resting in the passenger seat and smiled. Not a single penny of the laundered seed money had been wasted. The money would simply be added to other money he had at his disposal for boosting his career goals. The risk and danger of tonight's meeting has passed so there would be no anxious moments on his drive home. Maybe he could find a talk radio station with some commentator saying something favorable about him. Hell, maybe he would call in and stir the political pot a little. No, on second thought he wouldn't do that, not now. Instead, he would find a jazz or easy listening station and just relax.

CHAPTER 12

Once Frank and Charlie arrived back at the office, they busied themselves unloading the equipment. Frank locked the door and closed the blinds after everything was inside. If he had a "Do Not Disturb" sign, it would have been hung on the door. After unplugging the recorder from the Bionic Ear, he handed it to Charlie.

"A division of labor is what we need right now, Charlie. I want you to use the other computer to transcribe the recordings while I begin entering the report from my notes. We need to pay particular attention to the facts and record them accurately and objectively. I'm not going to call Felicity until we have everything correctly entered and printed out in its final form. Remember, an accurate and objective report is our testimony to the client. Felicity deserves our best effort. The better our report is, the easier it will be for her to digest and understand her situation. Our reputation for professionalism is established through our reports."

Charlie clearly understood what Frank was getting at and how important it was. "Okay. Will you do a favor for me and check my transcription before I print it?"

"You bet I will. And you will check my report, also. In fact, once we have doubled checked each other's work, you will copy your transcription onto a disk so we can transfer and copy and paste it into the main report. After we finish this, we will both do one final reading and edit any mistakes we find. I'll warn you up front, I'm a stickler for grammar. There's one more thing, Charlie. Both of our names go on this report. This is our joint investigation and that means we both get the credit or blame for how it turns out."

In spite of being nervous about the report, Charlie managed a smile. "So, this is what they mean when they say the job isn't over until the paperwork is done?"

"You have it, sweetheart."

Two hours went by without any significant comment from either of them. Finally, Frank stood and stretched. "Hey beautiful, can I interest you in a cold Pepsi?"

"You bet, hero. But that doesn't get you off the hook for buying dinner. I'm so hungry I could eat a whole steer."

After a few slips of the tongue, meaning curse words that were thrown out as self criticism they were finally ready to compare notes. All this was followed by three re-writes. At 8:20 p.m., they were ready to print the final report.

Charlie looked at the report with utter amazement. All of their work had been reduced to fourteen fact-crammed pages that told a story. She was beaming with pride and showed her feelings to Frank by way of a hug and a kiss.

"We have one more thing to do before we call Felicity." Frank was not about to leave anything undone or unaccounted for.

"What's that?" Charlie could not think of anything more that needed to be done.

"We need to activate our account and run a check on Matt's Ford Explorer. Hopefully, he will be close to it."

"I almost forgot about the poor guy. I bet he's scared to death. At least he got away before those two creeps could get to him." Charlie knew that Felicity would also be anxious about Matt's safety.

It took them almost twenty minutes to get the account activated, but it only took about two minutes to locate Matt's car. It was parked at a Marriot Hotel in Grapevine. Frank took the liberty to call the desk and ask the clerk to pass a note to Matt telling him to call his wife at 10:00 p.m. Frank figured that it was easier to leave a note than to ask the clerk to confirm if Matt was a guest there. Sometimes hotels are sensitive over privacy issues. Frank had all the confirmation he needed when the clerk agreed to pass the note to Matt.

"Hey, sweetheart, will you call Felicity and ask her to come here so we can brief her and give her the report?" Frank thought the message would be better coming from Charlie.

"You bet I will. I'm on it." Charlie liked being involved as much as she could be.

After calling Felicity, Charlie walked over and opened the blinds. She then opened the front door and glanced up at the sky. There were a million stars twinkling in the limitless depths of a blue/black sky. Strangely, the vastness of the view gave off a calm reassurance that things would work out for the better. She leaned against the door frame and took in a long breath. It was as though there was some supreme being up there that held the keys to all of life. Nature has a refined way of instilling a sense of reverence.

Frank walked up next to her and put his arm around her shoulders and joined her in gazing up at the sky. He also drank in its beauty and simplicity. "I think our world down here sometimes mirrors the one up there. The universe, like our world, is a circle and no one really knows where it begins or ends. All I know for sure is that everything we see and feel is a part of life."

"I know what you mean. There are so many wonders all around us, if we would only look for them." Charlie was sharing her moment with Frank and that was a wondrous feeling for both of them.

"I honestly believe you are right, Charlie. There are an infinite number of wonders between the birth canal and the grave. All that time, regardless of how long or how short our journey is, we will come to know it as our life. We certainly can't reclaim the time that we have already lived, but, we can focus and apply our energy on living out the time we have left. It's all up to us to make it count for something."

"What you just said may be deep, but, it is also beautiful. You're a remarkable guy and I feel very comfortable being around you." She twisted around and pulled him close to her and then kissed him with all the fire she had left in her heart. After all, it had been a long and exhausting day.

Charlie also realized that she had a past to confront and that task would not be easy. She knew that a deep spiritual love is enriched by sexual love, and it is certainly a necessary ingredient of any satisfactory relationship. Hopefully, this would not be an insurmountable obstacle. Yes, Frank deserved her love; he had earned it in more ways than one. She found herself saying a silent prayer for the wisdom and strength to do the right thing.

Frank sensed the intensity of her emotions so he decided to say something to her. "Look Charlie, I want you to know that I have a deep respect for you, on more than one level. I'm a patient man and that means we both have all the time in the world to build our love for one another. Love without trust is not love at all. You'll always be safe with me. The more I'm around you, the more I feel like we're soul-mates. I felt this same way about another beautiful person when I was in San Antonio. When I lost her, I thought I would never again find another like her. You are not exactly like she was, but no two people are exactly alike. There are no duplicate souls laying around for us to use to replace one with that we have lost. Nonetheless, after meeting you, I feel like a twice-blessed man."

"Frank, I'm beginning to feel the same way about you. We both have some emotional baggage that we're lugging around. Hopefully, we can lighten our loads and move on to another level. Yesterday, I had a glimmer of hope for us and now it is burning much brighter. When I get to the point where I can tell you about what happened to me in Arizona, you'll need to be honest with me. I hope you will still be able to look at me with love in your heart."

"Look sweetheart, we have to promise each other that we won't ever do anything for which we will end up feeling guilty about. Our honesty and openness will bring us to the right decision." Frank kissed her softly on the cheek to seal his commitment.

Frank's words told Charlie that whenever, if ever, they became lovers, it would be part of a magical journey. The only way their lovemaking would be meaningful, would be if it was unhurried and tender. It would also have to be done with the maximum awareness of each other on all levels. It would be the magic that fairytales are made of.

Traffic out on the street had slowed considerably with the late hour. Most people were already home watching their favorite late night show or the news on their televisions. Frank and Charlie had lapsed into silence as they watched the headlights with anticipation of Felicity's arrival. A slight breeze touched their faces and calmed their nerves.

Their patience was rewarded when a set of headlights bounced into the parking lot. Felicity wasted no time getting out and heading to the office. She began speaking as she entered. "You know, I've been a nervous wreck all evening. I thought you were never going to call..." She stopped short as her cell phone began to ring.

Frank waved a hand at her. "If that's Matt, just thank him for checking in with you. Tell him that you only wanted to know that he was alright. And don't let on how you knew where to call him. Just stall him, and tell him that you will explain later."

Felicity looked puzzled, but, she followed Frank's directions. She answered the phone with: "Hello dear. I just wanted to check on you to see if you were alright." She paused to listen to Matt's response.

"Don't worry and don't ask how I knew where you were. I'm with some friends right now. Can I call you back in a little while?" After more silence, she continued. "Really, I'm alright and I will explain later when I call you." She closed the phone and stuffed it back into her purse.

"This has been a long day for me and I really want to know what's going on. Is Matt in any real danger?" Felicity's voice wasn't so steady now and her tone went up a couple of octaves.

Charlie put her arms around Felicity and gave her a hug. They then turned to Frank, waiting on him to speak. Frank took his place behind his desk and put a hand on a manila folder. After a few seconds he began to speak to Felicity.

"I'm afraid your instincts have been right on the mark, dear. Your husband has gotten himself in the middle of a serious mess." He removed the report from the manila folder and slid it over to her. "I want you to take your time and read this report and then we will talk."

Felicity's hand began to tremble as she took hold of the report. Frank reached over and put his hand on hers. "Don't worry, dear. We are going to get through this, one way or another." He smiled reassuringly at her, but his set eyes revealed the issues at hand were grave, even more dangerous than first thought.

As Felicity read through the investigative report her jaw often dropped while her eyes widened with shock. The more she read, the more her heart filled with dread and despair. The whole ordeal was not only frightening; it was also exhausting, mentally and physically. It was as though her husband had been living a secret life. How could a small town minister from Kansas end up in the middle of an evil plot to overthrow the government? The world was getting larger by the minute and it was also closing in on her and her husband.

After turning the last page, she closed the folder and sat there staring at it as if it was some menacing monster. When Frank started to say something, she interrupted him.

"Frank, this whole mess looks so hopeless. Sweet Jesus, I'm so worn out and I'm afraid. I'm afraid for Matt and I'm afraid for myself. These goons, whoever they are, aren't going to stop until they kill Matt and maybe even me. I'm having trouble processing all this, it's so overwhelming. I'm so damn afraid of what this is all going to turn into. What can I do?"

Frank shook his head and downed a swallow of cold Pepsi. Even though his mouth was getting dry, he mostly took the drink to break the spell. "You're right, you are exhausted; mentally and physically. What you need is rest."

"No, it's not rest that I need. What I need are some answers and a way to deal with all this. I need a plan. This all has to come to an end; some kind of final conclusion where no one else gets hurt or killed. You're the expert, Frank. Tell me what you think. You're no stranger to all this cloak and dagger stuff."

Her eyes locked on Frank's eyes and then she reached across the table and held his hand. They sat there staring at each other as if they were locked away in some airtight compartment, oblivious to the world around them. Her eyes were potent green fires and her mouth was set, full of intractable tension.

"We're on thin ice here, aren't we, Frank? How can we get this cleared up so Matt and I can get on with our lives?"

Frank was unsure of himself so he couldn't be as direct as he wanted. Instead, he decided to talk himself through the issues in search of a way out.

"We all know that politics is a nasty business. In this case, it is worse than nasty. Judge Fullerton, and God only knows who else that are in The Order, are engaged in a gorilla warfare against our form of government. Their methods are nothing short of treason and sedition."

Charlie couldn't hold back any longer. "The judge and his pals are nothing but wolves in sheep's clothing. It looks to me like they pull honest folk, like Matt and Walter, into their little circles so they won't stand out so much. It's all camouflage to hide the bad apples among the good ones. They're camouflaged monsters; that's what they are."

Frank was grateful for Charlie rallying to his side as he searched for clever ways to express what should be obvious. "Thank you, Charlie, you're right on point. Some very bad people who are way up on the political food chain are using these local circles as fronts for a grass-roots movement that will inspire good folks to ask, no beg, them to save the country. Unfortunately, if they are successful, the country will end up being enslaved. We will no longer be a republic or a democracy."

Next, it was Felicity's turn to chime in. "Matt had a brother that was in the Navy. He was always using a term called: Keep your eye on the ball. It had something to do with guiding aircraft to a safe landing on a carrier. The people in The Order have their eyes on a ball, alright. Sadly, that ball is whirling through the air toward securing open-ended power for them. I'm scared that The Order is too powerful for the likes of us to do anything about them. Right now, I only want to save my husband. Doing anything about The Order is way out of my league."

A deathly quiet dropped down on the office as everyone thought about what could be done. Frank knew that both women were looking to him for answers. This was his area of expertise and that meant he was expected to lead. Unfortunately, all he could come up with was a comment.

"If only Walter hadn't died, we would have been able to put our hands on that file he had on The Order; especially the information on Judge

Fullerton. That option left this world along with Walter's dying breath. I don't have the faintest idea of where to look for it."

Frank's words were no sooner out of his mouth than Charlie was standing on her feet. "I'm no expert in these matters, that's for sure. However Frank, I do recall hearing you talk about getting information from anywhere you could as long as it pointed you toward successfully solving a case. So let's use all the resources we have at our disposal."

Frank was tempted to scratch his head, but thought better of it. The last thing he wanted to do was end up making Charlie look foolish.

"Where are you going with this, Charlie?"

"This may be a long shot, but, I do have an idea." She was ready to apologize if her idea was not an acceptable one. "You guys have done nothing but fill my head with all this Spiritualism stuff. Frank, you told me that you believe in séances. And Felicity, you said you're a medium. So why shouldn't we give this after death communication thing a try? Frank, if a medium could contact your dead grandfather and find out what happened to his sword, then why can't Felicity ask Walter where he hid that file?"

Caught off guard by Charlie's suggestion, Frank was at a loss for words. All he could do was relent to Felicity for any further discussion on the proposal. The only thing that Frank was sure of, at this point, was that Charlie had now put Felicity in an awkward position. This was going to be a test of faith for Felicity.

Felicity was a fighter on more levels than one. She was no stranger to having her faith and abilities as a medium challenged. Her commitment to Spiritualism had endured for most of her adult life and she had accepted it with a tenacious vigor.

"I have no doubt that Walter, now gone from this world, has survived his mortal life. That is the spiritual destiny for all of us, whether we believe it or not. I'm more than willing to act; in fact I would be honored to offer my services as a practicing medium. As a medium, I am an agent that bridges the gap between those that have passed on and those of us that remain behind, here in the physical world."

Hanging around Frank, Charlie was beginning to develop an inquisitive nature. "In general terms, explain the main points behind Spiritualism"

Felicity was more than eager to take this head on. "I would be glad to go over this for you. You see, the soul is a spiritual duplicate, with some differences, of our physical essence. Think of your physical body as a place where your soul stays when it is in the physical world. In broad terms, there are two worlds; the physical and the spiritual. We have to accept that there are a lot of similarities between these two worlds. For the most part, the spirit world is much nicer and more beautiful than the physical world. Inside the spiritual world there are sub-worlds or spheres. Our souls, once they cross over into the spirit world, continue to learn and advance, morally in search of enlightenment."

"Excuse me. What is it like in the spirit world and how do you know what it's like?" Charlie interrupted Felicity with her questions.

"Those are good questions and I'm glad you asked them. The surroundings in the spirit world are tranquil and enjoyable. The souls there help new arrivals work their way up through the spheres. The older souls are like missionaries. Also, the souls in the spirit world are generally eager to guide and assist the souls that are still in the physical world. If you are wondering how I know this; well, many of the souls in the spirit world that I have spoken to, have not been shy about telling me what it's like there."

Felicity's explanation was sinking in and what Charlie was gleaning from it prompted her to ask another question.

"If I understand you correctly, you are saying Walter will most likely be willing to help us."

"He will, if he believes we are trying to do the right thing. In fact, he will be morally obligated to help. I think Walter is a good soul just as he was a good man here in the physical world."

"As a side issue Felicity, I have another question about Spiritualism. Is there such a thing or place as hell?"

"I'm glad to see that you're interested. The concept of hell can be a point of contention for a lot of people. At this time, I don't want to enter into a discussion on this issue with you. We have more pressing matters to deal with. All I'm going to say is that my husband and I have debated that point on more than one occasion. Let me just say that the spirit world is not only filled with angels; it also has souls who want to become angels. Some have achieved enlightenment while others are striving to achieve it."

"You're right. We don't have time for too much chit-chat. Getting back on track, are you confident that you can contact Walter?" Charlie was creeping a little farther out on a somewhat shaky limb.

"Yes, I believe so. However, I'm not confident about the condition of his soul. Lately, he's been through a lot here in this world. I can clearly see that from the report you just gave me."

Charlie let out a long breath accompanied by a disappointing sigh. "So, it's still a gamble of sorts? I guess I thought a soul is a soul. A damaged soul is something I never thought of."

"Yes, that's a fair assumption. There can be a lot of damaged souls in the spirit world and Walter's could be one of them. The important thing, right now, is that we do something. Doing nothing at all leaves us up that proverbial creek without a paddle."

Felicity did not want to put a damper on Charlie's idea. In fact, she admired Charlie's enthusiasm and confidence. However, there was always the risk of disappointment. At this point in time, Felicity only wanted Charlie to understand that after death communication did have its draw backs and sometimes it took many attempts to make contact and still more attempts to reach a specific goal or to achieve a desired result. There's no way to second guess what is occurring in the spirit world or what spiritual mending is taking place. Damaged souls do need to be repaired.

Frank found the whole conversation stimulating, but not all that productive. He had kept his silence and politely allowed the women to talk. Even if a séance did not produce any credible leads, at least it allowed them to do something until something better surfaced. He couldn't think of a better way of killing time until he came up with something more credible.

"Okay ladies, is this where we all hold hands and try to reach into the spirit world for Walter?"

"No, this is not the time, Frank. I'm exhausted and somewhat overwhelmed with all of this. I need to be at the top of my game, you know, fit for duty when I take this on. You have no idea how physically, mentally and spiritually demanding a séance can be. Being a medium is hard work. I work for both the living and the ones who have passed on to the spirit world." Felicity looked at Frank and Charlie with pleading eyes.

Charlie managed to sparkle with a hint of enthusiasm in spite of seeing the séance drift out of the immediate timeframe. "So what's the plan?"

"I'm going to attempt to get a good nights rest and get myself together. This is going to be difficult because of the circumstances. I'm sure Matt is also a nervous wreck so I'm not going to involve him in the séance."

"So it's only going to be the three of us?" Charlie was already wondering about the mechanics involved in conducting a séance.

"I think we should all rest up tonight. I expect the two of you to help me with the séance. We need to approach the spirit world with sufficient power to connect with Walter and maintain an effective dialog. Together, we need to draw down a strong cone of power around us and we need to keep out any adverse or negative energy. There's simply too much at stake to approach this haphazardly. I need both of you to be strong and prepared to give it your best effort."

Frank drew the women's attention to him. "Speaking of Matt, I need to go over some things with you before you call him. He's going to wonder about Charlie and me and how we are involved in this mess. You're going to have to tell him that you hired us because you love him dearly and you have been sensing that he was in danger. He has to understand that we are not the enemy and that he has nothing to fear from us. You have to convince him that we are professionals and working hard to bring this to an acceptable conclusion."

"I'll call him right now and you can listen to what I tell him. He's going to wonder how I knew where he was at." She was stating a valid point.

"You tell him that we are experts and that's why you hired us. You tell him that you don't know how we do our jobs. You only know that we are the best and that we don't give away our trade secrets. You also tell him that he will like us when he finally gets a chance to meet us."

"Can I tell him that we are going to attempt to contact Walter through a séance?" Felicity wanted to make sure she didn't slip up and say the wrong thing to her husband.

"No, please don't tell him that. Just tell him that we are working on something." Frank silently wondered what Matt would think if the experts were putting all their investigative eggs into a paranormal basket. The poor man might run off into the night screaming in terror and never be heard from again.

Frank and Charlie sat quietly as Felicity talked to Matt and reassured him that his predicament and safety were in competent hands. The call appeared to go well and Felicity did a great job of convincing her husband to stay put and remain calm.

The three of them agreed to return to Frank's office at 10:00 a.m. the next morning. They also agreed to get plenty of rest. Frank and Charlie walked Felicity to her car and saw her off with all the appropriate hugs and reassuring words.

Hunger pangs reminded Frank and Charlie that they were neglecting their bodies. They stuffed themselves at an all-night diner with little conversation. Fearing that she might over sleep in the morning, Charlie decided to spend the night with Frank. Her sleeping over at his place was something that had an appealing aspect to it.

CHAPTER 13

By the time Frank and Charlie reached his house, the stress and strain of a long day was catching up to them. Frank was tired and only wanted to feed Leo, take a shower, and get to sleep. Charlie, on the other hand, exhausted as she was, wanted to sit and talk. When a woman wants to talk, there's no way out of it. At least they could first get ready for bed.

When Charlie headed to the bathroom to take a shower, Frank handed her one of his t-shirts to put on for when she came out. The t-shirt was the closest thing to a robe that he had for her. Sensing Charlie's hyper state of mind, he decided to pour two glasses of wine so they could unwind.

Charlie emerged from the bathroom looking like she was ready to attend a slumber party. The t-shirt she was wearing did little to hide her figure. Frank stared at her long enough for her to notice his interest and that set the stage for a discussion about male/female interaction.

Frank was wearing boxer shorts and a t-shirt and if an outsider had looked in on them, they would have portrayed all the casual characteristics of a married couple. They sat next to one another on the couch sipping wine and listening to soft music.

"Frank, there are a lot of differences between men and women besides the obvious physical characteristics." She was baiting him to enter into a debate of some kind.

"I have to admit, Charlie, that men and women approach things differently. How do women look at things and situations?"

"The nature of we females is one of synthesizing with a sense of diverse awareness. Wow, I can't believe I said something that sophisticated. Anyway, we tend to be cyclic and move forward as if we are a point on a car's wheel or rim. How does that compare to that of a man?"

Frank paused and analyzed the question so he could come up with something that fit Charlie's scenario. "I think men are more analytical and approach things with a sense of concentrated awareness. In other words, we're linear and move forward like the chassis of a car. We tend to take things apart to see what they're made of. Women, as I see it, tend to put things together to see how they relate."

"That's very interesting and I think you have hit the nail on the head, Frank."

"Well, little lady, what do you think this all boils down to?"

"I think that both approaches will get us to the same place. Depending on the circumstances, sometimes one approach might work faster and better than the other. With that said, I think that if we put both approaches together and work as a team, we can accomplish three times as much as if we worked separately. Left on their own, I think men have tunnel vision and women are easily disoriented."

"Charlie, you are an amazing woman. Most people go through life not ever learning what you just put into simple words. Now, what brought all this on?"

"I guess I'm trying to understand relationships between the opposite sexes. The better I understand, the better our chances are of making our relationship work. In the past, I took too much for granted and got myself into a mess. For me, recovering from my past is going to be a very daunting undertaking. I'm not ever going to chance repeating that episode of my life again."

Frank was keenly aware that emotional pain was every bit as real as physical pain. In fact, emotional pain can last much longer than a flesh wound; sometimes it lasts a lifetime. Once a person experiences a severe emotional crisis, they begin to live in fear that it will return and that dread is just as stressful as the original event. The natural thing to do is to plan out a life designed to avoid a reoccurrence. However, no matter how it is disguised, the memory of the original painful act will always be feared. Sooner or later, Charlie would have to rise to the challenge and deal with whatever happened in her past or risk damaging her self-esteem beyond redemption. The bottom line for Frank was that there would be no meaningful intimacy between them until Charlie resolved the issues she had faced in Arizona.

Charlie knew that Frank physically desired her and that meant intimacy. She was certainly tempted to make love to him. However, she wouldn't be able to put her heart into any passion of the flesh until she opened up to him about her dreadful past. Right now, there just couldn't be any negotiation with him when it came to sex. He would have to be patient with her. She would simply have to come around gently, little by little. No matter how much charm and finesse he had, it was not yet time for sexual intimacy. After all, she had once been violated by a sex crazed madman and that was not a footprint that could easily be swept away.

She snuggled over closer to him because she knew he would not grope her or otherwise force himself on her. He did care about her and earlier in the day he had demonstrated how much he cared about her by attacking that God awful man at the parking garage. Frank had rescued her because he cared about her.

The longer she sat there, the more her heart ached and the more confused her mind became and that was not a comfortable combination. A tear rolled down her cheek. She was so frustrated with herself and her life that she could hardly cope.

Sensing her discomfort and seeing the tear on her cheek, Frank reached over with his fingertips, and wiped that single tear away. Slowly and tenderly, he twirled his forefinger through a lock of her red hair until it curled into a ringlet near her temple. She closed her eyes tightly and turned her face into his shoulder. Soon she would talk to him about her troubled past.

After a few minutes, she snapped back to her senses, to a place where she felt more confident and in control. Noticeably, she changed her tone and mood along with the subject. "How do you think the séance will turn out?"

"I'm not sure how it will turn out, sweetheart. I do, however, think it will turn out a lot better if we get a good night's sleep." He sat up and yawned. "You go ahead and take my bed and I'll stay out here on the couch with Leo."

He was giving up his bed in order to give her some space. His gesture moved her to make an additional comment. "You're an honorable man, Frank. You deserve a good woman."

In response, he chose to add his own assessment. "There are good women everywhere, but, compared to you they are awful boring. I want a woman with spirit and depth; a gutsy woman. There's one more thing I have to say in regards to you. You're just as pretty on the inside as you are on the outside. If you haven't noticed, I do have strong feelings for you."

"I'm not sure what to say, Frank. I'm afraid that once you know the whole story, you might not feel that way." The frustration she was feeling rang in her words.

Leaning over, he rested his forehead against hers. "Then tell me, Charlie, about whatever it is that you are holding inside. Get this all out in the open so we can work through it and put it behind us."

Charlie knew she was quickly approaching the threshold, the point where her confession would be inevitable. However, this was not the time. "I'll tell you what, Frank. After we get through the séance and its aftermath, we will sit down and talk. You deserve my best effort and that's what you will get. Right now, we have to think about Felicity and her husband and our case. Discussing the burden of my past at this time would be too much of a distraction. We have to stay focused because people are counting on us and the stakes are high."

He smiled at her and ran his fingers through her hair. "You're right. I think we are about to go up against some heavy hitters and things could get rough. Our best weapons are clear heads and calm nerves. We can't afford to make any mistakes while we're faced with so many uncertainties. If we had more information, we could come up with a good plan. The best thing we can do now is get some well deserved sleep."

They held each other in their arms and kissed. Without another word they retreated; him to the couch and her to the bed.

CHAPTER 14

Charlie stretched until she was on her toes as she reached into a kitchen cabinet for two coffee cups. She had been quietly at work preparing breakfast for both her and Frank. She wasn't sure why, but she suddenly started humming an old tune from her childhood. The tune was one her mother used to hum and Charlie never new its name. The comfort and reassurance she was finding in Frank's home gave her a warm and secure feeling. This was closely similar to the same warmth and reassurance she had experienced at home when she was growing up.

The sound of bacon frying blended in with her humming. She had already broken four eggs in a bowl and pressed two potato patties and stacked them on a saucer. Smiling at her handy work, she inhaled deeply, enjoying the aroma of breakfast cooking. The thought of playing housewife and cooking for her man had an alluring feel to it. She was drawn to the simple things that made a family.

The kitchen opened into the living room and she knew it would only be a matter of time until the noise and aroma would awaken Frank. There was no rush because it was still early in the morning. In fact, the sun's bright rays were not yet up to bless the beginning of a new day. The coffee pot was beginning to perk and the added aroma complemented the smell of the frying bacon. A second frying pan was heating up, waiting on the eggs and potato patties. The toaster was primed with slices of whole wheat bread. Her cooking was coming together nicely so she turned her efforts to setting the table.

Frank thought he was dreaming when he began to smell the thoughtful preparation of a home-cooked breakfast. When his eyes opened, he realized that he had not been dreaming at all. After rubbing sleep from his eyes, he sat up.

Sensual was the only way he could describe seeing Charlie preparing breakfast wearing only one of his t-shirts. She appeared dazzling in his over sized t-shirt; and those legs, those smooth bare legs were a sight to behold.

Frank walked over and approached Charlie from behind. He cleared his throat to make sure he wouldn't startle her. He slipped his arms around her waist and pulled her close to him. She relaxed and leaned back into his embrace. Kissing her freckled cheek was a pure morning delight. At this moment, love was certainly lurking about in his house.

He whispered into her ear, "Sweetheart, are you trying to spoil me?"

She turned around, and facing him, she said, "I think we are going to spoil each other." She followed her words with a soft kiss to his lips.

They made a game, of sorts, out of eating breakfast. Each took turns feeding the other. Frank miscalculated and got jelly on Charlie's nose- the next thing they knew they were in a smearing frenzy. They were adults acting like teenagers. Following their playfulness, Charlie cleared the table and did the dishes. Frank dashed off to take a shower.

While in the shower, Frank heard a faucet being turned on and before he knew it Charlie tossed a glass of cold water on him. By the time the echo of his scream faded she was long gone. "I'll get you for that. You won't see it coming, either." He could hear her laughing from down the hallway. This was fun and Frank felt like a mischievous adolescent. A foolish act by the young at heart was a sign of innocence. Anyway, that was the way he saw it.

At 9:00 a.m., they finally emerged from the front door of Frank's house. The sun was no where in sight. There was nothing but dark billowing clouds hanging low in the sky.

"I think we're in for a big storm, Charlie. This is not going to be a very cheery day, I'm afraid."

"Hey, were going to a séance, this might be just the right setting. I mean, talking to the dead can't be a very cheerful thing. A good storm might just help set things up for Felicity."

"I hope you're right." He held her hand as they made their way to his pickup.

Traffic was light and the only people on the street were probably scrambling to avoid the storm. Tree limbs were swaying all along the street as drivers watched nervously. Frank turned on his headlights because it was so dark out. Fall had arrived and a few leaves were already falling from the trees. The mica-flecked pavement glittered in the beams of his headlights and shadows danced along the sidewalks.

A few heavy sprinkles of rain began to pelt the windshield like miniature exploding bombs. The windshield started to film over because of the temperature and the elevated humidity so he switched on the defroster to the low setting. The sky suddenly lit up and a few seconds later there was a clap of deafening thunder. It wouldn't be long now.

There was only one saving grace to the beginning of a very dismal looking day. They were rested and that meant they were alert to whatever the day had in store for them.

"Frank, honey, I just remembered that there's no more Pepsi left in the fridge at the office. We better stop at a convenience store and pick some up or you'll be edgy all morning."

"I know that I'm going to have to give up that stuff or end up dying from it. Thank you for reminding me, though. You're right, without Pepsi I could become awful cranky, especially on a day like this."

The wind was whipping and it blew a cardboard box across the street in front of them. Frank had to swerve to miss it. The street was now glistening wet from the rain and the truck skidded a little from him steering past the box.

He pulled into a convenience store and darted inside through a blinding wall of torrential rain. His speed was no match for the rain and he was soaked to the bone before he reached the door.

Goosebumps crawled all over Charlie's skin while she sat alone in the pickup. The only thing she could hear was the rain thrashing the roof while sheets of rain skewed her vision to the point where she couldn't see anything outside. Her mood became eerie and along with that came an anxious inner voice nagging at her. An out of control imagination was beginning to grip her otherwise calm demeanor. Maybe she had pushed too hard for this séance and if it failed the blame would be there to haunt her.

Frank yanked the door open and piled inside. His clothes were soaked and rivulets of rain covered his face. Cans of Pepsi were falling out of the soaked cardboard carton. Charlie busied herself trying to catch them and gather them up into her lap.

"I hope you have a change of clothes at the office."

"I do. In fact, I have a couple changes of clothes in case of long stays and foul weather. I only wish I kept a raincoat in the truck. Oh well, there's one at the office."

Frank turned on the radio while he waited for the defroster to clear the film from the windshield. Playing on the radio was a weather alert for all of North Texas. "Oh great," Frank's tone was one of disgust.

"That's just our luck; this storm is going to hang around until sometime tomorrow."

The street was flooding and the traffic was moving at a snail's pace. Normally, the convenience store would have only been a few minutes from the office. With the driving rain and street flooding, it took them nearly twenty minutes to make it the rest of the way.

"I'm going to dash inside and get the raincoat. We can share it. There's no sense in both of us getting soaked."

"Frank, you're living proof that there are still some good men out there. It's that chivalry thing again, huh? I was certainly blessed the night Beth introduced us. See if there's a plastic bag for these Pepsi cans, will you?" She was still trying to catch the cans as they kept slipping off her lap.

Following a considerable amount of effort, they finally made it inside. Charlie had dropped two cans of Pepsi and she had no idea which ones they were. "Sweetheart, be very careful when you open a can. I don't want you to get sprayed with Pepsi. In fact, let me open the cans. Can I pour you a glass while you change clothes?"

"Thanks, I appreciate that." He headed off into the back room to change.

By the time 10:15 a.m. rolled around they had taken care of answering all the phone messages and entering the new insurance cases into the computer. The lights had flicked on and off several times because of the storm.

"I hope the electricity doesn't go out and remain off. This is one hell of a storm, Charlie."

"It sure is a nasty one. I bet the weather is the reason Felicity hasn't made her way here, yet. I'm sure it has knocked out a lot of traffic signal lights and I'm sure there are accidents all over the place." Charlie was looking out the front window and shaking her head, nervously. A sense of anxiousness was beginning to pervade Frank's office.

"If we haven't heard from her by 11:00 a.m., I want you to give her a call on her cell phone." Frank figured Charlie would want to be the one to call Felicity since they were showing signs of a growing friendship.

Before Charlie could answer, the electricity went off as lightning lit the sky. In the dark confines of the office, Charlie's silhouette looked creepy to Frank. The thunder that followed was deafening and shook the office so severely that something rolled off a shelf and struck the floor.

Frank immediately got up and walked over to Charlie. He held her in his arms. Standing in the dark, they looked outside. The streetlights had gone out, also. Charlie spoke first.

"Come on, Frank, we both like a good thunderstorm so let's enjoy this one while we can. Once it's gone, we'll probably miss it. Besides, here in Texas, we're always living in fear of drought. I think all this rain is a good thing. I know my father's ranch is usually in need of rain. Right now, I think we should even toast the storm with a drink of Pepsi." She laughed and put her arms around him.

"You sure have me figured out and I can appreciate some optimism right now."

They spent the next thirty minutes staring out the window at the storm and drinking Pepsi. Frank thought about the way they were interacting as they frittered the time away. They didn't need a classy restaurant and a bottle of fine wine to enjoy each other's company. The simplicity of the moment was a treasure.

At 11:05 a.m. Charlie called Felicity's cell phone. After four rings she answered. "This storm is awful, isn't it?" Felicity's words were back dropped with the swishing sounds of her windshield wipers on fast.

"We were worried about you. After all, you're over an hour late. Are you okay?" Even with all the noise, Charlie's tone filtered through to disclose her concern.

"I apologize. I should have called to let you know that I had to pick up some things for the séance. When I get there, I will explain everything. Right now, I'm about fifteen minutes away. If this storm doesn't ease up, I'm going to need a boat." Next, she yelled "damn you, you jerk!"

"What's going on? Who are you yelling at?" Charlie was now alarmed and pressing for an explanation.

"These crazy Texans don't have any sense of courtesy. Some idiot just raced past me and the wave from his truck nearly washed me off the road. I'm sorry I scared you. Don't worry, I'm alright." Felicity was already calming down.

"Don't rush, Felicity. We want you here in one piece. Besides, the electricity is out right now."

"I figured as much; the whole city is dark. See you in a few minutes." The connection went dead at this point and that was alright. Talking on a cell phone is hard enough in good weather. In a storm, it was nearly impossible, if not foolish. Anyway, that was the thought that raced through Charlie's mind.

"Frank, you better get that raincoat ready. She's going to be here in a few minutes and she is bringing some things for the séance."

Without saying a word Frank grabbed the raincoat and joined Charlie at the window. Intermittent flashes of lightening lit their faces as they waited. Thunder continued and it reminded Frank of cannon rounds bombarding the area. He had always thought it was strange how a fierce thunderstorm sounded the same as a raging battle. However, this was not the time to dwell on the sounds of war.

Frank and Charlie's anxiety receded appreciatively when they saw Felicity's headlights swing into the parking lot. The séance was now closer to becoming a reality. The moment was like turning the page of a good book.

With the raincoat draped over his head, Frank made a mad dash to Felicity's Lexus. When Felicity turned off her headlights, her black Lexus disappeared in the darkness and Frank, head bent, had to run through the driving rain to where he thought it was parked. He nearly ran into the rear fender when the interior light came on. The light allowed him to regain his fix on the car. Felicity shoved the door open and Frank sheltered her with the raincoat. She clutched a knapsack in her hands while he ushered her to the office.

Charlie greeted her at the door. "Watch your step; the lights are out. Outside of a tornado, this is the worse storm I've seen in Texas. This thing must be setting some kind of a record."

"I hope this storm isn't an omen of things to come," Felicity quipped.

"Where on earth did you have to go that made you risk driving in this storm?" Frank's voice and tone slashed at Felicity's demeanor.

"I had to pick up some things for the séance. I want to increase our odds for making this work."

"Where did you go?" Frank pressed as his concerns began to rise.

"If you must know, I went to my home and after that I went to Walter's home in Argyle. I left early this morning before the storm rolled in." Felicity was already bracing for Frank's rebuke. She knew that the news went against his warnings and instructions and that would certainly irritate him.

"I thought that we agreed that you would stay put in the hotel. Storm or no storm, you put yourself at risk. You're paying me good money to look out for your safety and interests. You can't go gallivanting around and expect not to be noticed. In case your memory isn't serving you, there are a couple of killers out there and they want to get their hands on you, your husband, and a certain file." Frank felt like yelling, but was able to restrain himself.

"I'm sorry. I only want to hold the best séance that I can. In order to do that, I needed some things from my home and from Walter's home." Felicity knew that she was not going to win this argument. She also knew that she made it back in one piece and that should count for something.

Charlie saw that their exchange wasn't headed anywhere at this point so she intervened. "Since I don't know anything about holding a séance, what did you bring?"

Thankful for the chance to move on, Felicity began answering Charlie's question. "Since spirits like warmth and light, I brought some candles. I have six candles; three white ones and three purple ones. Other than spiritual light, these candles will be the only light used during the séance."

Charlie felt compelled to ask questions. "Why six candles?"

"The total number of candles should always be divisible by three just like the number of sitters. White and purple candles have always worked best for me. Everything in a séance is designed to set the proper mood for the sitters and for the spirits. If there are no further questions about candles, I would like to move on."

The looks on Frank and Charlie's faces made it clear that they had no more questions about candles.

Next, Felicity removed three small plastic bags and three brass cups from her knapsack. "We are going to burn three different kinds of incense in the room; cinnamon, frankincense, and sandal wood. As the incense burns, we all must be concentrating on contacting Walter's spirit."

She paused long enough for the importance of burning incense to sink in. Having the right smell present was important for setting the mood for any séance. All human beings, in physical or spiritual form, like an inviting smell. It has a soothing effect.

She pulled out a lightly colored table cloth and set it aside. No explanation was offered.

Reaching once again into the knapsack, she removed a battery-powered CD player. "This is a little relaxation music to help us along with a short guided meditation. We all need to be relaxed with our minds clear. Spirits should not have to compete with minds that are cluttered with irrelevant thoughts. Oh yes, Frank, I'm hoping you have a battery powered voice recorder. The séance needs to be recorded in case we have to analyze any spiritual messages."

"Yes, I would be glad to record the séance. Accurate records are important in most any kind of work. It's especially important in my vocation." He was appreciative of Felicity's request so he wouldn't have to secretly record the séance.

Looking at the knapsack, Charlie pushed for more information. "What did you bring from Walter's home?"

Felicity was eager to continue. "Well, when I got there I wasn't sure what I would be able to get, if anything. Luckily, Walter's caretaker remembered me. He was willing to support any type of spiritual endeavor so he gave me unrestricted access to Walter's home. The caretaker allowed me to take three articles." She reached into the knapsack and removed the first article.

She opened a small hinged photo frame. "These two photos are of Walter and his wife. Gracie was a precious soul and liked by everyone." She tilted the photo frame so Frank and Charlie could look at their photos. The lighting was poor so they couldn't get a good look until Frank clicked on a flashlight.

While Frank and Charlie looked at the photos, Felicity fished around inside the knapsack until she pulled out a fountain pen. "According to Hank, Walter's caretaker, this pen was a prized possession of Walter's. He always used it to sign important papers and to write personal letters. This is a Conway Stewart 93 fountain pen." Felicity held up the highly polished pen with gold trim to the flashlight beam.

Lastly, she removed an antique magnifying glass from the knapsack. The glass was framed in brass. "Hank said Walter always looked at old stamps and coins with this. I guess you're wondering what the point of these things is. These articles are links to Walter and hopefully he will be drawn to them during the séance. It is common practice for mediums to use articles like these to lure specific spirits from the afterlife. The only things better than personal articles would have been live family members. The only family member I knew was his wife, Gracie. Sadly, she has passed away." Felicity waited for a reaction from Frank and Charlie.

Charlie delivered the response. "Well, this all makes sense to me. How long will this séance take?"

"This could take a couple of hours so we had better eat a snack and have a drink of Frank's elixir." Pepsi was understood by all.

Outside, the storm was not letting up. The electricity remained off and Frank hoped the repair crews were safe as they struggled under challenging if not impossible conditions. Felicity handed him a large chocolate chip cookie while Charlie poured him a cup of Pepsi. Eating and drinking, they all looked outside at the horrendous storm, absorbing its ferocity. The weather provided enough goose bumps for everyone.

Following their junk food indulgence, they all gravitated into the back room. The next couple of hours were clearly in Felicity's domain. "Let's leave the door to the outer office open. I like the effects of a powerful storm. For me, it's an emotional charge. Don't you guys think it will add to the emotional atmosphere? I mean a chilling storm has to be an incentive for a spirit to be drawn to the warmth of the candle lights."

"You'll get no argument from us." Frank volunteered. He also thought that he and Charlie would represent the embodiment of respective attention as they enthusiastically supported Felicity's efforts.

Felicity spoke freely to her two newcomers while she busied herself with setting up the table. "My experience with the dead has given me a unique point of view. For instance, I see the dead as having a different vantage point when they look at things. They're not always more enlightened than we are; they just have a better vantage point. The longer they reside in the spirit world, they naturally become more enlightened than when they were here in this world, but not at first. They're just sitting up higher where they can see more and farther. This puts them in a better position to render advice and guidance.

"Additionally, the problem with most people here in the physical world is that it's harder for them to hear and understand those who have passed over into the spirit world. Someone has to clear the air for clear communication. My job, as a medium, is to help others, like you, to hear and understand what spiritual beings are trying to convey."

"I'm sure you are very good at what you do when it comes to Spiritualism." Frank was acknowledging his confidence in her abilities, albeit with a hidden degree of skepticism.

She smiled at Frank and then continued. "I have to point out one of the risks involved in conducting a séance. When we reach out to the spirit world, there is no guarantee that Walter will be the one picking up on our invitation. That's why I am trying to stack the deck in our favor by having some of Walter's prized possessions here with us. His spirit is the one I want to answer our call."

Charlie was listening intently to what Felicity was saying. Felicity's words were so earnest that Charlie felt a bit choky on the inside. Charlie knew Felicity was under a lot of pressure to make this séance a success.

"Okay, guys. I want to go over a few things before we begin. Once we start, none of us can get up and leave; not even to go to the bathroom. So, if you have to go you should do so now. Oh yes, we all need to turn off our cell phones right now before we forget. The last thing we need is a distraction. Once we make contact with Walter's spirit, or any spirit for that matter, don't get pushy. We should always be respectful of our spirit guests. We are going to them with our hands out, asking for information. Rudeness won't get us very far. These are the rules. Do you have any questions so far?"

"It all sounds like common sense to me." Charlie felt like she was in a movie theater and receiving the customary warnings before the movie began.

"When we begin, we will be sitting around the table holding hands. Unless you are losing circulation in your hands, try not to let go of the hand of the person next to you. We create and maintain our energy collectively. If you become so uncomfortable that you begin to lose your focus or get a muscle cramp, then you can let go as a last resort. The gist of our undertaking is to make it a team effort. We have to continuously consolidate our energy.

"I will begin the séance by conducting a short guided meditation to get everyone relaxed and their minds clear. Following that, I will call down a protective cone around us. Please remain quiet while I do this. I will ask for divine assistance to help us and then I will begin an invitational chant to Walter's spirit. Once I start the chant, I want both of you to join in. From that point on, we are playing it by ear."

Frank asked for additional guidance. "Once contact is made with Walter's spirit, are you the only one who can ask him questions?"

"Unless the spirit sets some conditions, any of us can ask questions. As long as spirits are willing to reply, you can carry on a question and answer session with them. Be aware that spirits can respond in a variety of ways. I have heard them tap or thump on something and sometimes I have felt a gentle breeze blow through the room. Naturally, the optimum response from a spirit is an actual apparition; second to that is a verbal response. On several occasions, I was blessed with having all sitters being psychically gifted. In those instances, the spirit chose to respond through one of the sitters. We'll just have to wait and see."

Frank could only draw on his experience with the medium who had contacted his grandfather to learn what happened to his sword. Currently, he was open to whatever might happen and with this openness came a sense of confidence. His skepticism was slowly fading.

Charlie was likewise ready for anything that would give her validation of after death communication.

CHAPTER 15

Felicity had finished preparing the table and briefing Frank and Charlie on what to expect. Their moment had now arrived. They were about to journey into the realms of the paranormal in search of information that was under the guardianship of a very nervous and apprehensive spirit. Everything that was about to take place during the next couple of hours was a gamble and the stakes were high.

In the dim light of the six candles their faces could be seen staring at one another with a sense of determination and hope. They clutched each other's hands while the rain thrashed down on the roof from billowing black clouds that defiantly blocked the warmth and brilliance of a mighty Texas sun. Occasionally, thunder roared like cannons from heaven. Will Walter's spirit find a way through on such a frightening afternoon? A higher power, a divine power, held the answer to that challenging question. Faith and hope were their strengths, and determination, along with their sincere desire to do what was right, were their goals. They sat there, aspiring to reach the supernatural world. There was no room for a skeptic or non-believer at this table. Frank finally cast aside his skepticism.

The gentle sound of waves caressing a deserted beach meshed with surreal, soul-stirring music; this combination now resonated from the CD player's speakers. The ambiance that settled over the room was in stark contrast to the chaotic world that most people had to contend with.

The words that began to pour forth from Felicity had the tone of a teacher; an ethereal master. "I want you to relax as you search for an inner tranquil calmness. The weight of your body is departing and you are becoming lighter. You can feel the weight of your body leave. It is all being absorbed into the floor beneath you. You should be feeling more comfortable, now."

Felicity paused for a few seconds to give Frank and Charlie time to relax, adjust and accept.

"Clear your mind of unwanted thoughts. Empty your mind as much as possible. Relax! Relax! Relax!" Her voice drifted to a soft, breathy whisper. "Close your eyes and drift into a blissful state where there are no worries, no cares, and no fear. The peace before you is for you to enjoy. Allow your face and neck to relax and focus farther down to that safe place, deep within yourself, that place below your heart, near your navel. This is your sacred sanctuary- that special place that only you know about.

"You are now passing through an ancient gate where you will step onto a spiritual path that you can only see with your mind's eye. There are other paths that intersect with your path. One path quickly draws your attention. There are many beautiful flowers on each side of the path. Among the flowers, you see a bright golden light. As you step onto that path you are absorbed into the golden light. This is your place of peace, comfort, and protection.

"Close your eyes. Listen closely and you can hear the gentle ocean waves rushing onto a beach of golden sand. Listen longer and you can hear the chirping of birds singing their love songs. A warm gentle breeze touches your face and you suddenly realize that you are being caressed by Mother Nature."

The aroma of the three incenses; sandal wood, frankincense, and cinnamon, floated through the air. In an incredible way, the aroma complemented the music and reinforced the mood.

"Smell the air around you. That aroma is the essence of wild flowers, and the sweet smell of the forest. The splendor around you is a miraculous wonder; a gift from heaven. Off to one side, you see a waterfall pouring into a crystal clear pool. You cup your hands together and scoop up a handful of water and drink it. The water's purity and coolness comforts and refreshes you. You have never felt so safe and so relaxed.

"You look around and see a meadow surrounded by large oak trees. The grove of trees is the enchanted forest that you have always dreamed about as a child. Perhaps, in your dreams, you have actually visited here before. The important thing is that this is your spiritual home, your haven. You see soft green grass growing in a meadow and without saying a word, it invites you.

"Across the meadow, in the distance, you can see majestic mountains touching the sky. Within those mountains are the gates to the greatest of all paradises. Now, you know where to find them. They are within you when your mind and soul are at peace. This is your sanctuary where you can come and relax, to escape from your troubles and fears.

"You have now let go of all your worldly problems and have found contentment. Your breathing is shallow and your mind is clear. Your breathing is soft, full, and easy. At this moment, notice how easy it is for you to be in your body. You have never been so comfortable in your life."

Now it was time to bring them back in a relaxed state so they could get on to the next phase of the séance. "You can now move your fingers and toes. You should feel the sensation returning to your body, but your mind is clear and you are free of tension. You have never felt so good. Breathe easily. Take the best feeling of this experience with you. You can open your eyes when you are ready."

Frank opened his eyes and saw that Felicity already had hers wide open. She looked extremely alert, in the gentlest way. Charlie, on the other hand, was still in a highly relaxed state with her eyes closed. Frank couldn't help but think that she was probably holding fast to a piece of her personal paradise; one filled with inner peace; one free of her past suffering. There was no telling what she had been through during her life.

Another minute, perhaps two, passed before Charlie opened her eyes. She gently squeezed Frank's hand to acknowledge that she was truly relaxed and at peace with the moment.

Felicity's warm eyes sent a clear signal to Frank and Charlie that the meditation had achieved the desired result.

The force of Felicity's expression intensified as she gazed up at the ceiling. Her voice was powerful as she pleaded. "I beg in your name, Lord Jesus Christ, to God in Heaven. I beg for your divine protection over this séance and those in attendance; both physical and spiritual. I ask that you send the four Archangels; Michael, Gabriel, Raphael, and Uriel from the Great Brotherhood of Light to ensure that there is nothing but light at this table. Command them to protect us all from evil and watch over our work on this day. We call on Michael for protection because he is like God. We ask Gabriel to bring order, clarity, and understanding because he has the strength of God. We ask Raphael to bring protection and healing to our work because he knows that God has healed. We ask Uriel for wisdom and peace to guide our work because he has the fire of God. We ask all this in your loving name. Amen."

Although Felicity's words were warm, loving, and devoted to God, they still sent chills up and down Charlie's spine. She flinched uncontrollably as the words settled in and touched her soul. This séance was not only a path to the spirit world; it was also a holy event in the most devout sense.

Satisfied that they were proceeding on course, Felicity advanced their efforts. She began to chant.

"Beloved spirit, Walter Welch,
Hear our cry,
Come to us across the great divide,
We seek your guidance,
We ask that you commune with us and move among us."

By the time Felicity had repeated the chant three times, everyone was chanting the words in unison. The chanting continued perhaps two dozen times before there was any sign that they were getting through. Each repetition came with more force and enthusiasm.

There was no rhyme or reason for what was occurring. Charlie's chanting suddenly subsided and she took on a new look. Her eyes were wide and her head began to sway, keeping time with the rhythm as her two friends continued to chant. Without warning, her head jerked violently and then remained still. She was there, and in a way, she was not there. She was assuming a different posture; one that was stern.

Aware of what was happening to Charlie, Felicity and Frank continued to chant the invitation to Walter's spirit. They had come too far to turn back now. This was their only shot so they had to give it their best.

Charlie was no longer herself. Her body was now occupied by some other entity. Hopefully, Walter Welch's spirit was in control of her mind and body. The last thing they needed was some unwelcome spirit bent on disrupting the séance.

A deeper voice was attempting to use Charlie's feminine vocal chords. The result could only be described as hybrid. Her demeanor was also changing. She leaned forward and spoke. There was gravel in her voice.

"So you want to speak to me, do you? Well, go ahead and let me hear your thoughts, concerns, and questions."

Frank took the lead. "Are you Walter Welch?"

"Yes, that's me. I remember you. You were there in the parking garage when I was dying. You tried to save me. I'm glad you didn't."

Frank was having some difficulty adjusting to the words that were coming out of Charlie's mouth. He told himself that Charlie was, at this moment, not sitting next to him. Somehow, this was all some kind of an illusion. He decided to question the voice and not Charlie's physical presence.

"Why are you glad that I did not save you?" The truth was that he did save Charlie that day and it was her body that was being used by the one he hadn't saved. The paranormal world just didn't make any sense. For Frank, it was defying logic.

"Right now, I wouldn't be living here with my beloved wife, Gracie, if you had been able to save me. Now, we will be together forever. I no longer have to close my eyes and dream about her. She'll never be out of my sight again."

"What's it like living on the other side?" Frank's interest was genuine.

"Oh, there are things to do here. There are so many damaged and scared souls here. Gracie and I, along with our life-long friend, Jonathon, work as a team. We do our best to mend wounded souls and remove ugly scars from spirits in need. There is always good that can be done, no matter where you are. This place is full of love and light. Some day, when our work is done, we will move on to the eternal paradise. Here, everyday is progress."

Frank was compelled to press for more information. "There must be millions, even billions of souls there with you. How did our invitation reach you?"

"That's a great and thoughtful question and I thank you for asking. All spirits that cross the great divide to the other side are linked back to those they left behind. They are linked by relationships, events, and places. As for me, I am linked to Felicity and her husband, Matt, by a long term friendship. I am linked to you because you were one of the last ones to see me alive in the physical world."

"What is a spirit guide?" This was purely an academic question for Frank and had nothing to do with his investigation.

"They are facilitators. Many people in the physical world have spirit guides they can call on to contact spirits or acquire information from the spirit world. The ones I have met here tell me that they often assist mediums desiring information for believers. My understanding is that mediums rarely make much money. Most of them only want to stay in business to help those who are trying to make contact with and learn from spirits. It's all a team effort based on faith and need."

Felicity could no longer sit idly by while Frank asked all the questions. She was driven by curiosity. "Walter, I have to know something. You are speaking in direct voice through someone you did not know before. Why did you choose her to facilitate your communication with us?"

"I suspect you have a right to know. The truth is she is not aware of anything I am saying to you. Her mind is in neutral. Her body only serves me as an instrument through which to communicate. I have a good reason for doing this."

"You are not answering my question, Walter. Why are you going through her? I don't understand why it is important for her not to hear what you are saying. You could have used me. I'm a skilled medium." Felicity was pressing for an acceptable answer.

"If you must know, then I will tell you. I will leave it up to your discretion to do what you think is best with this information. You see, she has a new link here in the spirit world. Early this morning, her father passed away and now lives here, among us. Charlene, or Charlie as you know her, does not know that her father has departed the physical world. I think that it is best that she learns of his death through members of the physical world. She should learn of his death through family members or authorities. As you must know, there are those skeptics that would cast doubt on you and your methods if you break the news to her. You and I both know that it is not evil to tap into the spirit world. There is goodness in our hearts."

Frank was caught off guard by the shocking news. He knew that Charlie would be devastated by the news. Silently, he vowed not to allow Charlie to listen to the recording of the séance. Whatever that dark moment in her past was about, her father had somehow interceded and gotten her through it. Throughout her life, he had been her mentor and savior. Her greatest love was for her father. His loss to her would be enormous.

Felicity was moved by Walter's sincerity and motive. "Thank you, Walter, for sharing this with us. You are right. You can rest assured that I will not divulge any of what you have said about Charlie's father."

"That goes for me, also." Frank interjected. "I see it as a matter of respect between our two worlds." Frank was the embodiment of respectful attention. The lasting power of the moment would hold this meeting captive forever in his memory.

Charlie's eyes scanned the table, but, it was Walter's sight and words that saw and spoke. "No matter which world a person lives in, that person only has one soul. I am not about to scar a single one of those precious souls."

Walter brought them back on point. "So, what is it that I can do for you?"

Investigating was Frank's domain. He had been so caught up in the spiritual aspects of the séance that he had nearly allowed himself to lose focus. Confident that he had achieved a working rapport with Walter's spirit, he got to the heart of the matter.

"I am going to be honest with you, Walter. Felicity has employed me to protect her husband, Matt. I'm a private investigator with a notable reputation for doing the right thing. I know about your affiliation with The Order. I recognize the violence associated with it and how it has used its power to promote an evil agenda. You and your best friend, Jonathon, have both forfeited your presence in this world and your loss has been noticeably felt. The Order now has its sights set on Matt. We have to put a stop to this, and do it quickly."

"I agree with everything you are saying. What can I do to help?" Walter's spirit was demonstrating a high degree of willingness to assist.

"On the day you died, Charlie and I were using a listening devise to monitor your conversation with Matt. Assassins contracted by The Order were also listening to your conversation with similar equipment. We know about the file you have on The Order. That file is Matt's bargaining chip to escape the tentacles of this evil organization. Once I have the file, I will deal with The Order on my terms and on Matt's behalf. Please, I need to put my hands on that file and I need to do it post haste. Doing something with that file is a task that you have left unfinished."

Walter was quick to respond. "I'm afraid the central theme of that file focuses on Judge Fullerton. There are some unsubstantiated documents in the file that deal with The Order. I don't know if they will help you. As for Judge Fullerton, he's a reckless man and highly motivated to perpetuate his evil agenda and enhance his public status. Outside of those in our small circle, I never knew or met any of those in the governing council. Every time I watched the evening news on television, I tried to speculate about the higher-ups. Oh, I had come by names. However, I never could prove there membership in The Order."

Although Frank was looking at Charlie's features, he was seeing the eyes of a dead man's spirit looking back. Flames from the six candles burned effortlessly throwing long quivering shadows around the room. For a brief moment, Frank clearly saw Walter's appearance shine through Charlie and it projected an image indicative of thought and power. Walter's face was sifting its way out of Charlie's like a creamy, misty fog. His big dark eyes were set widely apart and were quick and tender. Frank was convinced that in both life and death, Walter had always been a good man.

"Walter, I need that file. Where is it and how do I get to it?" Frank supposed that Walter could see the wish in his eyes and know what it is for. Both Frank's and Walter's intentions were of noble quality. "Please, Walter, you have to trust that I will do the right thing with that file."

"Oh, you can have the file. It's not doing me any good." Walter was a practical man with no time to waste, even in spirit.

In the background, Charlie's face had assumed the appearance of an old piece of porcelain. She sat there without emotion, staring through ice-green eyes fixed in a square face. Her blank stare showed an austere indifference to any emotion. The only thing lacking was a "vacant" sign hanging around her neck.

"Listen carefully so you will know how to find the file. It's at grandpappy's with my other woman. The key's under the welcome mat. Oh yes, remember this number: 1492." There! It was done. Anyway, that was what Walter thought.

Frank sat quietly, lost in thought, while listening to the relentless pouring rain and whipping gusts of wind as they attacked the roof, office door, and window. His mind raced as he willed time to stand still long enough to decipher and make sense out of what Walter had said. He only needed clarification; that was all.

His concentration quickly evaporated when he heard an awful crash in the front office. No sooner had he heard the noise, he felt the force of moist howling wind as it stung his face. The candles were unable to hold their own against the gale. Darkness filled the room. Illuminated by a flash of lightening, Frank could see paper debris fluttering everywhere.

Salvaging what was left of the séance was no longer an option. All hands were released as Frank and Felicity groped in the dark for flashlights. The thought of spending another minute in the dark was agonizing to Frank and Felicity.

Frank raced into the front office and using his shoulder was able to force the door closed against the wind. That single effort resulted in calming everyone's nerves. Once relaxed, he tried to analyze all the information gained from the séance as events replayed in his mind. Just when he thought things were coming together in a neat little package, he had a stupid riddle to figure out.

Flashlight in hand, he made his way back to the séance table and switched off the tape recorder since there was no longer anything to record. He retrieved the tape and stuffed it into his pocket. There were certain aspects of the tape that Charlie did not need to hear. There was no use getting her worked up over the possibility of her father's death. Such a confirmation needed to come from another, more conventional source.

Felicity was attempting to rouse Charlie back to reality. By this time, with the electricity being off, the ice tray in the fridge was probably filled half with ice and half with cold water. Frank soaked a washcloth and handed it to Felicity. Poor Charlie was pretty much still out of it.

Felicity had relit the candles so the flashlights were no longer needed. She began to sponge Charlie's forehead and face with the cold wet washcloth.

While Felicity was attending to Charlie, Frank grabbed a pen and pad. In cryptic fashion, he jotted down Walter's instructions concerning the file's location. While reviewing his notes, questions began to flash through his mind. Who was Walter's other woman? Had Walter's wife known about the other woman? At Walter's age, how could he possibly have a living grandfather or grand pappy, as Walter had put it? Where could they possibly live? What are the numbers 1492 for? Suddenly, everything was looking very complicated.

Charlie tried to set upright in her chair, but lacked the strength. "What happened to me? Did I pass out? Why am I so tired? I feel like I have been working all day on the ranch." She wiped her mouth with her shirt sleeve and spit at the wall. "What's that horrible taste in my mouth? It's yucky. What happened in the séance? I don't remember a thing."

Felicity smiled reassuringly at Charlie. "Sweetheart, you did a great job. You were the medium and not me. Walter's spirit came through you and you handled it well."

Charlie was bordering on being disoriented as she sat quietly with a puzzled expression on her face. "I'm no medium. This is the first time I've even been to a séance. I wouldn't even know what to do."

"That's the best part." Felicity smiled at Charlie. "You have the gift. You're a natural."

"If I'm a natural, why do I feel so exhausted?" Charlie looked at Felicity, her eyes wide with wonder.

"Being a medium is quite a burden and it drains a person both physically and emotionally. Sometimes I sleep for hours following a sitting. That's why I insist that people leave as soon as a session is over so I can recuperate."

Charlie wiped her mouth again with her shirt sleeve and made a face. "I need some mouth wash. I have to get that taste out of my mouth."

Felicity knew exactly what Charlie was experiencing. "Does your mouth feel dry like you have been breathing from an oxygen tank? What about smell? Does it have a pungent odor to it?"

"Yes, that's it. What's causing it and will it make me sick?" Charlie hadn't felt this nauseated and worn out since she had been hospitalized in Arizona.

Felicity assumed the position of lecturer. "What you are experiencing is the effects of ectoplasm. When a medium goes into trance, like you did today, a spirit will sometimes attempt to appear or manifest its presence to the sitters. Ectoplasm is the transparent corporeal presence of a spirit. It came through your mouth and nose. In this case, it appeared in a creamy off-white color and bore the startling features of Walter Welch's face. True apparitions, like this one, are rare. Sadly, the storm stopped the transition before he could assume a full length state. He was doing his best to appear normal to us."

Charlie scooted up in her chair and put her elbows on the table. Like waking up from a long nap, she rubbed sleep from her eyes. "Did we find out where the file is?"

Felicity took in a long breath and then exhaled. "I'm not sure what we learned. The storm kept Walter's spirit from explaining his message. Now, we have a riddle to solve in order to get to the answer. We keep coming up with more questions than answers. Somewhere hidden in Walter's message is the clue to the file's location."

"Are we facing failure or success?" Charlie directed the question across the table to Frank.

"We need to do a little digging, Charlie. Otherwise, we will never understand Walter's message." Frank slid the pad over to Charlie so she could read his notes.

After perusing the notes for a few minutes, Charlie asked a simple question. "Where do we dig?"

Frank looked at Felicity. "How well do you know Walter's caretaker? Didn't you say his name is Hank?"

"I've known him for years and I know him well enough to make off with some of Walter's personal property."

"Do you have a cell phone number for him?"

"I sure do. I have it right here in my purse." She dumped the contents onto the table and started sorting through it. "Here it is."

"This could be touchy, but, I think it is best that you handle this. I mean Hank doesn't know me from Adam."

"What should I say to him?"

"Ask him if Walter had ever mentioned his other woman at his grand father's place."

"Thank God for cell phones." Felicity began punching in Hank's phone number.

"You're right about that. On the down side, though, cell phones have pretty well put ham radio operators out of business." For Frank, everything had a cause and effect.

Felicity flipped her cell phone closed. "There's no answer. Maybe the storm is knocking out service. I hope Hank is alright. He's a very nice man. Walter once told Matt and me that he was worth his weight in gold."

Frank began tapping his pen on the desk. "Felicity, I want your word that you will follow my instructions to the letter. You took far too many chances this morning. Just because you made it here doesn't mean you weren't followed. I appreciate your zeal to think outside the box. But, if something happens to you all of our efforts are for nothing. Do you understand what I saying?"

Felicity leaned over and rested her shoulder against the wall. "I'm sorry I went off on my own. I only wanted to do more to save my husband and to be a part of what you and Charlie are doing. You have been sticking your necks way out. You have even put your own lives in jeopardy and you have no idea how much I appreciate you guys."

"Do I have your word that you will follow my instructions, explicitly?"

"Yes, you have my word."

Frank began scribbling little circles on the pad while he searched for the right words. He wasn't nervous. He was only being thorough. "When you leave here, I want you to give your hotel key to Charlie and I want you to check in at a different hotel. Charlie will ride with you in your car and I will follow to make sure no one is tailing you. Once we are sure you're not being watched, Charlie and I will go to your old hotel and get your things and bring them to you. While we're picking up your things, I want you to call Matt and make sure he is okay. All of this will be the first order of business. Do you have any questions so far?"

"No. It all sounds pretty good to me."

"First thing in the morning, I want you to try calling Hank again. We're going to have to put our heads together tomorrow and see if we can solve this damn riddle. We need to get our hands on that file and review it. Hopefully, we can put it to good use. Let's be careful out there. This is a bad storm and those two killers are still out there somewhere."

The lights began to flicker and then suddenly the electricity was back on. Charlie responded for all of them. "Well, this is promising. Look outside; the streetlights are coming back on. One ray of hope is better than nothing. Don't you think?"

Felicity started stuffing things back into her purse. Frank and Charlie began tidying up the office. Everyone was contemplating what they needed to do.

Frank looked at all the empty Pepsi cans and wondered if he should start saving them for recycling. Oh well, there was no use in doing that because he intended to quit drinking Pepsi and work on a better health regimen. At least he wasn't a smoker. He also knew he needed to focus on Charlie and getting their relationship moving along. There was always something to do.

CHAPTER 16

All the debris left behind from the storm's ravaging made travel around the area a daring undertaking. Trips that would normally take fifteen to twenty minutes seemed to take hours. No matter where they went, there were flashing red, blue and yellow emergency lights and the air was filled with the sounds of whaling sirens. At least the rain was lighter, reduced to a steady shower. According to the radio, the rain would not move out of the area until 11:00 a.m. tomorrow.

Once Felicity was tucked safely away in a different hotel, Frank and Charlie found an Italian restaurant open; one determined to defy the forces of nature. They feasted on lasagna until they couldn't stuff another bite into their mouths. With a lackluster effort, they dragged themselves back to the truck for the trip back to Frank's house. Charlie was so worn out that Frank wondered if he might have to carry her inside. However, she managed to sprint to the door under his watchful eyes.

Frank convinced her to jump into the shower first while he tended Leo who was a bundle of nerves. Cats never care much for water even when they watch it from a safe distance through a window.

By the time Frank got out to of the shower, Charlie was already curled up in bed. She was completely exhausted; her energy drained by the séance.

As for Frank, one crucial thing was weighing heavy on his mind. If Charlie's father really had passed away, then when would she be notified of his death? Naturally, she would have to leave to take care of the ranch and to make funeral arrangements. On another level, Frank hoped there had been some big mix-up in the spirit world and her father was doing just fine back on the ranch. Surely, mistakes and mix-ups did occur in the spirit world just like they did in the physical world. However, the tone in Walter's message had been one of conviction and that troubled Frank. Any news that had ever arrived with a lingering doubt attached had been followed with an anxious moment.

Even though Charlie was fast asleep, Frank leaned over and whispered to her with a voice half-stifled with the agitation of regret. "Sweet princess, sleep well and wake up knowing that I will be there for you, no matter what happens." He pulled the sheet up around her shoulders and switched off the light.

Frank made his way to the patio door and gazed quietly into the dark and listened to the rain's drumming on shrubs and stones. He was lost in thought. There was an occasional flash of lightening veining across the sky followed by hollow thunder echoing in the distance. Why did there always have to be so much potential for despair? Perhaps such moments of anxiousness were nothing less than normal for all conscientious investigators. Anxiousness and impatience were the perils of his profession- they were a vocational curse. Overcoming these emotions were all part of the journey; a reward in itself. Semantics always seemed to come about as a result of perception. All answers and resolutions don't arrive in a neat little package in a timely fashion.

After awhile, Frank made his way to the couch and stretched out in search of rest. What a day this had been. All he had drawn from the day was a weird and solemn feeling. He had people to protect and a silly riddle to solve. He would not sleep well tonight as his mind sifted through the grimness fostered by the séance. Somehow, this whole case appeared to be some bizarre chapter in his life, and as such, would only be of interest to those who have a feeling for life at its extreme. When he closed his eyes, his mind replayed that eerie vision of a transparent, creamy off-white substance oozing from Charlie's mouth and nostrils. No, there would be little rest for him on this night. There were just too many uncertainties and things that defied logic.

Frank began to philosophize about the realities of this investigation. One recurring and unfortunate theme was that his fears were outnumbering the actual dangers. Albeit true, most investigators tend to lean toward paranoia until all the facts are established. If he didn't push harder for results, he would become lost in his own despair. That was not a comfortable place for an experienced investigator. He had to have an end in sight and that end had to be final. Loose ends had a way of strangling a person.

Frank replayed all his fears, over and over, and that blocked the arrival of sleep. The sum of all his fears did not include any for himself. Everyone looked to him for leadership and answers. He worried that he had over sold his expertise and unavoidable failure was looming just around the corner. Tossing and turning during the night did no good. All leaders are aware that success or failure was their responsibility and they alone would be held accountable.

The last time Frank noticed the mantle clock, it was nearly 1:00 a.m. The slumber that finally arrived was thankfully sound and dreamless. The rain was steady and lacked the ferocity it had wielded the day before. When Frank opened his eyes the room was still dark in spite of the time being 8:30 a.m. The same issues were still there demanding his attention. However, they appeared less threatening with a clear head and a rested body.

He wiped the sleep from his eyes and then felt the stubble of a day's growth of beard. This was his opportunity to shower, shave, dress, and surprise Charlie by preparing breakfast for her. She had earned the extra attention by becoming the central figure in the séance. Unwittingly, she had become a spiritual medium. Again, she was worth her weight in gold.

Frank had gotten ready in less than twenty minutes. He had been nothing short of a whirlwind of activity as evidenced by his heavy breathing. Getting into better physical condition had to become one of his highest priorities and he vowed to get started as soon as this case was wrapped up.

All the necessary ingredients for a good breakfast were spread out on the counter when he heard the shower being turned on. Hopefully, she didn't know he was about to prepare breakfast for her. He wanted it to be a surprise the same way she had surprised him the day before. He decided not to put the eggs into the skillet until he heard her turning off the shower. He wanted his timing to be precise and he did not want to leave anything for Charlie to do except enjoy a warm meal when she entered the kitchen.

Five minutes after he heard the shower being turned off, the bathroom door could be heard closing. Only a few short minutes would pass before she came down the hallway to let him know she was up and getting ready.

Frank tuned the burners on to heat the skillets. It didn't take long for them to get hot enough for the bacon and he arranged the slices on one side of the skillet leaving the other side for the eggs, sunny side up, of course.

Calmly, he watched the hallway for any sign of Charlie. He had gotten use to seeing her mill around his house. Over the last week they had shared many happy hours enjoying each other's company. They always seemed to communicate with the soft murmurings that newly wedded couples were accustomed to. They couldn't be more comfortable together.

He poured two small glasses of orange juice from a bottle and sipped from one of them. As the cold nectar touched his taste buds, he visualized lush orange groves in Florida. He grabbed two coffee cups after filling the coffee carafe. He liked doing things for Charlie that reflected his attentive and caring side.

Frank was standing proudly next to the stove, gloating over his handiwork, when Charlie finally wandered into the kitchen. She smiled sheepishly and then walked over and put her arms around him. "You're too good to be true, Frank." Her voice was reassuring and tender.

They sat down across from one another and held hands over the table. Their hands were warm to the touch. No words were spoken, but, Charlie could feel Frank's sincerity when she looked into his eyes. She wondered if they would continue to share mornings like this once he knew about her past. Naturally, she feared that she would lose his love and respect once he knew the truth. She did not want to hurt him or herself, however, that was a possibility. Losing him would surely push her over the brink into a dark swell of despair. Where was her optimism when she needed it?

The only reservation, outside of her past, that carried any weight or impact on their future was that they may be moving too fast. She wondered if she had the emotional savvy to recognize the difference between real love and infatuation. After all, they had only known each other less than two weeks. Her mother's words kept bouncing back from the past when she always hammered the same warning: "Don't marry any man until you have dated him for at least two years." Maybe that warning was outdated. Contemporary life tended to move along a lot faster than it did when her mother had reached the marrying age.

She was also sensitive to the fact that they were both vulnerable in the sense that they had already lost something dear to them; he had lost his last love, and she had lost part of her dignity. She had never been able to commit to any relationship because of her career. She wondered why Frank wasn't more reluctant to begin a new relationship. After all, he had faced a tragic incident where his girlfriend lost her life. They both had skeletons in their closets and demons to deal with. Why does life have to be so complicated? When would her own emotions stop testing her?

Following breakfast, they wrapped their arms around each other. She felt good when he held her close. The strength of his embrace generated heartfelt visions of them strolling along a deserted beach at sunset.

Notions of romance always had a way of surfacing when two people were beginning a courtship. Some uncontrollable urge made her press her breasts into his chest. She was keenly aware that he cared for her and wanted her. She arched her neck until their faces were about to touch. The kiss that followed was full of passion. Somehow, their relationship had to work out in spite of the odds against it.

The heat of the moment was shattered by the ringing of Frank's cell phone. At once, they both knew that the call would be from Felicity and that meant their moment of intimacy and affection would have to be put on hold. The spell was broken and the moment was lost.

Frank flipped open his cell phone and answered. "I hope you have some good news for us."

"Well, not exactly, Frank." She was setting the groundwork for something. "I was able to get in touch with Hank this morning. He told me that he doesn't know anything about another woman. So I told him that I wanted to return the things that I had borrowed yesterday. He said he would be there all morning, but he would be gone this afternoon. He also told me that Walter's whole life is recorded, in some way, in his den. There are photo albums, movies, and journals all over the place. If we promise not to take anything, we can go through it all this morning. After today, that will be out of the question because Walter's attorney is coming to look over the estate."

"Charlie and I are ready to go. Since my truck is only a two-seater, can you come by and pick us up? We can be at the office within ten minutes."

"I'm on my way. Incidentally, I had a long talk with Matt last night. I convinced him that we're all on the same team and you have a handle on the situation. I told him that you're nothing short of par excellence when it comes to this kind of a case. After telling him that you had been a counterintelligence special agent in a previous career, he now feels more at ease. You know, I'm lucky that I found you." Felicity paused for a reaction from Frank.

"Maybe I need to hire you to market my business." He didn't want to give the appearance of being patronizing. He only wanted to show a degree of confidence in Felicity. Yet, he knew a little patronizing strategically placed couldn't hurt business. At least he used a tone that sounded up beat and energized.

At the office, they all greeted and hugged like old friends. Frank and Charlie had assembled a few pieces of equipment and tucked them away in a cardboard box. There was no telling where they would end up or

Dan Morris

what their needs would be. Charlie was drawn to the Boy Scout motto of always being prepared.

Because of the time constraints, they wasted no time getting on the road. Felicity explained that the ride to Walter's place at Argyle would take at least forty minutes. Fortunately, law enforcement was busy with the remnants of the storm so Felicity pushed her Lexus faster than the law would normally allow. They were on a mission of exigent importance; one of life and death importance.

Felicity's driving made Frank nervous. He had to admit, though, she handled the driving with skill and confidence. However, there were too many rolling stops at stop signs to count and that was not comforting. She skillfully swerved around debris and skirted large puddles. Still, Frank, who was riding in the front seat, continued to clutch the overhead handle with a vice-like grip.

The exciting drive aside, they all thought about what they may or may not find at Walter's. They were all conscious of the probability of failure. The fact that so much was riding on them finding the crucial link that would give clarity and understanding to Walter's message was gnawing away at their nerves.

Frank knew well that everything they did from this point forward had to be productive. Everything was also time sensitive. Every clue they could acquire needed to be turned into an actionable lead. He also wondered what those two assassins were up to.

The outskirts of Argyle produced new thoughts for Charlie. The people who lived in the Argyle area represented big money. Magnificent homes on prime land spoke not of farming and ranching like back in Childress County. She realized that the people who occupied these homes had not acquired their wealth through the hard labor and rigors of ranching. The barns she was seeing were more elegant than most homes where she grew up. Even the fences, fancy gates, and stone paved driveways reflected the eloquence of wealth. No, these weren't ranches; they were symbols of wealth. These were trophy ranches. Still, she was astonished by the scene and knew that such wealth must have been the result of intellectual endeavors and wise business practices. She tended to give credit wherever it was due. On the down side, she wondered if all these wealthy people were truly happy.

Charlie attached a great deal of importance to being happy. Most of the happiness in her life came from growing up in a rural setting where everyone did their share of the work. For most of her tender years, ranch life was all she knew of the world. The ranch was like a sacred flame that always drew her to its warmth. Her family's ranch house was perched

170

on a knoll and from the front porch she could look out across lush green pastures to where tree tops touched a beautiful blue sky. When she looked out the kitchen window, she could see a flowing creek winding through huge stones until it vanished behind the barn.

When her mother had died, Charlie remembered finding her diary. Glancing through the entries she came across something her mother had written about her. She recalled the entry as: "Even though Charlene is now a teenager; a cute thirteen year old, I can see that she will grow up to be an exquisite and caring woman. She has fine-boned features, sparkling eyes, and an easy self-assurance that suits her good looks. And, it doesn't hurt that she has the voice of an angel. Someday, she will make some lucky man very happy." Yes, her mother had been the greatest mother on earth.

Only God knows what the mothers in these elegant Argyle estates think about their children or what they write about them in their diaries. The rich and elite always appear so aloof and out of touch with the rest of the world. As common as her family is, there is no doubt about the love and understanding they showed her when growing up on that little ranch. All these things understood, there is still a question about how Frank will handle her other past; the dark one. If Frank really loves her, will that love be unconditional? This same question kept teasing her mind and she kept pushing it back, not wanting to know the answer just yet.

Suddenly, Felicity turned the Lexus onto a long paved driveway that twisted through large trees. The trees blocked the sun that was only now coming out of hiding from the storm. It was like driving through a tunnel. When they finally left the trees the road took them to a courtyard where the driveway circled around a fountain. Felicity brought the car to a sudden halt in front of a huge entrance with carved oak doors like one could find at some European castle or French chateau. Charlie welcomed the distraction so she could escape her worries over her life.

A huge grey haired man wearing a baseball cap came around the corner of the house carrying a piece of plywood. In spite of his size the man had soft, kind eyes. Felicity wasted no time running up to him and gently hugging him. If there was ever an image of the legendary Paul Bunion, this man was it. He was broad shouldered, at least six foot five, and every bit of three hundred pounds.

Looking at Frank and Charlie first, Felicity began the introductions. "I would like you guys to meet Hank." She paused and shifted her eyes back to Hank. And Hank, I would like you to meet two of my friends, Frank and Charlie. They are tagging along with me today because of the storm. Oh yes, I have the things I borrowed yesterday so I can return them."

Frank's hand disappeared in Hank's huge callused hand. Here was a man who was no stranger to hard work. "I bet school yard bullies didn't pick on you when you were a kid." That was all Frank could manage to say in the way of a greeting.

"Oh, those drill instructors in the Corps managed to take me down a notch or two when I got to Paris Island." He smiled.

"So you were a jarhead? Did you make it to Vietnam?" Frank was already taking a liking to Hank.

"Yes, I vacationed there with the 3rd Marine Division back in '65 and '66. I was a 60 gunner." Hank smiled with pride. "That is until I took a round in the leg. I couldn't get around very well after that so they gave me a ticket home."

"I'm sorry to hear about the leg. I still want to thank you for your service, though. Myself, I was in the Army and in country the same time you were. It's too bad things didn't end on a better note over there." Frank apologized.

"Yes, it was a mess alright. It seems like politicians keep writing checks that the military end up cashing. It really hits home. I lost a son in Afghanistan two years ago in March. It broke my wife's heart and now she's gone, too. It seems like war is just another way of life these days. It'll never end." Hank turned toward Charlie because he was finished talking about war and politics.

"Hank, we call her Charlie. It's sort of a nickname for Charlene." Felicity was right on cue to keep the introduction moving in the right direction.

Charlie extended her hand to Hank, slapping it into the middle of his, then she pumped it like an old water pump handle. "I'm pleased to meet you, Hank." She looked him in the eye.

"You're a country gal; aren't you?" He asked confidently.

"You bet I am. I was born and raised on a ranch in Childress County." She beamed with confidence and old fashioned country pride.

"Well, I'm pleased to meet you, Charlie. It does me good to meet a real Texan who knows what it's all about."

Felicity gathered up the things she had borrowed the day before and headed toward Hank. He put up one of his huge hands to say stop where you are. "Go on, honey; you can put those things back where you got them. You know the way. Try not to make a mess when you look around for whatever it is you want to find. That attorney will be here either this afternoon or tomorrow and I don't want him to know you guys were here poking around in Walter's things."

"Thank you, Hank. You're the best. We'll make it as quick as we can and we'll tidy up as we go. If you ever need anything, you have my number." Her words were in keeping with their previous arrangement. She also knew Frank and Charlie were in sync with Hank, also.

There was an odd feeling between the three of them as they entered the sanctity of Walter's den. Unofficially entering a dead man's home sliced at a dark nerve somewhere deep down in some shadowy cave in their souls. They meant no harm; only good. Surely, Walter's spirit would not have any objection to their snooping. After all, he had pointed them in a certain direction during the séance. However, this implied consent would be a tough sell in any courtroom. Frank isolated the thought of having to explain it in Judge Fullerton's courtroom. He would probably have them tarred and feathered.

Inside the den there were three lights; one on Walter's desk, one on a nightstand, and one overhead light. Felicity went around and switched all of them on. The trio went off in different directions to rifle through drawers, bookshelves, and folders. Working both quickly and efficiently they managed to put eyes on every piece of paper.

Charlie voiced an idea that bordered on being a miracle. "It's too bad that folder isn't here in the den. I know that would be too easy."

Felicity responded to her remark. "With the file in hand, I would still be wondering who the other woman was and where his grand pappy is. Sadly, we're looking for clues here and not the folder."

Charlie pulled out three photo albums from a built-in book shelf and began flipping pages. "Wow, some of these pictures must be close to a hundred years old judging from the clothes these people are wearing. I wonder if there is anyone left alive in his family."

Frank's eyes scanned the paintings and prints on the walls. "That's strange. We're land locked here, yet there are all these paintings and prints of seascapes and ships."

Felicity perked up at Frank's comment. "No, it's not surprising. I remember Walter saying something about his grandfather being a ship's captain and when he retired the family moved to Texas. In fact, I think Walter said that there were several generations of ship captains in his family dating back to the 1700's."

Charlie continued to flip through the photo albums focusing on pictures of women. She hoped that one might stand out as not fitting in with the rest. She glanced at her wristwatch and shook her head in disappointment when she saw it was nearly noon and none of them had been able to come up with any credible clue. Her patience was running thin and despair was taking over.

"There's got to be something here somewhere. We're just not seeing it. It's probably so obvious that we can't see it. You know, it's that old saying about not seeing the forest for the trees. Come on guys, it has to be right here under our noses." Frank's frustration was mounting.

"What if I tell you that I may have found the key to solving this riddle?" Charlie was nearly jumping up and down with excitement. She was so excited that she was beginning to stutter.

Frank and Felicity both dropped what they were doing and went to Charlie's side. Felicity shook her head with a puzzled expression on her face. "These are nothing but more photos of boats. It's just a bunch of sailboat pictures."

"What do you see, Charlie. What is it that we aren't seeing in these photos?" Before she could answer, Frank's eyes focused on what Charlie had found. "I'll be damned. I think you found the other woman."

"I don't see any women on any of these boats." Felicity still didn't comprehend what they were looking at.

"The other woman is the boat." Frank pointed to the transom of one of the sailboats and the fancy lettering on it that read "The Other Woman."

"Do you think this boat belonged to Walter?" Felicity asked the obvious question.

"The man's family is entrenched in sailing history. Some of that history had to rub off on him as a boy. All those stories of the sea and boats running through his head when he was growing up had to have an impact on him. Walter certainly had enough money to buy a boat. Why wouldn't he buy a boat?" Frank didn't have to try any harder to make his point.

"Frank, why do men always refer to their boats like they're women? There has to be a reason they refer to their boats with pronouns like "her" and "she." Sometimes they even give them female names."

"I'll give you the short version of what I think, Charlie. I can think of a couple of theories that make sense to me. One, when men first went to sea in crudely made ships, they were afraid. They needed a psychological crutch of some kind to deal with their fear. Sailors needed some protective spirit living aboard their ships, and what could protect better than a mother? They needed that life force in the hulls of their ships to inspire the timid and weak at heart to go forth and challenge the sea." Frank was pleased with his presentation.

"What's your other theory, Frank?" Felicity asked.

"Oh yes, my other theory is more relational. Look at these photos and you'll see certain design characteristics that tend to have a feminine nature. Look at the sleek angles of the hulls, the distribution of her various weights, and the soft billowing of the sails. I see these as feminine aspects of ships, especially sailing ships. Yes, ships are dignified with the spiritual essence of a beautiful woman. Like all women, ships have personalities and temperaments that distinct them from other vessels. A friend of mine in Louisiana has a sailboat and he loves the sea. I think he planted some of the seeds of what I just shared with you in my head." Frank didn't wait for any further comment from the girls. He just headed over to Walter's computer.

"What are you going to do, Frank?" Felicity was doing her best to process Charlie's discovery while trying to understand how they could make any use of the information.

"I have a hunch that I need to check out before we move on to uncharted waters; sorry, no pun intended. It just came out that way." He sat down behind Walter's computer and started the standard search engine that was installed. He simply typed in the word: GRANDPAPPY'S.

Searching the web for information, simple as it had become, is still a marvel by any technical standards. Even a child could access millions, perhaps billions of pieces of information and do so within seconds. Where would the world be now if it had this technology a hundred years earlier?

Charlie and Felicity were surprised at how fast Frank had seized control and fired up Walter's computer. "I thought so." Frank said. His voice was crisp now and the girls knew he was on to something significant. They made their way around to stand behind him so they could view the monitor.

Frank articulated what was instantly apparent to them all. "Grand Pappy's is a marina on Lake Texoma near Dennison, Texas. It must be a big place because there's a restaurant, ship store, yacht sales office, boat rentals, camping, and cottages for rent. This place is a resort- a real playground. This is quite an operation, ladies."

"Congratulations Frank. Looks like you may have solved the riddle of the other woman. I think it's funny how things can turn out when they end up being something different from how they sounded in the beginning." Felicity was excited over the development. Then she looked flushed like a child caught with her hand in the cookie jar. She saw Hank walking by the window heading for the front door. "Oh my, Hank is coming in. It must be time for us to leave."

"Quick, Felicity, go stall him long enough for me to do a map quest search for directions from Argyle to the marina." He didn't wait for her to answer. Instead, he began tapping away on the keyboard.

Felicity and Charlie both dashed out of the room to intercept Hank at the front door. Charlie couldn't restrain herself from speaking to Hank first. She spoke loud enough for Frank to hear. "Hank, I don't suppose you grew up on a ranch, too. Come on, what's your story?" Hank almost recoiled at her aggressiveness.

"Oh, I worked on my uncle's ranch when I was a kid. Actually, my dad was a carpenter and he taught me how to use hand tools and how to frame a house by the time I was sixteen. When it comes to ranching, I know just enough to be dangerous. If it wasn't for this bum leg, I would be out there building houses right now. I don't know what I would be doing if Walter hadn't taken me on as the care taker for his estate. He always allowed me to take my time getting things done and he paid me more than any handy man could make. I'm really going to miss that man. As for right now, Walter's attorney just called and he is going to stop by this afternoon. You guys need to high-tale it out of here, pronto."

"Good men, especially bosses, are hard to find these days. I guess I have known the worse and the best." Charlie was thinking about Frank when she mentioned the best.

Frank overheard Hank as he was entering the room. "Come on, guys, we better get going. I don't want to do any explaining to a lawyer." His comment put everyone on notice that it was time to leave. His words also took them off the hook for covering for him while he was on Walter's computer.

"Thank you, Frank. You know it's nearly lunch time and the lawyer could show up at any time now." Hank hugged both women and shook Frank's hand, then ushered them to the door.

"Thank God." Charlie blurted out as they headed to the car. "Now, we can move forward with a real lead. At least this trip was better than sitting back at the office wringing our hands and scratching our heads."

Once they were back in the car and making their way back down the drive, Frank removed the map quest directions from inside his shirt. "Looks like were in for a long ride. We have over eighty miles ahead of us before we get to the marina."

Charlie was bemused over the prospect of a nice long drive in the country. "The novelty of big city life has a way of getting old, fast. I like the peace and tranquility of open fields with horses and cattle grazing in them."

"I have to agree with you." Felicity was quick to pick up on what Charlie was expressing. "Just the other day, Matt and I were discussing how much we missed the fresh air and slower pace back in rural Kansas. There's just too much drama and pressure in the big city. I hope we go back to Kansas some day, and that day couldn't get here too soon."

Charlie sat quietly alone in the back seat processing Felicity's words and that made her want to evaluate her personal circumstances; an occurrence that was becoming frequent. Maybe she wasn't cut out to be a private investigator in a big city like Dallas. Her thoughts had nothing to do with Frank and her feelings for him. Truthfully, she didn't enjoy or find it the least bit rewarding to be suspicious of people. For the most part, during her life, she hadn't been a particularly nosy person. In fact, she detested gossip. On another point, she didn't even know if she could ask a rude question. Ever since she could remember, her preference had mostly been to give people the benefit of the doubt rather than suspect them. The exception to that rule would be when it came to horse trading with some of the old timers.

Admittedly and importantly, her interest in Frank was her primary motivation for thinking about staying the course in Dallas. Secondary inducements included all the gadgetry and spurts of excitement. Regrettably, she knew the demands of rural life did not lend itself to any great need for private investigators. Outside of a few insurance cases, Childress County was passive and docile. She didn't see any way to entice Frank to settle in Childress. Although, she did believe Frank and her father would like each other.

Charlie saw two girls riding horses across a field and the scene brought back memories from her youth. Every Saturday morning she and Beth would saddle up a couple of horses and ride out. She longed to return to those days.

Frank was also caught up in watching the scenery. The North Texas countryside was not anything like where he grew up in Southeast Ohio. Back home a man would be lucky if he saw anything other than steep hills covered with a wide variety of trees. The only exceptions to that scene would be the cultivated fields and a scattering of small towns. He looked at the entrance to a ranch and saw what he knew was an enlarged replica of the ranches brand. He couldn't recall ever seeing a brand on any kind of livestock in Ohio. In fact, he never saw a branding iron except on TV. Texas and Ohio were two separate worlds with different histories. Defining the differences between the two areas was not worth the effort as far as he was concerned. He not only slipped into a deep power nap to rest, but also to kill time.

Felicity was tempted to start a different conversation with Charlie, but set the idea aside for fear of waking Frank. Charlie's undivided attention was required for the conversation Felicity had in mind. She had no doubt about Charlie having a natural gift when it came to Spiritualism. Charlie was so naïve and innocent that spirits on the other side could easily be drawn to her. Disbelief was the only way Felicity could describe her feelings toward Charlie's performance during the séance. The manner and enthusiasm in the way Walter was drawn to Charlie; a woman he had never met before, was nothing short of phenomenal. Other mediums may have been jealous of Charlie's natural gift, but that was not the way Felicity felt about Charlie's gift. Charlie would become one of the great mediums of the country if she would only allow herself to be mentored. As soon as this ugly mess was over, Felicity promised herself to sit down and have a long talk with Charlie.

Felicity saw the folded directions lying on Frank's lap and picked them up. She carefully unfolded the first page and scanned the directions. There was no use in bothering anyone until they were closer to the marina.

After forty minutes of driving, Felicity had worked her way onto U.S. Highway 82 East and was nearing the turn-off for FM 1417. Frank and Charlie sensed the car slowing to exit and that rallied their faculties and made them sit up to see what was going on.

There were a couple twisted stretches and groaning yawns by Frank and Charlie. Looking out the front windshield, they saw that FM 1417 was under repair for quite a distance. Orange construction cones lined the lanes in both directions and as far as the eye could see, the road looked like a long orange ribbon. No doubt, because of all the recent rain in the area there was not any work being done on the road today. Frank felt sorry for Felicity because of all the mud. It wouldn't be long until her beautiful Lexus couldn't be distinguished from the oldest and most beat up rattletrap on the road. This same situation would not have bothered him in his old Nissan pickup.

Frank realized that Charlie was being noticeably quiet and that caused him to look back at her. She was staring strangely at him and that prompted him to say something. "Is everything alright, Charlie?"

"Oh yes, I was just trying to shake some things out of my head. Seeing the countryside is making me a little homesick. Do you know that you snore when you're in your power nap mode?" Her voice slipped into a laugh. She needed to get off the topic of being homesick.

"You're not the first person to tell me that." Frank joined her in laughter. "This road sure is a mess."

Felicity nodded and smiled to acknowledge what was being said. She didn't take her eyes off the road, however. She was too preoccupied with her driving to look anyone in the eye. Driving on a mud-slicked road invoked a higher degree of caution.

Felicity's nerves were as much of a mess as the road was by the time they traveled the six miles that led to their next turn. The new road, Preston Road, was asphalt, dry and clear asphalt with no traffic. She took a deep breath and relaxed. "I'm glad that's behind us. We need to find a local map and search for a better way back."

In less than ten minutes, they were on Grandpappy Drive. Partially because the road was littered with storm debris and partly because it was narrow, curvy and hilly, Felicity maintained a slow, cautious speed. All of them were wide-eyed, as they searched the scenery expecting to see signs of the marina at any moment.

After rounding a tight curve they came to a split in the road. A sign told them to turn to the right for the marina. They drove through the marina area in order to get an appreciation for the terrain and buildings. The docks were tucked snuggly in a cove between two hills. The hillside and walkways down to the boats were steep and still shiny wet from the storm.

The women expected Frank to tell them what to do next and he didn't disappoint them. "We need to pull in and park in the parking lot at the ship's store. There's a paved walkway at the end of the building that leads down to the docks. Let's walk down and have a look. I don't want to blunder in blindly without some kind of an idea about what to expect; that means we need to do a recon."

"So this is our version of a recon." Charlie was first to react to what Frank had said. "Don't look at me that way, Frank. I know what a recon is. I've seen my share of war movies."

Felicity giggled at Charlie's playful comments. "You two sure get along well together. Are you sure you are not related?"

Frank didn't respond to Felicity's question. He only started walking across the parking lot. To him, what he wasn't saying was the most important thing. Hopefully, some day he would be related to her, by marriage. The last thing he wanted to do was change the way they interacted on and off the job.

There was a metal gate controlling access to the dock. Normally, a key would be required to gain access. That was not the case today. Luckily, the gate was tied open with a cord. Frank offered the best explanation. "They must be keeping the access gates to the docks open because of the storm. A lot of rushing around by both boat owners and marina

Dan Morris

employees was probably needed to deal with the effects of the storm. No one wants to be held up in a downpour fumbling around for a key."

They all looked around for any sign of people or activity. None were observed. The only noise that could be heard came from the boat rental building that was out where the marina cove opened into the lake.

Without any discussion among themselves, they stepped out on the dock as if they belonged there. The dock was numbered "10" and they chose this one because it was one of several that were dedicated to sailboats. Sailboat docks did not have roofs like motor boat docks did and that meant they would be walking about in the open. Should anyone be looking, they would be easily spotted. This was the first operational hazard they had to encounter, although, it was minimal because everyone would be busy with the storm's aftermath.

Charlie was quick to point out the second operational hazard that would challenge the team. In reality, what she was about to point out was extremely critical to their mission. "Hey guys, if I'm not mistaken, all these sailboats were pulled in bow first instead of being backed in. How are we going to see the boat names? Don't they usually put the names on the back ends?"

"By golly you're right." There was an edge to Frank's voice. "Rarely do small sailboats have their name lettered on the side." As Frank acknowledged the depth of the situation, he was eying the boat rental building.

The boat rental building was a floating building with a walkway connecting it to the shore. There were a few people walking around the outside and a neon 'open' sign was clearly visible. Like moths drawn to a flame, the three of them began walking toward the building. The people loitering around the building were the first signs of life. Even a storm would not deter the more adventurous at heart.

Frank wasted no time renting a small motor boat. It was the only one left. The sun was beaming through the clouds and the temperature was on the rise. The high humidity would soon make everyone feel uncomfortable, if not down right miserable.

They were all squirming into lifejackets as they made their way to the boat Frank had rented. An employee walked along with them giving instructions and a warning. "When you're in the marina area the speed limit is five miles an hour. In a little while you will see some activity and you don't want to go near it. There was a boating accident last night when some boaters were trying to beat the storm." He pointed towards an area off one end of the docks. "Some salvage divers and sheriff deputies will be here shortly. Just stay out of their way while they raise a sunken boat."

180

A few boats were beginning to gather in the area and many people were waving cameras around. Raising a sunken boat had a way of attracting onlookers looking for a photo op.

"This is perfect." Frank whispered to the ladies. "We should blend in nicely with the others."

Frank jumped into the rental boat first, followed by the employee. The instructions came quick like a barrage. There was no use concentrating on most of the rules and instructions since it was unlikely they would take the boat out on the lake. They would simply troll the docks until they found 'the other woman.'

Once the employee was out of the boat, Charlie pushed against the dock with enough force to clear the boat rental building. They were all anxious to get started. Wasting time was against their nature and doing the bare minimum served no useful purpose.

Frank pulled the throttle back and allowed the engine to idle as they looked at the transom of each sailboat. The process seemed to be taking forever as they poked along. Eventually, they made their way back to dock number "10;" the dock they first walked on when they arrived. "The other woman" was a 44 foot Island Packet, with a center cockpit. It was a magnificent vessel.

The lettering on the transom was burgundy in color and written in a fancy scroll. There was something about it that took everyone's breath away. The trim, rigging, and the way she sat there rendered her a sense of elegance. Frank wondered if he would ever own such a vessel.

Charlie climbed aboard and took the motorboat's line from Felicity. Once they were all aboard 'The other woman,' a feeling of reverence overtook them all. Frank had read about Island Packet sailboats and knew they had a good reputation for quality, even though they were a production boat. However, this was not a time for gawking in appreciation or slipping into a sense of wonderment.

Recalling what Walter had said during the séance, Frank reached down and flipped over the welcome mat. Not surprising, the key to the companionway was right there. The padlock was huge and a bit stubborn to unlock; a little graphite or oil wouldn't have hurt. Evidently, it had been awhile since Walter had performed any maintenance on the boat. Boats, especially sailboats, require a good deal of maintenance and upkeep to ensure everything is in good working order.

Frank led the way down below to the galley and chartroom. Naturally, Frank began searching the chartroom or navigation area. Men are normally drawn to electronics and gadgets. Felicity immediately assigned herself to the galley. She was curious about the cooking and food storage arrangements. She was also quite taken by the teakwood flooring.

Charlie made her way to the saloon where she began rummaging through the storage areas under the settee cushions. They all searched quickly and thoroughly. The last thing they wanted was to be challenged by some marina authority or a security conscious boat owner. They were especially cognizant of the threat of sheriff deputies arriving soon. Permission given by a dead man was not much of a defense when it came to breaking and entering.

There were areas under bunks that could accommodate larger items and bulky gear and it didn't take long to clear these areas. Felicity opened a hanging locker and when she brushed aside some clothing that was hanging inside, she noticed a sliding door to a small inner compartment. Sliding the door open revealed a small safe with an inline combination lock on it.

"Hey, guys, come over hear and see what I just found." There was a great deal of excitement in her voice.

Frank reached into his back pocket and pulled out a note pad. He simply said, "1492."

The number reminded Charlie of an old poem she had read in grade school:
"In fourteen hundred ninety-two
Columbus sailed the ocean blue."

"Sorry, I can't remember the rest of the poem. It's been a long time since I had to recite it. My fourth grade teacher, Mrs. Hooper, did her best." Charlie faked a frown.

Frank looked over at Charlie and smiled. "This number is appropriately fitting for a family of sea captains to use." He began lining up the numbers on the lock.

Inside the safe were documents for "The other woman," maintenance records, a photograph of Walter with his wife, a revolver, and a thick manila envelope bound by two rubber bands. Frank took a great deal of care in opening the envelope.

"We just hit the jackpot ladies. This is what we've been looking for." They were all jubilant and relieved over the discovery.

"Out of respect, we need to tidy up this place so it looks the same way we found it. It's the least we can do." No one could argue with Felicity's logic. In fact, she couldn't resist dusting the wood work in the boat's interior.

Fifteen minutes later they were chugging along in the small motorboat and heading back to the boat rental building. Frank cautiously forbade anyone from opening the envelope while in the boat for fear of losing any of the pages. Water soaked paper was almost always impossible to read.

Once Frank had settled up with the boat rental people, they started to walk back to the shore on the wooden-planked walkway. Their laughter and chatter was quickly reduced to a frightful silence.

Charlie's heart began to beat faster in spite of her taking a few deep breaths. She was noticeably shaken. Surely, her heart would jump right out of her chest if she couldn't get her fear and anger under control. Two figures stood, side by side, blocking the way to shore. One was tall and lanky and the other short and stocky. They were facing off with the two would-be assassins who had been dispatched by The Order.

Charlie's eyes were locked with the creepy eyes of the young lanky asshole who was now wearing a smirk on his face. Felicity and Charlie both stepped behind Frank as the two killers began to walk toward them. Even though they were wearing windbreakers, pistols were clearly visible tucked into their belts.

"They must have been watching Walter's home and followed us here. I'm sure they were hoping we would lead them to the file." Frank would allow them to state their intent or demands before attempting any action. He also silently chastised himself for leaving his pistol at the office. At this point, the best he could hope for was to somehow knock them into the water to create enough lead time to make a run for the car.

The two men stopped about six feet in front of them. It was the older, short stocky one that did the talking. "I think you have something we want. Things are about to get messy for you and the ladies. Hand it over now, before we have to hurt you. Ladies don't look very pretty when they're all covered in their own blood."

Before Frank could reply, Charlie assumed control of the conversation. "I think you and your skinny pervert of a sidekick need to reassess your position. The law would love to know the lowdown on you two idiots. You have to be the two dumbest killers on the planet. By the way, does stupidity run in your families? Now move aside."

"Look, you smart ass little bitch. Before I blow your brains out, I'm going to let my friend have some fun with you. Now let's move up the hill until we're out of sight." The older man pulled back his jacket and placed his hand on his pistol grip.

"Why don't you show that piece of junk to our friends behind you?" Charlie was not bluffing.

The young man took the initiative and glanced back over his shoulder even though he felt confident that the little redhead was all mouth about having any back-up in the area. When he saw two deputies from the sheriff's office and a state trooper walking down the path toward them, he touched his partner's elbow. "Cool it, the cops are here."

Frank wasn't sure whether it was fate or circumstance that had come to their rescue. Actually, he didn't care where or how help had come. The important thing was that it was here, and in force. He also admired the way Charlie had taken control of a bad situation. She acted with a sense of bravado and detached arrogance. Frank liked the way she had drawn a line in the sand and turned the killer's advantage into her own.

Frank vainly smiled and spoke with a cocky tone as he drove home the killer's new position in this developing situation. "I will be hanging on to this little package, thank you. You kids aren't quite mature enough to handle it."

The two deputies and state trooper excused themselves as they threaded their way between the two killers. When Frank and Charlie got between the two stunned miscreants they couldn't resist buying a little more time while enjoying themselves. Charlie looked the lanky young man in the eye as she shoved him off the walkway and into the water. Frank acted more aggressively and elbowed the short killer into the water. Naturally, they intended to add insult to injury with an outburst of laughter.

The three escapees scurried up the path and headed for Felicity's car. They all glanced back at the two killers who were slipping, sliding, and falling in the mud, time after time, as they scrambled to get out of the water. Even the antics of cold blooded killers had a way of providing a little comedy relief. In this case it was slap-stick comedy.

Frank recognized the killer's car, the same one they had driven on the day Walter had died. Using his pocket knife, he sliced all four tires on their car. The flat tires would certainly put a damper on their mission as well as infuriate them. The two killers were having an all around bad day.

Instead of looking for a better route back to U.S. Highway 82, they decided to take the same muddy one they had used earlier. Each of them took a turn at making fun of the two killers.

Once they had settled down, Frank began to speed read through the file, hoping to find something substantial for making a case against The Order. Mostly what he was seeing had to do with Judge Fullerton and it was highly circumstantial. Several pages jumped out at him and he quickly stuffed them into his shirt for safekeeping and later review.

Frank's concentration was broken when he heard the ringing of a cell phone. He pulled his out of his pocket and realized that it was not his that was ringing.

Charlie pulled her cell phone out of the front pocket of her jeans and flipped it open. "Hi, Beth, I'm sorry I haven't called lately. We've been busy as hell with a big case. I promise to make it up to you."

There was a long drawn out silence as Charlie listened to her cousin. Both Felicity and Frank looked on as the pallor crept across Charlie's face. She was noticeably striving to master some intense emotion. The message she was listening to was freezing her soul. Frank and Felicity didn't have to second guess what that terrible message was all about; the content was not new to them.

Charlie dropped her cell phone into her lap and covered her face with both hands to hide tears of bitter disappointment. Tears burst from her eyes like blood from a severed artery. The only redeemable measure of a good cry is that it clears the air just as the rain does.

Frank thought about Beth and what she had gone through when she broke the news to Charlie. Surely, the worse refinement of torture known had to be breaking bad news, gently. Frank was relieved that the task had not fallen on his shoulders.

After a few minutes of crying, Charlie began to collect her composure with an effort that made her tremble like a blade of grass in the wind. She picked her cell phone back up and murmured a polite word of thanks to Beth.

"I'm sorry I fell apart like that, Beth. I'll call you later after I have time to think." Charlie didn't wait for a response, she just ended the call.

Even though Charlie's world had just been frozen stiff, she managed to find enough strength to tell Frank and Felicity what had happened. "That was Beth. My father has passed away. He died at home sitting in his favorite chair. I didn't even know he had a bad heart. Otherwise, I wouldn't have come to Dallas. He should have told me that he had a bad heart so I could have stayed home to look after him. Oh my, I'm going to miss him. You have no idea how much I loved my father."

Felicity was the next to react to the news. "Charlie, honey, under ideal conditions our lives are filled with days of sunshine, giving us warmth and comfort. But, life is not always ideal. Some days are filled with stormy weather and when we are watching that storm, the best of us can easily realize that we have missed some important duty. We can only regret what we missed, but we shouldn't let the guilt consume us. Life is not always fair and it can be full of challenges and heartbreaks. Most of life's challenges only give us enough pain to appreciate them when we overcome them. Death is the one challenge that we rarely completely overcome here in the material world. There is only one thing we can do when the death in our lives is not our own; we grieve. Please, I want you to rest assure that your father's spirit will live on. I guarantee that he is not alone."

Charlie looked at Felicity as if searching for some universal truth that would bring understanding and answers to all the questions about life that begin with the word 'why.' After a long pause, she looked out the window. What she saw was drastically different from what she had seen the day before. The once black sky had turned clear and blue. The sky was like a canopy flung over the world as far as the eye could see. In spite of the spectacular view, she remained restless, with frightened eyes, like those of some hunted animal. Her life was going to be scary and lonely without her father to lean on. Why had such bad news arrived on such a nice day?

Frank was not one to sit back with nothing to say, so he ventured forward. "Charlie, the way I see it, your father died calmly, peacefully in his sleep while sitting in the comfort of his favorite chair. I'm sure the expression on his face expressed love and affection for those he loved and that included you. He is now reunited with your mother and everyone else he had loved who had gone before him."

Charlie had no more tears left so she resigned herself to accepting that which could not be undone- her father was gone. She certainly owed her two friends a few words of appreciation. "I'm at a loss for words, except to say thanks for being my friends. Life would be poor and bitter if it wasn't for having good friends. I know you both understand what I'm going through. The last few days have been wonderful and I owe that to your good company."

Frank saw Charlie's strength of character shining through and knew that she would be alright. She was a staunchly independent woman who wasn't quite sure what she wanted to do with the rest of her life. Sometime in the near future she would have to come to grips with her past and work through the challenges of the present. The tasks before her were daunting, but not impossible to conquer. There were so many things that needed addressing and she wasn't sure where to begin. The next couple of weeks would be emotionally difficult in the most mundane sense. There would be a funeral, bills to settle, and the ranch. Once everything settled down, she would sit down and harshly reassess events from her past. She would likely need some help in confronting the demons that haunted her. Somehow, she had to replace fear with love and that was not always an easy undertaking. Then, the big question would be what to do about her budding relationship with Frank. She had to decide where he fit into her life.

Frank continued to sift through the file while Felicity drove and Charlie was lost in her thoughts. Without alerting the others, he separated a few more pages and stuffed them into his shirt. He would study those select pages later, and out of sight of the others. There was a reason for everything and he had his own for what he was doing.

CHAPTER 17

Bennie and Ivan were stranded at the marina for two days while they waited on the tires to be replaced on their rental car. They had to rent a cottage at the marina and eat out in the marina's restaurant. They did their best to act like typical vacationers. Of course there was nothing typical about them. They were thugs, not average folks. At least they were savvy enough not to get into a braw with other patrons at the marina.

Their fading self confidence was a mounting problem for them. It was rooted in their ineptness and blunders and the combination was taking its toll on their nerves. The whole assignment could only be described as a litany of mistakes and miscalculations. They were failing miserably in their assigned work.

Bennie was so put out over his lack of success that he refused to answer his cell phone when it rang. He knew the caller would be their handler so instead of answering the phone, he simply turned it off. He figured he had severely limited his career options as a killer if not totally ruined them. Any likelihood of follow-on assignments was probably out of the question. Hopefully, the word on his blunders and failures would not get around in the underground community of hired killers. The last thing he wanted was to be an unemployed professional killer; blackballed forever and a day.

The first night, neither one of them felt much like eating so they hung out at the bar and drank like common, everyday boaters. Silently, they hoped the alcohol would deaden their senses to the point of numbness. Failure was not something they were use to. They knew that their reputations and pride had been severely damaged; maybe even permanently unredeemable. These were feelings that Bennie was sharing with Ivan, although, Ivan was not bothered as badly as Bennie was.

Bennie was beginning, although reluctantly, to form a superficial personal bond with Ivan and he even regretted the thought of having to kill the young man and dumping his body in some remote swamp. Misery loves company and at the moment they only had each other to lean on. Bennie was beginning to realize that he was no longer among the best of the best in the business.

They had both acted with arrogance and overconfidence when they should have been more careful and methodical. Between the both of them, they had been nothing less than clowns performing for adults. They continued to drink until they could no longer walk a straight line-so ended the first night at the marina.

Harboring hangovers, the two killers slept until 9:30 a.m. Due to the difference in time zones, Bennie knew that it was an hour later on the east coast. Soon his phone would ring and he would have to make a report to the handler. Following the report, the handler would apprise the client. New orders would come once the client had time to consider all the options. Maybe the powers that constituted the decision makers would see the failures as only bad luck. No, that wouldn't be the case. There were way too many setbacks for matters to be chalked up to something as simple as bad luck. There had to be consequences, even deadly sanctions. Maybe they would only have to forfeit some of their fee. The best fallout for Bennie would be that all the blame would fall on Ivan. After all, the handler already wanted Ivan dead, so what was wrong with Ivan ending up being Bennie's scapegoat? The poor guy; everything hadn't been Ivan's fault. Oh well, better him than me, Bennie concluded.

Ivan didn't like sitting around waiting on the handler's call. "Bennie, I'm going out for a walk. It's stuffy in here so I think I'll walk along the shoreline."

"Okay. I'll come get you if I get any news from the handler or something on the car being ready." Once Bennie was sure that Ivan was out of sight, he would call the handler. He just couldn't stand not knowing what was going on.

Bennie turned his cell phone back on and held it as he watched Ivan's silhouette fade down the road. No matter how many times he tried to rehearse his report it never seemed to sound palatable. He finally gave up and punched in the handler's number. One, two, three rings went by before he got an answer.

Bennie nervously muddled through his report and then waited for the details to register. Not satisfied that his report was adequate, he started to rehash what he thought were the important elements. Primarily, he wanted to shift as much of the blame as he could over to Ivan.

The voice on the other end interrupted Bennie. "That's enough, I get the point. Even if you get your car back, I want you to stay put until I get back to you. Do you understand? I don't want you to make a move until you hear from me." The call ended with an abrupt click. Bennie knew his report had irritated the handler.

Bennie walked down to the marina to see if any progress was being made with getting new tires. A pickup was parked next to his rental and the front end was jacked up. New tires were already on the rear wheels and a young man was replacing the ones on the front. Bennie was glad that he and Ivan were no longer stranded. Now, the only thing keeping them at the marina was the handler's strict orders.

After the tire man left, Bennie drove around to the other side of the hill until he spotted Ivan sitting on a huge boulder staring out at the lake. There was no use bothering the boy until the handler called back with new instructions. Instead, Bennie headed back to their cottage where he showered and shaved.

At noon, Ivan returned to the cottage. "I see the car is fixed. Is there any news from back east, yet?"

"No, there's nothing new. Why don't you get washed up and then we can go get something to eat at the restaurant." Bennie decided not to tell Ivan that he had already made a report to the handler. He thought it was best to be a little cagy until he knew what the handler had to say.

At 2:00 p.m., sharp, Bennie's cell phone rang. He had been in the midst of taking a nap and the ring shot through his nervous system like an electric shock. He planted his feet on the floor when he sat upright. After dropping the phone once, he finally gained control of it. When he looked around, he noticed that Ivan had gone off again.

The voice on the phone came across clearly, firmly, and officiously. "I want you guys to get back to your hotel room in Dallas and hang out there until I call and give you new marching orders. Try to keep a low profile while things get sorted out back here."

A split second after acknowledging receipt of his new instructions, the handler abruptly ended the call. Bennie always thought such abrupt endings were rude. Like all other calls from the handler, there was no underlying hint that there had been any heightened dissatisfaction. Calls were always businesslike and emotionally lacking. Bennie preferred to be told when his work was in doubt. If he didn't need the money, he would get out of this line of work and tell his handler where to stick it.

The drive back to their hotel nearly took two hours. The trip was boring with only a few comments about having bad luck. Between them, they were too vain to openly admit any degree of poor judgment.

At the hotel, they both showered and changed clothes. Ivan asked for the keys to the rental car. "I need to drive around for a couple of hours. That's how I get my head together. All that shit at the lake has gotten to me. If anything comes up you can give me a call on my cell phone."

The last thing Ivan wanted was company. Besides, he had already had two days of drinking and hanging out with Bennie and that was enough. Truthfully, he resented Bennie's fatherly nagging. If the truth was known, Bennie was no smarter or better skilled than he was. Anyway, what he had in mind for the night would only be spoiled by having Bennie tagging along.

Bennie, on the other hand, was equally glad to have some quality time alone. Ivan would be no help when it came to sorting things out and getting them back on track with the handler. In fact, the handler had already made it clear that Ivan was not to make it back alive from this assignment. Bennie decided that the best thing to do on this night was to head down to the hotel's bar and restaurant for some food and drink. First however, a nice nap was in order. He had plenty of time to kill and he needed to calm his nerves while analyzing his situation. Later, when he returned to the room, he would search the TV channels for a good movie. Hopefully, the handler wouldn't call until tomorrow. He only wanted things to level out and the assignment to end on a positive note, if that was still possible. He couldn't handle any more humiliation like being pushed into the lake. If the cops hadn't been so close, he would surely have killed that private dick and his two bitches. Once those three thorns were out of the picture, grabbing the file would be a piece of cake. If only he could get his hands on that file, the handler would be as happy as an addict with a new fix.

Yes, all this could have been avoided had he had the good sense to case the marina and size up the situation. Had he only known about the cops and divers heading his way, he could have picked a better time and place to confront his targets. Targets, now that's a joke. It looked like the real target was that stupid file. The only human target left was really this guy, Matt. Maybe he should ask the handler how much collateral damage was acceptable. The more dead bodies that are piled up, the more money the client would have to come up with. Numbers are important when it comes to killing. All the loose ends have to be taken care of. In the mean time, he would have to endure this nerve racking wait. Yes, once this mess was finished, he would never return to Dallas- that was for sure.

Ivan knew how to relieve stress and he knew exactly where to relieve it. He found out where to go for what he needed by looking in the yellow pages. Sitting behind the steering wheel, he fumbled with the page he had ripped out of the phone book. Mockingbird wasn't that far away and it wouldn't be long until he was doing what he enjoyed most. All big cities had places like he was thinking about.

Ivan's appetite for sex, any sex, was stronger than most men's. He saw his craving for the lewd and lascivious as a manly trait. First on the night's agenda would be a couple of hours in an adult video store where he would get his juices flowing. Then he would head out and find some real action. Any sexual contact would be alright, but his preference would be a prostitute. He didn't care if it was with a male or a female as long as he got it. One way or another, his sexual urges would be satisfied.

Before he knew it, he was pulling into the parking lot of an adult video shop on Mockingbird Lane. The place was abuzz with activity. At least he wouldn't have to worry about Bennie putting a damper on his needs and desires. Bennie was probably too old and feeble to have the same urges.

Once inside, he meandered up and down the isles searching the racks of DVDs and VHS's. Sex was an exciting enterprise with unlimited approaches, and an adult video store had all the possibilities ready for viewing. At first sight, some of the patrons appeared to be females, until they were seen up close. On close inspection, he knew they were really transvestites or cross dressers.

Ivan knew that sexually oriented businesses were lucrative. Perhaps, one day, he would own one like the one he was in. Momentarily rethinking that goal, he decided that would be a bad idea. For him, that would be like an alcoholic owning a bar- a formula for disaster and financial ruin.

A line had formed at the cash register; people were purchasing sex novelties and movies, or maybe they were only renting movies. At any rate, the cash was flowing. On this night, he did not fit that category. He was there for the viewing rooms; that's where the action would be.

He looked down the isle and saw a man wearing a hooded sweatshirt. The guy had a goatee, a thick mustache, and heavy eyebrows. He appeared trim and fit in spite of his graying hair. Brushing past the man, Ivan could smell perfume. There was no doubt about what the man was cruising for. Like many of the other patrons in the store, he had the same thing on his mind. There was only one reason for anyone to visit an adult video store and that was sex. Alone or with someone, the viewing rooms provided privacy for whatever the imagination desired.

Ivan paused a minute to allow his eyes to adjust as he entered one of the dark hallways leading from the well lit racks of movies. As he made his way along the hallway, there were other men leaning against the walls, their eyes searching the faces of others for any sign of a shared interest. The only light in the hallway emanated from red and green lights above the doors. Red lights meant occupied and green lights meant the viewing room was empty and ready for use.

Looking back over his shoulder, Ivan could see the man wearing the hooded sweatshirt taking up a leaning position along the wall. Two doors down was an empty viewing room and Ivan headed for it. He was already feeling some arousal beginning to well up between his legs.

Ivan walked inside the empty room, but, he did not close the door, let alone lock it. Instead, he walked to the viewing monitor and put a ten dollar bill into the flashing slot for currency. Before the screen came to life, he heard the door close behind him and the click of it being locked by someone who was also looking for a sexual encounter. He didn't look to see who had followed him inside. Casually, he faced the screen and dropped his trousers to his ankles and sat down in the huge leather chair. There were about half a dozen lighted numbers on a switch board and he began touching them so he could search for a movie that excited him and hopefully matched the taste of his visitor. He really didn't care if the visitor was male or female. Besides, it was so dark in the viewing room that he probably couldn't see what his visitor looked like. The important thing was what the person felt like. Thinking that his visitor was probably a male, he selected a movie with two naked men kissing each other.

Ivan began to fondle himself and wondered how long it would take his visitor to move in front of him. He hoped it was someone young with a firm body and a hunger for passion. Oh how he needed this. Sex was such a good outlet for releasing stress; in fact, it had to be the best outlet, ever. Not wanting to appear too anxious, Ivan once again fought off the urge to look over his shoulder. Besides, it would only be a few more seconds and then they would be touching and fondling one another.

Ivan did not see the gloved hand that came out of the sweatshirt and he certainly had no idea of what was about to occur.

In the palm of the gloved hand was a pistol and at the end of the barrel was a silencer. The first bullet struck Ivan in the temple and a few strands of his blood streaked the wall next to the recliner. Ivan never heard the next two rounds that were fired because he was already dead from the first. Firing a total of three rounds was customary for ensuring a kill. A gloved finger selected another movie of a man and woman having intercourse. The only sound in the room came from the speaker as some porn star's shrill voice mocked her ecstasy. That is if it was real. No doubt such moans and screams were pornographic theatrics for viewers.

The hooded figure reached down and retrieved Ivan's wallet. The hand removed a twenty dollar bill and inserted it into the money slot so the movie would continue to play for an extended length of time. The wallet and all the contents from Ivan's pockets were placed into a plastic bag and stuffed into the sweatshirt with the pistol. Then the hooded figure walked casually to the door. A small tube of super glue was removed from the sweatshirt and squirted on the door lock and jam. It would dry in seconds and no one else would be able to enter that room for some time, even if the light over the door turned green.

The hooded figure strolled out of the adult video store and through the parking lot. In less than two minutes the killer had faded into the dark and slipped quietly into a car that was parked out of the view of security cameras. The gloves were removed and then a cell phone was retrieved form the glove box. The voice that spoke into the phone simply said, with a breathy whisper, "The boy is no more. I'll be moving on to the next one."

The call was short and once the phone was back in the glove box, the hood was pulled back exposing a full head of gray hair. Slim fingers grabbed the hair and a wig was removed. Then the same slim fingers removed the goatee, mustache, and bushy eyebrows. Shiny auburn hair fell over the figure's shoulders and the once mature appearing male face was now smooth and feminine. The driver flipped down the visor and looking into the mirror she skillfully applied lipstick. She was thirty-three years old and had been in the killing business for nearly twelve years. She had been a rising star, and a very gifted one.

She was glad of two things. First, she had never met Ivan and knew nothing about him other than he was a target that practiced the same trade as she. Second, the kill had gone off without a hitch. A smile spread across her lips and if anyone could look into her eyes, they would not find any sign of remorse or hint of morality. Her only thought was an analytical one and it fringed on being philosophical. Simply, in this line of work, bad things happen to people who never expect it. The hunter never expects that he will become the prey.

After a twenty minute drive, the hooded sweatshirt was dropped into a storm drain. So far, she was pleased with her evening's work and proud to be an elite professional assassin. Being a master of disguise had always been one of her best attributes. Disguise not only allowed her to get closer to her targets, but it also promoted her personal security. Blending in with the surroundings was an excellent way of achieving the illusion of invisibility. She was also a gifted actress and that meant she was good at impersonation.

Female assassins have features and strengths that are often overlooked by those that see this line of work as only belonging in a man's world. Women have a psychological advantage over men when it comes to killing. The use of femininity as a means of getting a target to drop his guard or overlook a woman's potential to kill has sent many targets to their grave. Men just never seem to learn when it comes to a woman's normally weak and meek appearance. The deadliest killer is the one that the target trusts or takes for granted.

Sandra saw her life as a journey and until now it was one that lacked any definable end. Of course, she had an idea of what to expect from her efforts. In a strange way, her life journey was its own reward. Like most high-risk vocations, hers had been lucrative. Money was the driving force at this stage in her life. But, change was on the horizon.

She had never been married and that was a plus. The only time she had a romantic interlude resulted in her getting pregnant. It was a one-night stand and she never even knew the sperm donor's name. Her daughter was the most precious thing in her world. Soon, her daughter, Karen, would turn ten and during these years as a mother, Sandra had never been happier. Her daughter wanted for nothing and that would continue to be the case. Karen's college fund was doing so well that an Ivy League school was a cinch.

Being an assassin was no nine-to-five job. Actually, she only worked a couple of times a year and most of those assignments only took a few days to a week. Usually, Karen had her mother's undivided attention and their environment was upper middle class with a low profile.

Transitioning out of this line of work would be her biggest obstacle. Those who try to simply walk away had a tendency to become loose ends for another killer to clean up. Handlers in the assassination business were not prone to giving asylum to quitters.

Good handlers made it a point to maintain a diverse and experienced pool of killers. Unlike most careers, there were no retirement funds or healthcare programs. Employees were always doing their best to plan for an uncertain future.

Additionally, at retirement time, there were no gold watches presented for distinguished service or flowery speeches from a grateful employer. A new identity and a new life was the only safe way to leave the business. Her bank account was fat and there were no bill collectors nipping at her heels, so it was time to fade out of the picture and leave the ugliness behind.

There were way too many dead bodies left in her wake and their images were beginning to haunt her on sleepless nights. She was well aware of how callous she had become about life and death. She had walked among the dead without pity or remorse for so long that the dead appeared like flowers in a garden. This was no way for her to live. She needed pleasant stories to tell her daughter, not morbid ones.

She quickly refocused on what she had done tonight and what still needed to be done. There would be plenty of time to work on a new life for her and her daughter. Ivan had been a disastrous liability to the handler, and together, Bennie and Ivan had become a real headache to the handler's client. Sandra had to admit that Ivan had been a liability to the entire human race and the world would be a much better place without him. She wasn't sure about Bennie, though. All she knew was that Bennie was losing his skill and stacking up too many gambling debts.

According to the handler, Bennie was a veteran in the business and a bit of caution might be prudent when taking him out. Personally, her assessment boiled down to both targets being insignificant cogs in the wheel of assassins. This trip would be easy money and her last assignment, if she had her way.

Even though she had cased the hotel where Bennie and Ivan were staying, she did not have a room there. She opted to stay in the hotel that was next door. There were several nice ones along that stretch of I-35 and all of them were convenient for down town work and play.

She wasted no time getting back to her room to change clothes and apply some casual changes to her appearance. With any luck, she would also be able to scratch Bennie off her list this evening. Yes, two separate hits on the same night had to be a record.

Since Bennie was Italian, she decided to go for that look. She watched herself in the mirror with a heightened degree of scrutiny as she adjusted a coal black wig over her auburn hair. Silver jewelry, dark eyeliner and ruby red lipstick would do the trick. Carefully, she changed the color of her eyes to blue with artificial contacts. Her dress was red, sleeveless, and low cut in both the front and back. Her cleavage was perfect. She applied an artificial mole to one cheek and to one of her breasts. Anyone that might observe her would not be seeing her for what she really looked like. She had transformed herself into a hot Italian diva.

Within five minutes, she was waltzing into the bar at the hotel where Bennie was staying. She hoped that he would be there since Ivan had stranded him by taking the rental car. Sooner or later, he would go for a drink and perhaps even a meal. He would have to notice her because she would be the only Italian-looking woman in the place. Anyway, that was her plan. She had memorized Bennie's picture that the handler had sent.

Sandra spotted Bennie sitting quietly alone at one end of the bar sipping on a draft beer. He appeared bored and lost as he watched a local news station on one of the overhead flat screened televisions. She wondered why he hadn't asked the bartender to change the channel. There was no good reason for him to be looking at the local news. There had to be some kind of a sports channel available. Out of either boredom or nervousness, he was fingering a cigarette lighter with his free hand. She also noticed that there were no ashtrays on the bar or on any of the tables. A sign above the bar revealed that Dallas had a new City Ordnance that barred smoking in bars and restaurants. The world sure was changing.

Bennie's eyes couldn't miss the arrival of the foxy-looking woman in a red dress. Instinctively, he began observing like a deer hunter with a deer in his crosshairs. Not to draw attention to himself, he made good use of the mirrored backdrop behind the bar. He couldn't help but smile at the frustrated look on her face as she pulled a cigarette from her purse. The bartender pointed to the smoking ban sign and she shook her head in disgust. The disappointment on her face was Bennie's cue to say something.

When it came to picking up women, Bennie knew he was socially and romantically challenged. For him, coming up with a good line to break the ice was a recipe for complete disappointment. Oh well, nothing ventured nothing gained he told himself. "It looks like I'm not alone when it comes to wanting to smoke." His words lacked appeal; however, they were appropriate under the circumstances.

"It sure sucks when you have a cigarette at your fingertips and find out it's against the law to light it up. What are they trying to do, run off good paying customers?" She knew that asking a question was a good way to keep their conversation moving along.

Bennie, under most circumstances, loathed social settings and encounters with strangers. Like most men, he did not want to suffer any public embarrassment over rejection by a female. He attributed his vain pride to his Italian heritage. However, he did recognize that he had a growing interest in this dark-haired woman in a sexy red dress. Appearance-wise, she was worth pursuing; at least this was an acceptable way of killing time. Hitting on women was certainly a manly enough sport.

"So you didn't waste your time by coming in here, can I buy you a drink?" He hoped he wasn't being too forward.

"Sure, why not. If I can't unwind with a cigarette, at least I can with a drink. My name is Maria, by the way. What's yours?" She offered her hand. She also knew that lying about her name wouldn't be the only lie she would use during the night.

Bennie took hold of her hand and likewise lied about his name. "Glad to make your acquaintance. I'm Ricardo." He briefly massaged her hand before releasing it. He was encouraged when she gently squeezed his hand in return before withdrawing hers. She also scooted over to the barstool next to him and that pleased him, even encouraged him.

Bennie chuckled noticeably out loud and with a smile affixed to his face, he wrapped his fingers around his glass and hoisted it while gesturing to the bartender. "I'll have another and bring this young lady whatever she wants; put it on my tab."

"I'll take the same, thank you." She wanted to fit in as an equal at this point. She would up the ante later.

"I guess we should get used to smoking bans. Before we know it, there will be a law against everything people enjoy. That's just the reality of our times." She was not ready to let go of the smoking ban topic.

"Reality is not what it used to be; that's for sure." At this point, he was willing to talk about anything as long as the conversation kept going.

If he wanted to talk about reality, then that was fine with her. "Reality is only a perception that occupies our minds at any given time. When we lose our minds, we begin to altar our view of reality. You see, I don't think anything is set in stone, not even our concept of what is going on around us."

"Are you one of those worldly and educated women? I mean, you're not going to start playing with my head are you? It's bad enough that I can't have a cigarette." The last thing he wanted was to engage in a battle of wits with some brainy broad.

"No, I'm not incredibly smart. I just like reading about things and studying people and how they fit into this crazy world." She touched the back of his hand and smiled to demonstrate that she posed no intellectual threat to him. She continued with her comments. "I like to think that people like you and me have creative minds, to some degree. I think that people with creative minds are fortunate enough to have evolving perceptions and that means we can adapt and change to keep up with the rest of the world."

"Wow, that's pretty deep. Are you saying that we can have more than one reality going for us at any given time?" He was open to learning something from her as long as it didn't get too technical.

"Yes, I think so. You're edging on making a good point. In an odd way, we are living as though we are in some science fiction movie. I have to admit that I once heard that real life is stranger than fiction." She could tell that he was drawn to her on more than one level and that would play into her hands quite nicely.

"I don't know if I buy into multiple realities. Maybe we only have distorted views of what's real." He was scratching the back of his head as his words escaped.

She paused for a minute to think about what he had said. "If you are implying that most people are a little crazy because they have distorted views of reality, then you have a good point. Hell, everyone in the world is crazy in one way or another. Some days, we're crazier than on other days. We have to be crazy in order to cope with life. I think we're beginning to beat a dead horse here. What do you think?"

"Yes, I suppose so. The next thing you know, we will be talking about life, death, politics, and religion. All this thinking is beginning to give me a headache." He laughed to let her know that he was only joking with her.

"When it comes to death, I guess the older we get the more we begin to think about it. I hear that at some point in our lives, we even begin to get glimpses of our own death. I just hope that I don't begin to smell it. It would probably stink." This time she laughed to let him know that she, like him, had a sense of humor. She also laughed to herself because he didn't know the truth behind her words or what was really in store for him on this particular night.

Finally, he thought of a clever line and decided to toss it out to see if she would nibble on it. "The only thing I smell is your perfume and it's driving me crazy. How would you like to come up to my room for a friendly reality check?" He didn't care if his boldness offended her. Until she walked into the bar, he was only going to have a drink, eat dinner and then go watch a movie in his room.

She leaned over so he could get a birds-eye view of her cleavage and then she whispered in his ear. "I'm easy, but not that easy. The least you could do is spring for dinner and then we'll see about going to your room."

He was about to be hooked as he nibbled on her line. "Let's see if we can get a waiter to serve us here in the bar. There's a booth in the corner where we won't be bothered by anyone."

Hotel staff was always eager to accommodate guests so their order was promptly taken in a cordial manner. They ordered seafood at her urging because she knew it would be salty and that meant drinking more alcohol to quench their thirst. They both had another round of beer while waiting on their food.

Food is always more expensive at hotels compared to other places. However, Bennie was not about to complain, let alone give her the impression that he was trying to take advantage of her. Following a bad week, he was suddenly in the mood for a change and the thought of feminine intimacy was certainly more up beat. Yes, he was exuberantly aroused by her provocative nature and he would spare no expense to see the evening through with her. Truly, his eye was on the lustful reward at the end of the evening and not on anything else between now and then. He couldn't help it; he was a gambler at heart and gambling on women was no better or worse than betting on horses or cards.

Half way through the meal, she insisted on a bottle of wine for them to split. This was an easy sell for two reasons that were only obvious to her. They were thirsty and more alcohol meant less inhibitions. Everything was beginning to fit quite nicely into her scheme.

She insisted on personally ordering the wine while putting it on his tab. She selected a nice sweet red wine because the taste blended well with what she would add to it. The result would nicely conform to her intent. Bennie went to the restroom while she picked up the wine from the bartender.

Back in the booth, she plucked a gold tube of lipstick from her purse and removed the cap. There was no lipstick inside, only a vial containing a liquid. It was only another murderous tool from her toolkit. The bartender had already uncorked the bottle of wine for her. There was an aspect of the vial's contents that had a common thread to the evening meal; the substance concealed inside also came from the sea. The vial contained a highly deadly toxin in a distilled condition. The toxin originated from certain internal organs from a specific deep sea blowfish. She poured two glasses of wine; one for her and one for Bennie. Dumping the entire contents from the vial into Bennie's glass took only a split second. There was no known antidote for this deadly poison. A broad smile beamed across her face once she had finished setting the stage for the rest of the evening.

Bennie slid into the booth across from her and his face glowed with the expectation of romance. All he wanted to do now was polish off the wine and head to his room with Maria in tow. Perhaps Dallas was not all that bad of a place after all.

"Boy, you didn't waste any time getting the wine. You must want to get up to my room as bad as I do." He was playing right into her hand. He scooped up his glass before she had a chance to respond.

"Nothing gets past you, Ricardo. This is going to be a big night for both of us. Oh, one more thing. What happens in Dallas stays in Dallas." She hoisted her glass to make a toast. "Here's to the great night that awaits us."

She sipped a lady-like drink from her glass and he gulped the full contents from his. It wouldn't be long before the deadly toxin would begin to work its way into his system. The toxin was a neural poison found in the tiger puffer. Its technical name was tetrodoxin and it is one hundred times more poisonous than potassium cyanide. The toxin acts as a sodium channel blocker that paralyzes muscles while the victim remains fully conscious and eventually dies from asphyxiation. She would have to work quickly because death could occur within ten to fifteen minutes of ingestion. The molecules in Bennie's body were probably already beginning to expand. In some subjects, the expansion gave the targeted person the impression that he would explode.

"Let's pay up and get up to your room, Ricardo. I'm in a romantic mood and don't want to waste time sitting in a bar downing glasses of wine." She stood up and reached across the table taking his hand. He already had his credit card out, in spite of feeling a bit woozy; thinking he had drank too much too fast.

Much to her satisfaction, the elevator to the third floor was a quick ride. During the ride she fished the door key card from Bennie's shirt pocket. "What's your room number?" She fired the question at him with a sense of urgency. Her eagerness had a different goal than any he was thinking of.

"Three ten, it's on the left when we get off." He answered obediently. Already, he was beginning to choke without knowing why. Thinking that he could throw up at anytime, he scrambled to the door of room three ten. He wasn't about to make a spectacle of himself in front of onlookers. However, no one was watching except his new friend, Maria.

In a split second, she had the door open and she followed as he stumbled inside. He began to pull at the collar of his shirt. "Damn, I feel like I'm smothering." He gasped.

"You'll be alright." She forcibly shoved him into a chair. "Don't worry Ricardo. I'll take care of you. You'll be fine in a minute, I promise."

Made panicky by his inability to take a breath, the now agitated hypercarbic Bennie desperately grabbed at his throat and chest as though he was having a heart attack. Weakly, he attempted to stand, but, she only pushed him back down into the chair, in a less than gentle manner. Extreme anxiety flashed from his eyes as the decreased oxygen began to frighten him. His pulse was speeding up and his blood pressure was rising. Unknown to him, but well known to his female guest, the level of carbon dioxide in his blood was increasing rapidly to a state called hypercarbia. His skin was beginning to turn blue and that was a sign Sandra, AKA Maria, was glad to see. Within seconds, Bennie would be unconscious following a huge convulsion triggered by his un-oxygenated and hypercarbic brain.

His heartbeat quickly became irregular and then it simply stopped beating, altogether. He sat motionless in the chair with his tongue hanging out the corner of his mouth. It had never occurred to him that his date was a contract assassin, and that she had been methodically killing him during the past ten to fifteen minutes. Patiently, she had just applied her trade with all the confidence and efficiency of a true professional.

Sandra paused a moment to look at Bennie and then she conjured up a passing thought. His life had only amounted to being nothing more than a grain of sand on one of many thousands of beaches on the planet. If his life was missed at all, the void would hardly be noticed. In the grand scheme of things important, the only lives she cared about were the ones that cared about her and even that was sometimes conditional.

Without any lingering emotions, she busied herself with other important tasks. The handler wanted Bennie and Ivan's room sanitized so there would be nothing for the police to scrutinize. She pulled a pair of rubber gloves from her purse, and with a washcloth from the bathroom, she began the painstaking task of wiping everything in the room clean. All the drawers were checked for contents and the notepad on the desk was taken. Sometimes a thorough police officer would take the time to check for imprints on notepads. Any clue that might explain what a victim had been up to had to be explored. Painstakingly, she went through all the pockets of their clothing, to include dirty laundry. After the better part of an hour, she was convinced that she had done a good job of cleaning and sanitizing the room.

CHAPTER 18

Frank leaned back in his office chair and stared at the file that was causing such a ruckus. After concentrating on it for awhile, he was still left with more questions than answers. Maybe his concern was not so much what was written in the file as it was what was missing from it; some element of authenticity. Like many documents he had encountered in the intelligence world, it was those things that were missing from between the lines that told the real story. Explanations and corroborations were sorely needed in order to make decisions about any case. Complex investigations often generated more puzzles than uncovering actionable leads. After careful consideration, he decided to keep separate the few pages he had removed earlier from the file. Those pages would, without a doubt, cause a great deal of trouble if they were known to others. The last thing he wanted to contend with was being pressured into using unsubstantiated information- if you can't use it, why show it? Besides, clients didn't have to know everything; especially if it could get them killed. Sometimes information serves a higher purpose when it is kept concealed.

Charlie's absence left the office feeling cool and looking drab and empty. He was worried about her and wondered how she was holding up under the loss of her beloved father and the stress of family and the funeral. If he hadn't heard from her by dinner time, he would call her on her cell phone. Besides, she would certainly call him if she needed to talk. In spite of their short relationship, they had grown close. Calling Beth for an update on how Charlie was holding up was certainly another option.

Movement in the parking lot caught his attention. Two cars had pulled in and parked next to each other. The black Lexus was Felicity's and the Ford Explorer was her husband's, Matt. Once they got out they held hands and began walking toward the office. It was nice to see adult couples walking about in public holding hands. The whole reason for the investigation was centered on Matt's safety and yet Frank had not yet been introduced to him.

Once the two were in the office, Frank was able to size Matt up; that is according to his apparent physical attributes. Matt had short, neatly cropped hair and a round pudgy face. A sizeable double chin stood out. Matt was short in stature compared to his wife. He was at least an inch shorter than her. He was a portly man with sharp fiery eyes, a trait stereotypically attributed to many ministers, Frank thought.

Felicity was relaxed enough to informally introduce her husband. "Frank, I would like you to meet my husband, Matt. I think it is high time that you two meet, after all, Frank, you have been doing an excellent job of keeping him safe."

"I'm pleased to meet you, sir. I greatly appreciate everything you have been doing on my behalf." His voice was deep, resonating, and authoritative. Reaching across the desk, Matt clasped Frank's hand with a vice-like grip. There was power and strength in Matt's voice and that left no doubt in Frank's mind that Matt could deliver one of those fire and brimstone sermons without the assistance of a public address system. Country pastors were famous for those types of sermons.

Frank could only describe Matt's manner as unrestrained, effusive. Matt probably used a different handshake and manner with his elderly or more reserved parishioners. Ministers were usually very adaptable to a variety of people and situations so it was not surprising that they had the social skills of a politician.

"You appear to be holding up very well considering what you have been going through. You're lucky to have a wife like Felicity in your corner. She's strong and obviously loves you very much." Frank thought it a fitting tribute to acknowledge their devotion to one another.

Matt chuckled approvingly of Frank's assessment of their marriage. He then rubbed his hands together as a delaying tactic for considering his next words. "Let me begin by saying that sitting alone in a hotel room, day after day and night after night, is getting old. This whole mess has me so nervous that I can't even focus on a single television show. When I'm not reading scripture or praying, I'm looking out the window at the parking lot and opening the door to check the hallway for those two killers that are looking for me. I need to be engaged in some fruitful activity and I need to have time alone with my wife. I seem to need more than I'm capable giving."

Felicity interrupted Matt. "I understand how Matt feels. There's no doubt about how much my heart's aching for his company. Unfortunately, I've promised Charlie that I will go to her father's funeral with her. I'll be gone for a couple of days. She has endured a lot and gone the extra mile for me, so I feel obligated to be there for her."

The last thing Frank wanted to try was being a marriage counselor. However, an idea was taking root in the back of his mind. "First, let's think in terms of security. Those two killers are still out there somewhere and they want to get their hands on you and this file. Second, we need more information about what this file is all about. I have an idea about how to take care of all these issues, to include the tension you two are harboring."

Matt shrugged his round shoulders and without the least bit of delicacy, he plopped down in a chair without comment. Felicity, on the other hand, sat down gracefully in a chair and crossed her legs. She dignified her interest in what Frank was about to say with lady-like poise. Like her husband, she made no comment.

Frank leaned back in his chair and closed his eyes, searching mindfully for the right approach. After a long minute that seemed like an eternity, he slowly opened his eyes and looked at his two impatient guests.

"Matt, I need your undivided attention and insight. I want to go through this file with you at my side and glean whatever we can from it. We need an edge and that means we need critical information that's germane to your safety. Once we get through that process, we can put together a workable plan. We need to come up with a plan that convinces The Order that you are not a threat to their purpose and security. My goal is to get you out of this mess in one piece. I propose that you check out of your hotel and stay with me for the next couple of days. Working closely with me will give your wife the time she needs to honor her commitment to Charlie. Don't worry; staying at my house poses no inconvenience to me since I have plenty of room. I believe we can turn this into a win-win situation for all of us. What do you think?"

"Frank, my wife has the soul of a saint and the steely grit of a warrior. Currently, I am the weaker one in our relationship. I guess you could say I'm insecure. I don't have the right amount of gravel in my gut to stand and fight a couple of hardened killers. If it wasn't for Felicity, I wouldn't have come as far as I have in both my life and my career. You must think that I'm childish, a weakling that is easily bullied. You're asking me to be a team player for my own benefit. The least I can do is work with you in a cooperative manner. I accept your offer with a great deal of gratitude.

After all I have heard about you and what you have been doing on my behalf, I'd be a fool not to agree with you. As for Felicity, I think she does need a break from all this. She speaks very highly of this young lady, Charlie, and it is a Christian act of kindness for my wife to help prop her up in her time of need. I support my wife in this matter just as she has supported me." Matt's words were as much of a confession of his faults as they were an agreement to Frank's proposal.

Much to Frank's surprise and approval, Felicity walked over to Matt and embraced him warmly then delivered a loving kiss to his cheek. Relieved that their devotion to one another remained in tact was a heart warming feeling for Frank. He also wondered if he and Charlie would end up the same way.

"I already have my things packed for going off to see Charlie." Felicity's tone echoed triumph as much as it reflected a determined will. "I'll leave you two good men to work out your agenda. I need to get on the road. "I'll call both of you when I get to Charlie's to let you know that I made it safely. Please, don't worry about me. At the first hint of any danger, I'll call to let you know what's gong on. Thank you both for everything. Good luck with the file." She didn't wait for any reaction from either of them. She just turned and walked out the door heading for her car.

Once he immersed himself into the seemingly inextricable content of the file, Frank did not want to stop or be otherwise distracted by routine housekeeping chores. "Come on, Matt. Let's go get you checked out of your hotel and get you settled in at my home. Somewhere along the way, we'll either pick up some take-out food or sit down to a nice meal in a restaurant."

"That will be fine with me, Frank. I also want to thank you for being so understanding. You seem to have a flare for evaluating human nature. I could use a volunteer counselor at the church." Matt appeared sincere with his offer.

"No, I think I'll pass on that. Thank you anyway, though. I'm severely lacking when it comes to scripture and religious matters. I've yet to come to grips with my faith." Frank had wrestled with a lot of faith-based issues during his life and many of them had resulted in life and death consequences. "You can leave your vehicle here and we can take mine. The sky looks clear so we can put your luggage in the truck bed." He was glancing out the front office window as he spoke.

With a nod, Matt put a hand into his pocket and followed Frank to the front door. Looking over his shoulder at Matt, Frank could only think that there was an impressive sympathy and a sense of freemasonry among men of the cloth.

Once Matt's luggage was safely sitting inside the front door of Frank's home, he asked Matt, "Are you up to eating out? I think we can spoil ourselves a little."

"You bet I am." Matt was quick to answer. "I'm hungry enough to eat a horse."

"If you don't have anything against Italian food, I know a great little place that's off the beaten path." Frank's suggestion was delivered with an enticing tone. He also cherished a fond memory of eating at the same restaurant with Charlie.

"If you haven't noticed, I like almost any kind of food." Matt patted his stomach.

Frank steered clear of discussing the file, or any other aspect of the case, during dinner. Such discussions did not belong in any public venue. Besides, there would be plenty of discussion the next day. They enjoyed dinner and chatted leisurely about nothing of any importance.

It was 11:40 p.m. by the time they were ready for bed. The day had been filled with promise and encouragement. Tension between Felicity and Matt had dissipated and confrontation between them had been averted. Now, all they needed was a good night of rest.

There were no late night major discussions. Actually, they didn't even engage in any late night chit-chat. The sleep that came to them was restful and uninterrupted. Upon waking up, Frank made the decision for them to eat breakfast at a diner. His reasons were twofold. First, he didn't want to waste time preparing breakfast and secondly, they needed a hardy breakfast because they would have to work through a long, focused day. It was time for them to roll up their sleeves and get to work. The file was thick and Frank would press Matt to fill in, as much as possible, between the lines via his personal knowledge and insight.

They did not reach the office until after 9:00 a.m. They were both a bit edgy because they had not heard from Felicity or Charlie. Matt had opened his cell phone intending to call his wife when it rang. The ringing startled him at first since he was already thinking something bad had happened. He answered before the phone had a chance to ring twice.

Matt walked around the office in hushed conversation on the phone. Finally, after about ten minutes of conversing, he ended the call with: "I love you too, dear. Say hello to Charlie for us, okay?" With a sigh, he flipped the phone closed.

"Felicity said she got lost twice and when she finally arrived they got to talking. Before they knew it, the time had slipped away to after midnight so she decided not to call and wake us up. I don't care how late it was or how much they were carried away with talking; she should have called. By the way, she said Charlie is holding up alright."

The look on Matt's face told Frank that he was a little irritated over Felicity not calling when she arrived.

"Look, Matt, maybe Felicity did drop the ball when it came to checking in with us. However, you need to back up and take a good look at everything, including us. On the other side of that same coin, we also dropped the ball. Just like them, we were caught up in eating dinner and getting settled for a good night's sleep. The way I look at last night, we didn't exactly lose any sleep worrying about Felicity. I don't see where there's any harm done." Once again, Frank was assuming the position of being the designated peacekeeper. Besides, there was no way to undo what was done.

"You're right. I probably got a bit curt with her when we were talking. I'll call her later and apologize. This whole thing has been so unnerving."

"Well, let's get to work." Frank sat down behind his desk and opened up the file. "We need to go through this file, line by line, and extract all the pertinent and usable information." Frank smiled to let Matt know that all the little things would take care of themselves. Right now, they had bigger fish to fry.

"I think it's best that I read the file out loud. Over the years, I have learned that this technique will allow us to get the most out of the written word. I use the same technique when I'm editing for content." No sooner had the words escaped Frank's mouth, he was transformed into a human blood hound- he was in hot pursuit of a new scent. He was not a quiet thinker. Much to the contrary, he was an active interactive researcher. As he began reading, his face acquired a new manner. The tone of his skin took on a dark and flushed appearance. His eye brows were drawn into two hard, tight lines while his eyes shone out from beneath them with a steely glitter.

Matt looked on with respectful attention and marveled at how Frank had changed so quickly. Matt began comparing himself to Frank. Like Frank, he knew the benefit of reading aloud; that's what he did with scripture.

Moreover, Matt often watched his congregation when he delivered an important sermon, looking for body language that would demonstrate how his words were having an impact. Now, he was sizing up Frank the same way. Frank's face was bent downward, his lips tightly shut, and the veins in his muscular neck stood out like swollen rivers. Matt fully expected Frank's words to turn into impatient snarls. Matt was watching

Frank so intently that he caught himself not paying attention to what Frank was reading aloud.

"There, what do you make of that?" Frank asked.

"I'm not sure. Would you go over that part again?" Matt was embarrassed that he hadn't been paying close enough attention.

Sensing Matt's lack of attentiveness, Frank chose to paraphrase. "According to this, Judge Fullerton openly bragged about having a personal contact on The Order's High Council and that person had guaranteed him a key position in the highest chamber of the New World Government; that is once it was established. He thought he would become one of the most powerful men in all history. Look here," Frank pointed at a sentence. "Walter wrote that the judge once said, 'I'll be the Chief Justice of the Supreme Court of the World.'"

Matt's eyes grew wide with excitement. "Does he say who the judge's contact is?"

"No, I'm afraid not. That's the problem, we need a lead and there's none here. Walter hasn't even given us a hint, let alone something substantial. There's no conspiracy here. Walter's notes leave us with the impression that this is all in the judge's head. Maybe the judge is a nut case. Worse yet, maybe Walter is a nut case. This is all useless gossip." Frank sounded disappointed.

"Where do we go from here, Frank?" Matt's disappointment was also apparent.

"We're going to continue to read the file and search for anything that has merit. Truthfully, this file has to coexist with a credible, living person that can corroborate what is written in it. Matt, if that person exists, that person is you. Like me, those that are chasing you, and trying to put their hands on the file, are wondering if you are a credible missing link. Should you be unable to corroborate what is suggested within these pages, well, we won't have anything but useless theory. In other words, there's nothing. The Order has to separate you from this file until they have a chance to read and analyze it. I'm sorry to have to tell you this, but, if they can't see what's in the file, they will have you killed. They just don't have any other choice." Frank was blunt with his assessment.

Matt thought deeply for a moment and then offered an idea. "Why don't we rewrite the file and turn it over to one of those killers?"

Frank was quick to remove the notion of a rewrite. "Unfortunately, they have already read the version that Walter gave to his journalism friend. They know Walter's handwriting and his style of expression. They just don't know if this file is a duplicate of the first one or if it is a newer version loaded with revealing facts that points to someone in their organization. I think they can spot a rewrite and that would tell them you are trying to deceive them. That's our dilemma, my friend."

Frank saw no constructive reason to continue this line of thought so he resumed reading aloud. After several paragraphs of useless conjecture and impassioned platitude, he stumbled onto something more thought provoking. "On several occasions, the judge claimed to know the identity of the person on The Order's High Council that is the conservator of The Order's written manifesto. The judge insists that this highly and critically placed person is a personal friend of his. Once, when drunk out of his senses, the judge swore that this friend also maintains the only roster of all the Inner Circle members, to include their biographies."

Matt appeared shocked as he listened to what Frank was reading. "This is the first time I have ever heard anything remotely like this. All I can say is that the judge has an overly inflated ego and he loves to brag about his importance. I know that he has been a member of The Order and of our local cell longer than anyone else that I am aware of. I guess it is possible that he personally knew someone at the top, but on another level, I have my doubts. I don't know what to make of this."

"I notice that Walter wrote most of this file in the first person. Unfortunately, he never identifies himself as the author. There is no signature or any proof of authenticity other than an unnamed author stating that he had composed a file on The Order and the judge's affiliation. In fact, we don't even know if this is the file that he compiled. I suppose the hand-written parts could be analyzed by an expert to support that this was his work." Frank was struggling to come up with some workable alternatives.

"Frank, I thought Walter told you where he hid the file and it was right where he said it would be." Matt seemed to miss the reliability factor. In his defense, one would have to admit that ministers tended to support their ideas as a matter of faith whereas juries and judges worked from demonstrative facts.

"I'm sorry, Matt. Obtaining factual information from dead spirits is not a concept that many rational people buy into. It would even be a tougher sell in a courtroom. I'm afraid we are grabbing at straws and coming up empty-handed." Even though Frank was tempted to use a sarcastic tone, he fought off the urge, preferring not to embarrass his client.

Frank took time out to reflect on his abilities as a professional investigator. For more than three decades, he had investigated many strange and interesting cases. He was a private man that loathed publicity and preferred praise and recognition only from his peers and clients.

Regrettably, not all of his cases turned into glowing success stories and those failures sliced at his pride. Truthfully, some cases had simply baffled his analytical skills and stonewalled his resources. They had been cases begun in earnest with great enthusiasm which had ended without resolution. Facing clients and supervisors with empty hands verged on disgrace for an investigator known for his successes.

This present case had the potential to go in a variety of directions. Already, lives had been ruined, people had been killed, and decent folks were being put through an emotional wringer. Personally, he was riding a circumstantial rollercoaster and everyone was looking to him for a smooth ride, one that may not come to fruition.

The case had all the ingredients of a suspense thriller that seemed to mock real life. He was in the middle of an adventure that included things like a secret order, outlandish conspiracies, assassins, the occult, and egos galore. He was a trapped man, but not a beaten one. When the time to fight came, he would be the first one in the foxhole. At least the weather had changed for the good.

Since Frank had no hand to play at this point in the game, the next move would have to come from elsewhere. The file was not turning out to be a good bargaining chip. In order for him and his client to survive, he desperately needed to communicate with some credible and influential leader in the upper echelons of The Order. Some kind of a deal needed to be brokered so everyone could walk away with some degree of confidence that guaranteed no further harm would be done. Both sides of this equation had to feel safe and secure.

Frank wished that he could lay his hands on one of those two reckless killers before they had a chance to do any more harm. Every man could be made to talk if properly induced. Surely, those two killers were nothing more than hired talent. There was no apparent indication that the two men were fanatics with any degree of unshakable loyalty to The Order. In fact, they were probably contract killers and didn't even know anyone in The Order. One thing they did have, though, and that was a contact with access to someone in The Order. Frank had to get to that contact and negotiate his way to the top.

Frank had to be careful to confine his raw, brute pressure to the lawless elements of the case; underlings that served only as witless soldiers for The Order. The only exception to that approach that might be workable was Judge Fullerton. Even at that, he would be working outside the law.

Considering law enforcement, Frank would be coming from a shadowy backdrop that would make him appear fickle. There was little hope of swaying the authorities to tackle some outlandish theory involving a secret world order. Such an endeavor had the earmarks of being viewed as a product of some nut case. Circumstances had to be backed up with credible facts that would stand the scrutiny of jurists.

Lacking a crystal ball, this case was now reduced to a wait and see game. His challenge would be coming up with something plausible in the way of a strategy that would put Matt's mind at ease. Frank needed to keep Matt and Felicity engaged until something either broke or there was some indication that the other side; The Order, had withdrawn.

"This isn't leaving me with a very comfortable feeling, Frank. I don't know if you can fathom how I feel right now." Matt threw his hands up as a sign of defeat.

Seeing Matt's reaction, Frank decided to do some prodding for a better understanding of his state of mind. "Matt, don't hold back. I want you to tell me how you feel at this moment."

"To tell the truth, Frank"- Matt sank his face into his pudgy white hands- "I feel helpless. My situation makes me think of something I saw a few months ago. I was watching one of those wildlife shows on the Discover Channel. This poor defenseless field mouse was gnawing away on something he found to eat when he was surprised by a huge, slithering snake that was almost on him. That poor little mouse had no way to resist or escape. He was a trapped and condemned creature. The jaws of that snake crushed the life out of that mouse in a fraction of a second. The way I see my situation going, I have no idea where my snake is or how soon he will crush the life out of me. I can only hope that The Order will stop when they get me. The last thing I want is to have Felicity harmed in any way."

"Matt, if you have given up and resigned yourself to a death sentence, then you will surely die. Trust me, my friend; your life isn't over until you take your last dying breath. I need you to be a soldier and fight. You have to give it your all. In order to get through this, we all have to remain alert and vigilant. We can't go to the police because there isn't a chance in hell that they will find any believability in our story. They wouldn't even put this case on their back burner for one of their junior detectives to work on. Unless this case takes a drastic turn in our favor, it will stay in our camp."

"I want to do my part and I want you to be able to count on me. Just tell me what to do and I'll do it." Matt was beginning to show signs of courage and resolve.

Frank was quick to keep the momentum moving. "Up until now, we have been operating under the mind-set that we will be ambushed at any given moment. These killers or assassins or whatever the hell they call themselves have had the element of surprise on their side. I say, it is time to turn that scenario around in our favor."

"How do we do that?" Matt was bracing for some kind of a plan that had formed in Frank's head.

"We are going to surprise them with our own ambush. That's right; the prey is going to become the hunters. No matter what we do or where we go, we will have a plan. We have to anticipate every possibility for action that they could come up with. No matter what one of us might do, the others will be covering. All we have to do is get the drop on one of these guys and grab him. Once I get him alone and out of sight, I will test his loyalty and mettle. I'll bet you a ten spot that I can get him to talk. Once you convince someone to start talking you won't be able to shut him up. Once they cross that line, as obscure as it may be, there's no going back." Frank's confidence was promoting a gleam of hope and enthusiasm in Matt's eyes.

Frank and Matt sealed their solidarity and commitment with a manly handshake. This is the way men with honor and dignity seal a deal with one another. In effect, they were making a promise to their 'hope' in order to survive their 'fear.' This was the practical side of their agreement.

CHAPTER 19

Before Washington D.C. had been established as a city there was a neighborhood along the Potomac River called George Town. Today, George Town serves as a residential host to several embassies; France, Mongolia, Sweden, Thailand, Venezuela, and Ukraine. It comes as no surprise that George Town is home to some of the most affluent people and politicians in our country. Even John F. Kennedy was living in George Town when he was elected President of the United States. Certainly, George Town is a Mecca of national and international power and influence by anyone's standards. Noteworthy, is that George Town is not openly identified or advertised as a center of power. However, it is certainly a convenient place for powerful people to meet and converse.

On an obscure side street in George Town, between two stately buildings, a cobble stone walkway allows people to escape the hustle and bustle of ordinary urban life. The walkway is lit by reproductions of eighteenth century gas lights atop ornate iron posts. By deliberate contrast, the lighting creates a dimming affect compared to other public lighting. The result permits people to go about their business unnoticed; blurred from recognition.

Fall weather had already established itself as evidenced by the cooler temperatures. On this particular evening, men snuggled in thick topcoats strolled nonchalantly along the walkway. To the unknowing eye, they were businessmen taking a leisurely evening walk. Occasionally, puffs of white breath could be seen coming from between their thick coat collars that were turned up to block the cool outside air. The scene was common to George Town and it attracted no attention; not even to strangers.

A good twenty yards down the dim walkway a large oak door could be seen on the left, tucked away between huge green shrubs. One by one, pale, stern-faced, refined looking men with graying hair would stop and knock on the door. Each time, a small sliding security door would open and inquiring eyes from within would ensure the identity of each guest. The dark shadows from inside disallowed any recognition of those that were entering or those who were already present.

The group, that now reached eight in number, clustered together in the dimly lit foyer. The visitors loitered about muttering in low throaty whispers. Their conversations came in gushes and dealt with ordinary topics such as the weather, the health of relatives, and the status of friends and colleagues. Of course, there was some small talk about Thanksgiving since it was just around the corner on the calendar. It was as though they had gathered to gossip about trivial matters like old women at a sewing circle.

At 7:00 p.m. sharp, a door opened from down the main hallway. An authoritative voice beckoned to them. "Come on, we need to get this meeting under way. We can all stand around and jaw-jack after we meet."

All conversation trailed off into a restrained silence as the men filed down the hallway and disappeared into the room. The warmth of the room was sufficient enough for each man to remove his overcoat and drape it across the back of a huge stuffed leather chair. Each man seated himself around a long mahogany table. No one brandished a writing instrument of any kind; note taking was not permitted. If the truth was known, no one wanted his comments recorded in any manner. There was no need for introductions since they all knew one another. In fact, they all knew each other so well, that they could identify each other by simple voice recognition. Some voices of the attendees could probably be identified by the general public because of their positions in public service, which gave them a signature of notoriety.

At the far end of the table, the meeting's host initiated the discussion in the form of a report.

"As all of you are aware, we recently encountered a possible compromise to our work. In Houston, Texas, we managed to eliminate a significant and immediate threat with in-house personnel, through self help, if you must. An investigative journalist was taken out under the pretense of a simple burglary. His research material was thoroughly destroyed after being read and analyzed. The only hitch to this scenario has been the Dallas, Texas connection. Dallas is where this whole thing began. Collectively, all of us that are present at this table have unanimously agreed to bring in outside contractors to eliminate the root cause of this whole debacle. Unfortunately, the two contractors that were dispatched to Dallas turned out to be professionally inept. When their inefficiency was combined, it bordered on being moronic. In their wake, they managed to alert the target and create additional targets. The handler that is overseeing this mess had to dispatch a third contractor to eliminate the two imbeciles. Now, there is a private detective involved who has a counterintelligence background. He has a long distinguished career as an experienced field operative, a special agent in the U.S. Army. This whole matter is escalating out of control. To top off everything else, either a duplicate file of the one encountered in Houston or a more in-depth file has fallen into the hands of the private detective. This rather unconventional private detective is working for a minister and his wife. The minister is one Matt Whitman who is a member of our Dallas cell. The only good news I can report is that the first two imbeciles that we contracted have been efficiently disposed of." The speaker paused to allow his report enough time to sink in.

A man sitting mid-table asked. "What can we expect if this new file finds its way into the wrong hands, such as the FBI or the CIA?"

"That's a good question. However, the answer is not a simple one. I have to preface any response to your question with the words 'It depends.'"

Another voice from the far end of the table simply stated, "Please elaborate."

"It depends on several things. First, it depends on the content of the file. Second, it depends on whether or not the content of the file can be corroborated by anyone. Third, it depends on what this private detective intends to do with the file. In that regard, we are at a stalemate. To my knowledge, he is only holding on to the file for some future use. If we can't get that file away from him, we are going to be put in the awkward position of negotiating with him. I think we are now working our way toward a pretty sticky situation." All around the table, heads were turning and minds were assessing the matter.

A man at mid-table asked another question, one that was seeking an opinion. "What do you think is in the file?"

"I believe the content could go in one of two directions. For the file to be of any value to the authorities or opposing politicians there has to be a link in it to someone in The Order. The first file that we got from Houston seemed to focus on Judge Fullerton and his careless assertions of being aligned with some secret organization bent on overthrowing the government for the good of our country, and the world. At least two of us at this table have a history of communicating with the judge. I'm afraid our telephone records would establish these communications as fact and that would launch every conspiracy theorist on the planet into a wild frenzy. We could all end up having our backgrounds dug into and our trash sifted through, as well as our names and reputations tainted by every news organization in the world. Journalists and investigators are like bloodhounds; once they are on your trail, they will find something or manufacture it. None of us want to end up on that slippery slope."

Another voice at the table generated a new thought. "I think we need to address the value of Judge Fullerton to our cause. I don't really think he would break if he was challenged by law enforcement, but, I think he would grandstand before the news media. I doubt that he would corroborate anything in the file because the file places him in the middle of a criminal conspiracy with overtones of treason. His ego is a different story, though."

"You bring up some interesting points. It's high time we make some sort of a decision on the judges' value to our cause. We need to come to a consensus on this, tonight!"

Yet another attendee felt compelled to join in on what was slowly becoming a contentious topic. "We could take a chance on the file only being a duplicate of the one that came from Houston. Should that be the case, we should consider eliminating the judge quickly before he draws any attention to the rest of us. In my opinion, he has slowly become a liability to us over the years. His actions and voice have drawn a great deal of attention to him. Lately and in my opinion, he has demonstrated signs of emotional instability. He could be on the verge of jumping the gun without our consent. The man has no patience and has, on many occasions, embarrassed his office and smeared his judicial reputation. Let's open this up for a full discussion and resolution."

The host looked over to the man at his left and nodded for him to begin with his position. "Please, I want you to be candid because a lot is at stake."

The man began speaking. "I'm in The Order because I want to see the world united on all fronts. At some point in the near future people in this country, and the world over, will beg collectively for a social democracy. They will openly see the benefits and efficiency of a single world government that will look after them and care for them. Naturally, they will get their world government; it just won't be a true democracy-it probably won't even resemble one. My belief is that our lofty goal of uniting the world into a single government could be jeopardized by Judge Fullerton's impatience and enormous ego. I vote to have him eliminated."

The narrow gray eyes of the man that had stated his point shifted to his left signaling the next man in succession.

"Gentleman, our struggle is an uphill endeavor and not a path that we have lightly chosen. We are only now gaining momentum. We still have battles to face and risks to take. The challenges ahead of us are not for the faint of heart. We will prevail because we have to. I feel, with enhanced conviction that we are on the right side of this cause. I believe that we, in The Order, know what is best for all those who live on the planet. All of my conversations with Judge Fullerton left me with an uneasy feeling jabbing my gut. The man lacks leadership and judgment. We can't risk letting him take us down with him. I also vote to eliminate him." His words left no doubt about his stance on the judge. Through thick spectacles, he looked to the man on his left.

The next man was much older than the others, thus, he had seen and experienced more of the political realities of the world. As the elder, his views carried a great deal of clout.

"Our success has been gradual, calculated, and effective. I may be old, but I'm not an old fool. I've seen a lot in my time and I want to remind all of you about what we have accomplished in a modest and methodical manner. If it wasn't for The Order, we wouldn't have the Federal Reserve System; the International Monetary Fund; the United Nations; the World Bank; the World Health Organization; the European Union; Euro currency; the World Trade Organization; and the African Union, to mention a few. Without question, time and patience has been on our side. Regionalism is next on our horizon. We are not yet ready for an all out revolt; that would be disastrous. We have to be tacticians and choose our battles carefully. If Judge Fullerton was a ship's captain, do you know what I think he would be looking at on his radar scope? Gentlemen, I believe he is setting a course for martial law and we are not quite ready for that at this juncture. I vote to eliminate him. The man is not a team player, he's a rogue. Should he self-destruct, he won't go quietly or alone. I for one am not going down with him."

The torch was passed to the next man at the table.

The man was eager and quick to take up the issue at hand. "All of you are aware that my background includes being an Ivy League professor of Political Science with a law degree. The Order is a secret political entity with the aim of creating a single decision-making office for the entire planet; all of humanity, if you will. One of our goals is to dissolve the antiquated ideals of the far right and replace them with the progressive standards and culture of the far left. We need to correct our political and cultural inadequacies. The U.S. Constitution has not kept pace with the wants and needs of the country. For many years the world has been undergoing a cultural evolution and the Constitution was not designed to progress with that change. Our founding document has become out of vogue and useless. In fact, the Constitution, in my learned opinion, has contributed to regional chaos and that has set the stage for change. Our political system is a sham and must be replaced by one with a new and progressive focus. I am glad to see that we now have a president that shares our views and understands the importance of change. If he didn't believe in the tenants of our order, he wouldn't have joined us. In fact, he would have exposed us. He is an intellectual who is blessed with inspiring charisma. History will record his approach and support for world rule as a timely one. I feel he will be chronicled as the savior of humanity. He is the leader we have been waiting for. Judge Fullerton does not belong among us and he certainly is not on par with our president. The judge's presence will set us back decades. This is unacceptable. I vote to eliminate the judge." He relented to the next in line.

"Gentlemen, my focus and approaches have always been geared to the financial woes of the world. Our current financial crisis has opened the eyes of the world and those eyes are pleading for change. We need a new government that will take care of everyone. The solution to the world's problems is a global approach, i.e. a global government with a global economy. I'm afraid Judge Fullerton is conceptually lacking when it comes to the overall picture. He tends to jump into issues with both feet before he considers the consequences. He needs to be eliminated from the equation before he has a chance to wreck the whole train. I have nothing further to add."

All eyes moved to the next man for his input. "Everyone here at this table knows that I was elected to office by a liberal constituency. Prior to my political career, I am proud to say, I had been a draft dodger during the Vietnam era. I was an activist and openly demonstrated against the war and anything that hinted of conservatism or any movement to eliminate Communism. I have always opposed, and always will oppose, any form of nationalism.

"One of the primary reasons I oppose our system of government and favor a single world government is that I think all patriots are nothing but flag-waving neurotics. These people cling to an outdated heritage that fosters war and global discontent. In the interest of true equality, I believe we should do away with state sovereignty. I never could clearly understand why states need any sense of individuality. In fact, why do we need country individuality? Once state sovereignties are eliminated, their sense of nationalism is also dissolved and that translates into eliminating war between countries. Peace may not come quickly, but, it will come. In my opinion, Judge Fullerton is too far to the right and would be too quick to use the military for solving judicial disputes. I seriously doubt that *posse comitatus* is in his judiciary vocabulary. We all know that the *Posse Comitatus* Act of 1878 strictly forbids the use of federal troops for law enforcement on non-federal property within the United States. Additionally, when did the U.S. Supreme Court or any civilian court have military might? Use of force or military might is an executive option and not a judicial one. Judges do not have troops. The judge is completely out of touch with reality and needs to be eliminated." His liberal views garnered a few questioning smirks from around the table. At least he was onboard with the others when it came to Judge Fullerton.

The next man in line to voice an opinion had a tendency to be even more controversial. His views unquestionably tested a few of his comrades when it came to religion. "I was raised in a family of Southern Baptists and my father and grandfather were both ministers. All my life, I had religion crammed down my throat until I convulsively gagged at the mere suggestion of going to church. I have made no secret to any of you about my concerns over the president's religious upbringing. It's not that I oppose religion in government- I loathe it! Not one among us should be blind to what is occurring. Clearly, we all see what's happening in our country and in Europe. Soon, Europe will fall to Islamic zealots that are scurrying about changing the face of urban neighborhoods. I don't even like religion, let alone traditional churches. Science, not myth, is my religion and I've never read an account of a soul being dissected in a science lab. Traditionally, wars have not been fought over science, but, they have been fought over fanatic religious beliefs.

"Like some dreaded disease, mosques are popping up all over the world. Every big city ghetto in the world now has at least one mosque. Next, they will be mushrooming across the rural countryside. On worship days, there are men appearing everywhere wearing headscarves with women trailing behind them like little groups of figureless tents. Common names like; James, William, Jeffrey, John and Mark are disappearing from our youth and being replaced with names like Mohamed. I have fearful visions of a new global religion coming to pass and it will be Islam. What if our New World Government accepts Islam as the official global religion in order to eliminate religious conflict? I know, you are wondering what all this has to do with Judge Fullerton? Well, it has nothing to do with him because he could care less about religion. I only wanted to throw out a growing concern of mine. When it comes to Judge Fullerton, well I'll go along with the others who spoke ahead of me. I vote to eliminate him." With the wave of a hand, he relented to the next man.

The eighth man, sitting next to the host, now had his turn to speak. "At this point in The Order's history, I can't conceivably see any need for Judge Fullerton or his talent as a jurist. We all know that when the future finally arrives, we will need a stern judge to aid us in keeping our global goal of one billion in population. At the rate we are growing, we may have to increase that goal and then trim it back. The judge that is needed for our goals will have to have the will, strength, and stamina of demeanor to enforce laws we select as capital offenses. He can't be squeamish when it comes to sentencing people to death. Population growth can't go unchecked; our intention to limit the world's population is a reasonable one. As a global welfare state, those who are compliant to the government's laws, rules, and policies will be rewarded with a means to live. All others will be starved to death, denied healthcare or be sentenced to death as criminals. However, we are not to this point yet so there is no need in The Order for the likes of Judge Fullerton. A time for such a judge as Fullerton has simply not yet arrived. We can always come up with a judicial henchman to help control our population and maintain the semblance of order. Without a doubt, a good judge will come in handy to control family size, disease, conflict, and eliminate gun ownership by the common people. I think we will all rejoice when people can't hide behind the Second Amendment. The fewer guns that are in the hands of our citizens, the less we have to fear from armed rebellion. The judge we will need and depend on will have to articulate clear laws that achieve The Order's goals while keeping the ruling class separate from the servant class. We can never again chance having a middle class. Naturally, our chief judge will always be with the ruling class. I whole heartedly vote to eliminate Judge Fullerton before he has a chance to damage our cause." That last vote completed the discussion and voting. Now, it was up to the host.

"At last, it is now my turn to have my say and cast a vote on Judge Fullerton. A little more than ten years have passed since the judge joined our ranks. Initially, he demonstrated a great deal of zeal and passion for The Order's aims and aspirations. His hand was steady and his eyes were filled with caution and restraint. There was no doubt about him being as motivated and as idealistic as any of us now sitting around this table. He was earnest and worked hard on legal issues that stood as obstacles to us. In the early days of his service, he was as strong a link as the best of us and that earned him a great deal of respect. Unfortunately, his status has waned lately and his value as a link has weakened proportionately with his ever-inflating ego. Now, he has become our weakest link; a powerful liability. His emotional instability reminds me of nitroglycerin. The judge is about to explode with enough force to destroy everything we have built. We can no longer rely on him to do the right thing for The Order. His fate is sealed. He will be eliminated with the utmost haste and I will personally make the arrangements. I know this hasn't been easy for some of you, but, I appreciate your candor and fortitude."

One of the inner circle's members sitting at the far end of the table felt compelled to add his comments to those of the host. "The very nature of what we are working towards and accomplishing in The Order requires us to rule our ranks with an iron fist. For our own security and self preservation there can only be one punishment in our code. It is death. We have to send a clear signal to any doubting member of The Order that disaffection or disobedience will not be tolerated. Spilling some blood is justified to keep our mission alive. The history of mankind has nearly always been written in blood. The design of change and progress is often a ruthless necessity." A cacophony of agreeing whispers echoed like faint thunder around the table to illustrate their solidarity on what had been decided.

The high inner circle of The Order had met and unanimously resolved a developing and pressing issue. This wasn't the first time that this group had chosen death over life for one of its members and it wouldn't be the last. There is something inbred in the minds and hearts of men with power; something that overrides a moral or compassionate conscience. Once committed, the powerful become hardened to their cause, and do so without any regard to nobility or empathy for any man that stands in their way. They tend to see themselves as ruling gods that no other earthly man can hold accountable. They are always in judgment of themselves without holding themselves guilty of any meaningful wrongdoing. Their arrogance is one of their strongest traits. It could be said that they set their own moral standards. For these reasons, they fear the current judicial system, the U.S. Constitution, and the power of a citizenry that can remove them from power by voting.

Elected officials only have power until the next election. The objective reality is like a coin. On one side of this democratic coin, no citizen has earned a right to complain if they did not exercise their right to vote. On the flip side of the coin, no vote is as dangerous as a uniformed vote. No better proof of this fact is necessary than can be obtained from a glance into The Order's philosophy.

The men sitting around the table knew by the character of one man's smile that the meeting was not yet over. He shifted his body, leaned forward with an elbow planted on the table, and directed a question to the host. "What are we going to do about that damn file and that testy private detective?"

"Oh yes, I need to clear that up for us. The handler that oversees our contracts for eliminating special problems is going to personally take this for action. Currently, he is setting things up to backstop his work. He is going to keep me posted on his progress. Suffice it to say, he is well aware that he has to take care of this quickly. He is a very competent and resourceful man and can be counted on for success. I will report the outcome during our next meeting. I'll call an emergency meeting if any problems arise. Does anyone have any new or pressing business they would like to bring up at this time?"

The last man to pose a question asked a follow-up question. "Will that private detective be eliminated?"

"If at all possible, the private detective will be handled without piling up another body. The handler is a very resourceful man. We will just have to wait and see." The host would not elaborate any further.

There was no additional new business that required discussion. Everyone stood and gravitated over to retrieve their overcoats. The last man to leave the room switched the light off.

The meeting that had just ended in this obscure room in George Town was one of many similar ones that had previously taken place and most likely resembled an inordinate number of ones that would follow it in the future. Over time, the faces and names would change, but, their evil and inhumanity would continue. Those in attendance viewed themselves as enlightened revolutionaries. Deep in their hearts and souls, they believed their work would save the world, regardless of the pain their actions would bring to others. Only an accurately recorded history would justify or condemn their efforts. No doubt, even historians would analyze and subjectively and objectively come to competing conclusions and hypotheses concerning The Order. One thing is certain, however, and that is the winners of wars are the ones who write history. Hopefully, for the sake of mankind, the ends will not be justified by the means; but, by some caring and loving respect for life.

On the down side, the struggle between good and evil may never end. On the up side, if a struggle remains, then there is still hope. Maybe God never intended to end the struggle. Maybe He only intended to evaluate how we apply our gift of a "free will" which allows us a high degree of self-determination.

There was still another way to look at the men in The Order and their meetings; especially like the one that had just ended. If any of the attendees had a conscience, they would have felt better about eliminating Judge Fullerton had they known that he had ordered the assassination of a lieutenant governor. They would even have been exhilarated had they known that the judge had murdered the ones he had hired for the assassination.

If an ordinary citizen had been looking in on the meeting, he would probably have thought the attendees were nothing more or less than a bunch of gangsters protecting their criminal enterprise. Politics is all a matter of perspective. Turf battles and cover-ups will never end.

CHAPTER 20

Sandra was enjoying a soothing bubble bath when her cell phone rang. Since the phone was only a temporary one for use on this assignment, she knew her handler was on the other end of the call. It took her two rings before she was able to get to the phone. She answered with a simple "hello."

"Good evening, dear. I hope you are well rested because I have work for you. By the time you get to the front desk at the hotel where you're staying there will be a package waiting for you. After you review it, you should take the normal precautions and destroy it. If you have any questions, give me a call. Once you finish this one, there will be a fat bonus for you. You get the premium rate for this one, sweetheart. Let me know when you have things wrapped up." The handler hung on long enough to hear her acknowledgement.

"I certainly will let you know. By the way; thanks for the payment for my other work. I see my fee has already been deposited in my account. I'll get back with you if there are any problems." She did not wait for a response. She simply ended the call with a flip of the wrist.

She sank back into the tub until she disappeared in the bubbles. The package could wait a few more minutes. There was no need to get into a rush at this late hour. Finally, she was about to embark on her last assignment. Once she had the money for this one safely deposited, she would collect her daughter, empty her bank account and begin a new life; one free of violence.

Nearly an hour passed before she was on her way to pick up her package from the front desk. There was no need to dress up because she wouldn't be going out for dinner. Instead, she would be reviewing her assignment and working on her game plan. While at the desk, she would arrange to have dinner brought to her room. Staying out of sight was always in her best interest when she was on an assignment.

While at the front desk, she did purchase a copy of the Dallas Daily News. It was always nice to know what was going on in your area of operation. Her room was comfortable; it even had a coffee maker and a fridge with soft drinks and alcoholic beverages.

When she was working, she never drank alcohol unless it was part of some script she had concocted to set up a target. Having a clear head was a vital part of her success. Tonight, it would be bottled water and a salad; that way she wouldn't have to worry about her food getting cold while she studied the contents of her package.

When she returned to her room with the package tucked under her arm she decided not to open it until after her dinner was delivered. The package spun around like a small yellow flying saucer when she tossed it across the room and onto the couch. She walked over to a mirror and looked at herself. She could see the excitement shining in her eyes and her enormous smile was truly dazzling and that made her feel good. Yes, soon her last assignment would be over and that meant she could take up a legitimate life like most mothers her age. Once the deed was done and the money collected, she would positively shine with the prospect of a new life. Yes, she would radiate with goodness. She would look like anyone's favorite sister, a best friend, and the girl next door, all rolled up in one.

In her new life, she would stroll around a small town with her daughter in tow. She would be a wonderful mother, a perfect mother. She vowed to always be smiling and forever loving her daughter. Yes, her new appearance would be genuine, not some act to set up an unsuspecting target. She couldn't wait for the games and charades to end.

A knock at the door pulled her back from visualizing her future. Her food had arrived and her work was still there on the couch waiting for her. Now was the time to exercise patience. There were only a few more hurdles in her path before she would realize her dream. In the mean time, she would have to make sure her body and mind remained in sync with her final assignment.

She was in such a good mood that she handed the young waiter that brought her food a ten dollar tip. Hopefully, the tip would make the boy feel better about his day. Hell, maybe it would even filter on and in some significant way help his family. Giving an unexpected and gracious tip had to be something good people did. It's never too early to practice being nice to others. In the interim, however, she was a paid killer with a steady eye on her way out of a horrible life.

She sat down on one end of the couch and took a few bites of her salad and a sip of water. The yellow package seemed to be starring at her, calling her to reach inside and remove its contents. A few more bites and then she would have at it.

Once the salad was set aside, she picked up the package and tore open the end. Everything was neatly stacked with a synopsis on top. She read it with an intense focus; one that only a professional could maintain. "My God, the target is a judge." She told herself out loud. Considering the fee involved she should have suspected the target would be a high profile one. He certainly would not be a soft target.

During every aspect and phase of a hit, she always remained intently focused on the details. As with all of her assignments, she erected an insulating mental wall around her thoughts. This was a cleaver talent she had cultivated and employed through the years. This was not a child's game she was playing. Her business involved deadly decisions that, if flawed, could ruin her life; if not bring about her own death. Arduous study and painstaking application was what had kept her alive and anonymous. Her only insurance was her cunning approach to each and every aspect of her work.

At the heart of the challenge was finding some method to isolate the judge from his public domain. She had to invent some surefire way to get him alone and then figure out how to get away without drawing any attention to her.

Whoever furnished the information in the synopsis must have known the judge well. There it was, plain as day. The judge was egocentric. The key to getting him alone was to somehow play on his ego. Luring him sexually would be out of the question because he was a public figure. They were usually cautious about attractive women who made advances. Should he reject her, she probably would not get a second chance. There had to be a way to appeal to his ego so he would think he had a public platform to parade around on. Egocentrics, especially politicians, want to be publicly acknowledged; heard, seen, their words read, and their life praised. The embryo of an idea was beginning to form. She was certainly on to something viable.

The judge would have to believe he is being interviewed in a casual out of the way place and that the results would be plastered everywhere. He had to be a driven man, one that wanted his public image enhanced.

After a great deal of careful thought, she decided to pose as a magazine reporter looking for a scoop. The judge would certainly bite on that bait. She would promise the judge that his photograph would make the front cover of a magazine that favored political news and insights.

An hour had flown by since she had turned out the light. She lay wide awake, her eyes vacant of expression and fixed on the ceiling. Watching television or listening to the radio was out of the question. The last thing she needed was some distraction that would keep her from coming up with the perfect scheme. Finally, the details began to fall into place. First thing in the morning, she would shop for the right clothing and then she would make the call to the judges' office. Timing was important so she wouldn't call until afternoon. The last thing she wanted to chance was the judge wanting to be interviewed at the courthouse. Hitting a target in a government building was way too risky, not to mention difficult. A casual setting with privacy was more conducive to success. Saturday, was ideal; the best of all opportunities.

Also, she would go to the library and do some research on the judge and his political views. After all, how could she set up and begin an interview if she didn't understand the political environment and his beliefs.

No matter how a judge is killed, the act would draw a great deal of attention. She would come up with a list of locations that would serve her purpose and then she would survey them. The last thing she wanted was to be on unfamiliar turf. Just because there was a rush on the job was no reason to be foolhardy in carrying it out. Yes, tomorrow would be a very busy day for her so a good night's sleep was the best way to prepare. Just as she had turned out the light, she turned off her mind, and fell fast asleep.

She awoke early the next morning and after brushing her teeth, she headed to the hotel fitness center for a quick workout. In the line of work she was in, staying fit was just as important as it was for a soldier or a fireman. Her dress for the day would be casual; jeans, blouse, and tennis shoes. Blessed with a youthful appearance, she could easily be mistaken for a college student. She exhibited a boyish charm when she dressed casually, and that allowed her to blend in nicely with most Texans, regardless of where she went.

By noontime, she had wrapped up her shopping spree. Everything she purchased matched the persona she had set her sights on. The part she had chosen to play was the leading role in a suspense thriller. Hopefully, there would only be one other actor in the production and that person would play a duel role; one as a rising star on the political scene, and the other as an unwitting judge that was on a collision course with an early death.

During the next two hours she busied herself with background research at a public library. By the time she returned to her hotel room, she had formed a rudimentary understanding of what kind of a person Judge Fullerton was and what he professed to stand for. She had read many accounts of favoring commentary for the judge and an equal number that were not so complementary. Now, it was time to bait the trap.

Fearing that she might make a mistake, she jotted down some notes about the character she would be playing and the topics that would play on the judges' ego. He was a big fish, and a clever one. He would require some careful angling if she was going to reel him in without tipping her hand.

She decided to make the call from her throwaway cell phone. Anyone tracing the call would find a dead end when it came to identifying her. This was a Friday afternoon and most courts were already adjourned so people could make a break for home or leisure activities. In other words, they were getting a head start on the weekend. The late hour would undoubtedly rule out any meeting today. She knew that the judge would not want to chance any interruptions when being interviewed by a reporter. The time for her first move was now or she would surely be put off until sometime next week. She was hoping for a meeting at the judges' home or some out of the way place where there were no prying eyes or potential witnesses. Sure, she had a list of good places, however, the judge might have a better suggestion; one that would meet her needs.

She punched in the phone number and waited for an answer. After waiting what seemed like an eternity, someone finally picked up. "You have reached Judge Fullerton's Court. This is Irene, the Court Clerk speaking. How can I help you?" The voice was pleasant, yet business like.

Sandra cleared her throat and then spoke. "My name is Pamela Collins and I'm the senior reporter for a magazine called 'Politically Correct.' I would like to speak with Judge Fullerton about an exclusive interview."

"Please hold while I confer with Judge Fullerton." Irene's tone changed to a more officious one. There was a long extended pause before Court Clerk Irene returned to the phone. "Please hold while I transfer your call to Judge Fullerton."

Following a second of silence the phone was answered on the first ring. "Good afternoon, Pamela, this is Jeremiah Fullerton, at your service." The tone of the judges' voice was extremely cordial, even bordered on being familiar. The call had no doubt garnered his interest.

"As I told your clerk, Irene, I am Pamela Collins, the senior reporter for a magazine called 'Politically Correct.' We are based in Alexandria,

Virginia and as you might expect from our name, we have a political theme. We have a reader base of over one hundred thousand and growing." Her exuberance demonstrated a sense of confidence and pride as she addressed the judge.

"What can I do for you this afternoon, dear?" The judges' manner was charming and confident.

"Well, judge, I would like to do an in-depth interview of you. Lately, it has come to our attention that you are becoming quite the rising star in the political sky and our magazine would like to be the first to scoop your arrival on the scene. I was about to leave Los Angeles this morning when my editor asked me to stop over in Dallas and see if I could land an exclusive with you. We want to put you on the front cover of our next month's addition. So far, does any of this interest you?" Her marketing skills were being tested as she waited for the judges' response.

"I'm not sure what to say, Pam." He had already shortened her first name as if they were old friends. "This is all coming as quite a surprise. I believe anyone yearning to move along his political career would be interested in finding a few media platforms to speak from. What do you expect to get out of interviewing me?" His question was an obvious and subtle way to gain some insight into what to expect from the magazine. No public figure really wanted to stick his neck out too far if someone was waiting to whack it off.

"I'm a career reporter, judge. I have my eye on being an editor some day. If I can establish myself with a politician displaying some fresh ideas and I can hang on to his coattails, then it couldn't hurt my career; if you know what I mean. The higher and the faster you soar, the better it is for me." She was hinting that she was going to be a little bias on the favorable side when it came to him.

The judge was keenly aware that many politicians around the beltway in Washington D.C. had strategically partnered themselves with elements of the media. Even though he didn't know anything about a magazine called 'Politically Correct,' the name implied the right tone. His mind was already beginning to look for ways the magazine could boost his status.

"Pam, this is really very short notice and I know you must have a deadline to meet. However, I already have a previous engagement for tonight." He was lying. Actually, he needed some time to prepare himself for the interview. "I have a yacht moored at Lake Lewisville and in the morning I am going out there to run the engines and make sure everything is alright. Would you like to join me there? We could do the interview without any interruptions in a relaxed atmosphere. What do you think, dear?"

The setup would be perfect. Anyway, that was what she was thinking. "I think that your idea is excellent. This is also a great opportunity to show our viewers some of your personal interests. The public has an innate curiosity about the lives of high-profile celebrities. I know, sometimes that is good and sometimes it is bad. Bad is something like what happened with Tiger Woods. Good, is something like Ted Kennedy sailing his boat at Cape Cod with his sons. By any chance, do you like to fish? Don't worry, I don't mean to imply that you're anything like Sarah Palin."

"I haven't fished in years. I only like to entertain friends on my yacht. By nature, I'm a very social animal. As a side issue, I think you will find me to be very staunch in my beliefs. However, I also like to let my hair down and have some real fun. Once you get to know me, I think you will like me a lot." Now, he was having his hand at some marketing.

"Our meeting is a sealed deal so all I need to know is where do we meet and at what time?" He had taken the bait and that meant she was ahead in the game. Judge Fullerton's life clock was now ticking a little bit faster and he was not the least bit aware of it.

"Let's meet on Main Street in Lewisville. Just east of I-35 you will come to the old part of town. You can't miss it. There's a little strip center on the right. I'll be sitting there in my Escalade at 10:00 a.m. in the morning. How does that sound to you, Pam?"

"I can't wait. I certainly appreciate you giving me some of your personal time on such a short notice. I'm beginning to see that you really are a very nice and accommodating man. I'll see you in the morning." They both hung up their phones with the customary closing expressions.

Her invitation to the judge had been executed with the best of her ability. Her performance was the first act in her last performance before embarking on a new life; one lacking violence.

Next, she headed out to find a place to use a computer so she could write and print a sign. The end result would be in keeping with the instructions in the target synopsis. As follow-on, she went to a hardware store and purchased a five foot piece of thick rope; something like you would find on a farm. These were articles that she would carry to the interview.

When she returned to her room, she gathered other materials that she would put to use early in the morning. The last thing she did before retiring for the night was to check the local weather forecast. She had mixed feelings when she learned that the next day would be filled with high wind and cold rain. This, she concluded, might put a damper on her disguise- that was on the negative side. On the positive side, the bad weather would drive them down inside the judges' yacht; out of sight of wondering eyes. Hopefully, no one would come out to brave the foul weather.

She went to the hotel restaurant and ate a nice and expensive evening dinner. The meal was her way of celebrating the crafty way she had prepared for her final hit. When she finished eating she dropped by the hotel's front desk and put in an early wakeup call for 5:00 a.m. Her final preparations would take several hours and she wanted to get in a quick workout and breakfast before heading out for the interview.

Her nerves were a little jangled by the time she finally rested her head on a pillow. She turned the radio on to a station that played classical music. Meditation was a method she had learned over the years to settle her mind and relax. By the time her eyelids were closing and she was beginning to drift into her gentle dream-like visions, she managed to turn off the radio. The sleep that came was restful and sound.

She sat up with a jolt when the phone in her room rang. Like a startled cat, she was wide awake. After snatching the phone from its cradle, she saw the red numbers on the clock on her nightstand- it was 5:00 a.m., on the button. The voice on the phone was a digitized notice that it was time to wake up.

In less than five minutes, she was in the exercise room warming up on the treadmill. Following her normal cardio routine, she then turned to the free weights. An hour later she was eating a fruit salad, some cereal, and sipping coffee and orange juice. By all appearances, she was as normal as any other guest at the hotel. When it was 7:00 a.m., she had showered, but not dressed. The next two hours were nothing short of pure artistry for her.

Facing the mirror required intense devotion if the proper outcome was to be realized. In stages, her plan for the prefect disguise slowly began to take shape. The first stage focused on her hair. She had a human hair wig that needed attending to. It was dark brown, nearly black in color. She combed it out and then used a toothbrush to apply a blend of liquid hair color that would achieve a realistic silver-grey tone. The goal was to turn the hair into an older, more mature look. Overall, she was seeking to add twenty years to her appearance.

She knew from experience that when an actress wanted to alter her appearance, in this case aging her features, she would have to exploit the natural features of her face. One of the central features of using old age makeup is to create and accent wrinkles. It is always easier to create wrinkles where they would naturally occur with time. She turned on every light in the room and studied her face in the mirror. With an exaggerated effort, she scrunched up her face, paying careful attention to where the creases appeared. She smiled, frowned, squinted, furrowed her brow, puckered her lips, and moved them from side to side. The creases she noticed were actually where wrinkles would naturally appear with age. With a brown pencil, she drew lines in each of these places. Only a touch of liquid latex was needed to accent the wrinkles.

When using a foundation layer of makeup, she used a shade lighter than her natural skin tone to create a pale look. Not wanting to appear too old- that elderly look, she decided to be conservative when it came to shadows and highlighting. This completed the second phase of altering her appearance.

Slowly, and in a manner of speaking, she was transforming her appearance from beauty to beast. On the practical side, she didn't want to overdo it. The last thing she wanted was to appear too old for the senior reporter image she was wanting to project. There had to be some blending of youthfulness with the maturity and aging results. This she easily achieved by creating a couple of aging spots on the upper portion of her chest to show another sign of aging. She did this by using a stippling sponge. Then she added some shadow color to create two smaller aging spots.

In order to demonstrate a hint of lingering youthfulness, she used a stick-on tattoo of a butterfly. She placed the tattoo at the edge of her cleavage; a place where most men inevitably ended up looking. She would also change the color of her eyes with contact lenses- this was as good a time as ever to have brown eyes.

Once she adjusted the wig on her head, her metamorphosis was complete. Her own mother would not have recognized her at this point. Actually, she probably now resembled her mother. Additionally, she intentionally did not wear her wristwatch fearing that someone might remember what it looked like. The only jewelry she put on was a cheap set of costume earrings that she had purchased the day before. Once her assignment is completed, these would be tossed out the window as she drove along the highway.

She slipped on some dark blue slacks and buttoned up a long sleeve blouse that she left open at the top. The blouse was a lighter shade of blue than the slacks, but matched nicely. Next, she needed to pack and double check everything that she was taking.

Her pistol with its silencer was sterile and in perfect working order. Even if the police were able to put their hands on it, they would come up empty handed. The sign she had printed was fingerprint free. The rope was neatly coiled inside her oversized tote bag. Since it was cool and raining, the judge would have no reason to suspect any wrongdoing when it came to her wearing gloves. The gloves were not for the weather, they were for not leaving any fingerprints at a murder scene.

Once again, for refreshing her mind, she did a quick review of her research notes on the judge and rehearsed the political questions she planned to ask. She would play the part of reporter and interviewer right up until it was time to take him out. Acting was one of the things she had always enjoyed doing throughout her life. After all, weren't most people really acting out various roles when it came to living their lives? She wondered how many successful people just had a knack for arranging a repertoire of facades to accommodate different situations. Conniving car salesmen acted like honest car salesmen; inept doctors acted like experienced doctors, and academically challenged teachers acted like scholars etc.; always projecting the image that others expected of them, and rarely did they project their true character. Life was like one long theatrical performance and every person that came in contact with you ended up being your critic. Some people had stellar performances and others failed miserably. Imagine a doctor acting like a brawling sailor.

She put on a hooded windbreaker that was waterproof. Once outside, she would pull the hood up over her head. The last thing she wanted was to mess up her makeup and ruin her disguise. Before walking out of her hotel room, she glanced around and thought about how nice it would be to check out of the hotel and catch a flight out of town. She was missing her daughter, Karen.

In spite of the rain, there were no accidents and traffic was moving along smoothly. She pulled into the parking lot where the judge had designated as their meeting place at precisely 9:45 a.m. She was surprised to see the Escalade parked there and the judge sitting behind the steering wheel. In her opinion, he was early because he was excited about the interview and the prospect of getting national coverage in a magazine that was dedicated to aspiring politicians.

She thought about asking the judge what he thought of the magazine and then brushed the idea aside since there was no such periodical. The poor slob thought this morning was all a big break for him. She figured the judge would be putting on his own performance and that it would probably match or exceed his ego. Hopefully, he didn't become arrogant with her. Should he end up insulting her in the least way, the interview would end quickly, along with his life. Besides, it was better that she toyed with him for awhile so she would have more time to check out the surroundings and her situation. Her security was paramount.

She called the judge using her cell phone and confirmed that it was she who had just pulled up. "Good morning judge. That's me flashing my headlights at you."

"Good morning Pam. I'm sorry about the weather. You can either follow me or you can ride with me." His offer was only a ploy to get more of her attention.

"Well thank you very much, judge. I appreciate the offer. However, I don't want you to have to leave your yacht and come back out into all this nasty weather just to bring me back to my car. Besides, I have some expensive gifts that I purchased for family members stored here in the car and I would never forgive myself if anything happened to them. Maybe sometime in the future when we are doing our next interview, the weather will be better. Hey, if it's really nice for the next interview, you can take me out on your yacht." She was ducking the judges' offer.

"I certainly look forward to that day. For now, you can follow me. I'll take it easy so you won't have any trouble keeping up." No sooner had he spoke, he was backing out of his parking space.

Suddenly, there was a cloudburst of rain thrashing violently against the windshield. The roar of the downpour drowned out the music from the radio and the windshield began to film over. She put the defroster on full speed and made sure her headlights were on. She begged Mother Nature to go easy on her makeup.

Surely, there would not be anyone crazy enough to board their boats in this insane weather. At least no one would see her face tucked in under her hood. Her goal was clear and she had no choice, but to stay focused on every tiny detail in her plan. She wasn't clinging to hope; she was ensuring success. Her best insurance policy was having the element of surprise on her side.

She did her best to remember all the roads and turns in spite of the rain. Luckily, there was only one road into and out of the marina. As they headed down hill to the marina walkway, she was relieved to see that there were only half a dozen vehicles parked in the lot. Some of those vehicles probably belonged to employees. The marina was huge and not what she expected to see this close to the city. Easily, there were a thousand boats and yachts docked there. The walkways looked new. They were wide and made of concrete slabs that floated on huge drums.

She began visualizing the beauty of the situation as it was beginning to unfold around her. Her confidence and a sense of optimism were growing by leaps and bounds. If the rain would only let up a bit, she would feel much better about the state of her appearance. She was relieved and encouraged when she looked into the rearview mirror and saw that her makeup was standing the test of the stormy weather. Things were working in her favor- that was for sure.

She got out of her car and made a mad dash to greet the judge. "You have to be one die-hard boater to brave this kind of weather just to check on your boat." She peaked from underneath the hood as she spoke.

"My dear, I'm not an ordinary boater. I'm a dyed-in-wool yachtsman. I belong with my lady regardless of the weather." He laughed gingerly while stating his determination and devotion. "Come on, dear, and follow me so we can get out of this rain."

She was already sprinting toward the entrance ramp that led to the docks. He, on the other hand, lagged behind. There was little doubt about her being the fittest between them.

The roofs that covered the motor yachts were metal. When she passed under one, she was instantly shocked at the deafening roar of the rain as it thrashed down on the huge sheets of metal. Spine tingling shivers crawled all over her skin, and, in spite of her windbreaker, she suddenly felt cold all over.

Now that she was closer to the water, she was increasingly cognizant of the wind. Even under the cover of the metal roofs, the wind was noticeably more intense. Blasts of cold wind blew mist over her body. She was glad that she was wearing her gloves. Any blockage of the elements was indeed welcome. What she wouldn't give to be sitting comfortably in front of a blazing fireplace.

"We have to go to the far end of the second dock. That's where my yacht is. The quicker we get there, the quicker we can get out of this miserable weather." His tone showed signs of discomfort and that put an obvious dent in his dyed-in-wool yachtsman bravado. He knew that it was an extremely dismal day for an important interview, but, he was committed to doing it, and on his terms.

There were only two other souls in sight as they briskly walked along the dock. The two men appeared to be checking out each yacht to ensure they were properly secured in the midst of the storm. Occasionally, they would stop and cinch the ties up snuggly. She did her best to avoid eye contact when the judge spoke to one of the men. The man only said hello because his focus was elsewhere; securing the docked vessels was more important than visiting with the judge.

The yachts that were docked on both sides of the walkway blocked the main thrust of the wind and rain, yet it roared threw the overhead beams- there was roaring wind under the metal roof and thrashing rain on top of the roof. The combination was deafening. The huge yachts on both sides allowed them to escape some of the storm's fury and that was a notable, although temporary blessing. She figured that the judge was probably embarrassed, to some extent, for wanting to have the interview in the midst of such deplorable conditions. She was not about to complain, though. The conditions were ideal for what she intended to do.

She slowed her pace so as not to leave the judge too far behind. The sound of his labored breathing told her that he was trying to stay up with her. It probably had something to do with the judges' competitive nature. Politicians and lawyers rarely seemed satisfied with only finding the right and wrong of issues; winning was what really mattered to them. She remembered something that she had once read; "all politicians are bought." Along with that thought, she figured the closest thing to an honest politician was one that stayed loyal to whoever had bought him or her. The longer they remained politicians, the greedier they became, and the more loyal they were to their benefactors. She often wondered why lobbying was allowed. There had to be a way to lobby voters.

Once they neared the end of the dock they began to feel the full force of the wind and rain return. She stopped in the middle of the walkway and waited for the judge to lead her to his yacht. He was too winded to say anything- he just veered to the left and climbed aboard one of them. When he extended a hand to her, she clutched her tote bag to one side while accepting his help.

He fumbled with some keys until he found the right one. Once he had the door open, he stood back to allow her to enter. She noticed two heavy duty cords that were plugged into a receptacle on the dock. Hopefully, one of them was for a heater because she was chilled to the bone. At least the yacht's insulation was keeping out the roar of the drenching rain as it attacked the dock's metal roof.

"This is some boat you have here, judge." She knew that all men took pride in their toys.

"It's not a boat, Pam. It's a yacht. More precisely, it's a fifty-three foot Hatterus motor yacht. It was built in 1978, and in spite of its age, this vessel is in pristine condition. As for the size, it's about as big a yacht as this lake can handle. A vessel of this size is also suited for blue water cruising. I like the size because I like to spend weekends on her. Size equals comfort." The judge was beaming with obvious pride.

"What will you do with her once your political station is upgraded?" Her question was more stroking than substantive.

"Why, I will sell her and get one that matches my new political station. Upward mobility does have its perks; wouldn't you say?" As he spoke, he managed to get the heater going.

She felt the temperature climb and knew that she would soon be able to take off her windbreaker in order to conduct the interview. Without question, her makeup needed to be in order. "Where's the restroom at?"

The judge pointed. "The head is right down those stairs and to the left."

She scurried off to the head. She always wondered why sailor's called the restroom a "head." Once she was in the head, she removed her windbreaker and studied her reflection in the mirror. Everything was in perfect order and that was a reassuring feeling. She was surprised to note that there was a shower in the head, in spite of the cramped space. Within minutes, she was out of the head and making her way back to the saloon.

Wanting to set the judge at ease, she decided to engage him with some small talk. "Judge, I have a trivia question for you. Why do sailors and marines call a restroom a head? I never did understand the reasoning behind that."

"Actually, Pam, I happen to know the answer to that question. In ancient times, sailors had a designated area at the front or bow of a ship where they could go to relieve themselves. They chose an area at the bow for two reasons. One, odors would dissipate into the air before reaching the work areas. Second, there was more ocean spray at the bow of a ship. That constant ocean spray at the bow acted like a sanitizer. Now, let me give you the clincher for using the word 'head.' In those days, most ships had carved figureheads on their bows. When sailors had the urge to go, they simply said they were 'going to hit the head,' because the figurehead, had a 'head.' Over time, the phrase became part of their culture. And now, Pam, you know the rest of the story."

"Bravo, judge. It all makes perfectly good sense, now. Do you have any more of these up your sleeve?"

"Certainly, I happen to have another one at the tip of my tongue. Did you ever wonder why someone says they 'walloped' a guy when they hit him?"

"So you're going to tell me where the word wallop came from? I suppose it has some connection to the sea or to ships."

"I thought you would never ask and yes there is a subtle connection to the sea. Please have a seat across from me here at the galley table." The judge waved his hand as part of his invitation. "I'm going to take you back in time again, back to the reign of King Henry the Eighth. The French had burned the City of Brighton and King Henry was mad as hell over it. He vowed to make the French pay. The King sent Admiral Wallop to avenge Brighton's burning. The admiral did quite a job on the French; the damage to the French coast was so severe, that Wallop's name became synonymous with overwhelming force." The judge hoped they could now get down to the interview instead of playing silly trivia games.

"Are you going to take any photos of me during the interview?" His tone reflected a sense of uneasiness.

"No, there's no need for that. I have enough photos of you from other sources. Besides, this isn't a good day for taking photographs." She dismissed any need for photo documentation.

"Do you mind if I smoke? Someone gave me some cigars and puffing away on a good one helps me relax." He had already pulled a cigar out of a box and was beginning to unwrap it.

"No, go ahead and light up. I'm used to the smell of tobacco. A couple of my colleagues at work are smokers." She wanted him to be as relaxed as he possibly could be.

He puffed away on his newly lit cigar until his large frame nearly became a blur; lost in a fog of tobacco smoke. She could hardly see the judges' eyes, but, she knew that he was studying her image as both a woman and as a reporter.

Satisfied that he was on safe ground, the judge began to slouch in his seat.

She placed a note pad on her lap and picked up a pen. She wrote out her first question and then began speaking. "Judge, are you ready to begin the interview?"   •

"Sure, I'm ready. Go ahead and fire away with the first question."

"I'm going to ask some broad, general questions that will give you a chance to layout and define your approach to national government and how your views relate to it and to the country's citizens. Here's the first question: In your view and in your words, what is collectivism?"

The judge cleared his throat after taking a long drag from his cigar. He did not expect a question like this. "You certainly get to the meat of things, little lady. Next, you will want to go global. Okay, I'll lay the concept out for you in simple terms. Collectivism deals with the collective nature of government. It is the opposite of individual will. It is the collective will of the people as expressed and carried out by the government. Under collectivism, the government is the ruling class over the people. The government decides collectively what is right for its citizens. There is no individual identity. There is only the

239

collective identity. The government represents the 'common' good over individuality. This is what collectivism is." The judge figured she would not go any deeper on this topic.

She was about to enjoy some intellectual jousting with a professional jurist and politician. Drawing out the details was more fun than just shooting the man dead while he was puffing away on his cigar. "Now, for the next question, which is a follow-up to the last one; are you ready?"

"Go ahead, Pam, give it your best shot."

She knew he had no idea that he had just used a pun. She smiled, and after making what appeared to be a few notes, she continued. "Don't most totalitarian or authoritarian governments start out by saying they are here for the collective masses because individuals are only concerned about themselves?"

"I guess you could say that collectivists are a tyrannical, minority class that leans toward the realization that they know what is best for everyone. They are more experienced and knowledgeable about what the government can do for the common people. Simply, they are elitists."

She would come back to this topic later. This was the time to pull in the other side of the issues. "Thank you, judge, for your candor. This is all most enlightening. My next question is: What is a republic?

The judge smiled. "Thanks, Pam. You make me feel like a civics professor. A republic is a true representative democracy. The citizens of a republic operate under the authority of a constitution that, sadly, restricts the power of government. In a republic, individuals have individual rights that are set in stone and the government can't arbitrarily take those rights away. It's a cumbersome way of running a country that employs a long, drawn-out process of getting things done. Personally, I don't think it is very efficient. The average Joe on the street doesn't have a clue when it comes to knowing what is best for him. We need bigger governments consisting of gifted leaders, not smaller, weaker governments. Unfortunately, in a republic the people empower the government instead of the other way around. Our Constitution, simply, has not evolved and progressed with the rest of the world. We need to scrap it and start over."

Her dander was beginning to rise. "Judge, are you saying that you are a collectivist and not a Constitutionalist- is that a fair statement?"

"You are right on the money, sweetheart. Change will come, that's a fact. One of the first things that must be done away with is the Second Amendment to the Constitution. An armed citizenry sets the stage for armed rebellion. We just can't run the chance of mindless fools roaming all over the country with guns. Only the government should have guns and those guns should be used to put down revolts and protect the government and its assets. Pam, imagine for an instant how peaceful the world would be if the entire planet was under a single government that did not allow individual ownership of firearms." The judges' voice was beginning to vibrate with passion.

Her passion was now beginning to match his. "Judge, during the next few minutes I'm going to be the professor. I'm not a historian and I'm certainly not a reporter." She reached inside her tote bag and retrieved her pistol with the silencer attached to the end of the barrel. Without any hesitation, she pointed the pistol directly at the judge.

"Going back to my high school days, I clearly recall studying history and remember the importance of the year 1776. If my recollection serves me correctly, and I'm sure that it does, that was one of those rare times in our history when good and individualism was combined and organized in the political sense. The people revolted and challenged oppressive authorities that thought as you now do. The people won their revolt and adopted the U.S. Constitution; and then lived by it for a long time. They even added to it with amendments that further restricted government intervention into the lives of the citizens.

"In my opinion, during the last hundred years or so, we, and I mean we individuals, have suffered under the yoke of too much government. The country is deteriorating into a morass of more government and less individual responsibility and rights. People like you have always been around, lurking in the shadows, wanting to destroy individual liberty. From my point of view, you and your kind are doing a terrific job of organizing against individual rights and liberty.

"Most certainly by now, you're wondering why I'm sitting here pointing a gun at you. Well, I'm not exactly sure either. However, here I am, ready to zap the life out of your egotistical body. My best guess, after listening to your radical bullshit, is that there are people that think you're off track, and off your rocker, and the country would be better off without you. I don't know who's paying the tab for me to take your life. For me, it's only a job. This has been my vocation for quite some time now. Please, take a good look at me. I represent the armed revolt that you've always feared, all wrapped up in one neat little package, a feminine package. Make no mistake about it, I am a hired killer; an experienced professional. During my research on your background and reputation, I have concluded that you're the modern version of 'the hanging judge.' You have dispatched more people to their death than I have. So here we are; two killers facing one another."

The judge noticeably knew that he was in a weak position with little to no room for negotiation. The woman before him, whoever she was, had the advantage of surprise and the firepower to back it up. She also had a real dislike for him and what he stood for.

There was an intense edge to his voice as he began to speak. "So, miss professional killer, what are you waiting for? Why don't you just go ahead and pull the trigger?" He really didn't want her to shoot. Regretfully, he was not packing his pistol and there was nothing within his immediate reach that could be used as a defensive weapon. Maybe it was a long shot, but just maybe her heart wasn't into killing him. There was nothing he would like better than having her change her mind and then getting her to talk about her client. Who would dare put out a contract on him, a sitting judge?

"Oh, I'm in no hurry to go back out into that cold rain. I'd rather sit here and banter with you for awhile. Hey, I have another trivia question for you."

The judge had once read that the best way to sway a terrorist into sparing your life was to befriend him. As he saw it, trivia discussions were his best opportunity to establish rapport and bridge the psychological and adversarial gap between them. At worse, he at least had a chance to delay his death.

"What's the question?"

She extended a cursory smile toward him. "Truthfully, I know the answer to the question. I just want to see if you know it. What is the difference between a violin and a fiddle?"

"Wow, you have me on that one. I never really thought about that before. Both instruments sure look alike, but they can't really be alike because they sound so differently. I really can't tell you the exact difference between a violin and a fiddle. I'm sorry. What is the difference?"

"Oh, I thought a cultured man like a judge would know something about music and musical instruments. The reality is that a fiddle and a violin are one in the same; they are exactly alike. The real difference between them is in the way they are played. When played as a fiddle, the instrument projects a rhythm and energy that a person can dance to. When played as a violin, the instrument induces a sense profound passion and eloquence. It moves a listener to look into himself to solve some inner mystery or search out some enlightenment. A violin is an inspiring instrument. Now, are you ready for the second part of the question? That's right, this is a two-part question." She paused and searched his eyes for some emotion.

The judge began to perspire profusely and his eyes acquired that captive stare like a frightened animal in a car's headlights. Intuitively, he knew their discussion was approaching closure. His only chance at survival was some desperate, last ditch offensive. There was something in her tone that told him she was beginning to get tired of the game they were playing.

"Go ahead, I'm all ears." He was beginning to experience the same feeling a man felt when sentenced to death. He tried to swallow his fear, but couldn't.

"You see, you and I are like the fiddle and the violin. We are both the same instrument- we are both killers. When I kill, it's an art form that gives others pleasure and escape. I am the violin. I'm a master when it comes to killing and I can turn it off any time I want. In fact, you are my final masterpiece. I have learned not to let my trade control me- I control it. When I leave here, today, I will evaporate into one of life's many shadows.

"Now, you on the other hand, are the fiddler in this comparison. You enjoy, even revel in, making people dance to your tune. The judicial system has been your sanctuary and it has allowed you to kill with impunity. You have become addicted to the power over life and death. Like any addict, your craving or need continues to increase each time you use it. Your addiction has destroyed your patience to the point that you can no longer get enough to satisfy your hunger for power. I don't know who you have pissed off, but, I can understand why. The client wants you eliminated with extreme prejudice. You are to become the poster boy for setting the example so others will stay in line."

The judge leaned back in his seat and braced for his inevitable sanction. He willed his body to lunge at his would-be killer, but his body was too paralyzed with fear. The pistol jumped twice in her hand and the silencer kept the noise, the sound of escaping gases, to a whisper. The judges' widened eyes captured the last image of his life for his brain, and that image was a smirk on his killer's face. His final exertion was a single exhaling of breath. There was no lesson left for him to learn. His addiction was cured. Blood seeped from the two new bullet holes in his forehead. She moved to one side and added the customary third shot; this one to his temple.

She placed the pistol on the table in front of him and quietly studied his corpse. Briefly, she rationalized over the kill, concluding that dying a brutal death had always been the judges' fate- his true destiny. He should have known that one day he would have to answer for his unsuppressed need for power and misguided use of the law. In the wake of his murder, his critics and the client would have to silently and inwardly trumpet their rebuke of the judge over his tactics and behavior. As his killer, she saw the hit as a mercy killing for the good of humanity. When it came to government, she and the judge had been a world apart. He was a true hypocrite because he had forsaken his vow to the Constitution. She, on the other hand, had never taken any vow to serve anything other than herself and her daughter.

She stood and stretched. The job was not yet complete. Some finishing touches were now needed to ensure the message to others was a clear one. She placed her tote bag on the table next to her pistol. She removed the rope she had brought and sat back down with it. About eighteen inches from one end, she made an 'S' shape with the rope. One of the looping curves was designated as the noose. She coiled the free end around the noose a total of nine times. There was a deep-rooted superstition about the coils numbering thirteen to signify that a hangman's noose was an unlucky instrument for the one it was made for. Historically, thirteen coils did not make for a very good knot; in reality it made the knot unstable. Six to eight coils worked best when it came to insuring death. Symbolically, she decided to use nine coils since cats, like bad judges, only had nine lives and Judge Fullerton had used his up. Anyway, that was her opinion.

The free end was then poked through the loop at the top and cinched tight. Satisfied with her handiwork, she pulled the noose down over the judges' head being careful to place the knot behind his left ear, for that was the proper position for a hanging. For her, being as authentic as possible was important.

The final touch and tribute was still inside her tote bag. She removed it with care and held it out to admire. It was a piece of thin cardboard with a sheet of paper stabled to it. She leaned it up against the judges' chest and then stepped back to study the scene for overall effect. Typed in large bold face letters was this message: "Here sits The Hanging Judge; R.I.P.; Meow-meow."

Her immediate thoughts were about the impression the police and news media would have. Surely, they would have no problem figuring out everything, but the "meow" part. How long would it take them to associate the nine coils in the hangman's knot with the nine lives of a cat? Added to their problem was that cats are often associated with females. That should whittle their search down to half the population. Should they pick up on an older woman being the last person seen with the judge then they would have some difficulty with their search for a suspect. That's what her disguise was all about. Oh well, that would be their problem. Besides, the list of the judges' enemies would be enormous; accumulated over an entire career.

Next, she sanitized the scene. Every place she had been or touched was wiped clean. The three empty cartridges were deposited into the pocket of her windbreaker. Before she left the yacht, she switched off the heater. She couldn't help wonder how long it would be before the judges' body was discovered. That question would have to be solved by keeping an eye on the news channels. There was no way this would escape being a nation wide headline item. She had followed the instructions and improvised in her own way to demonstrate extreme prejudice. The noose and the sign would be the talk of the town.

After pulling the hood back up over her head, she made her way back out onto the dock. The wind was still blowing and had now reached gale force and the rain was still falling in sheets. In spite of the weather, it was a beautiful day for her. She was alone with her newly found freedom and on the cusp of a new life. Nothing could be better for her. Within fifteen minutes she was clear of the marina and clear of her old life- she left as a winner.

CHAPTER 21

Frank sat in his living room watching the morning news on his television. He could hear Matt's voice in the back of the house, most probably coming from the bedroom. Matt seemed to be doing a better job of staying in touch with Felicity. As for Charlie, Frank had only heard from her twice and the conversation was always labored and short. Obviously, she had a lot on her mind with the funeral and all. In due time, things should simmer down to some sense of normalcy.

At the same time the local morning news was wrapping up, Matt walked into the living room and announced; "I'm starved. Can we go somewhere and get a takeout breakfast? I'll pick up the tab this time."

"I have to warn you, the weather out there is awful cold and wet. Make sure you wear a jacket. After we pick up the food, we can go by the office and eat there. I have to check for phone and fax messages." Frank was always keenly aware that he was on the payroll when it came to Matt and the best place to justify the money he was getting paid was to have Matt involved in his case while at the office. Client involvement is just a good business practice.

Keeping a client in the right frame of mind was not always easy. Frank had to devote quite a bit of time to Matt in order to maintain his sense of calm. It seemed like he would have to reassure Matt at least twice a day. Frank wasn't sure how many different ways he could deliver the same message without sounding too redundant. Although, he was convinced that progress was being made.

The bad weather turned out to be a welcome distraction for both of them. They were both more concerned with their safety while driving in the storm than worrying about one of those two killers popping out of nowhere. Frank figured those two idiots would not risk something as foolhardy as making a run at them in the middle of a storm, especially in an unfamiliar city like Dallas. He did, however, wonder about where the killers were and what they were up to.

An hour later, they were safe and dry inside Frank's office. Matt had the coffee pot perking away without any urging from Frank. They gobbled their food as if they hadn't eaten in days.

Frank knew that time, and the patience to withstand it, would eventually bring about progress. Men in crisis were often reduced to being slaves to these concepts. Frank saw that Matt was having trouble adjusting to his wait-and-see predicament by the way he was pacing back and forth in front of Frank's desk.

Frank saw this behavior before so he understood what Matt was going through. He remembered being under that same spell, many times over, during his career. This was as good a time as any to engage Matt in some meaningful dialog.

"Matt, waiting is a critical part of the investigative process. The time we spend waiting for something to happen is not wasted time."

Matt's ears perked up with interest over Frank's words. "I feel like I'm not contributing anything toward moving my situation along."

Frank smiled at his distraught client to encourage him. "Patience is our way of grinding away at the center of our concerns. We're grinding away toward a resolution. Think of waiting in terms of baking a cake. In our situation, we are simply baking our case in the oven of everyday life. Like waiting on water to boil, we can't make our case heat up any faster by watching it and fretting over it. Everything comes about in its own time. Once things come to a boil, we'll have plenty to do. In the mean time, relax and rest up for the challenges that are waiting on us. There's a time for us to rush, but, it's not yet here. And when we rush, we have to do a calculated rush. We will have to be careful, prudent, and on the mark. Our time to act may not come in the matter of hours- it could take days."

Matt shook his head to indicate that he still had doubts about his case moving anywhere. "I don't know about all this. How are we going to know when this is all over? How do I know when it's safe to go home and that my wife will be safe?"

Matt's questions created an opportunity for Frank to apply some homegrown logic. "I don't like answering a question with a question, but, this is a good time to do just that. When someone in your ministry is troubled over something serious, don't you tell them to pray to God?"

"Yes. That's how we handle most crises in our lives."

"What do you tell them when they ask you how they will know that God has heard their prayers? I bet you have some hip pocket answers for such questions. I mean, isn't that part of your job as a minister; your calling to serve? Think about it, the longer you serve God, the more experience you gain in comforting and understanding people and their problems."

Matt was now fully focused and aware of Frank's insight. "You're right, I need to calm down and practice what I preach. Prayer is that common thread of handling any difficult situation just as it's a way of dealing with everyday life and its challenges. You're saying that having faith works for both ministering and investigating. Thanks for the lesson. I can see where we both carry out the dictates of our professions based on our experience and dedication."

"That's right, Matt, we are both experts in our own fields." With that comment, Frank stood up and walked past Matt. Staring out the office window, he changed the subject by commenting about the weather. "All this wind and rain is keeping us both on edge. I doubt if anything significant will happen on a day like this. All those involved are probably hunkering down to wait out the storm. By the way, what did Felicity have to say this morning?"

"Oh yes, I heard from her early this morning. She's on her way back here. Once the funeral was over, the girls sat down and had a nice long talk. I'm supposed to tell you that Beth and Charlie are also coming back today. I guess Charlie wants to have a private talk with you and then have a group meeting with everyone."

"That's interesting. I wonder what that's all about."

"I wish I could tell you, Frank, but, I have no idea what's brewing with any of the ladies. I got the impression that Charlie is holding her cards close and will play them when she's ready. I guess we have to resort to using our patience for this too."

The hands on the clock seemed to click by at a snail's pace. Both men were now having a problem with patience. Winning a race by waiting is a difficult concept to accept. Waiting can even be worse when one isn't sure what he is waiting for.

It was nearly 3:00 p.m. when the ladies arrived, each in their own vehicles. The rain had dissipated to a blowing mist and the accompanying chill made it feel colder than it really was. They filed into Frank's office with Charlie trailing behind the others. The women greeted the men with lingering hugs. Beth and Charlie each added a kiss on the cheek when it came to Frank. Matt and Felicity kissed with enhanced passion to celebrate the occasion.

Felicity spoke first. "I don't know about the rest of you, but I'm famished. I hate to suggest that we split up. However, I think Charlie and Frank need some time alone. Beth, why don't you join Matt and me for a late lunch so they can be alone?"

Beth sighed at the idea without revealing any insight as to why. She just followed Matt and Felicity out the door.

Frank had an uneasy feeling that he was about to have a stressful interaction with Charlie. Charlie took his hand and led him to the couch. She locked the office door before joining him.

Charlie looked Frank in the eye as she began to speak. "Frank, I made a promise to you that I would tell you about my past and what happened in Arizona. I'm going to keep that promise and I'm going to do it right now. This is not going to be easy for me so I need to have your understanding."

Frank was quick to react. "Charlie, you will find me very understanding. I think that once you get this off your chest you'll be able to move forward with your life and with me."

She thought about what he had just said and instantly knew that he was only partially right in his assessment. Deep inside her heart and mind, she was convinced that there was no escape from her memories, and in her case, the memories were of the worse kind.

"My career as a singer was moving along alright even though I was not headed for stardom. I was paying the bills and making a name for myself in Arizona. From time to time, I would do a gig in Yuma at a local country & western club. Oh, the patrons sometimes got a bit rowdy, but, there were enough people looking after me that I was never in any danger. Folks came in; listened to me sing, danced, and drank. Sure, they got drunk. Sometimes the alcohol added enough fuel to a situation for a fight to break out. The bouncers always did a good job of keeping things under control. That's just nightclub life."

Frank smiled at her description of the setting. "I've seen my share of bar fights and excessive drinking. I understand the scene you were working in."

"After performing a few times in that club, I was introduced to a guy by the name of Marty Collins. Marty was a disk jockey at a local radio station. We had a few good conversations after some of my gigs there. He wanted to know if I had any recordings that he could play on his radio show. You can only imagine how excited I was over the prospect of getting my work noticed by a radio audience. A performer moves up in the entertainment world with exposure."

249

Dan Morris

Frank had to agree with Charlie. "I would want the same thing if I was trying to advance a singing career. That is if I could sing." He laughed at his comment.

"Well, Marty and I never became close friends. Like many men that you find in the club setting, I caught him trying to peek down my blouse and watching my butt. You get use to that kind of stuff when you work in night clubs. Once we were sitting in a booth and he tried to rub the inside of my leg. I brushed him away and let him know that I had no romantic or sexual interest in him." Charlie was holding up well so far.

"I'm surprised you didn't slap his face." Frank was not about to let the incident slide without editorializing.

"I know that would have been the appropriate response from most women. However, I didn't want to be too quick to knock myself out of the local limelight. Looking back, I regret not putting an end to our association, right on the spot."

"Yes, Monday morning quarterbacking often makes smart critics out of the most inexperienced of us."

"For awhile after that, he stayed clear of me. That is until one Saturday night. Marty walked into the club while I was singing. He was strutting around like he owned the place. I guess he was a celebrity in his own right. Two men and two attractive women were tagging along with him. As usual, I was singing the best I could and when I finished there was a nice round of applause."

Visualizing the scene, Frank realized that Charlie still had some lingering pride when it came to being on stage. "That must be a good feeling, knowing that people appreciated your talent."

"Oh, entertainers live for recognition. Making money is important, but, knowing that people like your work is the most important thing. Anyway, let me get back to the story.

"During my break, Marty motioned me over to the table where they were all sitting. He made the introductions in a business like manner. One of the men was with a recording studio in California and he was there with his fiancé. You could imagine how I perked up with that little bit of information. I immediately sat down with them. I tried to ignore the fact that Marty was acting like he and I were an item. The last thing I wanted to do was cause a scene so I bit my tongue and let his lies about us being intimate pass.

"We had several drinks together, and before I knew it, I was feeling a little tipsy. After I sang my last song, I returned to the table and we drank until last call. The next thing I knew, we were moving the party to a local hotel suite. This is where things started to go horribly wrong."

Charlie paused for a few seconds as she began to struggle with what was coming.

Frank didn't have to be a trained investigator to recognize the situation that was developing. "Didn't you realize that you were getting in over your head?"

Charlie took a deep breath and then picked up where she had left off. "At this point, I thought I could handle Marty's advances as I had in the past. That was a big mistake. Look, Frank, all I had on my mind was gaining access to this guy that worked for a recording studio. Oh, I didn't come on to him. Besides, he was there with his fiancé. Everything I said to the man was courteous and of a business nature. I just wasn't prepared for the life style of these people. To say that they were morally loose was an understatement. Before I knew it, breasts were being exposed and hands were in places where they shouldn't be. Next, cocaine was on the table and things were getting really freaky. I may have been tipsy, but I wasn't up for what was taking place. I started to get scared."

Frank could hardly contain himself as he listened to Charlie's narration that was going full-throttle toward a disastrous conclusion. "By this time, you must have been ready to break and run."

"You bet I was. Marty was out of control. His hands were all over me. If he had any more hands he would have been an octopus. The other two couples were already in another room, and from the noise, I would say they were having an orgy. I was slapping the hell out of Marty and it wasn't even slowing him down. I couldn't fight too hard because I had too much to drink. I even tried kicking him between the legs and when that didn't work, I started to scream. The bastard slapped me with an open hand and then he punched me in the stomach. He knocked the wind out of me and that left me helpless. Before I knew it, he had my clothes off."

"Did any of the others come to see what Marty was doing to you?" Frank's voice was edging on anger at this point.

"They could have cared less about me. They were probably doing what they always did when they went to a party with their kind."

"Go on, Charlie, I didn't mean to interrupt you." He apologized.

"Before I knew it, Marty was on top of me. Frank, he was raping me and I couldn't stop him. I can still hear his grunting and smell his stinking breath. The man was an animal, a crazed and vicious animal, and I never felt this helpless in my entire life."

Frank sat there wringing his hands wishing he had been there. He would have surely killed Marty. Frank knew that rape was a vicious crime that had more to do with control than it did with sex. The emotional imprint on Charlie had obvious after-effects. Her current emotional state reflected the horror involved with the attack.

"I can't believe the others let this go as far as it did. They have to feel some responsibility for what happened to you." Frank was trying to make some sense out of what Charlie had gone through.

"One of the women did come out of the other room. The woman's name, as I recall, was Maxine. She was older than the other woman and had a deeper voice. She started laughing, can you imagine that? At first, she didn't speak to me, only to Marty. She told him, 'I see you finally have that little slut under control. My, she looks tired. You must have worn her out.' Then she spoke to me. She said, 'Hey, sweetie, relax and enjoy it.' Frank, I'm no little slut. If there were any sluts in that hotel suite, it was those other two women." Charlie began to sob. Her dark memory of that night was still very much alive and haunting her.

"It sounds like this Maxine was nothing less than a lust-filled Trojan horse working in concert with the men. In my opinion, she's an accessory to the act. That's the way I see it." Frank had a way of looking at things from a legal standpoint. "What happened next? I mean how did you get out of there?"

"No one tried to stop me. I just walked right out the door. Marty didn't seem to care one way or the other that I was leaving. After all, he got what he wanted. Next thing I knew, I was walking along a dimly lit street. My clothing was twisted and wrinkled and my hair was a tangled mess. I was so traumatized that I must have looked like a zombie or some stoned girl from the barrio. All sweaty and smelling of alcohol, I stumbled along. The street lights were spinning around like I was on some carnival ride." She was sobbing again, fighting for control and strength enough to continue her story.

Frank concluded that to an unknowing eye, Charlie must have appeared to be some disgusting wench that had partied too hard. Appearances are often deceiving and likely to prejudice an evaluation. So many times, appearances provide false impressions, even to a trained eye.

"Where did you end up going?" He knew things were not going to go smoothly.

"The local police drove up. They were not there to rescue me. Before I knew what was happening, two officers had me leaning up against their squad car, searching me for weapons and making wise cracks. I was too traumatized to be humiliated. I only wanted to be safe.

"Even though I was incoherent, I did my best to explain what had happened. I must have gotten through to some extent, because when they got me to the police station, there was a detective waiting to hear my story. He was courteous, but not quick to give any merit to my story. He grilled me on every detail like I was some criminal instead of a victim. This lasted for two hours and I must have been somewhat convincing because he had me taken to the local hospital for an exam. In the meantime, he went to the hotel with a uniformed officer to check out my story. I was admitted to the hospital for treatment and observation. A nurse gave me a sedative and I was out until mid-morning the next day."

Frank held her hand. "At least you were safe and being cared for."

"That's a matter of opinion." She fired back angrily. "Things didn't turn out the way I had expected. At lunch time, the detective came to my room in the hospital with a doctor. The detective had an extra day's growth of beard on his face and dark circles under his eyes. They were whispering among themselves while looking over some papers on a clipboard. When the detective saw that I was looking at them, he walked over to me and sat down in a chair next to my bed. He was obviously troubled by something and I knew it wasn't in my favor."

Frank knew that the scenario Charlie was relating to him was one that was often replayed during sexual assault cases across the country. "What did the detective have to say about your attack?"

"He told me that he had taken statements from everyone except Marty Collins. Marty's lawyer was there within half an hour and he wouldn't allow him to answer any questions."

"What about the other four; the two couples that had been in the suite when you were assaulted, what did they have to say?" Frank knew the story was not going to play out in Charlie's favor.

"What I am going to tell you now will explain my distain for the justice system. Maybe I should say the 'injustice' system. I've been told that every criminal can have his day in court. This is not true for victims. The detective told me that all four witnesses swore that the sexual exchange between me and Marty was consensual. They said that I had been all over Marty during the night. Essentially, they turned the facts upside down. They said that when I couldn't get some kind of a commitment from the guys for boosting my career, that I charged off ranting about getting even with Marty.

"I begged the detective to put those people on a lie detector and prove that they were lying for Marty. Frank, the detective told me that the prosecutor refused to take the case. He made it sound like I was the criminal and not Marty. I was brutally raped and had no recourse." Charlie was now crying uncontrollably.

Frank saw it coming. There was the word of five people against one. The law consists of written words and those words can't always guarantee that justice will be done. We are a nation of laws and the system works well, but not always perfectly. Still, Frank knew that the United States had the best legal system on the planet. Compared to other systems, the accused in this country have more rights. Our laws were written with the belief that it is better that ten guilty people should go free before one innocent person was convicted. Oh, without a doubt, our country has had bad laws on the books. Once they are realized, they are usually weeded out, either by legislation or through appeal courts. There was no way to adequately explain this concept to Charlie. As good as our system of law is; it is not foolproof. She had been wronged and no words would set things right.

"Charlie, I can't imagine the depth of your disappointment at that moment. You must have been devastated."

"I lost it Frank. I went over the edge. It was like my whole heart and soul had been ripped right out of my body. I screamed until I was hoarse and I cried until I was out of tears. That asshole, Marty, got away with raping me and there was nothing I could do about it. I never felt so helpless and alone in my life.

"The members of the band I had been with picked me up from the hospital and took me to another hospital in Phoenix. I ended up on a psychiatric ward for evaluation. The band members never came to visit me, not once. I can't blame them. They had to continue to earn a living so they probably found another female vocalist with a nice figure to take my place. I'm sure they also felt as though I had betrayed them for my own selfish reasons. Think about that for a minute. What if I had ended up with my own individual recording contract? I would have had to move on without them. I didn't only screw up my own life; I screwed theirs' up, too. By this time I was carrying around a lot of guilt; more than I could handle."

"What did you do? How did you get out of the psychiatric ward?"

"They let me make a call back home. I called my dad and told him where I was. He was there by the end of the next day. Daddy has always been my rock; my anchor. There are not enough words in my vocabulary to describe the love between Daddy and me. I wish you could have known him."

"Didn't you tell me that he had been a deputy sheriff? How did he handle what you had been through?"

"Daddy sat next to me and cried. Then I saw anger in his eyes. It was a raw anger that I had never seen in him before. It's strange, but

I wanted him to be just as angry as I was. I was glad to see him there, sharing my rage and my disdain for the judicial system. I swear that I saw him snarl like a dog gone mad. He sat there, breathing heavy for awhile. I could only imagine what was going through his mind. After dinner, he excused himself and told me that he had some business to attend to. I thought he was working on getting me released so he could take me home. Unfortunately, that would end up taking more than a week to get done."

"Where did your father go and what did he do?" There was no telling what an angry father was capable of doing.

"Daddy was gone for nearly three days. I was beginning to think he was going to desert me. Worse yet, maybe something bad had happened to him. My nerves were shot and I couldn't eat. I was going down hill. Then, there he was, standing in the doorway of my room. He had a haggard look about him and it looked like he had slept in his clothes.

"I started to get up out of bed to hug him and ended up getting tangled in an IV line. He untangled the line and sat down in the chair next to my bed. He had a folded newspaper tucked under his arm. I asked him what he had been up to and he just handed the newspaper to me. The newspaper was from Yuma. The headlines read: Local DJ found murdered. The article went on to report that some boaters had found the body of Marty Collins, a local radio DJ, along the water's edge at Senator's Wash in Imperial County, California. The exact cause of death was pending an autopsy report, but, deputies at the scene suspect his death was caused by a single gunshot to the head from a high caliber pistol. At this time, there were no suspects.

"I looked over at Daddy and I guess my eyes did the asking because he told me that justice had been served. We never spoke of it again. He took me back home to the ranch and that's where I have been until I ventured out to visit Beth. You can fill in the blanks anyway you want, Frank. Daddy's gone now so there's nothing anyone can do to him, especially the justice system."

Frank sat quietly and processed Charlie's story. An assortment of thoughts was swirling around in his head. Revenge was not always sweet like many people thought; it's cold and hard and rarely provides the slightest illusion of closure, let alone satisfaction. On a personal level, he felt that no evil deed should go unpunished just because the law lacked the capacity for justice. What does all this have to do with Charlie's story? Well, it has plenty to do with the destruction of a young girl's life. An innocent girl's life had been ruined, scarred forever. Frank couldn't help but wonder if there had been times when Charlie would have preferred death to remembering that part of her life. He even understood why she never sang again. Her beautiful voice had taken her on a journey, a dark one.

"Where do you and I go from here, Charlie?' His question was pointed.

"That's a fair question and you have every right to put me on the spot. I'm not only emotionally scarred, Frank. I may be damaged beyond repair. Truthfully, at this point in my life, I'm not capable of being intimate with any man. Somewhere down the road that may change. If it does change, it will be a long, long way down the road. Hell, it may never change and that wouldn't be fair for you. I treasure your friendship more than you could ever imagine. In my own way, I love you. Because I love you, I have to say we should never try to be intimate. You have taught me a lot and you have demonstrated that you care about me and I appreciate that. I believe we work well as a team. I like all this investigating stuff. Please, don't trap yourself by keeping the embers of your love for me burning when there is little chance of it going anywhere. I have some other things to announce when the others return and that should add some clarity to all this. As for you and I, we are no longer boyfriend and girlfriend- we're friends and that's all."

Frank was hurt and disappointed, that was for sure. He had fallen for Charlie way too fast and too hard. He had no one to blame for that but himself. He was well aware that the most coveted treasure a person could have was love. The most disappointing part of his life was that each time he felt he had love within his grasp, it somehow slipped away. If he couldn't have love, then he would have to settle for intervals of happiness and be thankful that he had that.

When it came to him and sex, the oddest comparison crossed his mind. Metaphorically, he was like a porcupine. It must be a difficult challenge for them to have sex. Like a porcupine, making love for him had too many challenges and it always seemed to be an awful painful pursuit. That must be why people didn't see a lot of baby porcupines running around. Most people would like to believe that they are at least like other people, but how does a guy know what the standards of normality are. He at least knew he was a survivor and that he would weather this emotional storm like the other ones in his life.

"You make a hard case, Charlie. At least you're allowing me to have some part to play in your life. I think we can say that we are better people for having known each other. Don't worry, sweetheart, I'll keep your story to myself. I'm loyal to my friends and I consider you to be one of the best ones I have. I hope we can continue to work many more cases

The Order

together." Frank meant what he had said because he was not one to go back on his word.

"There's one more thing, Frank. You are not the only one I have confessed my story to. I also confided in Beth. I should have had this talk with her years ago. You could say I have been piling one mistake upon another for way too many years. This is my week to begin lightening my burdens. I feel like an alcoholic on some twelve-step program." She stood up and walked over to Frank's desk for a tissue. Her eyes were red from crying. Crying is one of the things that can occur when a person submits to reality and change.

"I don't suppose you have a fresh pot of java or a Pepsi around do you? I need a little pick-me-up before the others get back."

"I sure do Charlie. Your voice is getting a bit raspy so I suggest a cup of hot coffee instead of Pepsi."

"Thank you." She sat back down and let Frank wait on her. She was getting tired. The day had been long and trying.

Frank saw no advantage or purpose to press Charlie about anything she had said. The only thing he could accomplish by challenging her would be to damage their friendship and that was one thing that he always valued from others. She had taken a stand and what was done was done. Besides, women have something in them that makes them rise above men's objections when it comes to matters of the heart.

The next half hour passed with a slow awkwardness. Frank wanted the others to return so he could hear the rest of Charlie's story. Charlie also wanted them to return so she could bring things to a close- two separate and distinct reasons for waiting. Finally, they both had their goal in sight.

Matt held the door for Beth and Felicity to enter Frank's office. Charlie smiled at them and then took a long drink of coffee. She admitted to herself that she felt somewhat guilty for placing her problems ahead of Matt's and Felicity's. After all, they were the clients and they were paying to have their situation dealt with. For her, guilt was beginning to take its toll on her. The next few minutes held new challenges for her.

She hoped that she would not come across to them as some camp counselor making an announcement about canceling an activity that everyone had been looking forward to.

"Okay, everyone, I need to get this over so all of you can get back to addressing your own situation. First, I want to say something special to Felicity because I know she has been waiting on me for an answer to her offer. In the short time that I have known her, she has clearly demonstrated her talent as a gifted medium." Charlie was now looking directly at Felicity. "In all my life, I have not met such a remarkable woman who is so dedicated to such a spiritual calling. I mean that; you are one in a million. I truly appreciate the confidence you have in me and for your desire to have me join the ranks of professional mediums. I have to confess that for most of my life I never had a sense for Spiritualism, especially something that is on par with your abilities. You have sparked my interest, but, the timing is off. I'll gladly meet with you whenever I have the time. However, at this time, I can't devote my life to learning and honing my skills in Spiritualism. Don't worry, I'll stay in touch and meet with you whenever it's convenient for both of us."

The level of disappointment in Felicity's eyes was noticeably apparent to everyone. She squinted, then frowned, and reluctantly projected a somberness that bordered on defeat. As expected, she bounced back quickly by not closing the door for future spiritual work with Charlie.

"I understand that you have been through a great deal, lately. My offer is a standing one and I look forward to working with you whenever I can. There's no denying that you're a special woman with a special gift. Just remember, I'm only a phone call away." Felicity had been keenly aware that Charlie may not accept her offer. At least she had given it her best effort.

"Thank you. I appreciate your understanding. Now, I want to let everyone know what will be on my plate for the immediate future. I have decided to keep the ranch and work it. The ranch has been my home and sanctuary for as long as I can remember. Some of my best memories are there and I intend to create more good memories there. Ranch work is not easy and it's something I can't do alone." She looked over at Beth and smiled. "Beth is not only my cousin, she's my best friend; she's what's left of my family. We have quite a bit in common. We both left home in search of Shangri-La; our hidden mystical paradise. After all these years, we have realized that we had actually left our personal Shangri-La when we left home. This is about as profound as I can get considering that I'm only a country gal. Like so many fairytales, ours has a good ending. Beth is quitting her job as a bartender here in Dallas and is joining me to work the ranch. Life in the big city has been a part of our journey, but it was not the destination we were searching for. As for everyone in this room, you have all been among the bright spots we encountered as we passed through. In more ways that you can fathom, you have all enriched our lives and for that we give you our eternal gratitude. God bless each and every one of you."

Matt was the one who spoke for the group. "You are a blessed and remarkable woman, Charlie. I think that I'm speaking for everyone when

I say that you have also enriched out lives. Your parting words have delivered a good message to us. I believe in miracles. Whenever a person finds their way in this crazy, topsy-turvy world; it's a miracle. I'll keep you in my prayers; that's a promise."

Charlie's meeting ended in a round of hugs, kisses, and best wishes. There must be something to that old adage that for every door that is closed, another is opened.

Once Charlie and Beth were gone to take care of Beth's departure, it was time for Frank to pay attention to Matt and Felicity. They asked to go home and spend the night there. Frank was not in favor of letting them go. After some debate, he finally agreed with the condition that he would go with them and check out their home for any breach of security, to include signs of entry and tampering. He could tell that they were worn out, both physically and emotionally. They wanted their lives to return to some degree of normalcy and that was understandable. He reminded them that the two hired assassins could possibly still be in the area targeting them. At least the weather was improving by leaps and bounds.

CHAPTER 22

After ensuring Matt and Felicity's home was secure and there were no signs of tampering, Frank returned to his office. He was still nervous over them being home alone so he made two follow-up phone calls to check on them. The last one was at 11:00 p.m. He was glad to hear that Matt had made arrangements with the local police department for his home to be checked during the night under the premise that he had seen a prowler near his house. The home was also equipped with a burglar alarm and Frank agreed to keep his cell phone on even while it was being charged.

The weight of Charlie's story and announcements were weighing heavy on Frank's mind. Sleep was not about to come easy for him on this night. Each time he started to fall asleep, snatches of isolated words would drive him wide awake. The words followed no logical order and they never seemed to complete any specific thought. The words came at him like a scattering of pellets from a shotgun blast. The words that kept popping up included: flashback; denial; self-blame; isolated; betrayed; bewildered; and depressed. Somehow, they had all become a part of his life. They were all linked, in one way or another, to the disappointments he had faced each time love seemed to be within his grasp. Like any leader worth his salt, he had to take responsibility for the failures in his life, to include lost loves. Although, love rarely followed any logical sequence and it certainly was not a science.

He always seemed to be making others feel safe and secure while never being able to do the same for him. Surely, the depression he was sinking into had something to do with the way he had always lived his life; always on the edge and unconventionally. The nature of his business was taking its toll on him. Although his life was often filled with excitement, it was also a grueling one. His career choices were leaving a harsh imprint on his heart and soul. His personal life was hedging on being a disaster. There was always one redeeming value, though; his work had always been necessary and meaningful to those he had served. He was forever serving some thing or some one and rarely serving himself. Like other military personnel, he had served his country well, time and time again. He never wanted medals or flowery accolades for his service; all these things failed in comparison to the love of a woman. Now, Charlie was the latest of his failures. He thought of that old Elvis song: "Only Fools Rush In." A person's resolve to cultivate the love of a soul mate was nothing like charging a hill to take it from the enemy. Yes, the only living creature that would warm his bed tonight was his lovable fur ball of a cat, Leo. That had to count for something.

Tossing and turning brought no comfort and contributed nothing to securing any answers. The last time he noticed the time, it was shortly after 1:00 a.m. Not long after that, his mind gave into the needs of his body and he fell into a deep, restful sleep.

Thankfully, he woke up rested and in much better spirits. He looked forward to moving this case along to some acceptable resolution. He skipped watching the local morning news on television, anxious to get to work where he could analyze and hopefully come up with a workable strategy.

Driving to work was a pleasure compared to the day before. Only in Texas could changes in the weather be so dramatic. It was an ideal winter day for North Texas with a light blue sky, flecked with little fleecy white clouds drifting along from the north. The morning sun was shinning brightly even though there was an exhilarating nip in the air. Everything was so energizing and that gave promise for a productive day. It was funny how the weather impacted one's life and mood.

Frank swung into the parking lot at his office just as Felicity was backing out of a parking space. When she saw Frank, she pulled back into her space. She was alone and that made Frank wonder where Matt might be.

"Good morning, Felicity." Frank called out with all the enthusiasm of a reinvigorated and optimistic man.

"And a good morning to you too, Frank." She sounded extraordinarily chipper for a distressed client.

"Come on inside, Felicity and let me put on a fresh pot of coffee."

"I would have to say that we both got a good night's sleep." Her words slipped from her tongue like those of a weary traveler that had recovered from a long trip.

Frank had the coffee perking in no time. "What brings you here so early in the morning?"

"Oh, you can call it intuition or you can call it a woman's prerogative. I only wanted to chat with you about yesterday afternoon."

Instantly, Frank knew Felicity's visit had something to do with Charlie's meeting and pronouncements concerning her future. "Here, I'll let you fix your own coffee." He was already stirring his. "Yes, I think Charlie caught us all off guard. I don't think I will ever understand a woman's mind. Whenever I think I have one figured out, I get blindsided. What's your take on Charlie?"

"Even though I'm a woman, I learned a long time ago that each one of us is cast in a different mold. When it comes to men and women, and how they relate to one another, the only thing I can say for certain is that when a man thinks he is falling into a woman's loving arms, he may, instead, wind up falling into her hands. Men tend to be too quick to turn themselves into putty for a woman to either mold or discard. Sometimes, women aren't even aware of what they are doing. What I trying to say, is that men tend to lack patience when it comes to women." Felicity was not sure she was getting her point across.

"Tell me, Felicity, what did happen yesterday?"

"When Charlie was delivering her speech, I could read hurt and disappointment on your face. If you would have taken your eyes off of her and looked over at me, you would have read similar emotions on my face; although for different reasons. You see, I had offered Charlie a chance to work with me in my spiritual pursuits. I even invited her to come live with me and Matt. That's one of the reasons I went to see her in Childress. She has a natural gift when it comes to after death communication and I didn't want to see her throw it away. On a spiritual level, she has the capacity and ability to do so much for others. Unfortunately and like you, I didn't see this change coming over her. Truthfully, I doubt that either one of us will see much of her in the future. I'm fine with that if ranching is what she really wants to do. On a deeper level, though, I believe there is more to her choice than meets the eye. Since you had a private meeting with her, you probably know more about what's driving her decision. I only want to be sure that we are all at peace with the way things have turned out. Also, I don't want you to be too hard on yourself. You didn't cause her change of heart. Everything happens for a reason. There's nothing for us to judge here. Do you understand what I'm trying to say?" She inhaled deeply while waiting on Frank to respond.

"When it comes to women, I'm as clueless as a hog looking at a Rolex watch. As far as gender is concerned, I don't know how much it has to do with her decision. To be perfectly honest with you, I think Charlie and I are two vulnerable people wanting to fill some sort of void in hour lives. Obviously, each of our vulnerabilities was created for vastly different reasons. She can't overcome what's behind hers and I'm not sure I'm ready to come to grips with mine. I'd like to think that I'm farther along in the process than she is, though. Anyway, I'm not about to sit and dwell on it when I have other things nipping at my heels." He turned away from Felicity to end the topic.

"Exactly what is the next step for Matt and me?"

Her question reminded him of the conversations he had with Matt the day before. "I'm going to review the entire case and compare my findings with Walter's file. There may be some link or hidden theory that I've overlooked. Outside of that, we all need to exercise a combination of patience and caution. This thing is not over yet, not by a long shot. We can't bet on these hired killers giving up that easily. This secret order is like a frightened snake; it's either going to slither away out of sight or it's going to strike at us again. As far as what our plans are, it's still too early to say."

He had stated his position and given his warning. Now, he wanted to get a feel for how Felicity and Matt were holding up. With Charlie bailing out, their ranks were reduced by one; by one fourth of their total force. "What's on Matt's plate today?"

"Matt is meeting with some of his parishioners this morning. He is anxious to get back into the pulpit and attend to people's spiritual needs. He's a man with a compelling faith. Like him, I want my life back."

Frank knew only well that when a person's enemy was out of sight for awhile there was a tendency to become lax and complacent- complacency was a deadly trap for the unaware. Frank gave a parting instruction to Felicity.

"Please, keep me informed of your whereabouts and stay vigilant. Likewise, I will keep you posted on what I'm coming up with. My gut is telling me that we're on the final stretch. Trust me, this case is about to come to an end and I want a happy ending for all of us."

Felicity hugged him and as she headed for the door she spoke confidently. "Don't worry, you're still in charge. Matt and I trust you and we realize that you're the expert in this business." She was out the door before he could respond.

Frank spent the better part of the next hour at the copier. Backup files had saved his butt in the past and this case was too important to take any chances. When he felt comfortable that he had taken care of the administrative part, he sat down to relax for a moment.

Soon he began to regret taking a break because the inactivity allowed his mind to once again wonder about sensitive aspects of his life. His office looked barren and that seemed to match his life. He was alone in an environment of his own choosing. There was no other human around to share his life with. All he had was a cat.

A sense of self pity was beginning to consume him. He couldn't help but think that his sadness was based on him recognizing his own failures when it came to having a mate to share his life with. The closest thing he had when it came to friends was some people he had met at a local bar. All the bar was accomplishing for him was providing a way of passing some idle time. What was the quality of such friendships? Throughout his entire life, friends seemed to come and go. No one, man or woman, was a failure if they had friends. Where were all the real, close friends in his life? Why was he asking himself questions that he could not answer? Figuring out his own life had to be his biggest mystery of all for him to solve.

Charlie! Charlie! Charlie! Why couldn't he get her off his mind? She could have married him if she had truly wanted to. Instead, she chose to marry her family's ranch. Oh well, he had chosen to marry the world of investigations over pursuing a human relationship. Like Charlie, he was serving a master that only lived in his mind. They were both married to a way of life instead of a real person. A career is intangible and not something capable of returning love. Frank had to ask himself why he was making his career the center of his life instead of a real person. All his personal concerns were like ping pong balls bouncing off the walls in his office; there was no telling where they would end up.

In Charlie's case, could it be as simple as her only wanting to keep the memories of her father's love alive? Did she really think that she could rekindle the lingering memories of her childhood by working the ranch with her cousin, Beth? That had to be the case for her. He hoped things would work out for her.

Frank wondered about himself. What memories was he trying to keep alive? Maybe he wasn't trying to keep any alive. What if he was trying to avoid the early years of his life by focusing on work? How could he solve a major investigation and not be able to figure out his own life? Would the questions ever quit mounting and bearing down on him?

All these questions were beginning to overwhelm him to the point that his surroundings had unconsciously been reduced to a blur. With his mind in such an un-alert state, he hadn't noticed the man that had entered his office and was now approaching his desk. He was wearing a dark suit and carrying a briefcase and his sudden presence startled Frank.

"I take it that you are Frank McLaughlin, the private investigator?" The man's tone was in no way cordial; in fact it was extremely business-like; even officious.

Before answering the stranger, Frank took a few seconds to study him. Experience had taught Frank to watch a man's eyes and hands when he was summing him up for the first time. "Yes I'm Frank McLaughlin. What can I do for you?" Frank matched the stranger's manner.

When the stranger reached inside his coat Frank remembered that he had placed his pistol into his desk drawer. He pulled the drawer open far enough to place his hand over his Taurus. The stranger was quick to respond when he saw Frank's move. "Don't get excited. I'm only reaching for my identification." He removed a black leather credential holder and offered it to Frank for examination.

"You'll have to excuse me. Things have been a little tense around here, lately." Frank examined the man's identification. The photo matched the man's appearance. "What can I do for the FBI, Special Agent Adler?" Frank already suspected that the visit had something to do with Matt and Felicity's case. Surely, the FBI was not interested in some innocuous insurance case.

"By any chance have you seen the news this morning or read the newspaper?" Special Agent Adler had a slight nervous twitch in the corner of his mouth when he spoke.

"I've been too busy with paperwork this morning to catch the news. Is there something going on that I should be aware of?" Frank was already regretting not watching the morning news before leaving home.

"If you don't mind, Mr. McLaughlin, I have a copy of the morning paper here in my briefcase. I think you should take a look at the headline on the front page." Special Agent Adler slid the newspaper across the desk at Frank before sitting down in a chair.

Frank was overtaken with shock when he saw the photograph and read the large print of the headline. "Local Judge Found Slain!" The photograph was unmistakably that of Judge Fullerton. Frank sank back into his chair and read the account without any interruption from Special Agent Adler.

Frank did his best not to display any outward emotion as he read and digested the sketchy details that the police had released to news reporters. Inwardly, his emotions were much more pronounced. He knew that his reactions had to be cool and calm even though he was fighting for distance from the dark cloud that was beginning to brood over him. Hopefully, he had not projected any lack of composure for his visitor to pick up on.

"I never met the man personally." Frank blurted out as he slid the newspaper back over to Special Agent Adler. "I hear that the judge was a rather unconventional jurist and was always stirring things up. It looks to me like he acquired one enemy too many."

"I'm going to digress here for a minute and work my way up to the purpose of my visit. I'm not a local FBI agent. I work out of our Houston office. There was an investigative journalist murdered in Houston and that case has been linked to one that is being worked out of our headquarters back in D.C. One of our masterminds back at headquarters came up with a conspiracy theory that has tied together several personalities, including Judge Fullerton. I'm not going to tell you how I came by my information, but suffice it to say, I do have information that you are involved in our case and that our case has something to do with Judge Fullerton and possibly his death. That's why I'm here; I'm following up a lead. Are you beginning to understand the importance of my visit?" Special Agent Adler's eyes were drilling deep into Frank's eyes; searching for a reaction.

Frank listened intently to Special Agent Adler. However, he wasn't buying in to what was being said. Twice he had seen that nervous twitch in Special Agent Adler's mouth when trying to make a point. Frank was beginning to suspect that something was not right. This morning's newspaper was reporting the murder of a judge and already the FBI was here, in Frank's office, all the way from Houston, trying to connect dots that shouldn't even be apparent, yet.

"What is it that you want from me?" Frank asked his question more to evaluate Special Agent Adler than to see how he could assist the FBI with their investigation.

"I'm glad to see that you're willing to help out. I'm going to get right to the point so we aren't wasting each other's time. You either have in your possession or know the whereabouts of a file that is crucial to our investigation. You can either hand that file over to me voluntarily or I can have a search warrant delivered here within the hour. Trust me; you don't want to end up being on the wrong side of this investigation." The message was more of a threat than it was advice.

Frank's instincts told him that only he, his clients, and members of The Order knew about the existence of that file. Maybe the two hired killers had bungled their efforts to get the file and Special Agent Adler, or whoever he was, had now acquired that task. There was no use in calling the man's bluff by telling him to get the search warrant. Instead, Frank would do some sparing to see how organized Special Agent Adler was. There went that nervous twitch again.

"Before we go any farther with this, I need a couple of things from you, Special Agent Adler." Frank knew he was getting to Adler because he was beginning another nervous habit; two of the fingers on his right hand were unconsciously tapping his leg.

"What do you want?"

"Why, I want to check you out. That's all. I want one of your business cards and I want a copy of your driver license to compare with your FBI credentials. I think that's a reasonable request since you don't want to waste any more time than you have to."

"I don't see any harm in you being cautious." Special Agent Adler was eager to provide what was asked of him; too easy for an experienced federal agent.

Frank knew that no agent worth his salt would ever allow a witness or suspect to see his driver license and divulge his home address, unless they were false. Obviously, Adler had taken the time to backstop his bona fides.

After making copies, Frank placed a phone call to the number on Adler's business card. The woman that answered the phone sounded awkward as if she was reading from a script. She confirmed that there was indeed a Special Agent Adler assigned to the Houston FBI office and that he was out of town on an assignment. She did not offer to put Frank through to Adler's phone to leave a message or to turn him over to another agent. This was all wrong and it certainly was not proper protocol.

Next, it was time for Frank to do a little acting. "Well, it appears that you are who you say you are, Special Agent Adler." Frank saw the anxiousness disappear from his visitor's face. Each man pretended to take the bait offered by the other.

Frank walked over to his file cabinet and retrieved a folder. "I'm afraid you're going to be disappointed with this file. It's a copy of a copy and only amounts to circumstantial references to Judge Fullerton being part of some outlandish conspiracy to overthrow the government. Any normal person would only see it as fodder to feed some comic book series or one of those supermarket tabloids. There's no telling who wrote it since it isn't signed. I'm sorry you wasted your time by coming here for it." Frank handed the folder to Special Agent Adler. "Here, you can have it. It's of no use to me or to my client. It's nothing but rubbish for some whacked out conspiracy theorist to play with." He laughed as he returned to his desk.

"You can tell your client to relax, Mr. McLaughlin. We get these things all the time and all they do is keep us from doing real work. We'll give it a good going over only because Judge Fullerton has been murdered and there will be pressure for us to do something. I appreciate your time and cooperation. Also, I have to insist that you don't discuss this matter with anyone." Special Agent Adler stuffed the folder into his briefcase and stood up.

Frank watched Special Agent Adler as he walked out the door and crossed the parking lot to his car. He couldn't imagine the FBI sending even a rookie agent all the way from Houston to accomplish such a trivial task. The man didn't even ask to interview the client, let alone ask who the client was. The whole thing was a half-baked scheme to get their hands on the file so The Order could do an assessment and some damage control. At least the guy who was pretending to be a FBI Special Agent was better than the two imbeciles that came before.

Frank could think of a hundred questions, but none of them really mattered. Once The Order examined the file, they would have to conclude that their organization had not been breeched and none of their identities had been compromised. Giving up an inept file was a small consolation for acquiring freedom for Matt and Felicity.

Frank left the office and headed out for a bite of lunch. Later, he would meet with Matt and Felicity to go over what had taken place in his office. Walter was dead so he couldn't corroborate any details. The file was useless without an author or anyone to reflect on it. All the ugliness of The Order had been focused on Judge Fullerton and now he had been murdered. There was only one thing left for The Order to look at. Their Dallas cell had been damaged and left fragmented and Matt was part of that. There had been too much killing already. Things needed to be left alone to simmer and finally die.

After lunch Frank would follow up on his theory about Special Agent Adler. In the mean time, a hot lunch was in order. He settled for Chinese takeout followed by a quick stop at a convenience store for more Pepsi. His craving for Pepsi was something that was easier to satisfy than his craving for a woman's love.

Following lunch at his desk, he slipped into one of his power naps. When he awoke, he noticed that the sun had taken a new position; one to the west. He looked at his watch and decided that enough time had lapsed for him to make a confirmation call.

He picked up Special Agent Adler's business card and punched in the numbers just as he had done earlier in the day. At the beginning of the third ring a recording came on the line. "You have reached a number that is no longer in service. Please consult your directory or the operator for assistance."

This was exactly the response he knew he would get. The man who had posed as Special Agent Adler of the Houston office of the FBI had already shut down the phone number he had set up to backstop any inquiries concerning him and his role. On numerous occasions when Frank was working counterintelligence in the Army, he had used the same technique. It was simple and effective for confirming a cover story. Now, he could call Matt and Felicity for a meeting.

Confident that he had handled the case skillfully in his client's favor, he knew it wouldn't be long until it had run its course. While reaching for his phone, it suddenly began ringing. On the other end of the line was a very excited Matt. He was nearly babbling as he tried to inform Frank that Judge Fullerton had been found murdered. His sentences were broken and verged on being incoherent.

"Calm down, Matt. I know about the murder and things aren't as bad as you think. I want you and Felicity to come to my office immediately so I can fill you in. You are going to be surprised at everything that has been going on." Frank was using his best effort and tone to calm Matt. Matt agreed that he and Felicity would be at the office within thirty minutes. The time provided Frank an opportunity to do some administrative work.

Frank initially had trouble concentrating. He walked around his desk about a dozen times while occasionally glancing out the window. His best efforts were given to putting his thoughts together. Finally, he returned to his computer where he stared at the screen in search of inspiration. He had to be careful when writing up the case notes because there was no telling who might end up reading them someday.

He studied, typed, read, and reread until he was satisfied with the product he had created. After thirty-five minutes had passed, he was relieved to see Matt and Felicity walking through the door. Matt was noticeably nervous. Felicity, on the other hand, was uncharacteristically worse for wear. Her voice was scratchy and her eyes were puffy and red.

"I'm sorry we're late, Frank. Matt and I are terribly unnerved over the judges' murder. We drove in circles and took detours to see if we were being followed. What kind of news do you have for us?" Her question was forced and her tone glared with panic.

Frank smiled at them reassuringly as if everything was fine. They both looked at him with anticipation while their silence grew heavier by the second. "I had a visitor today. The man said he was a Special Agent with the FBI. I can tell you unequivocally that he was not from the FBI. My assessment is that he was a representative or intermediary for The Order. I think that I told you before, that at sometime, The Order would have to reach out to one of us in search of information. I bet you can't guess what this guy wanted from me?"

"I don't get it, Frank. How did he know to come to you?"

"That's a good question. He opened his conversation with me by showing me a copy of the morning newspaper with the headline on Judge Fullerton's murder. He didn't even ask me who my client was. All he wanted was the file that we have been trying to unravel. Now, how did he know about me and the file unless he was privy to what those two goons were up to? He's not from the FBI. He's on the other side of this issue. The Order has to know what we know and they have to know if that information can come back to haunt them."

Matt pressed for information. "What did you say to this guy?"

Frank laughed. "I told him that the file was useless and then I gave it to him."

"Do you think that was wise?" Matt was wearing a baffled look. "I mean, I thought we needed that file as our bargaining chip."

"Oh, I believe I played that chip in your favor. After all, this settles our problem of finding a way for the file to end up in the hands of The Order. When they see how useless it is, they will drop their efforts to go after you. By now, they think they have tricked us out of the file without leaving any trail back to them. Doing it this way makes us the tricksters."

"I hope it's that simple, Frank." Matt was second guessing Frank's logic.

"At this point, everything we do is a game. All games have an element of risk to them. If our strategy was to hold on to the file, do you think they would have come to us and announced that they were from The Order and that they needed to have a look at the file? The way it stands now, they think they have 'one up' on us. However, it would be nice if we had one more sign from The Order to let us know that the game is over as far as you are concerned."

"What do we do next?" Felicity decided to engage Frank.

Frank was searching for some reassuring words when suddenly Matt's cell phone rang. Matt turned away from the conversation and took the call when he recognized the caller. The call was short in duration.

"I don't know what to make of that piece of news." Matt volunteered.

Frank and Felicity were both anxious to learn what the phone call was about since there was no sign of clarity in Matt's demeanor.

Frank leaned back in his chair and took a swig of Pepsi from a can. He knew he wouldn't have to wait long to hear the details of the call from Matt. The poor guy was probably totally mystified by now.

"That call was from one of the guys in our cell." Matt was shaking his head in bewilderment. "He just informed me that the Dallas cell of The Order had been shut down by higher authority. We have all been instructed to never mention our cell or The Order ever again. Just like that, it's as though none of this ever existed and that anyone that might say otherwise would end up being a laughing stock. Everything is back to where it was before I joined." Matt stood there shaking his head in disbelief.

"I would have to say that we now have that additional sign we were looking for. As far as you two are concerned, this episode in your life has run its course. There will be no syndication or reruns. It's simply over." Frank's smile was one of reassurance.

Matt, on the other hand, was having difficulty accepting the outcome. "I can't believe The Order has disbanded so easily. They had power and they were backed by money. My understanding was that they had their claws into every social, economic and political infrastructure in the country. I can't believe that one big scare has produced a challenge so big that they would pull the plug on the whole organization. I don't know what to make of their decision." Matt kept shaking his head back and forth.

"Matt, let me elaborate on this for you. That call was not about The Order dissolving. It was only a message to you that you are no longer a player. You are out of The Order because you are not of the same mindset that they are. Your dedication is in doubt and that makes you a weak link. The Order is a secret organization with a deadly mission. They have done their damage control and you came out lucky. Secret organizations tend to fear too much negative attention. The content in that file told them that they were back on safe ground. Consider yourself a winner in this deadly game." This was the ending that Frank had hoped for.

"You're telling us that The Order is not finished?"

"They are far from being finished. The Order's structure and secrecy makes them invisible to the average citizen. It's only a matter of time before they recruit your replacement. The Order will proliferate and continue to grow stronger. They have time on their side. The best we can do is to be vigilant of what our politicians are doing. As voters, we need to hold our politicians to the constraints of the United States

Dan Morris

Constitution. Beware of a government bearing gifts and entitlements for its citizens. These things are bait for hooking us. There are already people sounding the alarm and when the time is right we need to respond with facts and cool heads." Frank delivered his assessment as best he could under the circumstances.

Realizing that the case was over for her and her husband, Felicity gave her parting thanks. "Thank you for everything. In a million years, I couldn't have manufactured such a story. This whole mess has been one shockwave after another coming at me. I was a fortunate woman when I walked into your office and obtained your services. I have my husband back and I have learned more about people in a matter of days than I have during my entire lifetime. Please, send me your bill. This is one check I won't mind writing."

"Thank you, my dear, for the tribute. Like you, I have learned a lot. All of life is a learning experience and this case has enriched mine. I hope you still feel the same way when you get the bill."

CHAPTER 23

The ending of the case did not mark the ending of Frank's interest in The Order. Strife, whether public or private, tends to go on forever. Strife sort of reinvents itself in another form each time it shows signs of fading out. The Order will exist as long as there are men bent on seeking change through power. Time after time, they will bring about strife and then pretend to save us from it. The Order will always be rescuing citizens from the perils it creates. Politics will always be a matter of philosophical perceptions and greed. Government is nothing less than the arena where political opponents compete for power and control. All these tenants are fragmented aspects central to political life. Government should be our servant and the people should be the master; never should these roles be reversed.

Frank sat quietly on the side of his bed staring at the old military footlocker he had dragged out of the closet. It was worn and tattered from being toted around for over forty years. Crammed inside were remnants of his life; material things that described the way he had lived. Every trinket and souvenir had meaning to him.

Like he had done so many times during his life, he began sifting through the contents. There were the plaques that had been given to him by soldiers and marines he had served with. Some plaques were ornate and others plain. The real splendor was in the memories behind the gifts. Everything was a bright tribute to times lost, but not forgotten, and jobs well done, but no longer important. He couldn't help but think about how those tributes and warm farewells had moved him at the time. It's sad how old buddies, friends, and comrades in arms eventually drift apart in search of new lives.

There are many chapters to every man's life. Some he would like to reclaim and others he would like to forget. However, no life is perfect. In the end, we all have tried to learn from our past. Then we live for the present with an eye on the future until our time is up. One consolation we all should embrace while holding on to our memories is our recognition that most of the work we had accomplished, at any given time, appeared to be everything at that time. Sadly, the significance of our accomplishments tends to fade over the years.

Outside, the afternoon was leaning toward dusk. The shadows were beginning to lengthen and taking on a deeper hue. Frank had lit a candle and placed it on the dresser. Burning a candle had more to do with his mood than saving electricity. The longer he stared at the contents of the footlocker, the hazier the room became.

A chill came over the room and a curtain moved as if a breeze had passed through. He picked up a bundle of papers that he had placed on the bed beside him. The time had arrived to add one more memory to his footlocker.

He had printed out a copy of the entire case file on Matt. Every detail was included. He sat the file aside and picked up another bundle of papers and placed it in his lap with a hand over them.

A thin transparent vapor began to swirl around the room. Maybe it was only in his mind; a mere illusion. Hopefully, he wasn't going over the edge from sanity to insanity. It had to be the result of the flickering candle in a dimly lit room. His weary eyes must be playing tricks on him because he was beginning to make out a face forming before him; it vaguely reminded him of Walter. A quivering voice faintly whispered; "You are doing the right thing." Then the room was warm again and the vapor was gone. Even though he was exhausted, he couldn't help but dwell on the moment.

Could this have been a short-lived mini-séance? Did he just receive a vote of encouragement from Walter's spirit? Maybe he was only hallucinating. Then again, maybe the voice and message had been real. Life is full of greater mysteries than one as trivial as this one. Men have acted on less motivation than those of a spiritual nature. There had always been those hunches and those gut feelings that had driven men to act appropriately.

Without regret, Frank had deceived his clients for personal reasons. When he had handled the file taken from Walter's yacht, he had surreptitiously removed a few pages and concealed them. He had also deceived the FBI impostor by lying about the copy being a copy of a copy and about the uselessness of the file. Into his lap, Frank had just placed the entire file. Several pages were original ones and not mere copies. He had been holding them in reserve for some last ditch effort to deal with The Order. He also had an academic reason for holding on to it, along with a moral motive. A few pages of the file contained information that would some day have some historical value for our country.

Frank moved his hand and exposed the top page. In bold, Old English letters, the cover read, "The Order's Manifesto." On the center of the third page was written the words: "Roster, Inner Ruling Circle at George Town." Nine prominent names followed.

The reality of what he was holding was pithy, to say the least. Knowledge was power. However, it had to be applied at the right time to be of any benefit. This was not the right time. The country was teetering on the precipice for destruction. More eyes than ever were now on Congress. The Order's goal was not within its grasp as long as voters could cast their votes and swing the pendulum in favor of liberty. Nonetheless, this was a good time to check our powder to make sure it was dry and ready. The country was resilient and had bounced back from many challenges throughout its history. We had experienced a revolution, a civil war, two world wars, a cold war, and many undeclared wars. Terrorism had reached our shores and we were dealing with an enormous economic failure. In spite of all these challenges and distrust of the government, and with the grace of God, the file would never be needed.

He placed the file into his footlocker and vowed that he would keep a close scrutinizing eye on the activities of the people listed as members of The Order. As he closed the lid Frank thought of three pertinent quotes from some of our country's Founding Fathers:

Thomas Jefferson, the third President of the United States and principal author of the Declaration of Independence wrote: "A government big enough to give you everything you want, is strong enough to take everything you have."

James Madison was the fourth President of the United States and principal author of the United States Constitution and the Bill of Rights. He wrote: "I believe there are more instances of the abridgement of freedom of the people by gradual and silent encroachments by those in power than by violent and sudden usurpations."

Alexander Hamilton was a lawyer and author of the Federalist Papers. He was also General George Washington's Chief of Staff. He wrote: "It's not tyranny we desire; it's a just, limited, federal government."

Frank took one final look at his foot locker and simply said, "I'll be watching."